The Accidental Fiancé

Linda ~

Happy Reading!

The Accidental Fiancé

A Love Lottery Romance

Christi Barth

Christi Barth

TULE
PUBLISHING

Dedication

To my husband. Thanks to our roles on the stage, he got to play my fiancé *multiple* times, before and after our wedding. Every time with him is the best ever!

Acknowledgements

My undying gratitude to Meghan Farrell and Jane Porter, who fell for a one sentence description of this series and actually encouraged me to write the whole thing. They—and everyone at Tule—have been unfailingly supportive and wonderful. To my readers—thank you so much for starting another series with me. I promise the rest of it will be just as fun!

A *delicious* brunch at the Kent Manor Inn helped solidify my teensy idea as workable. A stay at the Brampton Inn in Chestertown helped me immensely in nailing down, well, *everything* for my fictional Three Oaks Inn. And if you swing by Maryland, you should visit—it is lovely there. Big thanks to Mary Vaughan for listening to me vent about unworkable plot points, and helping me sprint my way to the finish line. And to all those aspiring authors out there—know that I had people who tried to talk me out of writing this series. I want to say I waited too long to try and pitch it as a result—but on the other hand, waiting clearly brought me to the perfect time for it to find a home with Tule. So listen to your heart and write the stories that you *have* to get out of your brain. People will want them!

Prologue

Christmas Eve
Downtown Pittsburgh

ALEX KIRKLAND FISTED his hands deeper into his pockets. December in Pittsburgh was no joke. At least, *he* wasn't laughing about the below-freezing temps. Although he wasn't in the mood tonight to be laughing about, well, *anything*.

"Alex, you've kept us in suspense long enough. Tell us what happened at your interview," his sister pleaded, with a sharp tug on his coat sleeve.

One look at her hopeful face reminded him he wasn't alone. The moping could wait until he was. But right now, Amelia looked like a smiling angel with her pale skin and her red hair dusted with flakes from the snow she'd tried to throw at him. These Christmas Eve strolls to look at the downtown lights were one of her favorite holiday traditions.

Damned if he'd ruin it for her.

"I went in, I charmed 'em, and proceeded to wow them with my in-depth knowledge of the hotel industry." He tossed her an exaggeratedly slick, smarmy smile that he would never, *ever* actually use in an interview.

"So you got the job?"

1

"Doubtful," Teague Sullivan cut in, scrubbing his hand over his close-cut light brown hair. "He'd have led with good news. Alex here was stalling on sharing his shit news—am I right?"

The problem with a best friend who had known you since a third-grade playground battle? They knew all your tells. All the ways you hid yourself and your feelings from the rest of the world.

There was no hiding *anything* from Teague. Especially after his Army Special Forces training. The man could sniff out a weakness or a lie faster than Alex could identify a smoking barbecue grill with T-bones from six blocks away.

"I didn't get the job," Alex admitted with a shrug. Then he stopped to stare at a storefront window decorated with elaborate swags of snow and holly. Jolly. Festive. It set his teeth on edge.

"Oh, no!" Everleigh Girard, his sister's bestie since forever, threw an arm around his shoulders. "How could they possibly ignore the total package of experience and movie-star good looks that you'd bring to their hotel as manager?"

"Maybe that's what killed his chances." Amelia waved a fuzzy green-mittened hand at his face. "The chiseled jawline, the icy-blue eyes. The man who interviewed you would've felt insignificant, and a woman would've known you'd be impossible to resist."

Alex appreciated the teasing compliments. Because they all *knew* the real reason he'd been passed over. Again. "Thanks, guys. But it was obvious my résumé didn't matter. Someone had read the damned article between setting up the interview and today. They know I was fired for covering up a theft at the Grand Orion."

"You didn't cover it up." Amelia poked her finger into his sternum to punctuate each sentence. She could be fierce with her love *and* her defense of those she loved. Good thing his black wool coat cushioned her attack. "You protected a battered woman in need. You let her get away *to save her life*, and then you called the authorities. I'm sick of the world treating you like a co-conspirator instead of a hero."

"The damn magazine made sure that I came off sounding like a criminal in that article. Enough so that nobody will give me a chance to tell my side of the story, let alone hire me." He bent forward to put his shoulder at Amelia's waist, and then hefted her over his shoulder. "No big deal. As long as you think I'm a hero, I'm golden."

What's more, Alex *meant* it.

Yeah, his prospects of lining up another hotel manager job were slim. No, he had no freaking idea what else to do with his life. But it had been him and Amelia against the world for years now. The three people kicking at the sidewalk snow with him were all that mattered. As long as he had them, Alex would be fine.

Sure, the Orion had given him a place to live as a sweet manager perk, which meant he was now sleeping in Amelia's spare room. No job, no home…but he'd make sure his sister still had a magical Christmas Eve.

After Amelia squealed, laughed and kicked while he spun her around twice in yet another tradition performed every time it snowed, he set her back down. And hoped the break was enough to shift the focus off of him.

But her laughter cut off abruptly. This time she was the

one who turned away to stare at a window display of nut-crackers, oversized mice and overflowing bowls of walnuts covered in red glitter. "If it makes you feel better, you're not the only one with bleak holiday tidings. I'm losing my job as of the first of the year. Home Warehouse is closing twenty stores, and mine is one of 'em."

"Oh, nooooo," wailed Everleigh. "Amelia, that's terrible." She threw her arms around Amelia. Her heavy dark hair swirled around them both like an actual cloak of sadness as they rocked back and forth.

Yeah, Ever could always be counted on to bring the drama. For good and for bad. But this time Alex agreed with her reaction. Amelia loved Christmas time. She was one of the nuts who started watching holiday movies by Halloween. Losing her job was bad enough. Finding out today would ruin her holiday.

It'd been a lot easier to protect his little sister before she grew up.

"I heard you hated that job?" Teague said, lifting one eyebrow. "I mean, I'm bunking on your couch. Thanks for that, by the way. Christmas is a crap time to job and apartment hunt. So I don't eavesdrop, but I heard you venting to Alex every night this week."

"I don't have any secrets from you." Amelia beamed at him from over Everleigh's shoulder. "You're practically my brother! And I do hate it. It was supposed to be a stopgap after college until I got a full-time gig doing landscaping. But it's been three years now."

"Maybe this is a good thing. Karma kicking you in the ass to find a better job."

"Hey, you know the rule," Alex barked sharply. "No mention of my sister's ass. Or any body parts, come to think of it."

Amelia disentangled herself from Ever. "Teague, I appreciate a good Karma kick as much as anyone. But I've *been* trying. Doing side-hustle solo projects to build my résumé while applying at every landscaper in town. Alex was going to try and hook me up at the Orion, but I get the feeling they don't want to do any favors for someone with his last name…"

Hand slapping at his forehead, Alex said, "Shit. I'm sorry, Amelia."

He'd screwed up. Alex had been ready to be the hero and hand her the job on a silver platter by the new year. But he'd never even asked his boss.

That had slipped his mind what with the police questioning and the firing so that the hotel could have a scapegoat for the disappeared money. Even though they knew full well—because he'd given the confessional letter left on his desk to the police—that Elena Vasquez had stolen the money using his passcode to escape a violent husband who'd been abusing her and her children for years.

She patted him on the arm. "It's fine, Alex. I don't want to work for a place that would throw you under the bus like that."

"If we're going all in on the pity party tonight, rather than chugging eggnog…um…I got fired today, too," Everleigh admitted. Her head drooped down, swinging her long black hair to cover her face. If Ever was feeling an emotion, chances were you could peg it by reading the motion of her hair.

"How could Randall fire you?" Amelia pulled Ever closer to the storefront. Then she looked left and right at the deserted sidewalks. "Weren't you guys...you know..."

Alex found it adorable—and reassuring—that his little sister, even at twenty-five, blushed and stammered when talking about sex.

"Do you have to make me say it?"

Teague raised one ungloved hand. Guess after spending the last three years stationed in the desert, he was happy to trail his fingers through the snow. "I've been gone, remember? I need *somebody* to say it."

Alex emailed the guy regularly. But he hadn't bothered to fill him in on Everleigh's latest romance because...well...they never lasted. He'd assumed that by the time Teague shipped back home, this idiotic move of dating her boss would be over.

This was one of the rare times, though, that Alex hated being right. "Randall was Ever's boss at the art gallery. They were a thing. Dated for a couple months, then just moved in with him at Thanksgiving."

"And he fired you? While you're living together? Man, that's cold."

Ever tossed her head. Tried to look stoic, but that fell apart when she sniffed and her lower lip trembled. "We're not living together anymore. His, ah, fiancée found out about us."

After a quick *is she for real* exchange of looks with Alex, Teague said, "Did you know about *her*?"

"Omigosh, of course not! There's no excuse for cheating...unless you don't know you're doing it. I'd never consciously hurt someone like that. Randall's a two-timing snake."

Seconded. Alex wanted to pull a reverse Santa on the guy. Go break in, grab all the presents under his tree, and give them to a homeless shelter. Everleigh was a walking and talking bleeding heart who always ended up with men who treated her badly. It killed him to watch it keep happening.

"Did you love him?" Amelia asked quietly.

"No. But I thought that I *could*. So my heart's in one piece, pretty much. I'm just out a job and an apartment. My car's loaded up with all my stuff. I was hoping I could move in with you until I can sign a new lease?"

"You'll have to share my bed. But it won't be the first time we've had a sleepover. The only thing is...my lease is up in a week. The building is going condo. They're raising the rents by two hundred percent to drive out the people who don't want to buy in. We'll all be out."

Holy crap.

Worst. Christmas. *Ever.*

Alex rubbed a reassuring hand along her back. Even though she probably couldn't feel it through the world's puffiest coat. "Amelia, don't worry. We'll find a place. The internet doesn't close for the holidays. We'll start looking tomorrow."

"I got a jump start. Here." She dug in the pocket of her forest-green jeans, then handed him a piece of cardstock. "Merry Christmas."

"What's this?" Holding it diagonally to catch the flashing red and green lights in the display window, all he could make out was a drawing of a large brick building and a number.

"A lottery ticket. I bought it at the coffee shop while waiting for you all to show up tonight."

"It doesn't look like a lottery ticket."

"Not for money." She rubbed her hands together. "For something much better."

Even Everleigh rolled her big blue eyes at that. "Like what? Magic beans?"

"A distillery?" And Teague's guess resonated with a lot more hope than Ever's.

"It's to win a historic inn. It's my present to Alex, so he'll have his own hotel to manage that nobody can take away."

"Aww, that's so sweet. Thanks, sis." Alex leaned down a good six inches to drop a kiss on the top of her head.

Teague plucked the paper from Alex's fingers to examine it. "The coffee shop's running a lottery? Beautiful girl, I think you got played."

"No, it's real. The owner's helping out a cousin of a friend…" she circled her hands in the air "…there was a long story. But it's definitely for real. The drawing's tomorrow."

Alex agreed with his friend. It sounded sketchy. More like a half-assed plan to bilk customers of a few extra dollars.

On the other hand, it'd put a smile on his sister's face. It gave her hope on this shitstorm of a day, which was priceless.

From the only two cells of his brain allowed to be spontaneous, an idea emerged. "How about we frontload our luck? Let's walk back to the coffee shop right now and we'll each buy a ticket."

"Really?"

"Yeah. I mean, we've all hit rock bottom, right? There's

nowhere to go but up. We'll count on some old-fashioned Christmas magic to reboot our lives."

Teague and Amelia hard-packed snowballs as they walked, winging them at the ornate light poles. Everleigh started singing 'It's the Most Wonderful Time of the Year.'

And for some weird reason, Alex felt hope, too. Despite not having a job. Or a place to live. Not to mention the crap coincidence of the other three being in the same situation.

They were together. That counted for a *lot*, especially with Teague just having returned from deployment in one piece. They were all smart and stubborn—which also counted for a *lot*. Sure, life had yanked the rug out from under all of them. Things couldn't get any worse.

So the next year had to be better…

Chapter One

January 4
…or the first day of the rest of their lives

O N CHRISTMAS EVE, Alex had thought that buying an undoubtedly fake lottery ticket for an inn was the most impulsive thing he'd ever done.

Boy, was he ever wrong.

Agreeing to move to the Eastern Shore of Maryland and run the inn that they freaking *won* ten days ago? That had to be the most impulsive act of his entire life.

"Do you see that billboard?" Amelia asked from the back seat.

He looked left and right, but only saw the winter-dry remnants of a cornfield and…something that was shorter than corn on the other side of the road. "What? No. I'm busy staring into the abyss of my future," Alex said.

Damn it. That was too dark. Eight shots of tequila at three a.m. dark.

All four of them had ricocheted through every possible emotion over the last ten days. Alex had been the one leading the charge to do this crazy-ass thing. He'd been positive and pumped and kept everyone on track with believing this was an amazing opportunity.

Until they'd spent five hours in the car actually leaving their lives in the rearview mirror. Then the panic had set in. His gut had been clenched for the whole drive as if bracing for a kick from a muay Thai fighter.

Half-swallowing laughter, Everleigh said, "I saw the billboard. It was for The Family Restaurant. In, I quote, 'the center of town.' That's it. No street name. No address."

Teague glanced back at them over his shoulder. "Does that mean we're moving to a town with only one restaurant, or only one street?"

"It means we've lost our collective minds," Alex muttered.

"Dude, this was your idea."

"It was Amelia's idea to buy the ticket," he snarled back. In the rearview mirror, he glared daggers at her laughing green eyes. "She started this whole thing."

"What's wrong with you, Alex?" His sister dug her long fingers into his ribs and tickled. Despite his admonitions over and over and over again to never distract the driver. Luckily, he barely felt her through his thick black Grand Orion sweatshirt and turtleneck. "You've had a frown on your face the whole drive. If I didn't know better, I'd say you were freaking out. But my calm, logical brother *never* freaks out."

Chuckling, Teague said, "Guess that means you've never seen him watch a Flyers game. From the first moment that puck hits the ice, he's a nervous wreck." Then he gripped Alex's biceps in mock horror. "Do we have to become Caps fans now? As official Maryland residents?"

Were they *trying* to make him crash the car? "No. I draw

the line at that. I'll uproot my life, cram everything I own in a U-Haul and drag it across two states, but I'm not rooting for the Capitals."

"Ooh!" Everleigh waved her hand between the seats to get their attention. "It would be a nice touch if we do make sure to show local games on a big television for the guests. Without any heckling from you two. Do you think there is a big plasma-screen TV?"

How had his life become something where that was an actual question? Did she think they'd be pumping water from a well, too? The old website from when it had been a functioning inn had been taken down, but they'd found a couple of wedding photos that showed the ballroom and enough of the grounds to get Amelia excited. They knew it wasn't a *hovel*.

"It's a historic one-hundred-and-sixty-one-year-old building. But it exists in the twenty-first century, Ever. It has electricity and plumbing and if there isn't a TV, we're damn well buying one. Or ten."

"Huh." It was more of a high noise in her throat than an actual word. "Amelia's right. You *are* throwing off waves of nervous snippiness."

Making a conscious effort to relax his white-knuckled grip of the Suburban's steering wheel, he slowly stated, "I'm a thirty-two-year-old man. I am not now, nor have I ever been, *snippy*."

"Are you scared?" Teague asked in a low tone. "Plenty of men in my unit would bite off everyone's heads right before a dangerous mission."

"Of course I'm scared!" Wow. That came out a lot louder than intended. "Look, it all became very real, very fast, okay? It was easy to be optimistic back in Pittsburgh. But we're almost there. This is our new reality."

Alex ran back in his head what he'd just said.

This *was* their reality. So there wasn't any more time to be nervous. The car ride had been it. He wouldn't waste one more second registering all the ways this could come crashing down on their heads.

He wouldn't drag down his friends and sister like that. He was in charge, whether or not they acknowledged it, seeing as how he was the only one who knew *anything* about hotels. He'd be the leader they needed.

Because this had to work.

It was their only chance.

Hell, it was probably his *last* chance.

Thank God, that was the moment the empty countryside closed in with the edges of a town. *Their* town, now. Chestertown, Maryland, sprawled along the banks of the Chester River that led right out to the huge Chesapeake Bay.

Like so many towns, the first harbinger was a McDonald's. Alex shot his fist into the air in victory. Yeah, he jammed his knuckles against the ceiling, but the momentary pain was still worth it. "See those Golden Arches? That's good news."

Snorting, Teague said, "Didn't know you were such a fan of the special sauce, lettuce, cheese combo."

"I'm not. But for it to stay in business, that means this town gets traffic. Regular, year-round traffic, not just seasonal. That's a good sign that our inn will have guests even in the winter."

"McDonald's? Really?" Amelia sounded beyond skeptical. Which was exactly why he was in charge. Because he was the only one of them to recognize the intrinsic value and meaning of the drive-thru. "That's your scientific assessment tool of our chances at prosperity?"

"It's the first one. There will be more. Watch and learn, my young Padawans."

"Oh geez. I think I liked you better all mopey than quoting *Star Wars*," Everleigh said.

"Teague, find us a decent local radio station. We need a soundtrack for our first glimpse of our new home."

As soon as Teague switched over from Sirius, a jingle for McDonald's started to play. They all laughed. "See? I told you. A good omen."

"It may also end up being our dinner if you don't get a move on. Stop puttering like you're driving a golf cart." Teague banged the steering wheel with the flat of his hand. "Don't we want to get moved in before nightfall?"

Amelia's hand shot between the seats for a high five. "Yes. That's my vote. I haven't researched what wild animals are out here, but I don't want to find out with an up close and personal sighting."

Suddenly it was a jumble of hands as Everleigh's also flew forward to point. "Washington College—see the cute brick sign on the right? That's good, too, isn't it? Means we can pack in the people and charge twice as much for weekends like homecoming and graduation?"

"I like how you think, Ever. And you're right. Good instincts. I'm claiming you for the sales and marketing team."

"We're picking teams?" Dismay coated Amelia's words.

"There's only four of us. Should we really be competing against each other?"

The softness of his sister's heart rivaled that of a stack of half-melted marshmallows. "Don't worry. No losers. Remember, this is a business. With structure. An org chart, to disseminate the flow of tasks and responsibilities."

"An org chart? Might as well use this." Teague whipped out his phone and scrolled to the photo they took on New Year's Eve. The four of them were clinking beer bottles, holding the winning lottery ticket in the middle and grinning like crazy. "Done."

"Hardly. You're hereby excused from any team that uses spreadsheets and graphs, with that attitude. The org chart will streamline and clarify all our roles. You'll thank me later."

"Maybe. But I'm sure not thanking you now."

Teague's attitude made no sense. "You spent the last fourteen years in the Army. How do you not have respect and appreciation for a command structure?"

Everleigh jumped on his words before Teague could even answer. "Hang on. 'Command structure' sounds even more ominous than 'org chart' did. We're not your corporate lackeys, Alex."

A deep laugh slipped out of his lips. "Trust me, there's not a chance I'd ever blur the lines enough to see you as that."

His sister and Ever were two of the least corporate types he could imagine. Hard workers, sure. Trustworthy and reliable. But ass-kissing, climb the corporate ladder grinders? No way. They'd burst out laughing on the first rung.

The buildings were quaint and old, and even on this first Monday after a holiday weekend, there was foot and car traffic. It might feel like they were in the middle of nowhere, but Chestertown was clearly a bustling destination.

Another surge of relief washed through him as they turned, just a block from the water. Glints of it sparkled in the bright winter sun. Alex was no longer forcing his good mood—it had settled into his bones.

This would be fun. Profitable. Successful. A fresh start. No, it sure as hell wasn't a metropolis like the Steel City, but they'd learn to appreciate the small-town charm.

The GPS gave the quarter-mile warning, but Alex didn't see a sign. Or a driveway. He slowed, taking in the thick wall of trees lining the road. Off to the right, in the distance, the triple blades of a wind turbine also caught the sun.

"There!" Everleigh shrieked, throwing her hand out and practically stabbing him in the eye. At the last second, Alex turned into the narrow, rutted driveway. It was completely overgrown, even in January. He barely missed clipping the edge of the sun-faded sign that read *Three Oaks Inn*.

"Christ. The only person who'd call this an entrance would be Indiana Jones. And then only if he was being chased by a spear-wielding tribe."

"Clean out the underbrush, take a whack at the bushes, and repaint the sign." Teague tapped a finger against his temple. "Got a mental list started."

"I just did half of that careening the U-Haul around the turn," Alex muttered. Still, they'd made it. They were finally home. The place that would solve all of their problems. It fixed the no jobs/no homes issues in one fell swoop.

For as much as Alex detested doing anything on impulse, using this winning lottery ticket *had* to be the right move. Things had crashed down around them in December, but January was all about rebuilding. Restarting.

"That's all cosmetic," Amelia pointed out. "Easily fixed."

"Yep. And easier to do in January with all the leaves gone and not dripping sweat," Teague said, making a face like he was remembering those 120-plus-degree days in the Afghan desert.

"Hey." His sister's voice turned unnaturally stern. "Nobody touches a leaf or twig without checking with me first. You can't just go hacking at plants. Some can be pruned during hibernation, and some can't."

"Simmer down. Nobody's pulling out a chainsaw. We know you're in charge of Team Plants."

"Oh, from the looks of it, landscaping's going to be an all-play," she murmured softly as Alex braked to a stop in front of the enormous, four-story brick building.

The yard that stretched out on both sides was so out of control that it almost blended into the edge of the surrounding forest. The bushes lining the side porch were higher than the railing—which was good, since the railing was cracked and peeling. Not to mention missing more than a few spindles.

"Does anyone else notice that it doesn't match the pictures we saw online?" Everleigh asked in high, thin voice.

That was the understatement of the year. Alex's fingers tingled with the urge to grab his phone and text the man who'd given them the inn. He wouldn't go so far as to call it a bait and switch, but it wasn't what they'd been promised, either.

Not by a long shot.

One by one, they got out of the car, yanking on coats. Their feet crunched on a thick carpet of dry leaves. A few birds chirped, but otherwise it was totally silent.

Shock.

It was a collective instance of knowing nothing could be said that would come close to what they felt.

The inn was a *disaster.*

Alex dragged a hand through his tousled dark curls. What had he dragged them into?

No.

This wasn't the time to freak out, or worse, let anyone else do it. Lead by example, that was Alex's way.

He pulled on his black leather gloves. "Look, we knew it had been empty for a while. Since the guy's—Marshall's—grandmother died."

"Yes, but did she die *this* century?" Teague wisecracked.

The thing was, it definitely hadn't been abandoned since 1999. But Alex couldn't swear from the state of the inn that it had been inhabited in the last decade. "Let's walk around to the front. Nobody expects to be impressed by a side entrance."

"Oh, right. I say that all the time." Amelia pulled her long braids out from the collar of her coat. "I even had it spelled out in magnetic letters on my fridge."

They followed the stone path. It was uneven, but again, easily fixed. Alex only hoped that was the theme for the rest of the property. As they turned around the end of the side wing, the sunlight hit him first.

In front of them lay the wide, sparkling Chester River. The inn was situated at a bend and a little offshoot of a bay, so their view was more expansive than other properties they could see along the water. The three giant oaks that gave the inn its name were in a triangle just at the edge of the embankment, and the steps down to the river.

The trio of stately trees slammed hope back into his heart. "Those oaks might as well be the pot of gold at the end of a rainbow."

Teague frowned into a *have you lost your damn mind* look. "Nobody's paying top dollar for acorns these days, Alex."

"They do pay top dollar for wedding sites. This one's a doozy." Alex waved an arm at the bucolic vista. "Can't you picture the bride and groom standing right in front of the trees, the guests facing the river?"

"Ooooh, yes," breathed Amelia and Everleigh in tandem.

After looking side to side, Teague nodded. "Yeah. I see it now. Sorry to be slow on the uptake. My head hasn't been in a wedding-planning space in the last, well, *ever.*"

"Well, get there." He bumped shoulders with his friend. This had to be surreal for him. Going from being a Special Forces Weapons Sergeant to thinking about the best spot for a bridal arch. "It barely matters what the inside looks like. Trust me—this view will have bridal parties lining up to get in—and filling the inn."

"That sounds good." Teague chucked a branch overhand into the water. "Also sounds like a futurecast, as in the far, far future, from what I'm seeing."

He wasn't wrong. But hopefully, he wasn't *completely*

right, either. "Let's keep going." The thought of what bad shape the inside might be in had Alex leading the way to the rest of the property.

Also situated on the water was a pool, with a pool house. It was empty for the winter—or however many years this place had been unoccupied—but it looked like an infinity pool, taking advantage of the straight shot to the river. Leaves and mud and water filled the bottom by at least a foot. Ice shimmered in patches.

Cautiously, Everleigh sat on a lounge chair, propping up her black Uggs. "I've never had a pool before. I feel very fancy."

Habit had Alex barking out the reminder he'd used constantly on his staff at the Orion. "It's for the guests."

Teague shrugged in his fleece-lined leather jacket. "Why can't it be for us, too?"

"It...it wouldn't—" Alex broke off.

The man had a point.

They weren't working for a corporation. They were running their *own* place, however the hell they wanted to. It gave them more possibilities, more options. More freedom.

It also meant Alex needed to run less on autopilot, and more on instinct.

He gave a slow nod. "You're right, T. Guests first, but we should enjoy it, too."

Amelia clapped her hands together, beaming. "I think we just made our first official policy. Well done, guys. This whole working together thing is going to be a breeze."

What the hell?

If the pool had been full, Alex would've pushed his sister

in for saying that. He'd give up his life for the people on the cracked pool deck with him. But working with them? And living with them, on top of it? That was a huge unknown.

And an almost bigger worry than the state of the inn.

Because he'd let the whole damn thing fall apart before he'd let it tarnish their relationships. Amelia, Teague and Everleigh were the most important people—the most important parts—of his life. Yet their complete lack of experience with hoteliering promised more than a few bumps along this road.

He glanced at the tennis court. Didn't have the heart to discover if it was cracked from unruly tree roots or...*whatever* could go wrong with a tennis court. Instead, Alex tromped past an oval garden he'd bet was situated off the kitchen toward the L-shaped row of cottages. All the curtains were drawn, so they couldn't tell much about the eight buildings.

Looking across the wide-open space, Amelia volunteered, "This looks big enough to set up a volleyball net. Or a croquet lawn. Depending on if we lure millennials or baby boomers."

"We can do both." Everleigh began ticking off ideas on her fingers. "Think girls' weekends, bachelorette parties, fiftieth birthday trips, babymoons. This place can appeal to everyone."

She really did have a mind for marketing. Good to know.

Because with every step he took over this vast property, Alex wondered more and more if he'd bitten off more than he could chew. A little natural PR talent was ammunition to be hoarded against more panic about whatever they might discover inside.

But he had to keep things light. Keep everyone positive. And because explaining his growing panic would just come off as insulting. So he teased, "*If* we have those TVs I mentioned. Then all the people will come."

"What about horses?"

Amelia's hands flew to cover her heart. "You mean like a Shetland pony to be the inn mascot? Be available for petting for the kids?"

"No. *Horses.* For the stables." Everleigh walked forward a few steps and pointed.

Sure enough, what the lawyer had called 'outbuildings' looked to actually be stables and a couple of barns. Hopefully they held helpful things like lawnmowers and ladders.

Not freaking horses. Alex didn't know how much it cost to take care of a horse, but he'd bet it was out of their budget. By a long shot. Besides, this property had clearly been left empty for years. There couldn't be horses in there.

There *shouldn't* be, anyway.

Deliberately, he turned his back on the stables. "Let's call that the long-term plan. After we've had a full reservation book for at least two seasons. Because I don't know anything about horses. And my plate's full enough with things that I *do* know about."

"Don't worry, Alex." Amelia linked her arm through his as they headed for the main inn. "In my professional opinion, the grounds aren't in horrible shape. There's an obvious footprint to follow. I've got this. With the help of some strapping sets of muscles." Playfully, she squeezed his biceps. "Know anywhere I could find some of those?"

Oh, she'd pay for that dig. Alex dropped his shoulder and crouched. He caught her off-balance and tipped her over his back. Both of them laughing, he half-ran around the garden and up the steps.

"You bounced too much," she complained as he dumped her into a porch swing.

Uh-oh. Too late, he remembered the state of everything else they'd surveyed. Would it hold her?

Thankfully, the wood only squeaked a bit. It needed fresh stain, but seemed to be structurally sound.

Okay. He hadn't broken his only sister, and he also hadn't broken their newly inherited furniture. The day was looking up.

Alex inputted the code he'd memorized into the lockbox. Removed it…and held his breath.

"Here we go," Teague said, pushing past him to open the door.

It was bright by the windows, but dim in the adjoining hallway. A couple of fruitless flicks of the light switch made him realize the power probably hadn't been turned on yet. No power also accounted for the deep chill in the air.

From the rows of farmhouse-style tables and chairs, he'd peg it as being the breakfast room. All the chairs had cushions tied on…but they were faded from the uncurtained windows. Everleigh drew her finger in a line through the dust coating a wooden table. "Yuck."

"Everything's going to need to be cleaned," he cautioned. "Probably more than once."

Without saying anything else, they crossed the hall and found the kitchen. Its industrial-sized appliances were probably necessary for the volume of guests when the inn was full. But it intimidated the hell out of him. Things were oversized—even the double sinks. And why were there two ovens, too? Out of the four of them, only Amelia could really cook. Let alone *bake*. The kitchen basically mocked them with its double-threat.

Still wordlessly, they all filed out and down the hallway. It forked off into the two wings they'd seen from outside. Turning right took them into the sunroom...or the *cold* room. Its wall of windows did nothing to keep out the January temps. It was full of faded furniture. Faded wallpaper.

"It just looks sad," Amelia said in a near-whisper.

Yup.

Crossing to the other wing brought them into a ballroom. Another potential cash cow, in Alex's opinion. *If* you ignored the deep scratches on the floor, peeling paint on the windowsills, a disgusting number of dead bugs along the baseboards, and some sort of animal droppings just about everywhere.

From Everleigh's shudder, she was unable to ignore any of it. At least the cold kept it from smelling bad.

How was *that* the best thing about this room?

Teague turned on his phone's flashlight when they got to the small, windowless office. Hanging on the wall were rows of keys. Not just for the rooms upstairs, but for the cottages, too.

Alex seized on that as a means for escape. He could tell from everyone's faces they'd seen enough. "We'll stay in a cottage tonight. It'll be easier to heat up with a fireplace than this enormous building."

"Shouldn't we keep going?" Everleigh flung an arm to point at the wide staircase. "Look at the whole thing?"

Should they? Yes.

Could they bear to see anything else as crappy as what they'd already seen? Nope.

Doing a half spin on his heel to reverse course, Alex said, "We're practically camping. Which means the smartest thing to do is to use the sunlight while we've got it. Let's unload the basics, get the fire prepped and set up in a cottage. Make a grocery run, grab dinner. Tomorrow can be the first day of the rest of our lives."

It wasn't an *actual* stampede past him to return to the back door, but it felt like it. Alex didn't mind bringing up the rear. It gave him the chance to clench his fist around the cottage keys. And to pinch with his other hand at the tightening band of pain from temple to temple.

Alex had convinced everyone this inn would be their salvation. Promised that his experience and their enthusiasm could make a success out of it, no matter what.

The problem was…now he had to convince *himself* that was still true…

Chapter Two

S YDNEY DARROW WASN'T a particularly religious person. But she knew, without a doubt, that a salad spinner was an instrument of the devil.

It didn't work. At *all*. The handle was too short to hold on to for more than five spins. And every time she checked, the lettuce inside was just as drippy as the *last* time she'd checked.

Screw it. She ripped off an arm's length of paper towels and dumped the soggy greens onto the middle of it. And at her break, she'd toss the thing in the dumpster behind Marina Mercantile.

After traveling the world several times over, Sydney had eaten in less than sterile conditions. A *lot*. Enough to know that a little dirt on vegetables never hurt anyone. She'd be happy to personally impart that globally honed experience to the small-town minds of the populace of Chestertown, Maryland.

Or, you know, just *not* tell anyone that she skipped rinsing the damned lettuce.

She was one hour into her first shift at the Mercantile and already ready to run screaming into the street. Which was a whopping forty-five minutes longer than she'd predicted lasting.

The family business was for her father, her grandmother. It was *not* her jam. Not her scene. And, btw, a huge part of the reason she'd fled Chestertown with wings on her feet the day after high school graduation.

To say she'd never dreamed about the day she'd be standing behind the counter washing greens for the lunch rush wasn't just an understatement. It was entirely backward.

Most of Sydney's girlish dreams revolved around a reality where she never again had to stand behind this counter, let alone darken the door of the Mercantile at all. But she'd also never dreamed that her grandmother would get cancer, almost die, and need her back here to help during the chemo treatments.

She hadn't waited to be asked. Because her grandmother *wouldn't*. She knew Sydney's job producing travel shows was demanding. They also knew she had a chip on her mental shoulder against her hometown—proven by the fact she hadn't been back in years, preferring to meet her family in far-flung destinations.

Sydney had immediately offered, though. No, *insisted*. The woman had raised her. Coming home to help her gran was the literal least she could do. That, and donating a pint of blood yesterday at the local hospital in her name.

"Hon, can you help me with a display?" her dad yelled down the length of an aisle.

"I'm still working on the last thing you asked me to do— prep the lettuce."

"That can wait five minutes while you help me fix this endcap. It looks messy. Messy products don't sell."

Sydney looked up. Saw where her dad was standing. And *shuddered*. "Nope. No can do. No way, no how."

"Syd…" His gelled, sandy-blond hair with the comb marks still in it was easy to spot above the shelves since he stood six four in socks. Especially when that head slowly wagged back and forth in the disappointed nod with which she was very familiar.

Well, it wouldn't work anymore. She wouldn't be manipulated by old routines. Yes, Neil Darrow was still her father. But here at the store, their dynamic had to be different. She had to lay down the law right now, day one, that she was an adult. A peer.

Sydney shoved at the hair falling forward past her ear. Which made her realize she'd forgotten to put on the rubber gloves.

Since when was hand-washing—which she of course *had* remembered—not good enough to rip off lettuce leaves?

Frustrated with the situation, the lettuce, and herself, Sydney dried her hands on a dishtowel embroidered with a grinning crab.

"No, Dad. I told you that I'm not going within six feet of the bait. That barrel of minnows is just creepy." They were in a holding pen for their death. Eww. Equal parts depressing and disgusting. "When I agreed to come and sub in for Gram for three months, it was with the stipulation of certain conditions, remember?"

"I thought you were kidding."

Sydney was *shocked*. Rocked to her core shocked.

Did he truly not understand what a huge deal this was? That she'd come back to Chestertown at all, let alone for three whole months?

How disruptive it was to her life, her career, to take a sabbatical and bury herself in this backwater town?

How soul-crushing?

"You thought I was kidding?" she asked in a flat tone. Because at this point, it was either strip all the emotion out of her voice, or let it fly with a screech of sour snippiness. Which wouldn't really underscore her whole *treat me like an adult and not your daughter* request. "Really? How many times have I come home in the last dozen years?"

Quietly, he said, "Not enough."

And then he put down the…boat thing…he was holding and came over to envelop her in a hug. A hug that felt so right, so grounding, so wistful for all the ones she hadn't gotten from him over the years.

Damn it.

She couldn't be mad about the minnows. Not when she knew how much he'd missed her.

To be fair, she'd missed her dad and grandmother and sister tremendously. Even her brother Campbell, more or less. But Sydney hadn't *ghosted* them as she globe-trotted. She video-chatted with them regularly, and always had. Staying in touch was important. She was a daddy's girl, through and through.

So Sydney sank into the hug. Reveled in it. Decided that it balanced out the horror show of the salad spinner.

"I love you, Dad. But I mean it. You and Campbell have to deal with everything in that smelly, fishy corner of the store. I'll stay up here and handle the money. Fumble my way through the food. Heck, I'll even shovel the sidewalk the next time it snows. Without any grumbling! But I'm not going near the bait corner."

"Stubborn Syd." He yanked at the messy braid she'd fastened with a twist tie off the bread bag so that he didn't force her into a hair net. "Always so sure you know what's best."

"Not by a long shot." That made it sound like she always thought she was right. And the hard left turn her career—and her life—had just taken proved how little she knew. "But I do know what's best for me."

Glancing down at the bulging paper towels and the half-plucked lettuce, he shook his head. "It's only day one. Working in the shop is like riding a bike—it'll come back on autopilot if you relax."

Wow, he knew just how to go in and plumb the depths of her nightmares. First the worms and minnows, and now the horror of remembering—and *settling* into—working at the Mercantile.

Being stuck in their small town.

Being stuck in the town that her mother had abandoned her whole family just to get out of…

"Don't count on me relaxing until my bags are packed and you're driving me back over the Bay Bridge to BWI." But Sydney said it with a winsome smile, to take the sting out of the words. "My autopilot isn't set to tending a store. Autopilot for me is zipping around the world. And you know darn well I could never cook."

"That's for sure." A high, barking laugh burst out of him. "Remember when you tried to make brownies? You shook the measuring cup to level it and got flour over every nook and cranny of the kitchen."

Yeah. That had been one of her *lesser* cooking misdemeanors. "I'll try, Dad. But when the lunch rush kicks in, it'd be smarter to keep me at the cash register while you handle the food."

"Gotta get your feet wet, hon. We'll compromise. You finish prep, and then I'll make the sandwiches. Because I think you need a trial run before we let you near the panini press."

"Since when are you *panini* fancy?"

"Since your gram explained that it's just a gussied-up grilled cheese that you can charge twice as much for." Another loud laugh accompanied by a knee slap of his navy corduroys, as though it was the best joke of the decade. Then he caught sight of a man heading to the register. As he hustled over, he said, "When you finish with the lettuce, start slicing the tomatoes."

"How many?"

"Until you're sick of it, plus five more."

Guess he had her pegged.

Sydney glanced down at her iPad. Thought about unlocking the screen for just a moment, to check email. To check for a certain email that would mean her career wasn't irretrievably stalled by taking this unpaid sabbatical. Or worse, one that declared her boss had decided *not* to hold a spot for her. Because he'd been quite clear that option was on the table. Shockingly, the dying grandmother story had garnered zero understanding or sympathy from him. She'd had to volunteer to take the time unpaid to get him to agree to it at *all*.

But checking would lead her down a wormhole of what-ifs and more emails, and nothing would get done. As much as she hated being behind the counter at the Mercantile again, she would do her part while here. Because she wasn't a sulky teen anymore. She was an adult with a work ethic who knew darn well that filling in the hours that were normally her sick gram's was necessary.

Compromise could be the word of the day, however. Sydney pulled out her phone, and tapped to the Duolingo app. Being fluent in English and French got her through a good swath of the world. But learning Spanish would ease her travels considerably.

Ten minutes later she had two full containers of individual and mostly dry lettuce leaves. A small win, but Sydney would take every one she got. Suddenly, a hand swooped in and waved right in front of her nose.

Startled, her arms jerked up. Lettuce flew…everywhere. Sort of a re-enactment of the flour episode her dad had just recounted.

Furious, Sydney looked up to level a lethal glare at the owner of the hand. And up…and up. The man on the other side of the high metal counter was as tall as her dad. Bundled in a wool coat that belonged over a suit—so it marked him as a non-local. Dark brown hair with a hint of chestnut at the tips looked like he'd slept on it. Strands that gel probably kept smooth normally were curling into thick waves.

Thick waves that she'd love to sink her fingers into, under any other circumstance. Great hair instantly amped up the attraction meter on a guy.

And this one also rocked high, knife-sharp cheekbones that blended with a straight nose to give him the look of an

English aristocrat. Or at least the way they were portrayed in the costume dramas she loved to binge on trans-oceanic flights.

Good hair, excellent height—yeah, he pressed all the right buttons. Except for two things: Sydney had zero plans to hook up with a tourist, *and* the way his ice-blue eyes were shooting darts of disdain her direction.

She yanked out her earbuds, and he managed to lob the first snark.

Raising one dark eyebrow, he asked, "When you're done juggling the lettuce, can you get us some coffees...*without* spilling them?"

Ah, the joys of being in a customer-oriented field. Where the odds were that at least a quarter of the time the customer would be a certified jerk. Sydney hadn't missed it one bit, and she sure as hell wouldn't miss it when the jetway closed behind her in three months.

"No guarantees. It's my first day. You might want to step back, out of the splash zone," she said through clenched jaws. "Or, you know, maybe not wave your hand in my face without warning."

"Maybe you should pay more attention to the job at hand than bopping along to your music."

"I'm learning Spanish," she snapped. And instantly regretted the words. She knew better.

Do not engage. Apologize and fix the problem.

Sydney's grandma had probably spoken that mantra to her while Sydney had still been swaddled in a car seat for her first trip into the Mercantile. It was the golden rule of customer service. And the golden rule of the Darrow family business. Besides, it wasn't his fault she was worried about her grandmother's health and had had to abandon her dream job to come home to help out in the Mercantile.

His icy eyes pointedly tracked from the scattered lettuce to her phone. "Does your manager know that you're focusing on self-improvement while he's paying you to assist customers?"

This man!

"Alex, a bad night's sleep doesn't give you free rein to be rude." The redhead next to him whapped his arm with the back of her wrist. "I'm sorry. My brother's not usually such a pain. But there's no electricity at our hotel, so we're cold, not showered, and grumpy. And by 'we,' I mean him."

The man scrubbed a hand over his face. To Sydney's shock, when he dropped it, the face he revealed looked ashamed.

"Man, I *was* out of line. Stress and no sleep are an excuse, but you deserve better. You deserve a full apology." He dropped a nod. "I'm sorry. I was a jackass."

So he had charm to go with those charming looks.

Interesting.

Intriguing. That is, if she was in the market for a hookup. Which she definitely wasn't. Not now. Not here.

Most of Sydney's anger fizzled right out. She set about picking up the escapee lettuce. "Thanks. And your hotel sounds like a nightmare. You should switch. Or better yet, get out of town as fast as you can."

"Please!" Laughing—which brightened his face and made him ten times more attractive—he ear-muffed his sister with his hands. "Don't give her any ideas."

The woman twisted out of his grip. "That didn't work when I was six, and it doesn't work now."

Dark eyebrows pinched together as he scowled down at her. "Since you did hear what she said, I'll reiterate that we're staying put. No matter how hard or how miserable."

That was…odd.

Sydney wasn't anywhere close to a first-string fan of her hometown. But the hotels and B&Bs in the area had solid reputations. Tourism was their bread and butter. Nobody could afford to screw up as badly as they were describing.

"I don't think you understand how hotels work," Sydney said slowly. "You're not supposed to be miserable. If you are, you certainly shouldn't have to pay for it."

"Oh, no. We're actually locals, now. That hotel with no power? It's ours. We moved in yesterday." She went up on tiptoe to offer her hand across the counter. "I'm Amelia. That's my brother Alex."

Wow. Never would've guessed that in a hundred years. Hurriedly, she dried her hand and shook. "Sydney."

"That's why we're here," Alex said, brandishing an arm to encompass the whole of the endless shelves of the Mercantile. "No power means no coffee, no breakfast. Our friends are waiting for us to grab sustenance while they sit on hold to raise hell with Delmarva Power."

Hmm. Retirees often opened B&Bs, thinking it'd be a relaxing second career in a beautiful spot. Aaaand then those B&Bs turned over to new owners within five years, because there wasn't anything relaxing about running a business. Especially one where you had to scrub toilets *and* cook.

But Alex looked to be close to her age, with Amelia a little younger. Basically, a lifetime away from retirement. It didn't add up.

Sydney looked back and forth between the two of them. "You bought a *hotel*? Here?"

"About a mile down the road. We actually won it. In a lottery. On Christmas." Amelia elbowed her brother in the ribs. "Best present ever, huh? Wonder how I'm going to top it next year."

"If we get it in the black by next Christmas, that'll be enough of a present for me." He pointed at the bakery case. "Can you load us up with one of everything? Or did I annoy you so much that you'd spit on the scones?"

"Initially? Absolutely. But I can restrain myself now."

"I'll go grab four coffees. Nice to meet you, Sydney." Amelia hurried away with a wave.

Sydney thought for a minute as she grabbed a paper bag. And remembered in the nick of time to also grab tongs to retrieve the pastries. A property a mile down the road that was empty? It could only be one place. "You won the Three Oaks Inn? *Won* it?"

"True story. Wild and wacky, but true." Another spectacular smile streaked across his face.

Spectacularly *sexy*. But knowing that he lived here made Alex even more off-limits.

Sydney wanted no extra ties to this town. She loved her family, and even *they* weren't enough incentive to bring her back here. Instead, she flew them out for visits wherever she was on assignment with the ridiculous number of frequent flyer miles she racked up every year.

"My parents got married at the inn. It's beautiful. Or,

well, it used to be."

"Ouch." He winced. Staggered back a few steps, hand to his heart. Adorable. "You're right, though. She's in rough shape. Doesn't mean she can't be rejuvenated."

"By you and your sister? Single-handedly?" Her skepticism was layered more heavily than the coating of streusel on top of the blueberry muffin that slipped out of her tongs. For the third time.

"You think we'd be that nuts?"

"Ah…maybe? Hard to judge based solely on our whopping four-point-five minutes of knowing each other." The muffin stayed in her tongs this time, but was so squished that the top popped off right as she centered it over the bag.

Was this a karmic test? Or a more straightforward one by her father, to see if she'd find and correctly choose the magic muffin-picking implement? Like Indy choosing the Holy Grail?

"First impressions are often right. Take my first impression of you. That working in food service is not your chosen profession." He pointed at the streusel crumbles cascading across the counter.

Talk about an understatement.

So yeah, he'd pegged her. Sydney would offer him a cookie as a reward for being right, but she'd probably just mangle that into sweet shards, too. "I told you it was my first day. First hour, actually."

"Want some advice?"

Oh, this ought to be *priceless.* Planting her tongue firmly in her cheek, she said, "From a guy who has owned a wreck of a closed-up hotel for twenty-four hours? Sure. Lay it on me."

"Use the wax paper. In the box. At the opposite end of the case."

Oh yeah. The folded half-squares. Because the tongs made pastries crumble, and were only supposed to be used on rolls and cheese.

Sydney *knew* that. It had just been locked behind the mental vault that housed all of her Mercantile memories. Darn it, her dad was right. It *was* coming back to her.

Crap.

She hovered between defensive and sheepish. But Alex had only tried to help.

He had no idea that Sydney simultaneously wanted to be competent enough to sub for her gram to help keep the Mercantile afloat, while also being so bad that her whole family would acknowledge that she did *not* belong here. And that her choice to leave town with her high school graduation tassel still swinging had been best for everyone.

"You're pretty savvy at the pastry-handling. Want to trade places?" she offered, reversing the tongs to thrust at him. "You can clean up my messes, and I'll run out to Three Oaks to clean up whatever a decade of neglect looks like?"

"Funny how you think rehabbing an eight-cottage, ten-room inn would be easier than scooping scones into a sack."

"Tomato, tomat-oh," she said breezily.

Great. A reminder that she still had the joy of cutting up tomatoes in front of her. Which didn't seem quite as bad after the break of this delightful verbal repartee with the far too good-looking stranger.

Alex dug in his back pocket to pull out his wallet. "While

I appreciate the offer, winning this inn is the opportunity of a lifetime. We're looking forward to doing all of it. Once it's back in the twenty-first century with power, that is. Without a power sander, we wouldn't reopen for another year."

"That coat emphasizes the width of your shoulders." Aaaand she'd said that out loud. That was…unfortunate. It only proved how off-balance she was being back. The only thing to do was to brazen it out the rest of the way. "What I'm saying is that I'll bet you've got enough muscles under there to buff and polish some floors. Cord-free."

Alex cocked one dark eyebrow. "Thanks for noticing. Just like I noticed how your hair is the color of a soft, sweet vanilla caramel."

A food reference flirt always weakened her knees. It led the mind to imagining his mouth on her, but without actually *going* there too obviously. Few men had the restraint or the tact to pull it off.

Yet Alex had managed it before the jump start of a single cup of coffee.

"Do you have a sweet tooth, Alex?"

"Average, I'd say. But special treats…intrigue me into wanting more."

Whoa. How did eyes the color of a glacier manage to smolder? Sydney popped an extra chocolate glazed into the bag and hurriedly—and loudly—crumpled over the top.

And then opened it again once she remembered to add a stack of napkins.

"The floors I could handle. It's the wallpaper stripping that I have to save my muscles for. Tedious and painful. But worth it. So far, it looks like just cosmetic fixes."

"You're giving the inn the Cinderella treatment?"

"Yes. And I'm worried about how right that reference may be when it comes to mice and birds being inside."

"You'd turn down a helpful army of woodland creatures?"

"We'll be banishing them day one. Don't need 'em—and God knows my sister doesn't want 'em," he said with another knockout of a grin. "Amelia and I are one heck of a team. Plus, we've also got our friends Teague and Everleigh. Teague's a workhorse and Ever…" Alex's mouth opened and closed, as if auditioning the right words before letting them come out. "Well, she's still finding herself. But I think she's an ideas person. She's certainly great with people."

Sydney handed over the bag. Their fingers brushed for a moment, maybe two. It sent tingles that reached all the way to her elbow.

Which was ridiculous. She brushed fingers all the time. Taxi drivers handing her luggage. Front desk clerks handing over keys. Waiters taking back the menu. There was nothing sexy about a finger brush.

Until today.

Until Alex—the obviously crazy lottery winner. Or the massively naïve, optimistic lottery winner. Either way, he was a complication she didn't need.

She yanked her hand back. "That'll be fourteen dollars."

"Plus the coffees," he reminded her, with a backward tip of the head toward his sister.

"Twenty-two, then."

"Yikes. We'd better load up on cereal and milk."

"Our pastries are worth it. And come back to try our

sandwiches." Sydney looked down at the half-filled bucket of lettuce. "On second thought, wait until tomorrow to come back for lunch."

"Something special on the menu?"

"Yes. I won't be the cook. So the sandwiches will be edible." Because Alex was nice. He didn't deserve her half-assed attempt that would no doubt burn the crap out of a panini. "You've witnessed my lack of kitchen talent." She brushed the muffin crumbs into the trash.

He slid bills across the counter. "I can make a sandwich. If I come back, it'll be for the beautiful woman who can't."

With that, he headed for the door, where his sister waited.

While Sydney just *gaped* at him. What had just happened?

"Hey, hon?" Her father came around to the sink carrying two empty coffeepots. "Don't forget that you're on chemo duty with Gram this afternoon. And take a couple of pairs of gloves with you. Your job is to hold the basin when she pukes. Her aim...well, it's not great."

That was a timely reminder of why she was here. Lettuce dryer and puke catcher.

Whatever *had* just happened with Alex?

It didn't matter.

Chapter Three

A LEX FINISHED PULLING on his gloves. Then he tilted his face up to the sun spearing through the pine trees. "This feels great, huh? We'd never be able to sit outside like this on January 5 if we were still in Pittsburgh."

"You're not in the Caribbean wearing just trunks and some sand. You're wearing a sweater under a coat. And a scarf. And a hat." Everleigh glared at him as she pointed at each article of clothing that clearly offended her.

She hadn't, ah, been on board with meeting on the inn's porch. Outside.

In January.

But it was fifty and sunny in the midafternoon. No snow, no wind. It felt great.

Better than being cooped up inside, without the warming sun. He'd insisted they throw open the windows in every room, on every floor, to blast out the stale air. Hopefully blow some of the dust out, too.

"Do you want a blanket?" Amelia offered.

Teague gave the railing a careful push before leaning his whole weight on it. "Or do you just want to whine for another minute to get it out of your system?"

"What I want is to be warm. I know you don't want to

heat the entire inn, Alex, but why can't we light one of the fireplaces and huddle in one room?"

With a patience he did *not* feel, Alex said, "They need to be checked by a professional before we use them."

Everleigh shifted on the wicker furniture. The cushion sort of gasped, and the frame of the couch sort of...wheezed? "For what? They're not ancient machinery. You light a fire and the smoke goes up. Basic since medieval times."

If she kept this up, Alex would tell her to do jumping jacks to stay warm. Because they had about two hundred things to discuss *besides* Everleigh's core temperature. "Animals could've built nests in them. You want to smell a roasting possum corpse?"

"That's disgusting. You're just trying to scare me into shutting up."

"A little, yes." Maybe a lot. He did *not* have the time to argue every single upcoming item. Alex sat in the chair next to her. "Look, we have no idea what could be in there. We have no idea if the chimneys are open at the top. If the liners are up to code so sparks don't slip through cracks and set insulation on fire. They need basic maintenance."

She turned her head to look at Amelia. Alex couldn't see her face, but he'd seen the move enough times in their years together to know that she was giving his sister an epically huge eye roll. "Fine."

It was ten kinds of strange *working* with people he'd known his entire life. That he'd gotten drunk with and eaten cereal in bathrobes with and, in Amelia's case, changed her diaper. If it was hard for him to recategorize them as colleagues? Probably just as strange for them to do with him.

Alex never got this frustrated, this fast, with his employees. He understood that people had lives outside of work that could be affecting their mood, their performance. In this case, he knew everything about their lives. Except for how annoyed they might be with their new boss.

He'd stop thinking of them as his favorite three people in the world. That made it too easy to bicker, too comfortable. He'd remind himself that for at least eight hours every day, they were colleagues, only. That should help.

Teague kept working his way down the porch, pushing at each section of railing with his black-gloved hands before sitting on it. "We can go through and close off the vents of the rooms we're not working in. That should redirect the heat when we do turn it on, save us some power. Or maybe just a couple of space heaters, if we're spending the day in, say, a bathroom."

"Good thinking." That was exactly the sort of thing Alex needed. Strategy. Right in line with his plan. He tapped the edge of the legal pad against his thigh. And, yeah, wished he had long underwear on beneath his jeans. "Teague came up with an idea the rest of us hadn't yet. That'll happen a lot in the coming months. It's what will make us a stronger team. And that's why we're out here; for a SWOT assessment."

"Like a fly swatter?" Amelia wrinkled her nose. "Alex, it's too cold for flies." She held up her hands, palms out, as if to hold off the tidal wave of his wrath. Yet another gesture he knew inside and out. "I'm not complaining like Everleigh, just stating a general insect fact."

"SWOT is with an O. It stands for strengths, weaknesses, opportunities and threats. We assess our team and our project for all of those things."

"Why?" Everleigh pounced with the question. Literally. She leaned over the armrest and drilled a finger into his thigh. Repeatedly.

Alex waved his pad. Which already had more than a dozen filled pages. "It'll allow us to appropriately divvy up this massive to-do list."

Teague made his way down the porch stairs, testing each tread slowly, all the way across. "It sounds annoying as fuck."

Really? The guy had spent his entire adult life in the military. Which was rife with rules, regs, ranks, and categorizing their members. Successfully. Where was this pushback coming from? He'd been certain Teague would be on board.

"Maybe a little tedious," Alex conceded. "But it's useful. A SWOT assessment will help us minimize risk, figure out where the holes are, and how best to optimize our knowledge base."

The idea had come to him while talking with the beautiful blonde who'd mangled their muffins. He'd stumbled over describing to her what attributes everyone brought to the team. *Not* just because Sydney was pretty and had attitude for days that would be so damn much fun to go up against.

In a perfect world, he would've stayed longer, flirted more. Then secured a date to see how her beautiful brown eyes warmed in candlelight.

In this world, though, he had to be the grown-up in the room, ride herd on his friends and work his ass off for the foreseeable future.

"I literally tuned out everything after the weird acronym," Amelia said with a wry twist to her lips.

Everleigh nodded her agreement. "Corporate speak will get you nowhere with us." Then she fluffed her hair forward in punctuation.

Come *on*. He wasn't asking them to take a four-day leadership seminar. He was asking for a couple of hours of frank discussion. It was day two already. It was time to buckle down and work harder than they ever had before.

"Stop making this more complicated than it needs to be." Teague leapt back up three steps to snatch the pad from Alex. He flipped through. Frowned. Flipped through more. "We'll run down each page of what has to happen. Then we'll each take a few pages and we'll do it. Simple as that."

"Really?"

He finished thumbing through, then tried to rip off all the written-on pages in one swift yank. Except that it didn't work. Because there were too many pages, too *much* to do in a single chunk.

And wasn't that just a damn metaphor—allegory?—*something* for what Alex was trying to explain?

Alex pushed to his feet. Then he whipped out his arm and snatched back the legal pad. "If we do it your way, just hand out pages and do what's on 'em, then you might end up having to come up with the design for the gardens. You up for that, buddy?"

"Obviously not," Teague said with a head tilt to the side that called him a moron. "*Obviously* I'd hand that over to our flower expert, Amelia."

"Okay. You sloughed off the landscaping." Deliberately, Alex turned over a page. "What about choosing the themes for each bedroom? Deciding on sticking with the old décor or getting new?"

"My 'décor'—" he made finger quotes around the word "—has mostly consisted of a camouflage tent with a Pittsburgh Steelers flag tacked to the wall. Of course I'm not the one to pick out paint colors."

Gotcha, Alex thought. He had to bite his lips to keep from grinning. "Then who is?"

Amelia stood up, too. She marched over to stand toe to toe with Teague and jab a finger in his face. "And be careful with your answer. If you go all caveman on us and say that the girls do all the decorating and the boys do all the construction, I might need to do some serious rehab on your *brain*. I spend my days hefting potted trees. I've got muscles and stamina, and I'm not afraid to use either."

"I'm more about stamina than muscles, but yeah, what she said," Everleigh chimed in.

Before he could answer—and dig himself further into a hole—Alex pressed harder. "What about reaching out to the Chamber of Commerce? Who's our expert on that?"

"You. *Obviously*, Mr. Hotel Manager," Teague snarled.

He let his buddy's irritation roll past him. This was a useful exercise. Talking through it all at once should get it out of everyone's systems. "Nope. I can't be the only one doing all the hotel admin things. Just like you can't be the only one painting, and Amelia can't be the only one planting. It's all too much for one person. We've got to work as a team."

To Alex's relief, the women nodded, getting his point. And Teague—well, at least he stopped arguing.

And, to his surprise, Everleigh went one step further. She

stood right next to Amelia, effectively boxing Teague in against the railing. "Don't be so closed-minded. How do you know you won't be good at choosing color schemes unless you try? Just like you can't assume you hate brussels sprouts until you try them. I always said I hated them. But then Jeremy took me to this gastro pub where they were roasted with balsamic vinegar, and crispy and caramelized, and now I'm hooked."

"Which one was Jeremy?" Amelia asked, tapping a finger against her lips. "The dermatologist or the investment banker?"

"The sommelier. And the wine we had with that meal was out of this world. The perfect wine for them is a Languedoc red. And all I know about it is that I definitely can't afford it."

Alex made two mental notes.

1) Everleigh was, indeed, good with the big picture and motivation. He wanted to nudge her toward doing their marketing.

2) She could derail a conversation in the freaking blink of an eye. Keeping her on task might be a challenge.

"Okay, okay already. I hear all of you." Teague threw up his hands and then scooted past the women. "Let's get this over with."

Amelia beamed at him. "That's the spirit."

"We can start by listing the special skills on my résumé." He ticked them off on outstretched fingers. "Operation and maintenance of domestic and foreign weaponry. Detonation and deactivation of explosives, sniper, and certified parachut-ist."

Smart-ass.

"I think I'd better make my presence known before you say anything else." A tall man came around the magnolia tree and stood at the bottom of the steps. His hands were in the pockets of his puffy black jacket.

And a shiny gold police badge was clipped to his belt. Right next to the holstered gun.

Great. Teague ran his mouth in front of a cop. Not the best first impression. Which meant it was up to Alex to fix it.

He held out his hand as he loped down the steps. "Alex Kirkland. Brand-new owner of Three Oaks Inn."

"Matt Halliday. Chestertown Police Chief."

Even better—Teague had put the *chief* on notice. He'd definitely gotten up on the wrong side of the very cold bed this morning. "Nice to meet you."

"Same. But let's get the official stuff out of the way so I can meet everyone." He nodded at Teague. "Are you mili-tary?"

"Ex. As of three weeks ago. Special Forces."

Matt's blond eyebrows shot up. "Impressive. Coast Guard, for me."

Teague flashed a smile as flat and shiny as quicksilver. "I'll try not to hold that against you."

Seriously? Now he had to poke at the police officer for belonging to the 'wrong' branch of the military? When he wasn't even *in* it anymore? What if Teague made a joke like that to a paying guest, six months down the road?

That voice of doom—or reason—that kept circling his

skull reminded Alex that this whole boondoggle of the four of them pulling this off might *not* work, after all.

Matt leveled a cool stare at his friend. "Maryland's got more shoreline than lots of other coastal states. And you now live in a waterman's town. Might want to dial back your obvious disrespect to the Coast Guard."

For the love of God, Teague, don't make this worse! Alex thought. Hoped. Repeated really fast three times in his head like a mantra.

Thankfully, his friend dipped his head in apology. "Sorry. I was on autopilot there for a second. I only mustered out three weeks ago. I'm still working on figuring out how to act like a civilian."

The chief shrugged one shoulder. "Been there, done that. It gets easier, I promise. Do you have a carry permit?"

"Yes. For Pennsylvania." He dug out his wallet and flashed the laminated card. "We just moved here yesterday, so I'll be getting one for Maryland."

The guarded stiffness disappeared from his frame. A warm smile creased his face. One so affable that it looked far more natural on him. But Alex wouldn't forget the initial sharpness to the man's brown gaze. Nor underestimate it.

"Good enough for me. Sorry to interrogate you, but it comes with the job."

"Understood." Teague also went down the steps to shake. "I'm Teague, that's Amelia and Everleigh. We actually all own the place."

"So I heard. You four are the talk of the town. It's why we came out here to introduce ourselves."

"We?"

Matt did a half turn on his heel, cursed under his breath, and disappeared down the path. A few moments later he reappeared, carrying an enormous basket wrapped in blue cellophane. Right on his heels was a woman with tight black curls close-cropped to her head, wearing a cream suit with pearls and stilettos. She had the hip-shot swagger of a fashion model, and the high cheekbones to match.

"Hello! Welcome to Chestertown! I'm Angie Hilliard, president of the Chamber of Commerce." Then she paused, looked at Matt, and finally nudged him with her elbow.

"Oh. Yeah." He handed the enormous basket to Alex.

"That's a small representation from our member businesses from the historic downtown. A way to introduce themselves to you!"

Wow. The woman actually talked in exclamation points. If this was *Sesame Street*, they'd be boinging above her head. There was enthusiasm…and then there was Angie, about seven miles past it.

But making nice with the chamber was on the very first page of Alex's to-do list. "Thanks for making the trip out here. We're honored."

"And we're all in *shock*. The general opinion was that a resort conglomerate would snatch this place up. Someone with the money to really do the place justice. Never in a million years did we think that Kenny's cockamamie lottery scheme would *succeed*!"

Funny how her 'shock' sounded a lot more like 'what kind of a dumb-ass would take this on themselves.' Sure, it was a lot of work. But unless all the pipes needed to be refitted, or the foundation was cracked, the work was hard, not high-priced. Not if you were willing to put in the time and the elbow grease.

"We're just lucky, I guess," Alex said with an easy smile that hid his gritted teeth.

"That's one way to look at it." Her tone and skeptical squint said that her viewpoint was the opposite.

"It's how *we* see it," Amelia said firmly, stepping forward to be shoulder to shoulder with her brother. "This is the best Christmas present we ever got. And that includes the year our parents surprised us with a trip to Disney World. Getting to rehab and then run this beautiful inn with the people we love most in the world will make this new career even more rewarding."

"New?" Angie latched on to that one word like a mosquito to a bag of O+. "You're new to the hotel biz?"

Also not a tidbit he'd planned to broadcast to the whole of Chestertown. Or, really, *anyone.* But Alex could gloss over that.

He set the basket on a wicker coffee table—one they hadn't tested yet for sturdiness—and hoped it wouldn't collapse. "Amelia's a landscaper. Hotel, estate, business park—it's her experience with plants that matters, not where she puts them."

"I was about to sign a contract with the most prestigious hotel in Pittsburgh." With a *what can you do* twirl of her wrists to end palms up, she said, "But then we won the lottery for the inn."

Alex thrust his hand into a pocket to prevent an accidental fist-pump. *Way to go, Amelia!* He'd set the conversational ball, and she'd spiked it as though they'd practiced the move a hundred times. Take *that*, subconscious voice of doom. "I've got all the experience necessary to run this place. And each of us brings specialized skills to the table."

If only he knew what those were…

"Great! Three Oaks is a special place. We're thrilled that anyone has decided to take it on as a project and bring it back to life!"

Again, it all sounded good, but listening between the lines, Angie thought they'd bitten off more than they could chew. Or wanted *them* to think that. Which made Alex extremely suspicious.

Sauntering around to the front of the basket, Alex made a big show of peering through the cellophane, poking things around. "Angie, you didn't say yet. Which business is yours?"

"I run the boutique hotel downtown, right on High Street. Our restaurant is Zagat rated. Perfect for your guests who are celebrating something romantic!"

Aha. She was here to size up the competition. Which Alex respected. It meant she did her homework.

"That sounds wonderful." Everleigh pushed in on Alex's other side. Once again, he was struck by her ability to read a situation. Her people skills would come in handy. As long as he could curb her self-sabotaging impulse to fall for every man between twenty and sixty who looked her way. "I'm looking forward to sending our hungry guests your way."

Her tone was saccharine and sincere. That took talent.

Angie sprayed them all with her smile, like a sprinkler head moving down the line. "It would be so nice if at least one of you could make it to the next Chamber of Commerce meeting. Outreach and reciprocity are the hallmarks of this business community. Our meetings are held the fourth Saturday of the month, in the Episcopal church hall."

"Which one?" Teague snorted. "We passed an intersection last night that had one on every corner. Felt like a turf war might break out any minute."

"St. David's. At eight sharp. Feel free to bring samples of your inn's breakfast and tea pastries." The fashion model façade slipped. Angie's smile became extremely shark-like. It was a challenge, and they all knew it. "All the information's on the website, and my card is in the welcome basket."

Matt cleared his throat, hooked his thumbs into his pockets. "I'm here to give you a heads-up. The local teens have been using your barns as a party spot. They figured it's far enough off the road that nobody would find out."

Everleigh swayed forward. Licked her thickly glossed pink lips. Alex had seen that two-part move before. About a hundred times before.

Holy hell. It had been five minutes, and she was already flirting with the police chief. How many more ways could this welcome visit go off the rails?

"But you're smarter than a bunch of drunk high school boys?" And Ever's voice was lower, breathier than normal.

Matt's lips quirked up on one side. "I like to think so."

"Did you run them off?"

"A few times. I added more regular patrols that drove back onto the property. It was just about under control, but now that you're here, they'll assume I'll cut back the drive-bys. You should rig up some motion-sensor lights back there."

Alex gave a nod. "Thanks for the tip."

"No need to use your advanced foreign weaponry knowledge on them," he said with a pointed look at Teague.

"Aww, you read my mind. Here I was going to rig a glitter bomb to go off on the next person who opened the barn door."

Matt laughed. Then laughed harder. "You know what? I approve that plan. It sends a message and embarrasses them. Go for it. Unofficially, of course."

"Chief Halliday, you can't condone an attack on children." Angie pressed her long fingers to her chest, just below the pearls.

"Simmer down. It's glitter, not buckshot. You can buy those things on the web and have them delivered to someone's desk. It'll be ten times as effective as sending one of my officers out here once a week."

The chief seemed like a good guy. Maybe someone they could call a friend, down the road. "We'll let you know if there's any trouble." Alex extended his hand to shake Angie's, then Matt's in turn.

"Nice to meet all of you." The pair headed down the path that led to the parking area.

"Changed my mind," Teague announced. "I'll volunteer to do reach-out to the chamber. A very...personal reach-out."

Everleigh rolled her eyes. "Because Angie looks like Lupita Nyong'o?"

"Yep."

Alex couldn't believe his friend. But he also couldn't

blame him. For all her carefully slipcovered attitude, the woman was gorgeous. Just…not as striking to him as Sydney had been. "No flirting with the president of the chamber," he ordered. "What if something goes wrong?"

With a wink and a cocky grin, Teague sat back down in the rocking chair. "I've got mad skills, Alex. No worries there. Road-tested in four countries."

Amelia thwacked him on the arm as she flopped onto the sofa. "OMG, he isn't questioning your bedroom moves. He's questioning what happens the *next* day, when you're ready to move on and Angie's gone all heart-eyes for you."

"Can I help it if ladies love me?"

"Yes," Alex said firmly. He braced his back against one of the poles on the staircase that would look amazing draped with garland and lights in eleven months. "You can. By not encouraging them in the first place."

"Alex, dude." Teague cupped his hands around his mouth and stage whispered. "You need to get laid. Soon. Then that stick might fall out of your ass."

"I've got no time for sex in the next year. None of us do."

Everleigh made a time-out gesture with her hands. "I don't recall celibacy being in the partnership contract we signed."

"It was implied." Alex waggled his notepad. "Due to the copious amount of around-the-clock work we'll be doing to open this place as soon as possible so that it stops draining our reserves. Now, can we get back to the SWOT assessment?"

Ever might've had a point. No sex would only make a

tough situation tougher. But it was no different than working overtime and not getting to watch a football game, or being too busy to hit the gym.

He just wished that he *hadn't* met Sydney today. Temptation was harder to ignore when you knew it was out there.

And she'd been very, very, tempting...

Chapter Four

IT WAS WEIRD for Sydney to see her father hovering. He'd always been quiet. Calm. Moving to the beat of his own drum without noticing what went on around him. But today, Neil was flustered. Repetitive. And hovered more than a hummingbird.

He paced a tight four steps back and forth in front of her gram. "I brought you a rocking chair, Mom. I'll just run out to the truck and get it."

"A rocking chair? With a cushion?" She glared at him over the top of the surgical mask he'd tied on her himself. "No. This isn't a resort, it's a business. I'll use the stool my butt's been parked on for twenty years."

This ought to be good.

And not just because it gave Sydney an excuse to stop pulling off lettuce leaves. Her gram was a spitfire on her most relaxed days. Today? She was so amped up to be back in the Mercantile that she was like a kid on Christmas who'd already knocked back four hot cocoas. *With* marshmallows.

Neil paced over to the register to stare down at the basic wooden stool. "It doesn't have a back."

"It's a *stool*, not a recliner. Do I have to explain furniture to you?" Gram crossed her arms over the purple turtleneck, cardigan, and fleece her son had bundled her into. In case she caught a chill from customers opening the front door.

"You need more support than that." He thrust his arm out to point disparagingly at the stool. It was so dramatic. So over the top. So *not* like her father.

It was a little bit adorable. Except that obviously her grandmother didn't see it that way.

The older woman let her head loll to the side to roll her eyes at Sydney.

"Nope. Leave me out of this. I have too much respect for both of you to pit a parent and child against each other. Although I'll happily take the rocking chair for when I do a shift at the register. I think you should bring it in, Dad, and we'll figure out who uses it later."

He pivoted, launching all his frustration about his sick mother into a fiery glare at Sydney. "You're a perfectly healthy thirty-year-old. You stand and look engaged and ready to hop to when someone walks in the door, young lady."

Wow. Back home for three days, and he'd already spit out his first 'young lady.' What was next? Being grounded for sassing him? This whole situation with Gram's illness really had him off-balance.

Gram struggled out of her top fleece layer. Her movements were cautious and yet jerky, as she was hampered by the lingering pain from her surgery two weeks ago. "Neil, stop treating me like I'm about to kick the bucket."

"But...Mom...you were. The doctors all said so."

"And they were all wrong, weren't they? I'm here. Which makes me the smartest, stubbornest person in the room. So go check the inventory on snow melt in the back, and give me some peace."

He huffed. Puckered up his mouth like he wanted to spit out a nasty response. But then, he shuffled forward to press a kiss on the top of her pumpkin-orange curls and headed to the stockroom.

Sydney kept watch, though. Noticed that as soon as his back was turned, her grandmother sort of deflated, folding in on herself as though their bickering had been the only thing keeping her upright. The older woman grabbed for the edge of the counter and leaned on it as she lowered herself onto the stool with a long sigh.

"Want me to hang up your fleece in the office?" Sydney offered. "I know, I know—you can take it there yourself. But you don't want to run into Dad. You both need to cool off for a few."

"Fine. Thank you."

Sydney hustled over to take it. At least this time Gram hadn't turned sheet white from the walk, like she had going from the house to her son's truck. "Have you two been fighting like this the whole time I've been gone?"

"Of course not." Gram shifted, winced. Shifted again. "Neil's an easy partner to work with here. He's just lost his damn mind since my diagnosis."

Oh, boy. Things were in a sorry state when *Sydney* had to be the adult in the room. So she'd wade into dangerous waters and point out the obvious truth. Better for Gram to be mad at her than at her son. "I'm pretty sure it's more about almost losing the mother he adores than losing his mind."

"Dwelling on what *didn't* happen is dumb. I'm fine for now, and I'll be better after I'm finished with chemo."

It didn't take a psych degree to see that the near-death slide was a topic being completely ignored by Gram. One that she'd probably been too terrified to even process. Although the fact that her globe-trotting granddaughter had returned after more than a decade ought to have hammered home some of the seriousness.

In a very calm voice, she said, "Being at the Mercantile stresses your already compromised immune system. You're not supposed to risk getting sick until you finish chemo. It isn't smart."

"Neither is letting you burn down the shop," Gram snapped back. "Neil told me about yesterday's incident."

Now it was *her* fault her post-op grandmother had left the house a week ahead of schedule? Sydney knew full well that was an excuse. That Gram had been climbing the walls, missing her store and her friends.

"It was one blob of cheese on the grill that started smoking. There was no fire."

"Let's keep that streak going. Maggie's going to keep baking and bringing the daily pastries over, but you're going to have to make sandwiches. Hot and cold. Knives and griddle and everything."

Sydney snuck a look at her watch. Not even ten. This would be a long day. "Well, I'm sure I'll learn it all fast, learning from the best."

"Ha! What about that fiancé of yours? Does he do all the cooking?"

Oh no.

Right before surgery, when the doctors were predicting the worst possible outcomes, Sydney had called, for what could've been the last time. Gram had asked the question she asked during every call with hope in her hazel eyes—*have you met the man of your dreams yet.* She had this idea that Sydney's travels would result in a love connection. This ridiculous, impossible, *outdated* idea.

But this time, Sydney had caved. She'd looked at her uncharacteristically scared grandmother, so fragile in the hospital bed with the IV stand and the monitors beeping…and she'd invented a fake fiancé. To put a little joy in the woman's subconscious as they wheeled her into surgery.

Then Gram…hadn't died. Cause for rejoicing, sure. But tricky for Sydney in terms of this lie that had spiraled out of control. She couldn't dump the fiancé until after Gram made it through chemo. No worries, no stressors—doctor's orders.

"Gram, I—"

"What's his favorite thing to eat? You should learn to cook that, at least. I can help."

"Gram—"

But the interrogation continued without even waiting for Sydney to answer. "Are you moving in together? Once you stop taking pity on your poor old grandmother and go back to your real life? Some old biddies say to hold out for a ring. But *I* say you need to test drive every aspect of a man."

She would lie about her imaginary fiancé as long as it took. Sydney drew the line, however, at hearing so much as another inference about her grandparents' premarital sex life.

What could she make up as his favorite food that would be easy to learn to cook? Was steak too cliché? Pasta too predictable? Stalling, Sydney patted the fleece still draped over her arm. "I…I'll just go hang this up. Be right back."

The door opened, bell jangling. She paused, and couldn't help but smile as Alex—the muffin man from two days ago—walked in.

His face lit up, their eyes connecting. Then his gaze tracked down to the fleece. "Going somewhere?" He thumped his hand over his heart, then dramatically whipped his head to the side. "After I came here *just* to see you?"

After a giggle at his obvious teasing, she said, "Me—or my unlimited supply of caffeine?"

"Sydney, you're breaking my heart. How could you accuse me of wanting coffee more than I want you?"

Gram's hand suddenly clenched with a surprising amount of strength around Sydney's wrist. "*That's* your fiancé?" she whispered.

No.

Nonononono.

Her grandmother leaping to conclusions made an already awkward situation even more complicated. How was this fair? A breezy, two-sentence banter with a handsome man. That's all Sydney had wanted. Yet now it had turned into so much more.

Without waiting for a response—*again*—she said more loudly, even though Alex was walking closer, "You came here on a visit?"

His dark brows crinkled together. "No, I live here now."

Clapping her hands together, she rocked so far back on the stool that Sydney thrust out a hand to catch her. "That's the most wonderful news I've heard all year."

"It's January 7th. You're setting a very low bar for the next eleven months."

"Nothing could top you moving here." She thrust out her hand. "You can call me Daisy."

With a bemused smile, he shook. "You can call me Alex."

In cartoons, a light bulb went off overhead when someone had an idea. Sydney felt like a lightning *bolt* crashed into her brain at that moment. Especially since her heart also started pounding like a jackhammer. Because she had an idea.

A crazy idea.

A no-way-would-it-work idea.

A reckless idea.

But…it *would* make things easier for the next few months. It'd get her grandmother off her back. It would also make the woman happy for at least eighty-eight more days. Relaxed. Distracted from the discomfort of chemo.

Which made it a completely necessary idea.

Patting the fleece, Sydney said, "Alex, would you come with me while I stow this jacket in the back?"

That look of bemusement teased another smile at the corners of his mouth. "Sure. I love sneaking behind the velvet rope and seeing off-limit spaces. Makes me feel like the president, going up the service elevator before a speech."

"Gram, I'll be right back. Keep your mask on. Don't go near the food prep. Just sit there."

Gram coughed out the word, "Spoilsport."

Sydney cocked her head to indicate the direction of the door into the back. Wordlessly, she led Alex past the bathrooms, past the locked alcohol stockroom, to the utilitarian office. And then she made sure to close the door behind him so her father wouldn't be tempted to wander in and join the conversation.

"This is…not as exciting as I would've hoped," Alex said, looking at the crammed-together file cabinets, shelves, a ratty, mustard-colored couch that had literally been there Sydney's entire life, and a wooden desk.

Draping the fleece over the rolling chair behind the desk, Sydney almost laughed. "It's about to get exciting, believe me. I have a favor to ask."

"First off, let's back up about two minutes. Why does your grandmother think that I'm your fiancé?"

"It's purely wishful thinking. With a soupçon of confusion. We were talking about him right before you walked in the door."

"You're engaged?" Sydney *felt* his gaze, like a thorough caress, rake up and down her body. She wore jeans and a cape-sleeved beige sweater, but Alex's heated stare made her feel like she was in La Perla lingerie. "Lucky man."

"Actually…no. I'm not engaged. To the unending consternation of my grandmother."

"I'm confused."

This was it. The moment to shake her head, laugh, and lead them back out. To not risk making a complete fool out of herself.

But she'd already made the ultimate sacrifice by coming home for three months. What was an awkward extension to that time?

Sydney sat on the couch. Patted the cushion next to her

for Alex to sit as well. Then she folded her hands in her lap. "My grandmother almost died a few weeks ago. Or, we *thought* she was going to. Cancer."

He angled more sideways, his knee brushing hers. "I'm so sorry."

"No, it turns out she's fine. Hopefully will be, at least. They read the scan wrong—or there was a shadow? It's unclear. There's a lot of CYA going on by the hospital staff as to the overly dire diagnosis."

"I'm not surprised. Are they hoping you'll skip the lawsuit out of sheer gratitude that she's not on her deathbed?"

"Maybe. I'm not really dialed into the details, since I just got here a few days ago. The surgery went well, but she still has a few rounds of chemo ahead of her."

Alex nodded once. "Ah. That explains the mask."

He unwound a pale blue scarf that perfectly matched his eyes. From its semi-bulky, uneven rows, it was obviously hand-knitted. It said a lot about a man's character that he'd ignore suaveness and fashion and instead choose sentiment.

"She shouldn't even be out of the house. She fell after getting up too soon after the operation, and tore her stitches. Now she's started chemo. That gives her the impossible task of needing to stay healthy in the depths of cold season. But...well, the Mercantile's her baby. Almost as much as my dad is. We literally couldn't keep her at home another day."

"Strong lady."

"You have *no* idea." Daisy Darrow had held their family together in its darkest times by sheer force of will. She was the one who'd told Sydney to go chase her dreams, even if it meant leaving Chestertown, when everyone else argued against it.

"She doesn't seem addled, though. So how about you circle around to why she thinks we're engaged?"

"Before the supposedly dicey surgery, I couldn't get back in time to say goodbye. I wanted to make her smile, though, when we video chatted. She's a bleeding-heart romantic. Every single phone call begins with her asking if I've met anyone special. So…I invented an engagement."

"That's a bold choice."

"Bigger than I knew." The anesthesiologist had warned them that she'd have some memory loss. Probably centered around right before and after the operation. So Sydney had assumed the white lie wasn't too much of a gamble. "As soon as I walked in the door three days ago, she remembered it."

Alex swiped his palm over his mouth. It didn't hide the fact that he was trying and failing at not snickering. "That's rough for you. When are you going to tell her that you lied? Because if it's today, how about you give me a twenty-minute heads-up? My friend Everleigh would be fascinated to watch."

"Very funny. And that depends on how you answer the question."

"What question?"

Taking a deep breath, Sydney focused on his blue eyes. The tiny crinkles at the edges. The super long, super dark lashes that probably made his red-headed sister bitterly jealous. He'd listened to her whole story patiently. Fully engaged. So many men would've not paid attention. Alex gave the impression that he was all-in on a conversation, whether arguing or laughing or sympathizing.

Yikes.

She'd spiraled out a little bit there. He was too handsome and she was clearly too easily tempted.

Steepling her fingers, she tapped them against her lips. "Would you pretend to be my fiancé?"

An easy grin widened his mouth. "You're hilarious."

"Sometimes. Especially after exactly one and a half moji-tos. But right now? I'm serious."

"You can't be."

"I am." It wasn't a good sign that the shock value of her request had sidelined Alex from answering. "Please don't keep going around in circles as to the truth factor. We don't have much time. Gram expects me back out there."

Alex half-stood to pull off his coat. "You barely know me."

Which made him a better candidate than probably the last six men she'd attempted to date. "I know that you're bold and passionate and a hard worker, if you're going to bring Three Oaks back to life. I know that you're loyal, to do it with your sister and your friends. And I know you're caring to have not already walked out the door halfway through my story."

He scratched at the back of his neck, just above the collar of his navy Henley. "What if I'm engaged already?"

"Then you wouldn't have been flirting with me." Cripes, what if she'd read him all wrong? "At least, I hope not," she amended.

"Correct. Which leads us to the next obvious stumbling block. If I'm pretending to be engaged to you, I won't be able to actually flirt, let alone date, anyone else." Alex cleared his throat, thrust out an arm as if orating to a crowd, and said, "'In the spring a young man's fancy lightly turns to thoughts of love.'"

Sydney's mouth dried up. Her handsome, almost-fake fiancé could quote Tennyson? That was as panty-melting as his smile. Maybe more so.

Then she realized he'd mentioned spring. Her mouth rounded from slack-jawed awe at his poetry pizzazz to shock at forgetting the main fact that would make him say yes. "Oh! I forgot the best part."

"I don't have to drop two months' salary on a ring? Or you have a deal worked out with the hardware store and you'll let me use your discount to purchase all our supplies?"

She held up one hand and ticked off yet another point on her fingers. "And now I know that you're extremely fixated on money."

Alex's expression morphed into straight-up solemnity, like he'd slipped on a mask. "The four of us have no incoming income until we get this inn running. Damn straight I'm all about the bottom line."

"I guess I can add practical to your list of traits." Which she appreciated. It was the people who pretended not to care about money but pinched every penny in secret that were difficult. Hiding things—anything, big or small—never turned out well.

In a tone drier than Death Valley, Alex said, "That is *just* what every man longs to hear during a proposal. That practicality came in ahead of good looks and sex appeal."

"I didn't say that." Did he truly not know that he smoldered with sex appeal? That he could be the man in a cologne/watch/champagne ad? It was actually endearing that he needed a bit of an ego stroke. "Alex, you're suavely handsome. Your smiles are rare, and all the more potent because of it."

Those icy eyes widened in...disbelief? Appreciation? Hard to tell. But then he dipped his chin. "Nice to hear. Was that so hard?"

"I didn't realize you needed a bit of flirting to consider this favor. It seemed...forward to lead off with cataloging your physical traits."

"Forward?" A huge belly laugh rolled out of him. It was warm and contagious, even though Sydney knew it was aimed at her. "You just proposed after a grand total of ten minutes of conversation, over two days."

Men had a tendency to be so darned literal. "I'm not proposing for real. I'm asking for your help. You will, in no way, be obligated to follow through into a fake marriage."

"Then where does the line get drawn?" Alex braced a hand on the back of the couch and leaned forward. He leaned in so close that his breath warmed her ear. "How interesting does this get?"

For a moment—okay, three—Sydney let herself enjoy the closeness. The heat pumping off him through the waffle-weave shirt onto her chest. The brush of his biceps against the back of her head. How their knees pressed together. It was all intimate and on the edge of...something. She just wasn't sure what.

"It'll be over in the spring. That's the best part. Three months. That's all I'm asking for. Then Gram's chemo will be over. She'll be out of the woods, and we can drop the charade. But now? It would make her so happy. It'd give her something to think about besides how utterly crappy she feels from the chemo." Sydney put her hand on his shoulder, locking them in a loose circle. "Please?"

This close, she could see the radiating lines of ice and midnight blue in his eyes. Could see his pupils flare wider, darken.

"Hon?" her father's voice echoed down the hallway. Sydney sprang into the opposite corner of the couch, in a move that she'd feel in her quads tomorrow.

"Yeah, Dad?"

"There's customers." The unmistakable squeak and clang of the rolling bucket punctuated his sentence. "And I just dropped a container of milk that needs to be mopped up."

"I'll head out front."

"Thanks, hon."

Sydney stood. Waited for Alex to say something. When he didn't, she put her hand on the doorknob. "Well?"

He crossed to the desk. Opened one drawer, then another. Once he grabbed a jumbo paper clip, he unwound it, then wrapped it twice into a circle that he then slid onto her ring finger. "It's up to you to come up with a cutesy story about why I proposed with this."

"Deal."

The overwhelming gratitude and relief *almost* made Sydney miss that Alex was still holding her hand with both of his. With fingers that were long, blunt-tipped, and enveloped her own with a warmth that made her think of lazy weekend mornings under a duvet cover.

The door swung inward a crack, almost clocking her in

the head. "Hon, I can hear Mom's voice all the way back here. She's getting riled up."

"Trust me, that's better for her than chicken soup laced with morphine."

Sydney hustled out to the front of the Mercantile. Two steps from the register, Alex caught her hand again. Interlaced their fingers. For a near-stranger, it felt amazingly right. Like a perfect fit.

Which was impossible.

Gram's eagle eyes spotted them, drawing her focus from the parents cooing over the newborn in the stroller. "Is everything okay with you two? Are you fighting? Did you go in the back to smooch?"

This was the moment she had to sell it. "Why bother? We can do that right here." Sydney went up on tiptoe, looped her arm around Alex's neck, and pulled his head down.

It should've been awkward.

Weird.

Perfunctory, even.

It was none of those things. Their kiss was as smooth as if they'd already rehearsed it a hundred times. His lips caressed hers, molded them, took their time with her. They were warm and welcoming and more than a little bit wicked.

Alex's arms cinched around her back, lifting her off of the floor.

Or so she discovered once he set her back on her feet and her ankles wobbled to steady herself.

"Bye, my angel." Alex raised a single eyebrow at her. It clearly taunted her in a *you started this* way. Then he squeezed her grandmother's forearm—quite thoughtfully avoiding a germ-laden handshake. "Nice to meet you, Daisy."

"I'm so happy you swung by for a visit, Alex." She beamed at his retreating back, throwing off happiness like sparks from a bonfire.

Sydney touched a fingertip to her lips. They were still tingling from his kiss.

Maybe this had been the right choice to perk up her gram.

Or maybe…this crazy favor she'd asked him was a million, billion times more dangerous than she'd anticipated.

Chapter Five

"HEY, DO YOU—" Alex broke off, annoyed. He sounded like a little kid's half-assed version of Darth Vader from under this mask. Sure, it'd keep their lungs safe during days and days of sanding. But it was only hour two of the sanding, now that they'd finished their initial cleaning push, and he already hated the thing. He yanked it down to protect his Adam's apple, instead.

"Do I wish we could've sprung for the full-sized industrial sander? Hell, yeah," Teague said. His voice was similarly muffled. Unlike Alex, though, he seemed to take it in stride. Guess after protecting himself from the punishing desert wind and sand, a little mask action made no difference to him.

"We will. For the big jobs. But it'd be useless here on the stair railing."

"I get it." Teague winked over the top of the mask. "Size matters."

"Don't say that in front of Amelia and Ever. They'll dissolve into giggles. Or a feminist mantra recitation. It is impossible for them to hear those two words and not take them out of context."

"You mean like us and how anything remotely fart-related turns us automatically into eleven-year-olds?"

"Yeah."

Switching off the sander, Teague said, "You sure about starting here? On the stairs?"

No.

Not entirely.

It'd kept Alex awake for the whole night. Well, equal parts that, and thinking about Sydney. The beautiful, big-hearted woman who apparently would do *anything* for her family. Including dragging him into a hip-deep lie.

It was easy to tell that the Mercantile, with its prime location right between the main historical drag and the marina, was an integral touchpoint for the small town. Which meant that lying to the people who ran it would no doubt come back to bite him in the ass.

But he'd been unable to say *no* to her big, pleading, honey-colored eyes.

Alex rolled off of his heels to sit on the step, leaning back against a pink-patterned wallpaper that would be the next thing they tackled. And reminded himself not to let his friend see his own indecision. He had to be their rock.

So he slid on an easy grin. "We have to start somewhere."

"The stairs don't feel important. Who books a getaway because of a staircase?"

Ah. Teague's years with the Special Forces gave him an entirely different frame of reference. Alex had barreled forward with the decision without explaining.

He never would've done that back at the Orion. Employees didn't work well in the dark. But he was so used to automatically being on the same page as Teague that he hadn't thought to talk it through.

Dumb.

He was *sucking* at the whole transition of friends-to-business-partners thing.

Alex reached between the railings to grab the travel mugs of water they'd staged. He handed one to Teague. Better to lose five minutes now to get him all the way on board.

"Look, there are two things that will make us money. That'll bring people here, as opposed to that inn on High Street, or the resort over on the Bay. The rooms, and the wow factor. The cottage rooms are in better shape than the main building, so Everleigh and Amelia are starting there. The wow factor is this grand entrance." Alex waved a hand to indicate the open staircase that circled up all five flights. "People go nuts for a dramatic, sweeping staircase. Bridal parties can take photos on it up the wazoo. The sooner we get it restored, the sooner we can start marketing it."

Teague shoved his mask to the top of his head. Wiped the back of his hand across his mouth. "Okay. When you break it down like that, I get it. But man, I don't think I've got the vision you do."

"Doesn't matter. Actually, it's probably for the best. Too many different visions muddy the waters. You bring the sweat equity. The drive to finish. The know-how, thanks to working with your uncle's construction company."

"That's me. Sweaty know-how. Used to have that on the name plate on my flak helmet." Teague leaned over. "Also what more than a few ladies call me."

"Ladies who only know English as their *second* language?" he ribbed back. God, it was good to have his friend home.

The front door slammed open, banging all the way back against the wall. Alex winced at imagining how deep a gouge the doorknob must've left. Guess he needed to add doorstops for every room to his never-ending list. Installing them would be an all-day project.

Amelia stopped at the threshold, hands fisted at her sides. Her face was almost as red as her hair as she yelled, "Alexander Graham Kirkland. Where are—oh. There you are."

Uh-oh.

Amelia *never* rocked his middle name. He was in trouble. And, much like many of the times his parents had bellowed it, Alex had no idea what for.

After another slow sip of water, he waved a greeting. "What's up, sis?"

She marched to the side of the stairs and glared at him through the railings. "Do *not* act casual."

"It's not an act." Teague snorted. "It's hard to be anything but casual when squatting over a sander."

Teague always had his back.

She white-knuckled her fingers around the railings. "I am your only blood relation on the planet. But you don't bother to tell me that you're engaged? Do you know how hurtful that is?"

Shit.

Teague dropped his travel mug. It bumped and clanged its way down seven steps before rolling to a stop at the door. "You're *what?*"

"I'm not. I'm nothing." Alex stood, back against the wall.

"I didn't think you'd find out."

"Really? So you weren't going to invite me to the wedding, either? Or Teague, for that matter?"

"Dude. You weren't going to let me throw you a bachelor party?" The disappointment that coated Teague's words was as thick as the pain over Amelia's.

This was spiraling out of control faster than a barrel going over Niagara Falls. He held up both hands. "Stop. Everyone stop jumping to conclusions. Let me explain."

"Oh, this oughtta be good." Everleigh strolled in, kicking the door shut behind her. Her hair twitched in the same rhythm as her hips. "Did I miss anything?"

With a one-shoulder shrug, Amelia said, "Just Alex turning as white as marshmallow fluff."

"Good. Then it's not too late for me to weigh in." Standing shoulder to shoulder with Amelia, she squint-glared at him. "You said we couldn't have sex for a year. A year, Alex! Yet somehow in five days you managed to leapfrog through hooking up straight to an engagement? Because none of us believe you'd put a ring on it without a test drive."

True. Not a deal-breaker, but definitely nothing he wanted to discuss with his little sister and her BFF.

Not that he'd wanted to discuss *any* of this with them. Because there wasn't supposed to be anything to discuss!

"I said stop," he bellowed. "I'm not engaged. I haven't had sex. And for God's sake, Teague, we've been talking about going to New Orleans for our bachelor parties since we turned twenty-one. Of course we'll do it. Together."

"Then I'm good." Teague leaned back, propping his elbows on the stairs above and stretching his legs out. "But I'm staying put, because I can't wait to watch you squirm your way out of this firestorm."

Evidently the 'having his back' portion of the day had concluded.

Alex jumped down the three steps to the floor. "Amelia, I'm sorry you heard about this from somebody else. But I swear it isn't true. It's a fake engagement. As a favor."

"A favor? A fake engagement to a stranger is one step below donating part of your liver. If you felt an impulse to do something good, you should've left your change in the tip jar at the gas station. That's what we call a proportional response."

She wasn't wrong.

Rather than trying to explain more, Alex jumped ahead to the point that ought to absolve him. "It didn't seem like a big deal because I didn't think anyone would find out."

Amelia pinched together her thumb and forefinger. "We live in a town the size of a microchip. Of course news like this would spread."

He hadn't accounted for that. They'd lived here for five freaking days. It wasn't like he was in sync with the town yet, after only talking to less than a dozen people.

However, it was obvious that he should've picked his head up out of the to-do list and paid more attention to their new ecosystem. Alex pressed the heels of his hands into his eyes.

"Sydney, over at the Mercantile, told her dying grandmother right before an operation that she was engaged. To make the poor woman feel better. Except it turns out that she's not dying anymore. Daisy *is* going through chemo, though. Which is hard, to say the least. So Sydney needed a fake fiancé. I just walked into their sightline at the wrong time and ended up getting cast in the role."

Everleigh wrapped her arms around herself and swayed side to side. "Alex Kirkland, that is the sweetest thing I've ever heard. *Of course* you had to say yes. You stepped up. I'm so proud of you."

That was a far more exuberantly positive reaction than Alex had expected. Or probably deserved. But he wouldn't look a gift horse in the mouth. "Thanks. Don't give me too much credit, though. I figured it would be an 'in name only' sort of thing."

Mostly.

Except for that kiss that'd knocked him back with its equal parts heat and sweetness. He didn't know what to do about it.

Hope for another? Or acknowledge it was eight kinds of trouble and hope there *wouldn't* be another?

Alex closed the gulf between him and his sister. Her gaze was locked on a knot in the floorboards. *Aka*, studiously not on him. She'd been riding the wave of red-headed temper when she stormed in. His explanation appeared to have stripped that down to the pain underneath.

Hell.

That was a million times worse than her anger. When Amelia still stayed silent, he pulled her into a tight hug. "I'd never hurt you like that. Not on purpose. Or keep something this big from you."

"But you did," she said in a small, quiet voice that pierced his heart.

"This engagement—it was a nothing. It didn't matter. It wasn't real. Unimportant. But what is important is that I *did* hurt you, so I'm very, very sorry."

"Okay." And her arms finally squeezed him back.

Thank God.

After wallowing in the hug long enough to be sure they were back on an even keel, Alex tapped her on the nose. "How did you even hear about the engagement? You've been in Heron Cottage all morning."

"On the radio."

What the *hell?*

His fake love life was a media story? In a place where he didn't know anyone? Yet *everyone* now knew him? The inn was supposed to be the story, not him. Alex literally could not imagine how this could get any worse.

Teague's laughter rolled off the walls and filled the four floors of empty space amidst the open staircase.

"Zip it," Alex growled.

At this point, Teague was laughing so hard that he had to grab on to the railing to keep himself upright. "You're breaking news, dude. This is hilarious. I wonder if anyone's going to roll out a location reporter to interview me about the inevitable bachelor party."

"I said, zip it."

The front door banged open. Again.

Dinging the wall. *Again.*

Guess that project needed to be air-lifted to the top of the priority list. Since knocking and doorbells weren't apparently the custom in Chestertown.

This time, it was Sydney who raced through the doorway

as if…as if her dad was about to turn this into a shotgun wedding.

Huh.

Maybe this whole thing *could* still get worse.

She threw her honey-streaked mass of hair over her shoulders with both hands, then looked down the hallway. Their eyes immediately connected. "Oh, good, you're here."

"For the next four months, I can guarantee this is the only place you'll ever find Alex." Amelia hip-bumped him. "He's as grafted to this inn as that giant magnolia out front."

"No, I mean *here*." One hand unwound a pink and brown plaid scarf, while the other gestured at his spot by the stairs. "I already knocked on half the cottages, because I saw your car over there."

"Well, welcome to the Three Oaks Inn. Officially." Alex bumped Amelia back—with enough force to bump her out of his way—and moved toward Sydney. "Or are you expecting me to carry you over the threshold? You know, to practice for our big day?"

And yeah, he let more than a little of his temper singe his words. This was not how he wanted to be introduced to the town. Also? Not a fan of other people making decisions on his behalf.

In other words, Alex was regretting this favor. *Big*-time.

"Alex, I'm so sorry." She twisted and untwisted the scarf around her wrists. "As soon as I heard the radio report, I raced over here to warn you. And apologize."

"Christ, Sydney, how are we a news story? What did you do?"

"Nothing."

He curled his fingers on the lintel of the doorframe. Angled his body to cage her in against the screen. And ignored—mostly—that it put him close enough to notice the sprinkling of cinnamon-sugar freckles that dusted across the bridge of her nose. "Really? If *you* didn't tell the DJ, then who did?"

"My gram's friend Hazel. Gram went to get her hair done one last time before it all falls out and told the entire salon, because she's so tickled. Hazel thought it was the most romantic thing ever. Couldn't pass it along fast enough to the station manager. Because *she* wanted to top her friend Myra who'd tipped them off on the mayor's pregnant daughter last week."

That was...convoluted. Small towns, man. They ought to come with an instruction manual.

"Romantic?" Teague heaved himself up, shaking his head. "It's barely believable. Hasn't everyone already heard that we won this place in a lottery?"

Or did logic get left behind at the town border? "Tacking on, after the fact, that we just happened to win it in the same town where my fiancée lives?" Alex spread his arms wide, palms up. "Come on. That stretches suspension of disbelief more than sitting through *Cats*."

"That's evidently what makes it so romantic. The unlikeliness of it all." Sydney shrugged out of her wool coat to reveal a pink sweater. One that hugged her curves and dipped low between her breasts. Her initial hung from a thin gold chain, and suddenly Alex was consumed with the idea of pushing it aside with his mouth and tasting her.

He took two giant steps backward.

Away from the temptation.

"Then people in this town are dumb. Or the biggest suckers who ever lived," Teague proclaimed. He came down the stairs with his hand outstretched. "I'm Teague. I hear you're going to marry my best friend. Any chance you want to reconsider now that you've seen another option?" He gave her an oversized wink, one side of his mouth cocked wide.

"Sydney." While they shook, she winked back. With an equally big grin. "And while I appreciate the offer, let me reiterate that I'm *not* going to marry Alex. I'm simply...borrowing him for a short while to perpetuate that illusion." Sydney pivoted to Alex. White-knuckled her scarf, her body drawn up as stiff and straight as if a puppeteer were pulling her strings. "That is, if you're still willing."

Sure, Alex was angry. Frustrated. But he wasn't mean. The reason they were pulling off this stunt hadn't changed. "Is your grandmother still going through chemo?"

"Yes."

"Is talking about our engagement making her happy?"

"God, yes."

What kind of a monster would he be to stop it all? Instead of his usual Giving Tuesday donation to the American Cancer Society this year, he'd make this his goodwill donation. "Then I'm still in."

Her whole-body stiffness resolved infinitesimally. "Thank you. And to clarify to all of you, this engagement is finite. I'm gone in ninety days. Eighty-six, to be precise."

Everleigh's mouth gaped open. "You're counting?"

Head bobbing up and down fast, Sydney replied, "I can't ever scrape this town off my shoes fast enough. You *bet* I'm counting the days. My dad says that's as long as they need me—through her finishing chemo."

"Oh, I'm Everleigh, by the way." She shoved her hands into the back pockets of her faded jeans. "Best friend to your fake soon-to-be sister-in-law, and co-winner-owner of the Three Oaks."

Amelia wrinkled her nose. "Gee, that's not confusing at *all*."

"Hi." Sydney beamed a smile at the other women. But it was so wide that Alex caught a portion of it, and it hit him like a two-gallon can of unfiltered lust straight to the gut. "I'm sorry to have interrupted your day with this nutty drama."

"No, it's good you came over." Everleigh took Sydney's coat and propelled her through the plastic-sheeted doorway into a parlor. Or what they were calling a parlor until they came up with a less stuffy word. Everyone followed them, dropping onto the flower-sprigged couch and chairs. Good thing they'd vacuumed the dust out of all the upholstery yesterday. "You need to make plans."

"For what?"

"For your date. You have to go on a date for this to be believable."

Everleigh was addicted to romance. She taped the Hallmark Christmas movies to watch year-round. Her love of *being* in love had led her into making crap decisions about bad boyfriends time and time again. But Alex had never expected her romantic idiocy to be inserted into his life.

A quick glance over at Sydney revealed rounded eyes and a half-open mouth that meant she was as shocked as him by the suggestion.

"No. We're not complicating this," Alex stated firmly.

Because an actual date would be one hell of a complication.

He'd have to sit across from a gorgeous, smart woman and *not* let himself fall for her. Ignore his already sky-high attraction for her.

Talk about no good deed going unpunished.

"Your engagement is *literally* the talk of the town. They'll expect to see you two lovebirds out together," Everleigh insisted.

Amelia curled her feet beneath her. "Ever's right. You can't drop a bomb like this and then not follow up. You two have to go on a date. As soon as possible. In front of as much of the town as possible."

Teague slapped his hands together, and then pointed them at Alex. "Why not just ride on a float down High Street while holding hands? Something tastefully decorated, with turtle doves and bows and puffy hearts? I could get right on building that for you."

Just because they were running this inn by committee did not in any way, shape or form mean that his life would now be run by that selfsame committee. "I'll bet you think you're hilarious, don't you?"

Smirking, Teague said, "Yeah."

"No way. This is an engagement in name only." Alex got up to rip off a cracked piece of wallpaper. Hideous paper with its ancient print of birds that looked like it came from an ornithology textbook. "A date would steal time away from all the work we've got to do. Do you know how many stairs I can sand in the space of a two-hour date?"

Amelia rolled her eyes. "No, and I don't care. You are not solely responsible for bringing this inn back into shape. The sooner you realize that, the better."

Ever pushed onto her knees to twist around and lean over the back of the couch to face him. "In fact, maybe we'd all be more productive, get more done in less time, if you weren't lording all your bossiness over us."

Good thing he'd known them both his whole life. Realized they were poking at him with the best of intentions. That knowledge was all that kept Alex from stomping out in a cold, stony silence at their words.

Huh. Which would probably just prove their point. Five days in, and he'd been pushing everyone too hard the whole time. Himself included.

Amelia snagged his hand. Gave it a squeeze. "You gave your word. You committed to this thing, so you have to do it right."

"Besides, it isn't healthy to work in fourteen-hour shifts." Everleigh never stopped with a single push. She'd beat you to death with a point, and then beat you *more* with it once you were flat on the ground. "If you weren't on a date, we wouldn't let you be working here, either. Resting and recharging is important. Vital to productivity."

Alex looked over at Sydney as he realized that she had yet to respond to Everleigh's suggestion. "Give us some space," he ordered.

"But this is my new fave reality show," Teague teased.

"Out."

Once the three of them vacated the room—although

he'd bet they were only two steps down the hall, ears pressed to the wall—Alex sat back down next to Sydney. "You're awfully quiet."

Her lips compressed into a thin line before she answered. "Just registering the snowballing implications of what I've dragged you into. I don't generally ask people for help. I only know how to do things by myself."

That was sweet of her. But unnecessary. He'd been taking care of himself—and Amelia—since their parents died in the middle of his freshman year of college. "Don't worry about me. I can handle it."

"I get the impression you can handle anything that gets thrown at you." Sydney slid him a warm look of interest mixed with respect.

"Generally speaking. Although you did throw me for a loop with your proposal."

"Good to know." She dropped her head into her hands, elbows propped on her thighs. "I wanted to stay under the radar as much as possible this trip. Help my dad at the store, and take care of Gram. That's it. Now everyone will find an excuse to pop into the Mercantile and drill me with a million questions. Questions I won't have the answer to, because we're not engaged."

Alex reached out to stroke her back, her oh-so-silky hair—then stopped himself right before making contact. "Do you want to call it off?"

"No." Sydney sighed, then lifted her head. "My frustration and annoyance doesn't tip the scale against what Gram is going through. This is the perfect distraction from her chemo."

"In that case…" This time he gave in to impulse. Wrapped both of his hands around the ball of her fist. "Would you like to have dinner with me tomorrow night? Because I'd really like to show my fiancée off to the whole town."

Her laugh was short and startled. "Really? Saturday night?"

"Go big or go home. You've got to choose the restaurant, though. I don't have time to read twenty Yelp reviews."

"Fair enough." Sydney brought her other hand to cover his. "I think I'd very much enjoy joining you for dinner."

Yeah.

That's what he was afraid of.

Enjoying himself.

With her.

Chapter Six

SYDNEY FELT LIKE she was back at summer camp in the mountains of Western Maryland. Back then, they'd spent a ridiculous amount of every night sneaking around to the boys' cabins. Tiptoeing. Giggling. Shrieking. Rarely working up the courage to actually knock on the windows and talk to the boys, however.

Twenty years later, she'd come full circle. The adorable cottages at the Three Oaks Inn might as well be cabins, tucked into the forest that butted up to the property. The only thing missing was the rest of her posse. Which, at this point, was a good thing.

The point of sneaking up to Alex's cabin was that she didn't want the *rest* of the inn crew to know that she was here.

It was easy to identify Sandpiper Cottage as his. Only two of the cottages had lights on. And someone had hilariously taped a sign with the symbol for the appropriate gender on each of them. That circle with the arrow popping out diagonally told Sydney she was in the right place.

A peek in the front window revealed Teague watching television. Great. They were already separated.

She circled around the screened porch back to the bedrooms. Peeking in there would be rude. And at least a misdemeanor. So she reached up, eyes pressed tightly shut, and tapped her nails back and forth on the window.

Then she did it again.

Maybe she'd guessed wrong and was at Teague's room? Giving it one more try, this time Sydney knocked with her knuckles, feeling foolish. At least she hadn't done the classic gravel toss at the glass.

Abruptly, the window pushed up beneath her fingers. "Sydney?" Alex glowered for another second, then his features smoothed into amusement. "What the hell are you doing out there? I thought we had a racoon trying to break in."

"They're generally not the breaking and entering type. They need the lure of food."

He looked down at her. Boots buried in a snowdrift up to mid-shin. Balanced sideways against the wall to arch around the out-of-control vegetation. "Do you really want to keep crouching in that bush in below-freezing temps talking to me about racoons?"

"No. I really don't. But I don't want Teague to know I'm here, either."

"Yeah—that's obvious," he said dryly. "My room connects to the porch. I'll meet you out there."

Sydney got jabbed in the ribs as she tried to back out around the bush. Maybe this hadn't been a good idea after all. Few ideas that hit in pjs after ten p.m. ever were worthwhile. But mid-pint of Häagen-Daz's Rum Tres Leches, it'd felt *brilliant*.

She let herself in the creaky screen door, then sank into

an Adirondack. Hoped—probably too late, the way her night was going—that it wasn't splintery or cracked. She pulled her knit cap down more over her ears. Then she pulled up her parka hood over it. They might be out here a while.

Alex came out looking...bulky under his terry cloth bathrobe. *Very* bulky, for her to see it at all in the shadows. The moonlight wasn't doing too much to illuminate the porch.

Sydney pointed at him. "Why aren't you wearing a coat?"

"You said you didn't want Teague to know you were here. He'd wonder why I need my coat to hang out in my bedroom. So I put on three sweatshirts under this. Oughtta be fine for a bit."

Guilt lashed at her. "I'm sorry. This was dumb. I don't want you getting frostbite. I should go." She started to push out of the chair, but Alex put a hand on her thigh to stop her.

A hand covered in socks.

Which was *adorably* hilarious. And just so thoughtful, that he'd go to these lengths after a crazy woman knocked on his window.

"No. Sydney, *something* brought you over here close to midnight. Stay and tell me." He snatched his hand back. "Unless you're here to break up with me. I don't so much want to freeze my balls off for *that*."

"That's exactly why I'm here. Well, not to break up. But to discuss our engagement."

There was enough light to see his eyes widen perceptibly.

And his teeth flashed as his jaw dropped. "This couldn't wait until our big Saturday night date?"

"No." Because she had a shift at the Mercantile in the morning. The only way this conversation could wait was if she stayed in bed all day with the covers over her head. Which was another moment from her pre-teen history, but one she did not need to re-enact.

"Hmm." He rubbed his hand over his chin. "Need to negotiate our prenup?"

Funny. If they were inside, bantering over spiked cocoa in front of a roaring fire.

"Alex, the longer you tease me about this, the longer you'll be out here in twenty-degree temps."

"Sorry. Why is this a secret from Teague, by the way?"

"He's fun."

"Yeah? I feel like that comment is going to boomerang into you needing me to *not* be fun?"

"I'm already embarrassed about this whole thing. It wasn't easy to be confronted by Teague and Amelia and Everleigh when I came to the inn to talk to you today. They were all nice, but I felt like an idiot. Probably because this whole fake engagement is a really nutty thing to try and pull off."

"Well, you can't be embarrassed with me. We're in this together. And I'll do my best to dial back my natural affinity for fun." He folded his hand together. It was probably an attempt to look serious, but the sock mittens killed that vibe. "What's on your mind?"

Sydney pulled off her glove and waggled her fourth finger at him. "I don't know why you gave me a paper clip ring."

"What else did you expect me to use from that back office? Did you want me to spend a buck on a soda can and rip off the tab?" Frustration sharpened his tone.

Not everyone was a night owl like her. Maybe having this conversation close to midnight with a tired almost-stranger really was a bad idea...

"I know why you did it for *real*," Sydney said slowly, with exaggerated patience she in no way felt. "I just can't come up with a cute story about why you'd *fake* propose with it."

"And that's a time-sensitive piece of imaginative crafting?"

His clever snarkiness would be fun if it wasn't so darned cold and late.

"Yes. Now that our story's been on the radio, everyone knows. Which means everyone will ask. I need to have an answer prepared. Also—"

"Oh, good, there's more," he interrupted. Alex shifted to stretch one long leg out in front and settle onto the armrests.

"I'm just laying out all the bullet points for the conversation up front."

"Maybe I should go grab my legal pad."

Sydney leaned forward, elbows propped on her knees. Hopefully he'd pick up on her seriousness. "*Also*, I didn't think this whole fake fiancé thing through."

A sharp, much-too-loud laugh burst out. Alex slapped a hand over his mouth as he tried to swallow it. Finally, he shook his head and said, "No kidding."

"I don't want to lie to my dad and brother." Her sister

Kim was away and could be handled via an email explanation. "Not just because it'll get complicated, but because this is the most time I've had in person with them in forever. I don't want to taint it by it all being a lie. I have to tell them the truth. They love Gram. They'll play along."

"Well, *my* family and friends know the truth, so I won't stop you." Alex cocked his head sideways. "Why don't you spend time with them, if it means that much to you?"

"I travel for my job. Extensively. Mostly foreign. I'm rarely even on this continent."

"Lemme guess. Astronaut? Grand Prix driver?"

Funny—only because she'd slept with one once. In Monaco. And it turned out that speed truly *was* his specialty.

It was already hard enough to resist the sexy, rumpled, funny man next to her. If they started opening up, it'd make walking away from him so much more difficult.

Sydney held up her hand, palm out to push Alex away, metaphorically. "I'll answer, but with a caveat. I don't want to do the whole 'deep dive into sharing' thing. Because we aren't really engaged. Or dating. My emotional plate's pretty full right now with my gram."

"Okay. I get that." His voice stayed placid. Like his ego wasn't ruffled in the least by her semi-rejection. "God knows my brain is past capacity with focusing everything I've got on the inn. Well, that and learning how to work with my friends."

"That's, um, got to be an adjustment. Trust me, I know. It isn't easy getting my dad to treat me like an employee instead of a daughter right now."

He nodded vigorously. "Right? So damn hard. But for

the record, engaged people usually know at least a few pertinent facts about each other. The best lies are based in truth. Otherwise, you run the risk of me asking people if they've watched you on the competitive ping-pong circuit."

Damn it.

Alex was right.

So not only did that make Sydney wrong, but it showed that this impulse, bolt-of-lightning idea of hers was turning into a gigantic pain in the ass.

"I produce a cable travel show. Not at all glamorous. I don't get to stay in luxurious hotel suites and sample caviar. In fact, I may not have a job to go back to once these ninety days are up. Which is another reason why I really don't want to talk about it."

"Understood." He clapped his hands together. Which, in the sock-mittens, she would've totally missed had she not been watching the motion occur. "Solves the problem of how we met, though. I worked in the hotel industry. We can say we met on the job."

"Unless you worked at a hotel in Dubai or Australia, that'd be a stretch."

"A conference, then. All sorts of crazy things happen at conferences. And they're often in far-flung destinations."

That could work. Brainstorming to the rescue! "I like it. I'll even make the fake jet lag easier on you, bring it to this hemisphere. We'll say we met at a conference in Buenos Aires."

"Great. I love a thick, rare steak and a bottle of Syrah. Sounds like a good time."

It did indeed. Which is why Sydney did not linger on

imagining it, but moved briskly on. "You romanced me for the entire week."

"Obviously I would. You're very beautiful, Sydney."

The matter-of-fact compliment threw her for a loop. Good thing an icy blast of wind rattled through the screens just then to literally slap her in the face. "Then you threw caution to the wind and proposed, knowing I was about to fly off to the other side of the world. You couldn't risk letting me go without a ring on my finger."

Alex sandwiched her gloved hand between both of his. "We were at the gate. Your flight was boarding. There was no time." His voice had deepened, slowed its pace. He wasn't brainstorming anymore. He was telling the story of their love. "So I pulled the paper clip off the wad of conference agendas in my bag and wrapped it around your finger. That conference brought us together—and a piece of it would help *keep* us together. Forever."

Wow.

Her heart pumped faster. Sydney realized that she'd angled toward him more. Put her other hand on his forearm to truly join them together.

That was totally off-the-cuff. For a person with whom he had zero emotional involvement. Imagine what Alex could come up with, given more than five minutes, for a woman he truly *loved*?!?!?

"That's...um...that's terrific. If the inn doesn't work out for you, you should move to Hollywood and write rom-coms. I'm sold."

"Good." Alex let go and leaned back in his Adirondack. "If you buy it, everyone else will."

"You think?" Sydney tucked her hands into her coat pockets. "Because this isn't a game. My grandmother raised me. She loves this town. And me. She'd do almost anything to keep me by her side. Except that she *knew* I was unhappy here. So she was the only person in my family who told me to spread my wings and go find my happiness wherever else it might be. I owe her everything. I owe her the life I've been living."

"Sydney. I hear you. I'm committed to doing this. We'll give your grandmother the happiest three months of chemo anyone ever had."

"Thank you." She sighed. Wriggled her toes that were slowly going numb in her boots. "Thank you just isn't enough. I owe you something really, really big."

"You don't. This is a humanitarian favor. Any other guy you dragged back into the office and proposed to would've said yes."

He really believed that. Alex didn't have any clue that he was one of the few, the rare—the genuinely *good* guys. "Don't sell yourself short. A surprisingly small number of people appreciate the behind-the-scenes access."

"Look, I hear small towns can sometimes be…reticent when it comes to outsiders. So when we're out together, just introduce me as your fiancé. It'll cut through that reserve. Give me status as a local. We'll call it even."

"Hardly. I'm far from the prodigal daughter returning. But yes, our having dinner together tomorrow should help. Everyone adores my grandmother. Her talking you up left and right will go a long way."

"Is that it?" Alex stuffed his hands under his armpits.

"Because I'm here to tell you that parkas are much more efficient at heat-trapping than my triple sweatshirt method."

It was official. She was the worst fake-fiancée ever.

This was why she never asked people for help. It complicated everything.

"I'm sorry. Yes. That's enough for tonight." Sydney pushed up from the chair. Made a less-than-subtle beeline for the screen door. Because how did you gracefully end such a weird conversation while the other person was quickly turning into a human Popsicle? "I feel much better. Ready to brave the hordes in the morning. Please, go inside. And thank you."

She slipped out the door without waiting for him to say goodbye.

Sydney vowed to herself to be very mature, composed, and pulled together on their date. Hopefully that—and a little frostbite to the brain tonight—would make Alex forget this had happened.

She wished she could forget. Specifically, how readily he'd come out to help her, no questions asked. No coat on. How he hadn't laughed at her. How he'd come up with the solutions to all of her burning questions.

Yes, Sydney would like nothing better than to forget exactly how wonderful Alex had been to her tonight.

No chance of that happening, though.

Chapter Seven

SYDNEY WENT TO college far from home, without any support network nearby. She then traveled the world for her job, by herself. Sure, she had a team for some parts, but there were too many instances to count of being a lone woman in a foreign place. She prided herself on not just surviving, but *thriving* solely on her own strength and merits.

Tonight's date tossed all of that out the window. Tonight, and for the next three months, she had to rely on Alex's help to pull off this fake engagement. That fit her about as well as if she tried to shimmy into her third-grade gymnastics leotard.

The waitress cleared their bowl of empty mussel shells, lingering to give Alex an obvious once-over.

Sydney didn't blame her. The man looked…edible. He wore a light blue button-down—the same blue as his eyes— beneath a navy argyle sweater. Sexy-preppy-yummy was how she'd label it. The sweater showed off the breadth of his shoulders. And licking the buttery garlic sauce off his fingers certainly gave a girl…ideas…

"There's a man at the bar staring at you. Did you line up any other fake fiancés, in case I said no?" Alex asked.

"What? No." She scrubbed at her fingers with a napkin.

It felt too weirdly intimate to copy Alex's licking. "There was no plan, and definitely no list of potential fake mates. It was purely spontaneous stupidity."

"Should I prepare to fight to keep my place across from you?" The twinkle in his eye was impossible to miss. The serious grump who'd pissed her off when he first entered the Mercantile had been replaced with a playful Alex.

And playful Alex was *maddeningly* irresistible.

Sydney tried to sneak a glance at the bar, but there was a large party slowly passing, weighed down with car seats and parkas and four kids. Which, of course, had been the point of choosing 98 Cannon as the setting for their public coming-out as a couple. Located on the Chester River, her dad had assured her it was one of the hottest spots on a Saturday night.

She drained the last of her beer. This night definitely called for a steady flow of alcohol. "Nobody would be dumb enough to try and pick up a woman who is obviously on a date."

"Maybe it isn't obvious. Maybe us ordering the garlic mussels threw everyone off the, ah, scent."

"No puns, please. Of *course* we look like a couple. You're all snazzed up." Sydney circled a hand at his face. He'd used gel in his hair, too, to tease out a couple of rugged curls in the hair she'd only seen drooping over his forehead.

"And you look absolutely—" He broke off to inhale deeply as he stared at her. A stare that drifted over her as softly as satin sheets. It made Sydney glad that she'd piled her hair into a messy chignon and worn an off-the-shoulder pink sweater. Long links of gold stars dangled from her ears.

Alex made the extra effort worthwhile. "—lovely. I'm sorry I didn't mention that before now. Believe me, I noticed it the moment you stepped out the door."

Either Alex was exceedingly well-mannered, or sweet…or he meant it. Probably all three, from the way his focused gaze had yet to drift from her face.

If he meant it, though, that would complicate things. Sydney wanted to be friendly with him. She did not want a repeat of the kiss they'd shared.

Okay, she very much *wanted* another kiss from him. And just as much knew it would be disastrous to a clean, quick exit when it was time to cut and run. Why the heck couldn't he be grumpy and irascible again?

Laughing lightly, she dismissed his compliment. "It only has to look like a date, Alex. We don't have to talk like we're on a date. No compliments required."

"Compliments are never required. But giving them is often necessary. Simply a statement of fact. Like, if you wanted to state factually that you weren't at all tempted to switch your fake fiancé to Teague once you saw him…"

"Have you two always competed for the same woman?"

"Never. Our friendship's more important. Whoever calls dibs gets to make a move."

So he really was exceedingly loyal. Interesting. "Here are the rules—no boring small talk. No date-appropriate conversations. Only honest answers and no fake laughs at unworthy jokes."

"And no accepting dates from other people? Because that guy from the bar is coming over here now."

What a pain in the neck. "I'll head him off." Sydney

tossed her head back, laughed, and then slid her hand ever-so-slowly to cover Alex's. The move was deliberate and sensual, and full of ownership.

How good it felt…well, that was something she'd think about later.

In bed.

A safe four miles away from Alex.

"Stop with the touching. Some of us are trying to eat. Or at least get drunk." A man glowered down at her.

But not a stranger. And definitely not someone interested in a hookup.

"Cam!" She jumped up to hug her brother. *Now* it felt like she was home. "It's so good to see you."

He rubbed his palm over the significant blond scruff on his chin. "Had to look twice to be sure it was you. You've grown out your hair."

"About a dozen times. Chopped it all off just as many." She sat back down. "Where've you been? Dad just said you were out of town."

"That's the pot scraping the kettle for info. You've been out of town for more than a decade." He tugged at her bun. "Me and Zach were hired to help out on a private sail in the Virgin Islands. A guy with a summer place here wanted to teach his kids how to sail for the holidays."

"So you got charter money and a tan? Not bad."

"You said it. Just got back, so we're posted up here to drink to our good fortune." Then he pointedly turned to Alex. "Hi. I'm Syd's brother, Campbell."

"Alex. Nice to meet you."

Cam leaned down, bracing himself on the table. Kept his

voice pitched loud over all the voices pinging off the ceiling in the long, open room. "Treat her right. Or I'll come find you and treat you to my left. Left hook, that is."

Sydney pushed at his shoulder. "God, Cam, that joke wasn't funny in high school, and it certainly hasn't aged well."

"I enjoyed it. Got my point across. So it's a two-fer. Your not liking it doesn't so much matter."

"I've got a little sister. So I get your point, loud and clear. No worries." Alex motioned at the chair next to Sydney. "Would you like to join us?"

"No!" How were they supposed to establish their romantic couplehood with her brother as a third wheel? "We're on a date, Alex." Sydney finished with a significant eyebrow waggle that he had to be capable of interpreting as *drop it.*

"Oh, that's blindingly obvious. I have zero wish to sit here and watch you paw at each other. Just wanted to say hey. I'll swing by the Merc tomorrow and catch up with you?"

"That'd be great." Whew. She'd gotten a reprieve in telling him about her 'engagement' here, surrounded by all the locals. Unless...someone mentioned it while he lingered at the bar. Better to tell him the unvarnished truth at the store tomorrow. "You should move on to the Retriever Bar. No kids. You sailors can be as salty as you like."

"Good idea." Cam dropped a kiss on the top of her head and moved off.

Narrow escape achieved.

Alex wiped the back of his hand across his forehead in an exaggerated gesture of relief. "Glad I didn't have to fight him for you."

"You'd probably lose. Cam's a boatman. Biceps like tree trunks from pulling ropes and lifting engines for his whole life."

His eyebrow shot up. "Wow, when you said no date talk, you weren't kidding. Insult duly noted."

"Sorry." Sydney's hands flew to cover her mouth. She'd gone too far. Because she was so comfortable with Alex. Because she wasn't treating him like a date at all, but an easy-to-talk-to friend. That was terminal honesty territory. *Aka* not at all appropriate with someone you barely knew. "Oh, God, I'm really sorry. I wasn't denigrating your manhood. I mean, I wouldn't. I couldn't, actually, seeing as how you're so handsome and, well, manly."

Oh, geez. In digging herself out of the self-created hole, she'd just made it crumble all over her.

Alex leaned forward, his voice low and dark and as velvety as a chocolate truffle. "Did you know that your cheeks turn a lovely shade of pink when you're embarrassed?"

No. But she did know that his words upped her core body temp by at least five degrees. "Is that another back-door attempt at delivering me a date-like compliment?"

"Just an observation. No different than admiring the blue-gray color scheme of this restaurant that must blend well with the river view when the sun's out."

Sneaky man.

The waitress delivered their plates of fish and chips. Nodded at Sydney's request for another beer, but fawned all over Alex long enough for Sydney to pour a pool of ketchup *and* eat six fries. The fries were excellent. Hot and crispy.

They were never as good in other countries, no matter how fancy the restaurant, as back here at home.

Once the waitress sashayed off, Sydney said dryly, "You did an admirable job of not flirting back at her."

"I'm having dinner with my fiancée. Who has instructed me to not even flirt with *her*, let alone any other woman."

Interesting that her *fake* fiancé had more integrity than some of the men she'd dated for real. "Flirting's okay. It'd make everything look more believable, seeing as how the whole point of dinner is to sell this engagement as the real deal."

"This is too good to be true. I don't have to exercise any caution around topics that aren't date-appropriate, *and* I get to flirt with a stunning woman? Who knew I'd hit the lottery twice in as many weeks?" Alex took her hand, brushing his thumb back and forth over the paper clip ring he'd given her.

Yes, it sent chills up the backs of her arms and legs.

No, Alex hadn't crossed a single line.

Yes, he'd done *precisely* as she'd asked.

No. Noooo, Sydney had not anticipated the effect a flirty Alex would have on her. How could she? He'd snapped and scowled at her about three hundred percent more than smiled in their short time together.

Until last night, really. But last night's helpful and warm Alex was a whole different level than *flirty* Alex.

How was she supposed to know that he'd transform in-to...into...this total package of male awesomeness? Or realize how susceptible she'd be to it?

Sydney propped her forearm just in front of the thick

white china plate. To the rest of the room, it'd look like she was whispering sweet *somethings* to him. Luckily, thanks to the busy buzz of the room, even the closest two-top couldn't overhear her say—for her own self-preservation, "As long as you don't expect it to go anywhere."

"Hey there!" The greeting from the town police chief startled Sydney. But Alex held tight to her hand to prevent her from yanking it away from him. "Keep it clean, love-birds. I don't want to have to book you on felony flirting."

"Hi, Matt." Alex looked ridiculously pleased with him-self. "You're the first person I've accidentally run into. That I know. That I recognize. This is great. I'm putting down roots here."

Matt nodded at Sydney with a smile, then angled back to Alex. "Glad you feel that way. Because I've got someone who wants to meet you. Our station dispatcher."

"Why does she want to meet me?" Alex pursed his lips (so sexy) then clicked his tongue knowingly. "Is she a fan of Michael Fassbender and noticed my striking resemblance?"

Matt crooked his finger, and an older woman with tight-ly shorn salt-and-pepper curls practically bounded to the table. "Alex, this is Debbie, who keeps my life collated and organized. One of these days she'll tell me what she puts in the station coffee to magically erase stress. She's a miracle worker on many levels."

"Debbie...Miss Debbie? From Maplethorpe Elemen-tary?" Sydney asked slowly. Wow. A blast from the past that she hadn't expected. And she was almost as thrilled as Alex at the spurt of recognition.

A brown hand fluttered up to her cheekbone, brushing

the wide plastic hoops she always wore. Tonight's were blue. With snowflakes painted on them. When Sydney had been nine, she'd thought the endless variety of hoops to be the height of sophistication. "Indeed. You were such an attentive student, Sydney. I do enjoy seeing how the finished product turns out, as it were. I'm so pleased that you remember me."

"Of course I do. You were my third-grade teacher. You had us make papier-mâché replicas of the wonders of the world. I think that's what gave me the travel bug."

Her hand fluttered back down to pat Sydney's shoulder, as if she were still a student. "Oh, that's such a kind thing to say. No wonder your young man popped the question."

"But you were a teacher. How on earth did you end up working for the police?"

"Have you been back in an elementary classroom since you grew up? It's a damned battlefield. I find criminals much easier to deal with."

Alex burst out laughing. "Do you have any kids of your own?"

"Goodness, no. It takes all my energy and then some to keep our police chief in line. But that's just me." Then her infectious smile turned sly. "I'll bet you two will make beautiful babies."

Omigod.

The *embarrassment*. The only bright side? If she actually was 'with' Alex, it'd be a hundred times worse.

"Miss Debbie." Sydney let go of Alex and grabbed on to her beer like it was the last lifeboat bobbing by the *Titanic*. "We're barely used to being engaged. Don't rush things. Didn't you used to tell us that cutting in line was bad?"

"I'm not rushing. I'm anticipating." The older woman rubbed her hands together. "Like Christmas."

"Christmas is eleven months away," Alex said dryly.

"Yes, but I'm already looking forward to it."

Matt took her arm. Grimaced his apologies over the top of her head. "We're here to celebrate your birthday, not freak out Alex and Sydney. Let's head back to our table. Everyone's waiting for you to order dessert."

"You mean you didn't get me a surprise dessert with a candle and all the waitstaff to sing to me?"

"Of course I did. But I also know you like to graze between two desserts."

"No wonder they put you in charge, Chief."

The moment their backs were turned, Sydney took two long gulps of beer. "Sorry about that."

"What? She's adorable. And after all, I'm not the one who'd lose the ability to see their ankles by the eighth month of pregnancy."

"Oh, you're hilarious." Sydney shook her head. "You don't understand yet how this all works. By this time tomorrow, she'll have told two dozen people that she talked to us about being pregnant. Some will start suspecting a shotgun wedding."

"You're exaggerating."

Maybe a little. "Okay, it'll take forty-eight hours."

Alex dug into his coleslaw. "The food's good. I'm meeting new people. And my non-date is delightful. I've got no complaints, no matter how hard you try."

She caught movement out of the corner of her eye. "Just wait. You won't be able to get three bites in."

"Before what?"

"Sydney! I hear you're engaged!" A man who could be a dead ringer for Ichabod Crane waved his long arms in the air. "Don't tell me it's to this scrumptious man?"

Alex's eyelids flared wide. Surprise, mostly, but she'd bet there was a touch of WTH scrambling through his brain. That was the reaction most people had to the director of the County Historical Association.

"Are you still with your partner, Mr. Lyndon?"

"Not only with him, but legal. We got married two years ago."

"Congratulations. And with you off the market, then, yes, Alex is stuck with me."

"Aren't you sweet?" He thrust out his hand. "Dr. Lyndon Calvert. It's a genuine pleasure to meet the man who is giving the Three Oaks Inn the respect she deserves."

Alex shook. "It's a team effort."

"Then I can't wait to meet the rest of the team."

Alex's smile stiffened. She'd already picked up on the fact that he wanted to eat, sleep and breathe the renovation, interruption-free. After tonight there'd be a non-stop conga line of visitors to peek at the inn and all four of its new owners. But…Alex was doing her an immense favor.

So she held her tongue. Took a bite of fish.

And noticed three more people blatantly *in line* to stop at their table. He'd be lucky to snag two more bites in the next twenty minutes. Even though he'd asked her to smooth the way with the locals, it seemed like his wish had been more along the lines of her waving a magic wand and telling people he could be trusted. He wouldn't appreciate pop-ins interrupting his work on a daily basis.

Which would, technically, all be her fault.

Guilt niggled at Sydney's brain.

Just not enough to stop her from popping in a few fries…

SYDNEY BREATHED DEEPLY in the crisp January air, so different from the stuffy restaurant. It helped clear her head. Which brought back a thought that had poked at her at least six times during the course of their extended dinner. "I couldn't find the right time to ask this inside because—"

"Because your hometown is chock full of very, very, *very* nosy people?"

"That about sums it up." His arm was casually draped around her shoulders. When was the last time she'd walked like that under the stars? And how was a walk across an icy parking lot suddenly romantic just from the weight of his arm and the pine scent that clung to his coat? "I know you put your charm into overdrive, too, instead of showing how much it annoyed you. Thanks for that effort."

"Sydney, my charm takes no effort. Just like my great hair and my ability to see through any poker bluff. Tonight was great. Killed two birds with one stone."

Why did he have to be so funny? And fun? "What second bird were you trying to knock out besides selling our engagement?"

He gave her a squeeze. "Everybody already heard the story of the outsiders who won the hotel lottery. Now they got to meet one of us. Curiosity thus assuaged. Hopefully, it'll stop them from trekking out to the inn to gawk at us like zoo animals. We don't need the interruptions."

Oh boy.

When Alex got it wrong, he got it the full one-eighty degrees *wrong*. Might as well break it to him now.

"You really think that'll slow the flood of visits you're about to get? That's priceless. They want to meet *all* of you. They want to grab a behind-the-scenes peek at the renovations so they can lord the info over their friends. All you did was put a match to a bonfire."

"Ah. Really? Damn." He pinched the bridge of his nose, then shook it off. "I still have a lot to learn about small-town life. Maybe we could work out a barter system? A hint on small-town protocol in exchange for every public endearment or hug I toss your way?"

No. Nope. He wouldn't distract her from her question. "That's what I wanted to ask. We both know you didn't move here for love of a made-up fiancée. And upending your life because you win an…unusual lottery is, well, *unusual*. So why'd you really go for it and come out here? What's the real reason?"

"Hmm Well, I guess you could actually say love."

Hands flying to her mouth in mock horror, Sydney wailed, "Oh no, are you cheating on me?"

"Let me clarify. Not of the marrying kind. My love for Amelia and Teague and Everleigh. They're…my circle. My foundation. My family—all I've got."

No extended family? No parents? Her heart stuttered. "That's both sad and lovely, simultaneously."

"I got over the sad a while ago. Now I'm just grateful for them. Every day. Especially with Teague deployed in danger zones for too long. He just got out. Special Forces."

"Oh my." That explained his confident stance. Like he was always ready for anything.

"You could say that all of our lives skidded onto a rough patch. Simultaneously. It'd be a comedy of errors if it wasn't our actual damn lives."

"I'm sorry." It touched a more than sympathetic nerve in her. Seeing as how her boss had been crystal clear that he didn't approve of her sabbatical and might not hold her job for the next three months. Let alone the promotion she'd been promised and then had yanked away right before coming here.

Sydney had skidded into one heck of a rough patch, career-wise. And she was still coming to terms with the fact that she'd almost *lost* her grandmother. While half a world away. It had almost broken her heart. And she had no idea how to deal with that going forward.

Alex tugged his comically long scarf away from his neck. Like it—or the words—were choking him a bit. "Long story short, for a variety of reasons, all four of us either suddenly didn't have a job or were about to lose it. Same with our living situation. The lottery ticket was a fun, cheap fantasy on Christmas Eve when everything was crumbling around us. Amelia's attempt to cheer me up."

It really *was* a great story. Something that should be immortalized in a cable holiday movie. "So it truly was happenstance?"

"Yeah. We'd hit rock bottom. Together. This inn was a

way out, a way up. Together." His smile flashed in the moonlight. "What could be more perfect?"

Um…a lot of things? That weren't so labor-intensive or money-sucking. But she did get the perfection of the timing and keeping four different people tied together in a single enterprise. Nevertheless, it seemed…risky?

"I don't mean to come off as negative, but why do you think you can pull this off?"

"Because we have to. There's no other option, no escape plan. No parents or trust funds to fall back on, or promised jobs hanging out there to be grabbed in six months. This is it." Alex stopped to lean sideways against her car. "Since we've officially abandoned proper date protocol, can I tell you a secret?"

"Sure."

"I cashed out my IRAs." Alex tipped his head back and let out a half groan, half laugh. "Feels good to share that with someone. It's been a lot to carry by myself."

Holy crap. Talk about risky. Trying not to reveal the panic that was her instinctual response, Sydney asked, "Why?"

"Because we need cash flow. To live off of. The inn came with a small operating account, but it isn't enough."

"That's…brave. Generous." *Ballsy.* "Nobody else knows?"

"I can't tell them. They'd worry. Want to do the same. Better to only have one of us assume the risk. I'm more of a business-oriented type, so they leave the books to me. Everyone's chipping in a little for food, but what we're putting into the rehab? That's mostly me."

Wow. They were all putting in sweat equity, but Alex was shouldering the actual equity all by himself? Talk about selfless. Sydney herself was incredibly anal about her savings accounts. Because they represented freedom. The more she amassed, the more choices she'd have. Which is what had given her the, yes, *freedom* to take this unpaid sabbatical. "No wonder you said this has to work."

"Yeah. It does." He leaned over to plant a hand by her side, caging her in. "It will. I'll make sure of it. You just watch." The intensity in his voice vibrated through her.

"I will. I believe you." In a near-whisper, Sydney added, "You're a remarkable man."

"Guess you know how to pick 'em." Alex chuckled. Then he lowered his head just enough so that their lips barely touched. The faintest pressure connected them. He stayed there a moment.

Giving her a moment? A chance to break the connection before it went any further? To stop him?

Sydney did none of those things. She probably *should* have. That would've been smart.

Sensible.

Boring.

Instead, she waited. Held her breath, not wanting to move even a hair in case it broke the mood.

Suddenly, the pressure changed. Intensified. With the swiftness of the initial drop out of an airplane when skydiving. And with the same jolt of excitement.

Alex *molded* his lips against hers. Sydney immediately opened for him, more desperate to taste him than chocolate bread pudding they'd just shared. His tongue thrust in, commanding, very much in the lead.

Which was okay—for now. If there was a next time, she'd change that. But she hadn't yet decided if *this* time was smart, so his taking charge made it feel less like her own bad decision.

And Alex very much knew how to take charge. His teeth pulled at her lower lip, sending a shock of pleasure up her spine. He leaned in closer, pressing his whole body against hers. It created their own island of heat in the sub-freezing night.

He slid a hand inside her coat, widening his fingers to curve around her ribs while the heel of his hand grazed her breast. "Thanks for not zipping up against the weather."

"Thanks for keeping me warm."

Sydney hitched a leg around his. Because she couldn't get close enough. From the way his other hand immediately boosted her butt so she could wrap both legs around him, neither could Alex.

And the long, slow kisses just kept coming. Wave after wave of licking and sucking and exploration. Her limbs felt heavy, her blood electrified. His strength thrilled her. His desire spurred her on. His low, sexy growls popped up goose bumps on her arms, even beneath a sweater and coat.

But then it occurred to her—what if this was part of the ruse?

What if Alex was just playing the role of the attentive fiancé?

Sydney stiffened. Let her legs slide back to the ground. "You're not required to kiss me, you know."

Alex instantly eased back. And frowned down at her.

"There's no windows on this side of the restaurant. Only the wall facing the river."

"So?"

"So nobody can see us. I'm kissing you because, despite our best intentions, this turned out to be an actual date. A good one. Which means I'm kissing you for *me*, not for anyone else."

That simple statement steadied her. Just as much as it surprised her.

Oh. Laid out like that? She'd had a pretty great night, too. It *had* morphed into a real date at some point.

Rats.

That was a…massive strategic error on her part. Even though Sydney had a sneaking suspicion it'd been unavoidable.

But there were two ways to handle mistakes. Try to ignore the whole mess. Or…lean into the mistake and *own* it.

She tunneled her hands beneath the heavy folds of his overcoat. And leapt back up, locking her arms and legs around him. "Count me in on that action, too."

Chapter Eight

ALEX MADE SURE to keep his eyes straight ahead, glued to the god-awful speckled linoleum of the Chestertown High School's hallway.

Because if he stopped concentrating, for even a second, he'd have to look over at Sydney. Pretty Sydney, with pink in her cheeks from the cold wind and a sparkle in her brown eyes from the warm welcome they'd received in the administration office.

He wouldn't be able to resist. He couldn't resist her.

That had been proven three nights ago, in the freaking parking lot. He was thirty-two years old. He had zero business making out with a woman in a parking lot. Sydney deserved better. Deserved more respect than that, for sure.

Not to mention how much more complicated this fake engagement would be if it turned physical. Well, *more* physical. The level of entanglement deepened. Her leaving in eighty-three days would be harder to handle.

Alex didn't forget an extra round of self-flagellation for his hypocrisy, either. For telling his crew that none of them had time for hookups, let alone relationships. *And* then being the first one to dive right into a lip-lock.

What had he been thinking?

See, that was the problem. There'd been no thought.

He'd gone with his gut. With…feelings.

Alex had felt pretty crappy the last few months, after unjustly losing his job. After fighting to make it right and getting nowhere. Even after discovering that the dream lottery prize that fell into their laps was so much more decrepit and more money-sucking than they'd imagined.

Being with Sydney felt good. Great. Kissing her felt even better.

He'd given in to that. Been self-indulgent. Selfish.

No *way* could it happen again.

Sydney stretched her arm to trail her fingers across the bright red lockers. "They changed the color. I think these used to be gray. Maybe? It's not like I came back for any of the reunions. I could be wrong."

"I never understood those people in TV shows who remembered their high school locker combo when they take their kids back. I don't remember which wing mine was on, let alone the combo."

"Me, neither," she said on a breathy laugh.

Oh, great. Another connection between them. *Crap.*

"The principal and vice principal didn't both need to come out and inquire about my gram. I'll have to be sure to mention it to her."

Sydney sounded surprised. Which surprised Alex right back. "Isn't that one of the biggest selling points of small-town life? Everyone cares about everyone else?"

The muffled thud of their sneakers was the only sound as they passed four classrooms. Interspersed with two more banks of lockers.

Finally, Sydney said softly, "I didn't believe there was anything good about it. Or else why would my mom have left?"

Shit. That was nothing but lousy. Alex's hand automatically reached out to stroke across her shoulder blades. "Your mom bolted from here? When you were a kid?"

"Yep. When I was seven. No explanation. Not to my dad, or Gram, or me, Kim and Campbell."

How would someone be so callous? "It wasn't something your dad hid until you were older? She really didn't leave a note or anything?"

"No, she did not." Sydney matched her stride to Alex's. Leaned in a little until his arm was draped around her. "I adore my family. But I can unequivocally say that none of them are particularly high maintenance, or troublemakers."

"What? You don't want to throw your brother under the bus as being a handful?" he teased, trying to lighten the awful memory.

"Well, there was a stretch of years in there where I would've, but now in hindsight? Cam was just a normal kid. And normal kids annoy their little sisters."

Alex remembered a time when that had been his daily goal, in fact. "I'm going to plead the fifth on that one. I'm sure Amelia would jump right on board that theory, though."

"I'm not broken by it or anything. Gram and Dad were wonderful. I never thought that *I'd* driven her away. So…if it wasn't me, or one of us, it had to be this town, right? This tiny, claustrophobic closet of a town. I became more sure of that with every passing year."

Sydney didn't sound mad. Or bitter. She sounded settled. As if what she stated was as much fact as Guinness tasting great poured over vanilla ice cream. "Maybe. Or…"

She stepped out of his embrace, holding up both hands. "If you're going to tell me that you majored in psych in college and want to pick through my brain, stop right there."

They rounded the umpteenth corner. Apparently the joint junior/high school had gone through a few growth spurts, so wings were just tacked on. And their destination of the shop classroom got moved to the furthest corner, for safety.

"No. Not that. No training, never had any therapy myself. Just another way to look at it, with the objectivity of a total outsider. Or I can keep it to myself." For two people who were supposed to be keeping things shallow and impersonal, he'd almost jumped in with both feet. Alex stuffed his fists into his jean pockets to tamp down his stupid, reckless new habit of reaching for her.

Sydney stopped at a water fountain. Unlike the basic stainless steel variety he remembered, this one had a drinking spout and a platform to fill a bottle. She slurped at it, holding back her long spill of hair to expose her neck.

The neck he'd nibbled on the other night.

He so *damn* badly wanted to crowd up behind her and do it again.

Upright once more, she licked at the single drop clinging to her lips. "You're right. You barely know me. There's no personal bias on your part. And, if you piss me off, we're about to walk into a classroom full of saws and welding torches."

"Wow. I thought the modern woman *wanted* a man who could talk about feelings. Without being threatened with power tools."

"We want men to talk about their own feelings. Never to try and interpret ours." Sydney planted her hands on her hips and cocked one leg out. "Go ahead. Hit me with your wisdom."

This conversation ought to come with that yellow caution tape they put up around open manholes. And he really wished that all the students in the cafeteria for lunch would start a food fight or a rumble to get someone, *anyone* to rush down the hall and interrupt him.

"Maybe a part of you, when you were little, was worried, deep down. That your mom left because of something you did. But the rest of your brain didn't want to acknowledge that. So it tamped it down. Transferred all your bitterness over to blame the town."

She didn't even blink at him.

"*Maybe* as an adult, you stop blaming the town. Look at it with fresh eyes. Like I am. Open to seeing the good and the bad. Like the friendliness of the administrators. How excited Debbie and Dr. Calvert were to see you the other night."

This time, she did blink.

Three times.

"Just because you presented a smart, reasonable argument doesn't mean I'm not annoyed by you right now."

"Duly noted."

She yanked on the big handle of the double glass doors. The room smelled like freshly cut wood. A circular saw whined in the back corner under what looked like a steady-handed boy in goggles. Wooden box frames containing light switches ran in rows four deep on the high worktables. The whole room was immaculate.

A giant of a man—easily topping Alex's six three by a few inches—with an equally gigantic bushy black beard made a hand signal for the boy to stop cutting. Then he pushed his own goggles up to his curly hair, revealing a black eye patch, and barreled forward.

"Syd! You came back!"

"Despite your concerted efforts at tormenting me," she teased. "Not to mention your hideous taste in music. I don't know why my brother chose you for his best friend."

"Mostly because I'm a great wingman. Women get intimidated by all this—" he waved a hand up and down his red plaid flannel shirt "—and see Cam as the safer choice. Plus, he saved me from a bully once, so now I owe him a life debt. He's never getting rid of me."

Alex didn't bother waiting for an introduction. He was too flabbergasted. "*You* needed saving from a bully? You're as big as Kilimanjaro."

"Thanks to puberty." A shrug pulled his black suspenders taut. "But before that hit, I was a scrawny stick. My nickname was Minnow. Kids would put them down the back of my shirt. Cam stopped one, and stuffed it into the bully's mouth. He was so surprised that he swallowed it. And then threw up his lunch all over the other kids in line for dodgeball."

Man, Karma could be a beautiful goddess when she wanted to. Alex guffawed. "That is a fantastic story."

"And the beginning of a beautiful friendship," he responded in an exceedingly bad Bogart impression.

Doubled over in laughter, Sydney waved an arm back and forth between them. "James, this is Alex. And vice versa."

James pointed at the bag dangling from Alex's hand. "Is that the promised bribe?"

"Double liverwurst, coleslaw, pickle and swiss. Times two." Sydney grabbed it and laid it gingerly on the nearest worktable. And then gave a full body shudder. "You know, I remember you eating these a dozen years ago. I remember how bad they smelled. And now that I made these with my own two hands, I can attest that they're every bit as disgusting as I remember."

"Come on. You're the world traveler. Cam told me you've eaten lots of weird things. Like blood soup."

Really? Alex wanted to call a time-out on the conversation with James and do a sidebar with Sydney. Find out the backstory to that comment.

Huh.

Maybe there *was* a reason that first dates followed a standard progression of questions. Because it occurred to Alex that he had only the vaguest idea what Sydney did beyond starting at the Mercantile six days ago. Everything he knew about her was in the context of Chestertown, and her relationships here. Like her crappy, selfish excuse of a mother that she'd just blindsided him with.

Of course, that also meant she had no info on him. That he didn't have to get into how he was fired, and why it was utter bullshit.

This *knowing each other only in the moment* thing could be a nice change of pace.

Laughter spilled from Sydney's pink-glossed lips. "Only once. In Vietnam. The guy I was with told me the blood soup was an aphrodisiac. Specifically, when mixed with rice wine."

Alex loved hearing about different international customs and traditions. Both because they were fascinating, and because it paid to know something about all cultures when you were in the hotel trade. "Did it work?"

"Dunno. The guy, however, was the *opposite* of an aphrodisiac." Sydney shoved the plastic bag a little further away. "The blood soup did, however, smell better by far than these stinkwiches."

"Must be why the Mercantile is the only shop in town that'll make 'em for me. Your granny's always had a soft spot for me." James pulled one out and unwrapped it. "One now, one for dinner. Thanks, Syd."

"Thank Alex. He paid for them. He's the one trying to bribe you."

Enough joking about the bribe. The last thing Alex wanted to do was cross any lines. James and Sydney might've been joking, but there was no guarantee the kid back in the corner would know that. And no telling what he'd pass on to his parents about this conversation.

"Well, I'm here to ask for a favor. Figured doing it over a meal would be more conducive to you saying yes." Holy hell, but that thing really did reek. Like cheap dog food. "I presume Sydney filled you in on the less than stellar condition of the inn."

"She said it's a total mess," James said succinctly around a giant bite.

The corner of his eyelid tried to flutter into a flinch at the insult.

Okay. Alex could forgive her the overstatement. That had been their first reaction, too. But the bones of the inn were good. Plumbing seemed to work, for the most part. Cosmetically it was a mess, but functionally they were in decent shape.

Knock on wood.

"Things aren't that bad," he said grandiosely, with a large swat away of the mostly false statement. "The inn looks worse than it really is."

"Looked pretty bad, the last time I drove by. So I hope you're right."

Man, this guy was a font of downers. Bet he didn't get Most Inspirational Teacher in the yearbook come May. "But updating her look will be labor intensive. It'll be a lot of work to get in shape before tourist season kicks off in April. If we don't make it by then, well, any chance of our turning a profit is gone."

Alex had done the math. Counted up the projects, the man-hours, the hours in a day, divided by his team.

It wasn't enough.

No matter how you sliced it.

Then Sydney's memory had been jogged by seeing her brother at the restaurant. That his friend James was now the shop teacher at the high school. Talk about a good place to get cheap labor.

Alex saw it as a long shot, but Sydney insisted James was

'mostly cool' and worth asking.

Oh, and also? He was *desperate* at this point.

"Yeah, you lose even one month of filled rooms, and you'll never make up for it come winter. Too bad you didn't get started until January. Every day will be crunch time." There was no sympathy in James's tone. Simply a recitation of facts.

Alex had been hoping for at least a smidge of sympathy. "We thought a couple of your kids might be willing to help. For extra credit? For on-the-job training? Like an internship? Nothing dangerous, I promise. Painting. A lot of painting, mostly."

"My kids can handle more than the basics," James said proudly. "Look around. We're not just sanding down scrap wood here."

"I noticed the welding booths. This is a lot better setup than my high school had. I'm impressed." He wasn't blowing smoke. The room was at least four times the size of a normal classroom.

James wandered up to the whiteboard and grabbed the bottle of soda off the marker tray. After taking a swig and doing a swish with it, he said, "Lemme guess. You went to school in a big city."

"Yeah. Pittsburgh."

"See, that's the difference. We put more emphasis on the trades out here on the Eastern Shore. Don't get me wrong— our academics are strong as anywhere. But the way of life out here focuses on fishing, carpentry, things where you use your hands just as much as your brain."

"It's a smart approach. My buddy Teague learned from

working on his dad's construction sites. Starting at way too young an age."

"You do it, you learn it. Simple as that."

Sydney hitched herself up onto a high stool. "James is quite the handyman, too. In case you ever get in over your heads on a project out there."

The big man thumped his chest. "You can't keep all this bottled up. I go out and share my talents with the world."

Funny guy. "I'll keep that in mind. We'll definitely need all the fireplaces and chimneys inspected."

"Not my thing, but I know the right guy. I'll put in a good word so he gives you the local rate, rather than the official hotel rate."

"Thanks." For a second, Alex flashed back to his old life. The automatic response would've been to hand over a business card.

But they didn't have one yet. They hadn't fully decided yet on whether or not to keep the name of the inn. Hadn't paid to get the telephone line up and running. Hell, he didn't even know what the current number was. Not to mention the lack of a logo to put *on* the card.

And all that wasn't due, according to his master List of All Things, to be discussed for another few weeks.

They were never going to make it.

Then Alex strode forward to the whiteboard. Because he only allowed himself one moment of panic a day, and ruthlessly tamped it back down after one breath. He picked up a green marker.

Of *course* it squeaked. After making a jagged smear, it popped out of his hand. How the hell did teachers write sideways on these things?

If a few-hundred-year-old building couldn't defeat him, a pen sure wouldn't. On the third try, he figured out the angle. "Here's my email. For you—or for any students who might want to come lend a hand. If you'll let them."

"Aww, I was just seeing how you stood up to a little poking. Gotta have a thick skin to work with teenagers, you know. Of course I'll encourage them to help. Well, a few of them. Those I can trust. This'll be a great opportunity for them to get some real experience. It's a win all the way around."

"That's—ha—that's really great of you."

"Let's try it out for real. Brody," he shouted toward the boy in the corner. "C'mere."

After carefully hanging his goggles on a peg board, he bounded over to them. "What's up?"

"This is Mr. Alex and Miss Sydney. Alex and Sydney, this is Brody Wickes."

"Hey," the kid said with a dip of his chin. Between his oversized hoodie over a sweatshirt and slouchy jeans? Brody wore enough fabric to clothe two kids.

And didn't that just prove that Alex's thirtieth birthday was long since in his rearview mirror?

Uh-oh.

Alex didn't know thing one about talking to teenagers. How was he supposed to pitch *come do menial labor for zero dollars to reduce my stress levels*?

James crossed his meaty arms over his chest. "So we all start on the same page, why don't you tell them what you're doing in here over lunch?"

"I'm doing work-study detention. Probation." He shook his head. So much hair in a retro-Bieber style that it looked like the tail of a large rodent slid down his forehead. "Serving my time."

"This isn't Shawshank Prison, kid. Explain more."

Alex didn't want a juvenile delinquent having free range in their inn. This explanation had better be good.

To his credit, Brody met Alex's searching gaze head-on. Without any attitude, either. "I put a snowman in the principal's office. Then I slid on the puddle from it and broke my wrist when I cracked it against the desk."

Yowza. The broken wrist seemed like punishment enough. Talk about bad luck.

James rolled his outstretched arm sideways, gangster-style, and pointed. "What did you learn?"

Spitting it out like a mantra, Brody said quickly, "Never pull a prank on a person in authority."

"No, it was never pull a prank on a person with *more* authority than you. If you get elected to student council, they'll all be fair game." Turning to them, James added, "He's a solid student. First-time offense. Had to take an incomplete last semester due to the broken wrist, so he's squeezing in extra hours to make up for it. Your project would help him get there."

Alex thought about it. It wasn't as if Brody was selling meth out of his locker. Pranks went wrong all the time. Some would say it wasn't the action that mattered as much as the reaction.

He exchanged a look with Sydney. Hoped the one he got back from her was interpreted correctly as *give him a chance.*

"That's a lot of snow to get indoors. You must've had help. Why aren't they in here, serving time with you?"

James gusted out a sigh that would probably topple a cat. "He won't rat them out."

Brody rolled his eyes. Clearly they were retreading familiar ground. "It was my idea. I take all the blame. If I'd thought to bring towels, I wouldn't have slipped and gotten hurt. Nobody would've known. My fault, my punishment. Nobody else's."

It was a good answer. Alex respected him stepping up. And for covering for his friends. Integrity mattered.

Besides, when he was in high school? He'd put all the football tackling dummies on the roof after those no-necks had insulted the basketball team. Along with the balls. And dyed their white practice jerseys hot pink...*and* left them on the roof, too.

Who hadn't pulled a prank in their time?

Decision made. "Brody, we need help out at the Three Oaks Inn." Alex crooked his thumb in the direction of the inn. Maybe. Hard to tell in this windowless bunker of a room. "You know it?"

"Yeah. The place is kind of a mess."

Why did everyone lead off with the obvious? And was Sydney really snickering behind him? "Hopefully not for long. That's where you come in. We're looking for someone who knows their way around tools to help with rehab. Would you be interested?"

That brought out the first real smile from the kid. "Heck, yeah. The whole point of this class is to help me get ready for a real job over the summer. That'd be great."

James cleared his throat. "It would also work off your probation faster. As well as count toward your mid-semester project."

Wow. Alex had just been hoping that James would *sanction* the request. Giving the students an incentive would no doubt entice more volunteers to end up on the inn's porch.

"I knew you'd come through for Alex." Sydney poked James in the belly with a grin. "I remembered that big ol' feather pillow of a heart below all those layers of muscle and pizzas."

Relief coursed through Alex faster than the burn from a shot of Jäger. "Thank you, James. So much. We'd be thrilled if only Brody shows up, but if you could wrangle up to five students to send our way, we wouldn't say no."

Picking up the other half of his sandwich, James said, "I'll use that email on the board to hash out the logistics. You may have to talk to some parents. For your own sake, you should probably have the kids sign liability waivers, too."

"Already prepared."

James gestured to the big, empty classroom with a wide sweep of an arm. "Feel free to swing by and hang over lunch anytime. Update me on how everything's coming together at the inn. It gets boring in here by myself."

"Why not go to the teacher's lounge?" Sydney asked.

James did a whole-body shudder that shook the floor. "That's for people counting the days until retirement. All they do is complain about the kids, the lesson plans, the other teachers. I'd want to quit after a week cooped up in there."

Brown eyes wide, Brody said, "You mean Mr. Stanley,

don't you? He always says that teaching us sucks the joy out of his days."

"What a di—" Alex caught himself. Mostly due to Sydney's well-timed plant of her foot across the top of his. "Dismal, horrible thing to say. The man shouldn't be in charge of children."

"Volunteer to take his place and the job's yours."

"Brody didn't say what he teaches."

"Doesn't matter. That doorbell over there could do a better job than Stanley Long. We're always looking for fresh blood to replace dinosaurs like him."

For a split second, Alex was tempted. Maybe three whole seconds. Because the thought of anyone treating students with such disdain and lack of care made him hot under the collar.

Then reason prevailed. "Thanks, but I've got my hands full."

Sydney beamed a smile at him warm enough to melt a stick of butter in ten seconds. "He's talking about me, not the inn. Being newly engaged is a full-time job."

Oh. Yeah.

That.

James snorted. "Keep it clean, Syd. There's an impressionable young mind here, and his hormones are already at DEFCON 5."

"Once we're open, though, I could volunteer. We all could. As a way to pay back for your stepping up to help us."

"Don't think I won't hold you to it."

Alex didn't mind the promise/threat. As they walked back down the hallway, he said, "This is fantastic. Everything was so easy. Thanks for smoothing the way. Seriously, Sydney—I don't know why you're so down on Chestertown."

"Just wait," she said in an ominously deep voice.

"You like James."

"I adore James. I'm also positive he wasn't responsible for my mom running away from here. From us."

It might be twenty-three years since her mom left, but the residual pain pulsing off of Sydney still felt fresh. And it made sense. Alex just wished that pain didn't have to be a mash-up with her hating Chestertown.

"James likes it here. Your family does, too. I'm just saying, it probably isn't as bad as you think. Seeing it through the lens of an adult rather than a child can make a difference. I'm determined to learn to like it here. What if you gave it a try *with* me?"

"What if...I make a concerted effort to stop being so negative about it? That feels like enough of a huge leap."

"Fair enough." If she was hitting the road again in three months, did it really matter?

It did.

Because Alex didn't like seeing her obvious unhappiness.

Even a fake fiancé couldn't let that lie.

Chapter Nine

SYDNEY WINCED AS her dad's voice followed her down the Mercantile's hallway. "Hon, don't prop open the back door. That cold air breezes right in and cools down our coffee. Walk back around after your trash trip."

Riiiight. Because she needed instructions on how to take out a damn garbage bag and toss it into the dumpster.

Sydney had stamps on her passport from thirty-two countries. She'd lugged bags and equipment over trails…and things that claimed to be trails but were just rain ruts in the dirt up the side of a mountain. She'd been in charge of helpless, whiny pseudo-stars and frog-marched them through customs. It was generally known that a location producer could make *anything* happen and get *everything* done.

So Sydney could take a single bag twenty steps and out the door.

At least, *she* was quite certain of it.

Her dad was driving her insane. Not in a way that she could legitimately blow up over. No, it was all helpful nudges. Reminders, like with the trash bag.

They were reminders that, in person, she and her dad had reverted to the same dynamic they'd had when she left town. As a teenager.

Oh, they'd talked plenty over the years.

Sydney kept him filled in on the ups and downs of her career. Neil kept her up to date on the goings-on of Chestertown, even when it was obvious that she'd stopped paying attention. They talked about the Orioles, the Ravens, and whatever Olympic hopeful caught the world by surprise every two years.

But she'd quickly discovered that physical proximity changed everything. Sure, she knew part of it was worry about his mom going through chemo.

Worry about how things would stand at the Mercantile once Sydney left again.

Worry about if and when his daughter *would* ever come back again.

She loved him enough to acknowledge all of that. And, therefore, to tamp down any visible irritation when she was around him. But she *was* pissed off and frustrated enough to let out a tight, long whine as she hip-checked the bar across the back door.

Without putting on a coat first. Even though it was a whopping twenty-one degrees on this January 14th. Why? When she wore only a long-sleeved tee?

Solely because the first thing her dad had said, after asking her to take out the trash, was a reminder to put on her coat for the twenty-second trip outside.

She'd be mature later. For now, she'd make it a point not to care that her fingers were already going numb around the straps that cinched the top of the sack. And maybe do a little dance step over the cobblestones that made up the alleyway behind the shop.

Because Dad would no doubt tell her not to dance. That the slick, uneven stones might be icy.

It was more of a shimmying skip than a dance. The bag threw her off-balance. It still made her happy, though.

Until…

Lo and behold, there was a freaking icy patch. That her skipping steps skidded right over. The momentum pulled her feet out from under her as if she was on a swing, suspended in midair.

Which Sydney was, both legs extended, until she landed.

Hard.

Right on her butt. The, ah, well-padded part, thankfully, not her tailbone. It still sent waves of pain straight up her spine. As well as through the wrist where she'd tried to catch herself.

Ow. Ouch. Even with the ice already melting into wetness soaking through her pants, Sydney didn't move. She sat and caught her breath. It took a few shaky, hitching attempts to get it back on track. Things hurt, but didn't require medical attention. If it'd been summer, Sydney would've sat there for a good five minutes, collecting herself and letting the pain subside.

But not only was she getting wetter by the second all along her legs—and getting colder—Sydney saw that when she flung out her arm to catch herself? She'd let go of the bag. Trash was strewn around her in a splash zone of disgustingness.

Unless she did require an ambulance, that had to be picked up ASAP. Chestertown was stringent about their historic downtown. They knew that tourists kept the town alive. And tourists came to see a beautiful, historic vision of what life looked like back in the 1700s—albeit a thousand percent cleaner.

The trash codes were both simple and extravagant. Simple? Keep the area in front and behind your property clean. Extravagant? If any trash was reported or seen, the fines were three figures. By the third offense? That popped up to *four* figures.

The fact that Sydney was in the alley didn't save her. The alley was cobblestoned. Had quaint architecture and window boxes and little silver plaques identifying what historical happening occurred on the seventh freaking cobblestone from the crosswalk.

So she rolled onto her knees. Flexed a few things in abominations of yoga poses, and then settled onto her shins, rolling her wrist gently back and forth.

"Welcome back, Sydney. I see you've gotten…comfortable."

Oh, *crap*.

Sydney slowly looked from the black leather pencil skirt up to the red cashmere sweater topped off with a diamond solitaire pendant in a circle of more diamonds.

The only thing worse than running into your high school nemesis while you were dressed very much down? And her being dressed like she'd just walked out of Bergdorf's in Manhattan? Was doing so with a pile of wadded-up paper towels by one knee and a slimy assortment of dead worms by the other.

"Nora," she said with the merest incline of her head in greeting.

"I see you've gotten…comfortable back in your old stomping grounds." The tip of a leather boot poked at the trash bag. "You know, I think my most vivid memory of you would be the eight hundred times you swore up and down that you were escaping to bigger and far better things than this tiny town."

Damn.

The zing was deserved. Sydney had repeated that assertion pretty much every time she opened her mouth from age thirteen on. And here she was, more than ten years later, working in the family store again.

At least, that's what it looked like on the surface.

Looks could be deceiving.

Gathering the shreds of her pride, in the haughtiest tone she could muster, Sydney said, "I did get out. I traveled. Had experiences. Met people who had experiences beyond living in the same town for seven generations. I gained a world view far more broad-reaching. I *lived*, Nora."

"Oh, don't go all Katharine Hepburn on me. Your family brags about you endlessly. I'm well aware of the 'fabulous adventures of Sydney Darrow.'"

"Then why are you hassling me?"

It genuinely didn't make sense. Yes, she'd had a knee-jerk *ugh* in reaction to seeing Nora. But Sydney didn't actively hold a grudge against her. Certainly wouldn't have launched the first attack, given the opportunity.

Nora tossed back her perfectly styled raven hair. It literally rippled over her shoulders. "You may have packed on a few pounds on that globe-trotting diet of yours, but your skin's sure gotten thinner. I'm not hassling you. You *are* back

139

home. And you're looking pretty comfy sitting in that trash, rather than scrambling to get out of it."

Comfy was stretched out on a pink-sand beach in Hawaii. Or nestled in for a nap on a hammock under a banyan tree. Or even the oh-so-comfortable warmth of Alex's embrace.

Despite the cold, Sydney put her other hand down on the slick cobblestone. Because she was *reeling* at that last thought that had popped into her brain. Alex? While sitting in wet pants in a girl fight with her ancient nemesis?

Why had she thought of him?

Now? Of all times?

Her brain had started doing this weird thing. If she didn't think of Alex consciously at least once, oh, every hour, some sort of subliminal alarm went off, popping him into her awareness.

For no reason whatsoever.

Aside from how attracted she was to the man. How much she liked him.

Aargh.

"You know what looks like super trashy behavior to me?" The voice came from behind Sydney. She had to twist around to see who it was, and was shocked to discover the cutting tone belonged to Everleigh. Sweet, bubbly Everleigh. "A woman who thinks she's too good to help someone. Who can only muster up the effort to denigrate, rather than pitch in. That's someone without an ounce of goodness, in my book."

Amelia, who stood beside Everleigh, thrust a pair of gloves at Sydney. She pulled them on in a heartbeat.

Gesturing at her outfit, Nora said, "Do I *look* like I should be wallowing in the trash?"

Amelia nodded. "From here, you sure do. I think you'd better take your snooty, sorry ass out of this alley."

"And once you're gone? Spend some time thinking about if being a jerk is really how you want to live your life. Because we don't want to have to explain to you again that this?" Everleigh made a wide semicircle with her arm. "Is a no-bitches zone. And if you're not in this zone, you're missing out."

Nora huffed. Looked between all three of them, then huffed again. "Your new friends need to learn who matters in this town, Sydney. You ought to enlighten them."

She sashayed off—with an enviable amount of grace in icepick heels that never once faltered on the uneven stones.

Amelia and Everleigh each grabbed underneath Sydney's arms and hoisted her up. "Are you okay?" Amelia asked.

"Of course," Sydney replied automatically.

That was the answer she'd always given over the years. Traveling *was* her profession. And when you traveled for a living, things went wrong. All the time.

You got sick. Sucker punched by jet lag. Run into by a tuk tuk. Bitten by hundreds of ants when someone thought a hilarious prank would be adding sugar to your bug spray.

The only rule? No complaining.

If you complained about every little thing—or even semi-big things—then you weren't cut out to work for a media empire that revolved around and worshipped travel.

And Sydney was *literally* counting the days—eighty left—until she got back to that job.

"Are you sure?" Everleigh pressed, with a frown. "I'm assuming you fell. That you didn't choose to sit down on the ice. Because then we'd need to mock you." But even as she spoke of mocking, the woman pulled off her coat and wrapped it around Sydney.

The warmth was *blissful*.

"It was my own fault. I deserve the bruises," she said ruefully.

Amelia shook her head. "Actually, my question is are you okay from being verbally slapped by that woman?"

Yet again, the answer was automatic. Thinking about it didn't matter. Feeling hurt by a few slings and arrows? That was a luxury that she couldn't afford. "Of course."

"She's a bitch," Everleigh pronounced.

"She was in high school," Sydney agreed. "We've all grown up and hopefully matured since then, though. I can't say if she *still* is one way or the other. Nora could be a perfectly lovely person—just not to me."

"Nope. She didn't offer to help *and* was rude to you." Everleigh wedged her hands into the back pockets of her jeans. "We caught the whole thing. She's on our blacklist. Nora, was it? We'll remember," she said, exchanging a glance and a nod with Amelia as if swearing a vow together.

That was…nuts. Appreciated, sure. But wholly illogical. Not to mention detrimental to a business they were trying to grow. It appeared that they were as oblivious to how small towns worked as Alex was. They'd rescued *her*—not that she'd needed it—and now Sydney needed to rescue *them* from making a mistake.

"Look, you just moved here. It's too soon to be picking

sides in feuds, for crying out loud."

"Too late. Already did," Amelia said with a grin. One that was very similar to her brother's infectious smile. Oh geez, there went her subliminal Alex alarm going off again. "Team Sydney all the way."

Everleigh linked her arm through Sydney's in solidarity. "Yup. Nora does not give good first impression. And my first impressions are right a solid eighty-two percent of the time."

"Except when it comes to men," Amelia corrected in a dry tone. "Then your rate drops to something like four percent."

Everleigh dropped Sydney's arm to whirl on Amelia, heat flaring in her blue eyes. "That's an unnecessary clarification. Just because you think I have horrible taste in men doesn't mean every single guy I'm with doesn't share something special and wonderful with me."

Amelia held her ground, both verbally and literally, despite Everleigh jabbing an emphatic finger in her face. "We're not talking about orgasms—which you've told me are not automatic, by the way, with your *vast* array of scuzzy men. We're talking about how you have a propensity to choose the worst human beings to hook up with. Cheaters and losers and selfish jerks. And it hurts me, as your best friend, to see you soaking up all that bad behavior. You deserve more. You deserve better."

"Well, according to your brother, I don't deserve anyone for the next year. None of us do. So it's a moot point."

This was…fascinating. She was learning so much about her new friends. Sydney swiveled her head to look at one, then the other. "You *all* agreed not to date? For an entire year?"

Amelia's eyelids flared wide. "Agreed? Heck, no. Alex laid down one of his innumerable pronouncements. Stemming from his immense panic about us getting up and running in time. He equates dating to a time-sucking distraction."

"But if he thinks I'm going a year without flirting—and following up on said flirting—then the man has lost all of his marbles." Everleigh did a whole-body shudder that sent her hair dancing over her shoulders. "It's been three weeks since Randall broke up with me. I'm already twitchy."

Amelia's green eyes narrowed. "In your case, a break might be warranted. What do people in Hallmark movies say right before they fall for the hero? *I need to date myself for a while.* Maybe you *should* take a break and figure out a better system for picking men. And take the time to figure out why you're okay with being treated horribly. Because it needs to stop, Ever. I mean it."

After hanging her head, she replied, "I know. Deep down, I know that you're right. I just enjoy the fun of it all so much."

Sydney could've watched this all day. This look behind the curtain was better than a movie.

Female friendships were something that had never evolved for her. In college, the emphasis on sororities and parties had seemed like a waste of time. After that, she traveled too much, and her industry's makeup skewed heavily male.

And men just…did *not* talk like this.

"Regardless, we're done with Nora," Amelia vowed.

Oh. Right. Back to her *own* mini-drama—which wasn't nearly as interesting as the one she'd just watch unfold.

Sydney held up both hands, palms out. "You can't be making blacklists in a town this small over a single incident. One that wasn't even about you. You have to play nice with all the businesspeople. Maintain a basic level of cordiality. And for non-businesspeople, too. Word of mouth is everything."

"And the words that came out of Nora's mouth weren't fair to you. As well as the lack of basic courtesy in helping you—and you with no coat—pick up the mess." Everleigh gathered the trash bag and started refilling it.

Sydney appreciated that. But the more she thought about it, the more she was *baffled* by their interaction. "In fact, I can't believe you two stepped in at all. Why would you do that? Why make an enemy?"

With a soft, warm smile, Everleigh responded, "I think of it as making a friend. Of you."

"Besides," Amelia chimed in, snickering, "you're practically family."

"No. Do not blame this on my stupid plan of the fake engagement."

"Stupid, huh? Does that mean you didn't have fun the other night on your date with Alex? Because I saw his washcloth in the bathroom the next morning. Sure looked like he'd wiped off lipstick from his face. And the shade was all wrong to be his own," she deadpanned.

Sydney bent to scoop up one set of coffee grounds. She wasn't ready to admit that they'd compounded their stupidity by making out.

Repeatedly.

Including after their jaunt to the high school two days earlier.

She'd meant to just brush a peck on his cheek as they left. Alex had turned his head at exactly the wrong time…or exactly the *right* time, depending on how you looked at it…and they'd fallen onto each other again.

Somehow.

"You are…you're…ah…his sister," Sydney stammered. "I can't talk to you about kissing your brother."

Everleigh's hand shot into the air. "I'm not his sister. Feel free to tell me all the juicy details."

"No details. It happened. It should not have happened. It's a complication layered onto an already complicated situation."

"Mmm-hmm." Everleigh nodded, knowingly, as if she'd hovered a drone over the high school parking lot and watched them make out. "Let me go ahead and state the obvious. Alex is *hot*. And thoughtful. I'll bet he kisses like a dream."

Amelia cleared her throat and clapped her chest, like she'd swallowed a bug along with Everleigh's words. "Do you secretly have the hots for my brother? I thought that was a one-day weirdness back in sophomore year?"

"It was. Believe me, over and done with. Long gone." Probably wisely, Everleigh backed away a few steps. "But given, as you put it, my experience with a vast array of men, I can spot a worthwhile kisser. And Alex has those gorgeous eyes and a really well-shaped mouth."

"Stop." Amelia waved the empty paper towel she'd just

picked up before chucking it into the bag. "We have the same mouth, so I'm stopping this entire discussion right here. Except to say that if you and my uptight brother have fun together, Sydney, well, then, please have *more* fun together. The less stressed Alex is, the less stress he unloads onto us."

Sydney was both semi-outraged and completely tickled by Amelia's plea. "Your case is that for your health and well-being, I *should* keep kissing your brother?"

"In a nutshell, yes."

"I'll take that under advisement. As a favor to my friends who so heroically had my back today." Sydney was *not* a hugger. But she could just tell that *they* were. And that even with all their hands full of trash, this was an appropriate moment. So she pulled them into a tight group hug. "Thank you."

Everleigh patted her back before they separated. "Nora's just a bully. You have to stand up to bullies, from the start, or they'll always think they can push you around."

"Why *was* she so bitchy to you?" Amelia asked.

Sydney opened her mouth to respond. But came up with a blank. Closed it, thought again, and then let out a hollow laugh. "I don't know. High school was just one long exit ramp for me. I wore a chip on my shoulder for all of it."

"Tough girl? You were the Rizzo of Chestertown High? All smack talk and sass to the teachers?"

"Ha! Completely not that." And although Sydney never opened up about her family history, she felt compelled to be as honest with Amelia and Everleigh as they were in front of her. "My, ah, mom left. With no explanation or warning."

Amelia's jaw dropped to the floor. "Omigosh, that's horrible. You poor thing!"

Her shocked sympathy was preferable to the soft-voiced pity that Sydney used to receive when people in town tiptoed around her for two years after it happened. "I'm not scarred for life or anything."

With more shrewd observance than Sydney would've guessed, Everleigh asked, "You sure about that?"

Mostly. Maybe not. Sydney just didn't think about it. Ever.

Until coming back.

Yet another reason she had not done so for over a decade…

"I was angry. I blamed this town for driving her away. Everything about it, and almost everyone in it. So I probably wasn't nice to Nora. Or…wait…" A hazy memory of a guy in a baseball uniform poked into her brain. "Maybe we dated the same guy?"

"Ouch. Breaking of the girl code. We'd have put *you* on the blacklist, back in the day," Amelia teased.

"Trust me, I don't do that anymore. But the upshot is that I didn't—I *don't*—have many friends here. Mostly adults who were good to me."

"You've got us," Everleigh declared stoutly. "Whether or not you keep kissing Alex. We're friends now. How about you come over later and help us paint? And by paint, I mean hang out debating paint colors and eating pizza."

"We take turns with who is in charge of tunes. It's very equitable. That was a rule Teague instituted about a million years ago." And Amelia rolled her eyes. Was there a story there? "So you're guaranteed good music every half hour, and lots of laughs. Only partially from the paint fumes."

She was having a great time talking with them. And if they had a great time chatting over trash pickup, didn't it guarantee that chatting over anything even a little less smelly would be even more fun?

It would get her out of the house. Give her something to do to distract her from the looming career decisions that occupied her brain whenever her Alex alarm wasn't going off.

And, speak of the devil, if it garnered her a glimpse of her fake fiancé, Sydney wouldn't be at all disappointed...

Chapter Ten

ALEX HAD NEVER once cheated on an expense report. Never swiped extra food from the hotel kitchen, even in those super lean years after his parents died. He followed the rules. Never cut corners.

Until tonight.

Tonight, he was skipping ahead on the inn's to-do list. By a *lot*.

Exactly what he'd told the others they could not, would not do under any circumstances. Because he'd prioritized the tasks. Varied them in arrangement so that difficult and easy-but-laborious things were always available so that whoever had the knowledge level and time could dive into the next thing.

The list was sacrosanct.

Following the list was the only shot they had at being able to at least partially open by the start of tourist season.

The list was to be respected and honored.

Tonight, though? To hell with the list.

Alex needed an easy win. And he needed relief. He'd spent all day scraping cracked paint off the moldings in the ballroom ceiling. Upside down for some of the time. Working over his head for the rest of it.

His back ached. His shoulders and forearms throbbed. They didn't have a working hot tub on the premises, so he made the executive decision to act on the next best thing.

A multi-headed shower. Twelve jets in total, to be exact. With *two* rain showerheads at the top of the beautiful water beast. Not to mention the added bonus of the fan not working in that bathroom, so it automatically turned into a steam shower.

Nobody would find out. This bathroom was on the second floor of the main building. In the opposite wing from where everyone else was working. He'd just make sure that when, in *March*, it was finally time to officially change out the washers on the leaky heads, that he volunteered to do it.

It'd taken Alex all of ten minutes. Which was less than half of the total time he spent luxuriating under those hot, fabulous jets. He could rationalize at least one of those minutes as a test of the facilities.

Alex knew that it was the small touches that bumped a hotel up to luxury status. He didn't want their guests to have an ordinary stay. No, in order to lure guests into repeated stays out here on the Eastern Shore, they had to provide little unexpected things that made a guest feel spoiled.

A dual showerhead didn't cut it. And now that he'd tried all twelve jets, he knew that had to be their standard. At least in the main building. Being able to list that in the website room descriptions would absolutely drive traffic.

Now, as he dried off, he felt human again. Loose. Happy. The only thing that could make it better was a cold beer while he got dressed. Especially since they'd stocked a minifridge near the landing and he wouldn't have to sneak all the way down to the kitchen.

Alex cinched the towel around his waist. For sitting in a linen closet for seven years, it was still plush and soft. Another win. He'd just opened the door into the bedroom when he heard a piercing female scream.

He was across the room in three long leaps. Threw open the door into the main hallway so fast that it sucked a cloud of steam out ahead of him as he rushed out.

And was almost barreled over by Sydney.

Thrusting out his arms, he caught her. Momentum spun them together in a half circle. They ended up standing in the doorway, sideways.

"What happened? Are you okay?" Still gripping her shoulders, Alex did a quick up-and-down scan. Didn't see any blood.

"Alex? What are you doing here?" Her fingers flexed, pressing harder where they'd landed on his still-damp chest. "Why are you…practically naked?"

"Huh-uh. Me first. Are you okay?" he repeated, slowly emphasizing each word.

"Oh. Yes. Oh, I'm sorry. I'm fine. You heard me scream, didn't you? That was stupid. I thought I was alone."

"Do you scream often when you think you're alone? Is it a therapeutic thing?"

"No. In fact, right now? It's a quite embarrassing thing. Can we pretend you heard nothing?"

"I'm going to have to go with a hard no on that. We'll be opening this place to guests. If there's something in here that made you scream, I need to know. And if you tell me that you saw a ghost, I'm going to do everything possible to convince you it was either the wind, a bad vent, or an animal."

He should let go of her.

But if he let go, then *she'd* stop touching *him*. And Sydney's touch was even better than that cold beer he'd been craving.

"Don't make me tell you," she pleaded. And flashed him the big, woeful brown eyes that *almost* worked. Would've worked if he hadn't gotten the big-eye treatment from his sister all his damn life every time she wanted something.

"Sydney." With one hand, he smoothed the hair from her face. "As the business owner, and as your friend, and especially as your fake fiancé, you've got to tell me what just happened."

Her teeth worried at her bottom lip. "I saw a snake."

Okaaaaay. That had been a big scream, though. Really big. While Alex might be new to the area, he knew it wasn't Florida. No pythons lurked along the edge of the Chesapeake Bay. "A boa constrictor escaped from the Baltimore zoo a hundred and fifty miles away and snuck in the house?"

"No. It was maybe as long as my hand. Skinny." She shuddered again.

"*That* we can deal with. Without calling in animal control or an exterminator." Which, God help him, they hadn't budgeted for. At all.

"Technically, I think you already did. It was on a white piece of cardboard? Like a glue trap?"

That made things simple. "It wasn't moving? Wasn't chasing you? I don't need to douse the place in gas and toss a match over my shoulder? Burn it all down?"

Her eyes narrowed. Dangerously so. "Are you making fun of me?"

"Only because I know that you're not in danger up here. And because you're adorable hanging on to me, all flustered. I kind of like stepping into the role of protector. Maybe, if we go digging around in the attic, we'll find a suit of armor I can put on."

Her hands dropped to her sides as fast as if he'd given her a shock. "Did you *know* about the snake?"

"You mean Reginald? The inn's long-standing mascot?" Her mouth dropped open, and Alex bellowed in laughter. "No. I didn't know about your snake. We were warned that they're a known nuisance here at the edge of the river. And that having the heat back on in this place might draw them out initially. So we laid traps."

"It can't wriggle up the stairs?"

"Not if it's already stuck on the trap. And more than likely dead." Alex shuffled them inside, then kicked the door shut. "There. Now there's a solid door between you and the snake, in addition to an entire flight of stairs."

"Thank you." Tension visibly drained from her face and body. Sydney no longer appeared locked in fight or flight mode. Well, just flight, given her sprint up the stairs.

Alex retightened the tuck of the towel at his waist. Because he was suddenly, intensely aware that they *were* behind a closed door.

In a bedroom. Even if the bed's comforter hadn't been washed in seven years.

They were alone.

And if he kept circling around that single fact, his towel

wouldn't be able to contain certain…parts for much longer.

He eased closer to the still-steamy bathroom. Put the depth of a tall armoire between them, angling his hips into the wood and away from her view. "Not a fan of the creepy-crawlies?"

"No. Not at all." Sydney moved to the opposite side of the bed—*aka* as far away as possible from the door. "I had a snake in my bed once. In Thailand—where there's a better than average chance that they're poisonous, rather than the garden variety."

"Yikes. Full disclosure? I would not be anywhere close to calm if I discovered a snake sharing my bed."

She interlocked her fingers. Twisted them out and circled them around each other as if rubbing on lotion. Back and forth. Over and over. "I can handle mice. Bats in caves. Bears crossing the path when I'm hiking. Just not snakes. It *scarred* me. I mean, it didn't bite me. But emotionally—yeah, I can't handle snakes."

Even though he'd only spent a handful of days with her, Alex had picked up on the fact that Sydney had some spitfire in her. Mostly from the way she'd aimed that temper at him during their initial meeting. Aside from that, though, she gave the impression that she was in control of herself. All the time. Even when throwing herself on his mercy to beg him to pretend to be her fiancé.

She was thoughtful. Reasoned. Not impetuous—again, aside from the fiancé ask.

Seeing her so visibly disturbed…well, it disturbed *him*. It didn't fit. It wasn't right.

Alex abandoned the relative safety of the armoire to cross

to her. It put the significantly narrower poster of the bed as the only thing between them. "I'll take care of it. Before you go back downstairs. You won't have to even glimpse it again."

Sydney dipped her head, sending that waterfall of streaky blonde hair cascading past her cheeks. "Thank you."

"I admire you, you know."

Her head popped back up. "No, I *don't* know," she said in an amused tone. "Why?"

"You're brave."

After a self-deprecating laugh paired with an eye roll, Sydney crossed her arms. "Did you block out the time, oh, three minutes ago, when I screamed at the top of my lungs and ran into your arms?"

"C'mon. Everybody has a phobia or two. A ton of people share yours of snakes. But you spoke so blithely about not being scared of other animals. Experiences you've clearly had. That's admirable."

Alex wasn't scared of snakes. Had encountered a bear once in the woods. Which had always seemed cool, in theory...until it actually happened. He'd held it together just fine. Until it was over, and he spent the rest of the night sleepless in his tent, contemplating how easily that bear could've had him for a snack.

And another three years passed before he went on another hike.

"I saw a ton rafting down the Puerto-Princesa Underground River in the Philippines. Bats get a bad rap. You can share a cave with them without any trouble. I mean, we're the ones invading their homes." Sydney batted a hand at the underside of the deep yellow canopy. "Go in respectfully, like you would if visiting your boss. Quietly, not flashing lights or screaming."

The analogy was perfect.

But it gave Alex the chance to have a seven-second day-dream about driving to the wealthy suburb where the Grand Orion's owner lived outside of Philly.

Where he'd stomp inside, proclaiming at the top of his lungs that it wasn't okay to care more about the bottom line than people's lives. That staff ought to be as respected and treasured as guests.

That he did not, under any circumstances, deserve to be fired.

"See? You're brave. Like I said."

"Maybe."

"Beautiful, too," he added. Alex *almost* reached out to her silky mass of hair, where it lay just grazing the top of her breast.

Then he remembered the towel. That he *only* wore a towel.

"You're, ah, not so bad yourself. All slick and sexy." Syd-ney did not seem at all concerned about the tensile strength of his towel. Because she *did* reach out. To stroke a finger down the line of hair along his sternum, whisking at the few drops of water left.

Her fingertip was soft.

The tip of her nail scraped *just* enough to raise goose bumps and harden his nipples.

Hell.

Alex grabbed for the towel. And mashed himself against

the wooden poster. While mentally lunging for a verbal distraction. "You're nice, too. Yes. Nice. That's why else I admire you."

Sydney brushed her palm lightly across his pec. "Why do you think I'm nice?"

Damn it. She kept touching him. When they'd agreed on not kissing again.

Well, they'd agreed, again, to not kiss, again. Agreed that it raised the complication level exponentially. They'd come to this agreement—*again*—just two days ago.

After they'd finished kissing—*again*—in the high school parking lot.

Where there'd been zero reason/excuse to kiss because class was back in session and nobody was around to witness the newly engaged couple putting in the effort to appear in love.

Zero reason…aside from the fact they couldn't, for some reason, keep their hands to themselves.

On Alex's part, there'd been a certain level of gratitude. Sydney had come up with the idea and more than delivered in her introduction to James and Brody. Not to mention that she'd taken time out of her busy day to accompany him.

If that didn't deserve a few kisses as a thank you, what did?

Now, though, there was no audience to convince that their relationship was real. Nothing, in fact, but trouble if they stayed in this room. Alone. Together.

Alex made one last attempt to be a gentleman. As opposed to a walking, talking erection. Which was becoming harder to hold back because *she kept touching him.*

"You, ah, came over to help paint this heap of a house when you don't have to. Voluntary manual labor. That's nice."

"I came for a paint *consultation*," Sydney corrected. "No actual fumes inhaled or drops splattered. Plus the promise of pizza and wine, select good music and many laughs. Pretty sure I'm getting the better end of the deal."

The skinny wooden poster wasn't cutting it any longer to hide his reaction to her slow strokes. Alex fig-leafed his hands. "Any help—no matter how big or small—is much appreciated."

She patted his chest before finally dropping her hand. "I'm paying back my new friends."

For God's sake, he just wanted to help distract her grandmother from chemo. Any man with a shred of decency would do the same. There was no quid pro quo.

"Sydney, you don't have to pay me back for posing as your fiancé."

A single eyebrow arched up. "Good, because I was talking about your sister and Everleigh. Or are you one of those men who think the world revolves around them?"

Hell. He'd really stepped in it without even realizing. "No. Nope. Definitely not. Just setting the record straight."

"Okay." Her response was more dismissive than wholly believable.

Alex needed to be sure she didn't lump him in with egocentric jerks. It shouldn't matter. If their 'relationship' wasn't actually going anywhere.

But it *did*.

"I, ah, didn't realize you'd gotten so friendly with them.

That's all."

"Me, either. And then, suddenly, we were. It's…nice," she said, with a laugh.

"Good. I'm glad. They left behind a big circle of friends. It was hard for them, even if they were too excited about the move to admit it." Every time he watched them work through challenges, small or big, it *hurt*. Hurt that he couldn't help. Couldn't protect them. Alex had already been worrying about how few people they knew here—and how few chances they had to interact, spending all their time inside the inn. "Any day now, the novelty of what we're doing will wear off. We'll enter the grind portion of our schedule. And they'd be lonely."

Sydney's other hand drifted slowly up until it landed on his bicep. "You really care. Deeply."

"When it comes down to it, they're both my sisters, in my heart. There's no differentiation just because Everleigh doesn't share our genes."

She'd drifted closer. Now her warm breath puffed onto his shoulder when she spoke. "A lot of men wouldn't muster up anything more than mild annoyance at their baby sister's BFF."

True. "Didn't we just establish that I'm *not* other men?" Yeah, Alex let more than a little dark and devilish swagger drop into his voice. He was no saint, after all.

And Sydney was pushing him dangerously close to his limit.

"Yes. That's becoming more and more clear." Sydney lifted her chin to meet his gaze. "Which is why I plan on coming back to help with the actual painting. Because you deserve it for helping me—even if you don't expect it."

So there'd be the chance of more private encounters like this one? Sharing moments and jokes and intimate details in that way that always happened when a man and a woman who were attracted to each other were thrust together?

Oh, *hell.*

Alex shoved his hand through his still-wet hair. If he was lucky, that spiked it up. Made him look silly instead of sexy. "That's really not necessary. Especially with the high school kids on tap. We're all set."

"Hardly." Sydney waved her other arm languidly to indicate the entirety of the rest of the building. "I've seen this place, remember? Amelia and Everleigh gave me the full tour while we contemplated color palettes. It'll be a good stress-break from the constant stream of customers at the Mercantile. Painting will be…meditative. Soothing." As she spoke, her fingers mimicked a brush stroke up and down the outside of his arm.

It was the last straw.

The match to the enormous pile of tinder on the bonfire about to rage in his veins.

Alex could hear the snick of the lock opening on the gate he'd been trying so damn hard to hold shut on his desire.

His hand shot out to bracelet around her wrist, stopping the stroking. "Maybe I don't want you soothed. Maybe I want you riled up. Every bit as much as I am."

"Is that what you want, Alex?"

"Right now? It's what I *need.*"

"Me, too," Sydney whispered, going up on tiptoe to breathe the words against his lips.

Lips that were right there, for the taking.

So he did.

Alex kept one hand anchored on the poster. And one side of his body canted behind it. With his other hand, he pressed against the hollow between her shoulder blades. Momentum had her body flush against his before he blinked again.

It was in that blink, the moment where he saw nothing and felt *everything*, that Alex took her mouth.

He felt her quick, indrawn gasp at his first touch.

Felt the noticeable arch of her soft breasts against his chest.

Felt the immediate give of her lips as he plumped them with his own. Nipped at them. Sucked the lower one in, and then scraped his teeth over it.

And then Alex *really* began the kiss.

After a gulp of air, he went in. Freaking *plundered* her mouth with his tongue. This time there was a little bit less calculated skill, replaced by a lot more heated need. Because with every lick, every swirl of his tongue against hers, fire raced through his body straight to his groin.

Then Sydney started moaning. Sweet little high-pitched, breathy mewls of delight. And her hand slid down his still-damp back to rest right at the quickly loosening edge of the towel. She kneaded the fabric in her hand. Her thumb scraped against his skin, and her fingertips grazed his ass.

That shot more heat through him, faster than a volcano spewed lava.

Alex abandoned the relative safety—at least in his mind—of keeping the poster between them. Threw caution to the wind. Because, in reality, they'd abandoned caution the moment that they entered the bedroom and shut the door.

He tightened the hold on her back and put his other arm around her waist. Lifted. As soon as Sydney's feet were off the floor, he pushed forward, putting one knee on the bed as he laid her across it.

Her hands locked behind his neck, pulling him closer. Good to know they shared the same objective. Alex still didn't lower his weight onto her, though. No, he'd put Sydney on the bed so he could touch more of her. He tunneled his hand up under her fuzzy brown sweater.

But...it was the depths of winter. So he discovered a thin tank under *that*. Alex was too determined to even be frustrated. He just started again, down at the waist of her leggings, and ruched up both her tops.

The wait was worth it. Every sliver of skin that got slowly exposed was soft, pearly perfection. As sensual to his eyes as his fingers. Alex skimmed across her belly, savoring the smoothness. He didn't want to rush through. Hit the five erogenous zones and call it a day.

No, he wanted every inch of Sydney.

Until her back arched again, drawing his attention back to her breasts. Aaaaand he refocused, just that fast.

"Kiss me," she demanded.

"On it," he replied. Alex trailed a string of butterfly-light kisses across her stomach, enjoying the way it flexed and tightened under his mouth. But at the same time, he palmed her breast with one hand. Squeezing. Caressing. Pinching her nipple through the layers of fabric and bra just enough to hear her breath stutter.

With his other hand, he slid beneath her to echo those motions on her tight ass. Then he swirled his tongue in her belly button, and Sydney bucked her hips.

"Points for misdirection and cleverness, but I need you to *kiss* me," she reiterated.

Thank God she was as eager as him. And as vocal. Alex far preferred a woman who verbalized what gave her pleasure. "I'm getting there."

He crawled up her body, only remembering at the last second to yank the towel along, too. Then Alex scooped her breast into his palm and out of the confines of all the clothing. He laved his tongue all around her dark pink nipple before sucking it into his mouth.

Sydney responded by digging her fingernails into his back before shifting to scrape them along his scalp. She pressed his head tighter to her. "Mmm, that's it," she murmured. "That's…delightful."

Talk about an understatement.

"We'll call that a good baseline," Alex said. "But plan on things getting exponentially better from here."

If he hadn't lifted his head to speak, Alex would've missed it. The faint slam of a door.

Christ on a three-humped camel.

Dropping a soft, deep kiss that wasn't nearly long enough, Alex pushed up with both arms. "They're back."

"Who? Where?"

"Whoever left. I'm presuming to grab dinner? Amelia and Ever?"

Sydney managed to sit upright and simultaneously scoot back and out from under him. "I forgot about them."

"Good. Because I was working on getting you to a state where you forget your own *name*."

She tugged off the comforter and draped it across his back. Her movements were jerky, verging on frantic. Which matched her furrowed brow and pursed lips. "You're practically naked."

"I'm well aware of that detail," Alex said dryly.

"Well, fix it! They can't know…we shouldn't…I'm going back downstairs. Wait five minutes before you follow me." Sydney scrambled off the bed, straightening her tops. "And, um, thank you."

Then she all but *sprinted* for the door. When her hand landed on the knob, Alex said, through laughter—because what else was there to do *but* laugh, "What about the snake?"

Haughty disdain at his reminder rolled off of her like fog off the Monongahela River. "It's as dead as you'll be if you mention what just happened."

All in all? Alex didn't regret his decision to use the shower—or anything else that had gone down in this room.

Not one bit.

Chapter Eleven

"THIS IS A nice library," Amelia said, looking out through the arches over the bookshelves to the carpet in shades reminiscent of the river and bay. "Bigger than I expected."

Sure, Sydney had spent half of her life dismissing her hometown. But now, she was driven to defend it. "Chestertown is the hub, the seat of Kent County. We have better services because of it than some of the surrounding towns the same size."

"Well, they did me just fine." Amelia hefted a stack of five books. "Step-by-step guides to almost everything we'll need to do at the inn. Because it's super annoying to hit pause every six seconds on a YouTube video while you try and follow along. Everleigh and I plan to study. We're not wild about Teague and Alex only dispensing basic jobs to us. We're capable of learning. Of not screwing up."

"Of course you are." Sydney believed it, one hundred percent. However, she'd spent the last ten years working in a mostly male field. She'd observed...*a lot* of similar behavior. Had figured out many of the reasons behind it. Mostly to keep from screaming at them in frustration. "They probably just didn't want to put pressure on you. Because all of you already have sooo much pressure weighing on you."

"They're fairly forward-thinking men, so I hope you're right. But both of them have been known to go full-on caveman when it comes to our boyfriends."

Sydney had no trouble believing that. Alex's fierce loyalty to these women was one of the attributes she admired the most in him. "I'm sure that's out of a desire to protect you. Out of love. Not because they think you can't take care of yourself."

"You have a brother, right?"

"Yep. Campbell. He's two years older. Likes to think those two years gave him twenty IQ points more than me, but he's wildly wrong."

Amelia nodded vigorously, sending the ends of her braids dancing against her lime-green and black plaid flannel shirt. "No matter his intention, it's still annoying when he tries to shield you from things, isn't it?"

Intensely so.

Yet another reason that Sydney had bolted right after graduation. Their dad was often stuck for long hours at the Mercantile. Campbell had decided it was his duty to step in and be in charge of Sydney once she became a teenager—and embraced all the trouble that went along with it.

"Oh, he was beyond annoying. It infuriated me. Still does—not that I think he'd dare try to pull that crap anymore. But I know all he wanted to do was keep me out of trouble. Prevent me from getting hurt."

"I'll welcome the first blood blister I earn at the inn," Amelia proclaimed. Probably a tad too loud for a library, but she was speaking of a principle. It deserved to be heard. "It'll be a badge of honor. And I'll wave it in Alex's face. Maybe not even put a bandage on it, just to drive him nuts."

Sydney waggled an index finger back and forth. "Don't go overboard. An infected blister would just prove him right."

"Good point."

Sydney ran a nail down the spines. Then she tapped a much smaller paperback. With a much more colorful cover. Laughter bubbled in her throat. "What's this one going to teach you? How to beguile a duke in eighteenth-century England?"

Amelia twisted, angling the books away from her. "Don't mock. The romance is every bit as important as the how-tos. It'll help me set aside my stress every night. Relaxation and recharging—that's the key to surviving a long, arduous project."

"Yes, but why historical? With the ridiculous layers of clothes and inane class consciousness and the serf-like position of women with no vote and no bank accounts?"

Not to mention the lack of air-conditioning. Codeine cough syrup. Netflix. The unwinnable but life-sustaining argument over the ultimate Chris being Pine, Evans, or Hemsworth...

Amelia leaned her hip against the edge of the shelf. "Those are valid counter-arguments. All those things bother me in general. I totally would've been a suffragette. Thrown in jail at least a dozen times for protesting."

"Then I repeat—*why?*"

"I don't want to read a contemporary romance. Those have a perfect man on every page. A perfect man I'd love to fall for—but can't. A perfect man who ought to be with *me*. Regency England gives me a believable reason why the hero isn't knocking down my door, pledging his love."

Uh-oh. "Are you getting over a bad breakup?"

"What? No."

A perfect man who ought to... "Even worse. Are you *pining* for a man who's too blind to notice you?"

"No. A little. It's...complicated. And it's never going to happen. Which I've come to terms with. Except for when I read a book that shows me seventeen different ways that it should've been easy to be with the guy I want. Wanted."

Sydney smelled far more of a story beneath what Amelia actually said. It'd be a lot easier to tease out of her with alcohol, though. "Then I hope you enjoy your book. Sorry that I teased you about it."

"You wouldn't be the first, trust me," she said with an eye roll. "How about we talk about a more current romance?"

"Who?"

"You and my brother, of course. I believe there's an update you have yet to share with me? Which, you know, frankly hurts. Since I'm your sister-in-law-to-be. I deserve to be dialed in to all your secrets."

An update? About her and Alex?

Sydney's temper—along with an equal measure of embarrassment—flared. She slammed her own stack of books down. Then picked them back up, and grabbed Amelia's wrist. A few steps later they were in the enclosed—and more importantly empty—magazine reading room. Nobody would be able to hear her vent in here.

"I can't believe he told you. I specifically asked him not to. I *threatened* him. He is a low-down snake."

Amelia half opened her mouth. Closed it. Then grimaced. "Well…"

No. Wait. This was actually good.

Sydney had been up half the night, tossing and turning and wondering how to interpret what had happened yesterday. Amelia *knew*.

On top of that, she knew *Alex*. Knew his history, his patterns. She could provide clarity on the entire situation.

Sydney sank into a cushy blue wing chair. "The thing is, I'm freaking out. Because I don't know what it *means*. I don't want to squick you out with the details, because he is your brother, but you have to know that he's drop-dead sexy."

"Um…objectively…I guess so?" Amelia crossed her legs and dropped onto the carpet at Sydney's feet.

"And when I saw him covered in droplets of water, all steamy, in only a towel…" Her voice trailed off, because her mouth went dry just at the memory. "He was like a hero in a movie. Muscled. Wet. Mostly naked. How could I not kiss him back?"

"Of…of course you had to? On behalf of all womankind?"

"It doesn't feel like a hookup. Not *just* a hookup. Not when we're becoming so enmeshed in each other's lives. If you hadn't come back with dinner, we'd be moving into an X-rated conversation."

"Do I get smacked for that? Or thanked?"

"At the time? I would've given you every dollar in my

purse to turn around and go back out the door. Now, though, it seems prudent that we stopped. Since we have no business doing anything to deepen this farce of a relationship."

Amelia propped her chin on her hands and leaned forward with a delighted grin. "You and Alex made out last night? That's...that's fantastic."

Oh, God. Sydney white-knuckled the arms of the chair. "You didn't know? He didn't tell you?"

"Of course not. When Alex gives his word, he keeps it."

"Then what details were you asking about?"

"Your trip to the high school, to meet with the shop teacher. It got mentioned on the local radio station while I drove here this morning. They ought to rename it the Alex and Sydney hour for how closely they're tracking your engagement."

Sydney had thought she'd been embarrassed, oh, four minutes ago.

Wow, she'd been wrong. Because this shaking and sweaty chills covering her body—*that* was embarrassment. "Can we pretend you didn't hear anything I just said?"

"Do we have to?" Amelia gave Sydney's knee a few kind pats. "It sounds like you need to talk."

Sydney tipped her head into the corner of the wing chair. Looked out the high windows, flooded with morning sun that sparkled off the few icicles still hanging from the eaves. "I don't know what I need. I thought I did. Then I came back home, and immediately things turned inside out. It feels like I need Alex, but the rational part of me knows that I can't have him. He doesn't have time. He can't emotionally invest in anything besides the inn right now. And I'm out of here in exactly eighty days."

They sat in silence for a bit. Sydney consumed with her own confusion. Amelia probably wondering if there was any chance Sydney could leave town early and put an end to this drama. She must want Alex solely focused on rehabbing the inn, too.

Which just made Sydney feel guiltier for her, well, *feelings*.

Finally, Amelia rolled up to her knees. "To answer the question I'm pretty sure that you're dying to ask, no. Alex does not usually do this. He *does* hook up. As you pointed out, the guy is man-candy, and lots of women want a piece of it."

"That's even worse. He's a player?"

"The opposite. Alex doesn't hook up with women he cares about. Drive-by, no-strings fun only. That's his MO. I can't name a serious relationship that's lasted more than a few months. His priorities have always been clear. Me, then his job. That's it."

Just as she'd thought. His intensity for the things he did care about shined out of him like a lighthouse beacon. Ergo, no further intentional or accidental lip-locks with him. No matter how you sliced it, there wouldn't be a happy ending.

"Thanks for sharing your perspective. It helps."

After another awkward pause, Amelia poked at Sydney's stack of books in an obvious attempt to switch subjects. "What's with all the cookbooks?"

"I'm terrible at cooking. I'm great at research, however. I love learning everything I can before I hit a new place, so I can soak it all up. To me, the kitchen might as well be a foreign land."

Laughing, Amelia said, "Oh, that's a great analogy!"

"So I'm researching how to cook. Hopefully that will stop me from alienating our customers and pissing off my gram."

"I like that you're shifting your mindset. It might just work."

"Here's hoping." Because she was still more of a liability than a help for anything beyond basic prep work. Why were sandwich presses so complicated? Why did they turn a sandwich from raw to incinerated in the blink of an eye? "Can you cook?"

Amelia shrugged one shoulder. "Standard stuff, sure. Nothing complicated or exotic. I learned from my mom, before she died. Then I stepped it up to feed Alex while he worked two jobs, sometimes three in those first few years."

"He worked three jobs? Simultaneously?" Sydney couldn't imagine the level of exhaustion that would create.

"Once our parents died, the financial burdens were overwhelming. He was only a freshman in college. He had to drop out and work. A *lot*."

Wow. A nineteen-year-old drowning in grief stepping up like that had to take an untold amount of strength. "And he became your guardian?"

"Mmm-hmm. There's a seven-year age gap between us— I was an accident, they liked to say to my immense horror, involving being stuck in a parking lot after a Smashing Pumpkins concert without any condoms."

Sydney's jaw dropped. "I can't believe they told you

173

that!"

"Mom and Dad were still head over heels in love to the day they died—and very open about it. Which gave us good role models. We were a tight family. That's why Alex fought so hard not to have me put into foster care. Including working so hard that he'd fall asleep eating the meat loaf I made."

Alex had told her last night that she was brave. But Sydney thought *he* was the brave one, after hearing all of this.

Brave beyond all telling. Determined. Strong. Pretty much an emotional superhero. No wonder Alex was so certain he could make the inn a success. He'd already succeeded against worse odds. And he'd done it alone, with no support system.

Yet here she was, holding a grudge against Chestertown, when the people in it had done nothing but support her and step up to help when her mom left. Suddenly that felt extremely narrow-minded. Petty.

Unfair.

"Maybe I'll try my hand at a meat loaf," Sydney mused out loud. "Turn that into a daily special sandwich."

"That's the spirit. Let us know and the inn crew will be over to try it."

See? There went Amelia being kind. Supportive. Growing their friendship. Enmeshing all of them into Sydney's life.

It felt surprisingly wonderful. The female friendships she'd pooh-poohed her whole life were turning out to be extremely worthwhile.

What was she supposed to do about that? How was she

supposed to just walk away?

And why did Chestertown suddenly feel more like home now that she'd gotten to know these strangers?

"WHICH PLANT DOES Gilroy, California, celebrate every summer during a three-day festival?" Sydney didn't bother flipping over the Trivial Pursuit card.

She knew the answer. Had, in fact, been to the Garlic Festival. Which was fun, but proved that there could, indeed, be too much of a good thing. She'd gagged through the garlic pineapple upside down cake.

"We're skipping that one," her grandmother replied tartly. For someone hooked up to an IV full of essentially poison, she still had plenty of vinegar in her attitude.

On an average day, it was one of the things Sydney loved most about her. Today? When Sydney was supposed to be helping take care of her? It made things difficult. It had only been an hour and Sydney's patience was already stretched to the breaking point.

But her annoyance didn't matter. It was nothing compared to her grandmother's discomfort and fear. Not that the woman would cop to either.

So Sydney swallowed hard, and plastered on—hopefully—the semblance of an indulgent smile. "That's not how the game works. The whole point of playing is to distract you from getting chemo. If we skip all the hard questions, it won't be a distraction at all."

"I'm not skipping the hard questions. It doesn't count as

a win unless you earn it."

Agreed. Sydney hadn't won a chess match until she was ten, because her family refused to 'let' her win. And she'd never once complained. "Then answer the question."

"No. I'm skipping all the travel questions." She started to metaphorically push them aside with her arm, but the taped-down IV tubing flapped against the side of the recliner chair. "You have an unfair advantage. You've been everywhere with that job of yours. And where you haven't been, you've researched. It's no different from insider trading."

Wow. How many different ways could she get kicked in the ass by her company? When the job they weren't even promising to hold for her made her a liability at *Trivial Pursuit*?

But that violated her vow not to think about her job. Which, honestly, had been working much better than her vow not to think about Alex.

"Okay. That's fair." Sydney put both of her forearms on the tray table and leaned forward. And was relieved that the surgical mask she wore hid her sly grin. "As long as I get to pick a category of questions to skip where *you've* got the advantage."

Twitching the edge of her *Star Wars* fleece blanket (a gift from Cam, to remind her that if Darth Vader could be defeated, so could cancer), her grandmother harrumphed. "That's acceptable."

"I get to skip all food and cooking questions."

After making a clucking sound, she said, "My darling granddaughter. You are *so* predictable."

Perhaps. But after staying up late reading four cookbooks, Sydney was even more aware of how little she knew. "We've got an even handicap now. No trashing the why or wherefore of it. Are you ready for the next question?"

There wasn't an answer.

Alarmed, she looked up from the card box to discover her grandmother's eyes had closed. It being winter, it was hard to tell if she'd gone any paler than normal. Sleeping? Passed out?

She was sorely tempted to hit the call button for the nurse.

But...there'd been a long lecture by her father about not panicking if anything seemed to go wrong. Or at least, not *showing* panic. A promise that Sydney wouldn't hover, wouldn't nag, and wouldn't pass out if the IV site spurted blood.

Relentless positivity, yes.

Panic and fear, hell, *no*.

So she waited. Held her breath. Did allow herself the indulgence of resting her hand on her gram's arm. And exhaled hard in relief, puffing out her mask, when the older woman, eyes still closed, patted her hand.

Okay.

At a snail's pace, she curled her fingers around the arm-rests. "Sorry about that unscheduled break, dear. A touch of vertigo."

"I thought the chemo didn't cause a reaction until hours from now?" Sydney was, in fact, quite certain of that, having not only done the reading but peppered the staff with questions the first time she'd come. Maybe she *should* ping the nurse?

"Oh, I've had vertigo for ages. A less than splendid souvenir from menopause that stuck around. Stress brings it on. I suspect the threat—however slim—of you beating me today shot my stress levels sky-high."

Ah. There she was.

Only Daisy Darrow would count a loss at a board game as more stressful than having poison pumped into her body that would make her miserable for the next three days straight.

"My bad," she conceded with a gentle squeeze of her hand. "Next time Cam should do this. He never beats you."

"So true. The boy's a hard worker. Considerate. But his retention of historical and pop-culture facts is right up there with a colander holding water."

"Do you need medicine for the vertigo?"

"Not unless it gets much, much worse. I'm used to these episodes. They're something you can look forward to down the road. In about, oh, twenty years."

Sydney pinched the edge of her mask tighter along her nose. "Thanks for that shining glimpse into my future."

"Would you rather hear about how many stitches I had after giving birth to your large-headed father? That'll probably pass down to you as well."

"Stop. Now *you're* stressing me out. Maybe enough to induce vertigo two decades early."

"Some water would be nice."

Grateful for the task, Sydney all but leapt out of the visitor chair. "I'm on it."

She made it two steps out the door before almost plowing into...Alex? A mask covered most of his face. But she was sure it was him. After all, she'd been plastered up against his body. His almost-naked body. It was branded on her psyche.

As was his dark hair with that bit of a curl that defied the gel, right in the center of his forehead. And most of all, that pair of pale blue eyes twinkling at her like lights on a Christmas tree.

"Alex?"

"Glad you recognize me. There's a lot of doctors in lab coats running around this hospital. I hear that those men tend to, ah, *distract* women."

Ugh. Such a cliché.

"Do you secretly watch hospital dramas? Because they're fiction. Every bit as much as shows about superheroes and families capable of solving all of their arguments over one well-cooked roast chicken."

"I…do not. My partners do share that addiction, however. So I've heard chapter and verse about 'hot docs.'" He made finger quotes in the air.

"The doctor I saw today is about sixty and terrifying. A pixie cut that shows off amazing bone structure, blood-red lipstick and statement earrings as big as silver dollar pancakes. She intimidates the hell out of me."

Dr. Morrison had been nothing but kind to her *patient*.

The patient's caregiver, however, had been at the receiving end of barked orders that made Sydney think she needed to take a crash course in advanced first aid just to keep up with the doctor's expectations. But she was thrilled that her gram was in such capable hands.

"Are you leaving already?"

"Not for a few hours still. I'm on a water run." She brandished the plastic pitcher in that hideous shade of burned mustard that seemed to only exist on hospital plasticware. "Um, what are you doing here? Is everyone okay?"

"You mean, did we have a power tool mishap? Did I sand off Teague's thumb?"

With a smirk, she said, "You read my mind."

"The inn crew is fine. I'm here to see Daisy."

"Daisy…my grandmother?"

A deep line crinkled between his brows. "This is a pretty small town. I doubt there are *two* Daisys. Unless it was a hippie commune about sixty years ago."

"I'm just startled. It takes a minute for the brain to sync up when you see someone in unexpected surroundings."

"Let me help you sync up with me." Alex tugged his mask down. He carefully crooked his finger in the top of hers to lift it out and down. Then he brushed the pad of his thumb back and forth across her lower lip. Her mouth eased open a bit at his touch. Alex pressed a kiss on her mouth.

They weren't joined anywhere else. His hands were at his sides. Their torsos and legs weren't touching. Yet Sydney felt deeply connected to him. As though a string passed from her heart to his.

Oh. Wow.

It was one heck of a kiss to spin her into a hearts-and-flowers haze like that.

"Hi."

Sydney licked her lips, tasting him on them. "Hi, your-self."

"Can I go see her? I called first, and the nurse said visitors were allowed. But if she's not up for it, I don't want to insinuate myself in there."

"Gram would be delighted. She *does* watch every hospital show ever made. When you walk in there with a mask on and that determined walk of yours, her monitors are going to spike so high the nurses will come running."

"In a good way?"

"In a *she might try to pinch your butt* way."

He put her mask back on, then his own. "I'll take it as a compliment."

"Let me take you in, then I'll pop back out for the water." Sydney pushed through the extra-wide wooden door. "Gram, look who's here."

For someone who'd been all vertigo-ed and limp a few minutes ago, the woman popped to attention like Sydney had announced the Pope had arrived. Escorted by the Queen of England.

"I'm so tickled to have a visitor." She patted the purple Ravens ski cap pulled down to her eyebrows. Gram got chilled very easily these days. "If you'd let me know you were coming, Alex, I would've put on my hat with the fancy pink puffball on top."

"Maybe I should step back out until you do. Seeing as how I'm a die-hard Steelers fan."

Hand fluttering at her mouth, Daisy said in a shocked tone, "Did my granddaughter know that *before* you proposed?"

"Oh yeah." He cocked one hip and fisted a hand on it. Winked obnoxiously. "Guess that tells you just how impressive I am that she could overlook it." Then Alex handed her a gift bag.

"You didn't have to bring me a present." Her delighted smile said otherwise.

"Of course I did. Sick people need presents to get better. It's a universally known fact."

Sydney knew that her gram didn't like to use the arm with the IV in it. So she hurried forward to help with the bag. The first thing she pulled out was a coffee mug stuffed with daisies. The mug was painted with a unicorn leaping over a rainbow.

"It seemed safe to assume that someone with your name would have an affinity for the flower."

Daisy sniffed the flowers deeply. "They're my favorite."

"The unicorn's so that you have a little magic in your day. That ought to help kick cancer's butt."

"I love it."

Sydney loved that he'd put such thought into the gifts. How many men could nail *whimsy* like that? Next, she pulled out a box of saltines and a bottle of ginger ale.

"I figure it's like bringing diapers to new parents. These are necessities for chemo patients, right?"

"Yes…unless there's a baggie of weed in there. That would negate the need for the crackers and soda." She tried to yank at the gift bag's tissue.

"Gram!" Sydney said sharply. Yes, she was losing patience. Again. Because this was the third time they'd gone round on this subject. "Alex is not your drug mule."

"If he wants to ingratiate himself with your family, he could be…"

"You *agreed* to see how this first round goes. Then we'll investigate getting you a medical marijuana card."

"Sydney, you get some water. I'll check my pockets and see if there's anything more…recreational to cheer up your grandmother."

Daisy laughed uproariously. Over her bent head, Alex mouthed *don't worry*.

Oh, Sydney had plenty to worry about. Because every single additional thing she discovered about Alex, every layer that got peeled back, revealed him to be a truly remarkable man.

Suddenly? This engagement didn't feel so fake. He was doing more than his part. There'd be no forgetting about Alex. No handing back that paper clip ring, tossing off a wave, and jaunting out of town without a second thought.

What was she supposed to do about these very real feelings for him?

Chapter Twelve

ALEX CUT ACROSS the frost-spiked lawn between the cottages and the main building. Because man, this property was *big*. And he was *wrung out*.

Yeah, Amelia would yell at him for damaging the 'tender shoots' or some such nonsense. But the grass had gone to hell after seven years of no real maintenance. How would she be able to tell what he'd walked across versus everyone and everything else that had tramped across this property?

Okay, she'd know.

She *always* knew. His sister was the freaking Dr. Dolittle of plants. But that was a problem for future Alex to deal with.

Present Alex had pried up the warped floorboards from the leaking pipe...after replacing said pipe...walked them out to the furthest outbuilding to look for replacement boards, cut them, then circled back to the cottages to check on the shower regrouting.

And it wasn't even lunch yet.

Lots of forward progress, sure. All good. But he wanted a break. And if he was too much of a freaking taskmaster to give himself one, then yeah, he'd shave off twenty steps by cutting across the damn croquet lawn.

"Alex," a big voice boomed. It was James, rounding the side porch, with Brody in tow.

A reprieve!

Alex didn't care *why* they were here. Just that it meant he had an excuse to not *do* anything.

"Hey there," he called out, arm upraised in greeting. "What brings you two out here on a Saturday?"

James hooked a thumb at his student. "Brody has an idea he'd like to run by you."

Initiative. Even better than a reprieve. Alex made a *bring it on* gesture with his hands. "Okay. Great. Hit me."

Brody didn't look like the owner of a great idea. He looked…nervous. Jittered on the balls of his beat-up Converse. Kept shaking out his fingers, too.

"Mr. James was talking up your project to some of the kids. Describing the kind of work it'd be. He mentioned that anyone who was specifically good at woodworking would be helpful, because your spindles, no, *balusters*," he said after James shook his head at the first word, "would probably need replacing."

"True. The ones inside are mostly fine, aside from a few that are loose. But the porch—those didn't hold up so well to the weather. I've heard stories about that hurricane you all went through a few years back. Anyway, between the wind gusts and whatever the wind shot into them, a ton will need replacing."

Brody looked at James again. Waited. Shifted from one leg to the other.

"Don't fizzle out on me now," James prompted. "Keep going. You won't get in trouble."

Hmmm.

That didn't sound promising. Or like a promise that James could legitimately give on Alex's behalf.

Bracing for whatever came next, Alex crossed his arms. And tucked his hands in his pits to keep them warm.

"Nobody's lived here for a long time. There were rumors it was haunted. That brought a lot of kids out to sleep overnight. Just on the grounds," Brody finished in a rush.

No big deal. The chief had warned them about that. And Alex had been Brody's age. Done silly stuff like that with his friends. James was right. He wouldn't bust Brody for it.

With a reassuring clap on Brody's parka, he said, "To test your bravery. Sure, I get it. Did you see a ghost? Because between you and me, we could use one. It'd make for terrific marketing."

"No ghosts. But a racoon came out of that top turret thing—" He looked to James again for the right word.

"The cupola."

"Yeah. It ran out of that, lost its footing and slid down the roof. Scared the pants off of us."

Alex hadn't surveyed the cupola yet. It'd been locked. Also, it wasn't big enough to be anything more than a novelty. That put it down the priority list until at least April. Unless a window was cracked, making it open to both the elements and animals.

Damn it.

Now he'd have to *deal* with it. And whatever else Brody was about to throw his way. Alex had learned that when it came to knowing what needed to be fixed at Three Oaks? Ignorance was definitely bliss.

He forced good humor into his voice. "No ghost, but a scare? I'd call that a fifty-percent win."

Brody's lightning-fast smile dropped five years off the grown-up façade he was projecting. "It was epic. Anyway, as we got older, we gave up on the sleepovers. Your stables and barn? Those are perfect for parties."

"I like how you state that as a fact, without actually letting slip if you've *been* to a party here. Almost like you were coached on what *not* to say…" Alex turned to James. But it was hard to stare down a guy with only one working eye. Especially when it was squinting against the sun's glare.

Brody's Adam's apple bobbed noticeably a couple of times. "I want to be level with you, Mr. Alex. I did go to some of those parties. Only when nobody lived here, though. We made sure to stop all of that once you guys moved in."

"Okay. I appreciate the honesty. And shutting down the parties. Is that all you wanted to tell me?"

"Huh-uh. There's lots of cool stuff in those outbuildings. We'd poke through it. Um, I'm sure I saw a box full of spare spindles. Balusters."

That good news balanced the news about the cupola. If true, it'd save a ton of man hours. "Wow. That would be so much easier than carving new ones. Do you remember where you saw it?"

"Sort of." His freckle-covered nose and brown eyes crinkled. "I think so? That's why I asked Mr. James to bring me out today. Is it okay if I go look for it?"

"Brody, it is more than okay. You'd be my hero."

"Great!" The boy raced off in a burst of energy that Alex envied.

"You're not upset about the sleepovers and parties?" James asked.

"Nah. Who could blame 'em with this huge property sitting empty for so long?" Alex eased down into one of the faded and cracked Adirondacks around what was left of the fire pit. He moved slowly both to test if it would hold him, and because the seat would be damn cold through his jeans.

James sat opposite him. Far less carefully. And with far more bulk. "I knew you were reasonable."

"Well, you guessed. You didn't *know*."

"I do now."

Alex appreciated the simplicity of his approach. "Thanks for bringing Brody."

"I did it for you as much as for him. He's one of my best students. This prank thing rocked him back on his heels. Made him realize there are consequences to his actions. He'd skated through on being naturally good for so long that I don't think it really hit him until now. Knows he screwed up. Wants to make amends."

Alex yelped out a stifled laugh. "So I'm the shop class equivalent to saying a couple dozen Hail Marys?"

"Sure."

"Glad it can be a win for both of us."

James slapped his knees and leaned forward. "You know what I think would be cool?"

"In general? Like dogs that can bring you ice cream? Or going a full season of any sport without a cheating scandal?"

"Both of those. And teleportation. I've been on a lot of cramped, crowded flights. There's gotta be a better way."

Not currently a problem he could fix. "Is there anything

a little closer to home you wanted to mention?"

"A game room. Here." He waved a meaty hand, encased in a red wool mitten, in the air. "In one of those buildings Brody's nosing around."

"Jonesing for some pinball?"

"Always. But you're here for the community, not just visitors, right?"

Cautiously, not sure where this was headed, Alex went with a line from his Orion days. "We'll strive to be an integral part of the community."

"Drop the canned bullshit. There's going to be nights—especially in the winter—when you aren't full. You want some other way to bring in cash, right? Besides weddings and baby showers and fiftieth reunions?"

"You bet." 'Want' didn't begin to cover it. More of a freaking desperate *need*.

"An independent game room would be great. The school could rent it out when the track team wins State. Bachelor parties. All you'd have to do is unlock it. It could be BYO everything else."

Whoa. Dollar signs started floating through Alex's brain. It *would* be easy. They'd have to drop a sizeable initial investment, though. So not as a part of phase I. He couldn't wait to float it by the others. "I like it. A lot."

"Good."

"It's a shame you missed Teague. He's on a supply run. I bet you two would get along."

"I get along with almost everyone."

"Which would make me right. But I think you've got something more significant in common." Alex pointed at the eye patch. Today's had a turtle painted on it. "Lemme guess—you're ex-military?"

"It's not like I have an eagle, globe and anchor on here," James said referencing the iconic symbol of the Marine Corps. "How'd you know I'm a jarhead?"

"How many people are missing an eye at your age without being in the military?"

"Good point. Just don't tell my students."

"Why not?"

"I told them I lost it in a shop accident when I didn't wear goggles. Make up a new story for it every year. Then I tell it on the first day. They *all* wear their goggles after that."

Alex laughed so hard he had to lean over and brace himself on his knees. "I love it."

"Your partner, he's a vet?"

"Special Forces. Just mustered out at the end of last year. Teague didn't have a clue what he wanted to do. Winning this inn…now he's got a job and a purpose. Best thing that could've happened."

James made a big deal of craning his neck to look from the cottages to the barns to the main building. "So…ah…did he go on the supply run alone?"

That was a random question. "Why?"

He rubbed his hands up and down the armrests. "Just wondering what the deal is with your *other* two partners."

"Amelia and Everleigh? What do you mean?" They certainly didn't give off a military vibe, if he was looking for more Oorah vibes.

"Are they…available?"

Ah. Now it made sense.

Yet one more complication he hadn't given a glancing thought to before going into business with his family and closest friends. He'd certainly never had to deal with it in his years at the Grand Orion. Alex kept his personal life in a cordoned-off bucket from his business life.

Which was no longer possible. The two were as messily smeared together as peanut butter and jelly on a sandwich.

Even though they were both adults, Alex felt awkward fielding that sort of question about his baby sister. That seven-year age gap between them never got any smaller. Amelia would, however, verbally slap the stuffing out of him if he tried to, ah, *shield* her from the opposite sex.

Which he'd done in the past.

Which had never, ever gone well.

Alex scrubbed a palm across his dry mouth. "Sure? I mean, we just got here. Nobody's had time to scope out the local scene and hook up."

"Except for you and Sydney," James said with a sly smile.

Wait.

Why a *sly* smile? What was he insinuating?

Alex immediately gave a hearty chuckle. A hearty, *fake* chuckle. "Well, that's not a hookup. There's a story there."

James gave an openmouthed, oversized wink. "I'll bet there's more to the story than the official version."

"Huh?"

"It's one hell of a 'coincidence' that you win a hotel in her town. The town she hasn't been back to in over a decade. What're the odds on that happening?"

Crap.

He'd clearly guessed the truth about them faking the engagement.

Well, Alex wouldn't lie to him. Not anymore. Not now that he'd been more or less deliberately challenged. What sort of a friendship starting gate was that to run through?

Shifting his feet over the crackling, frozen grass, he said, "You got us. I don't know how, but you did."

James rolled his lips in until nothing showed but beard, then pushed them back out. "Did what?"

Now he was being toyed with. Like dangling a piece of string just out of reach of a cat's swiping paw. "You're going to make me say it, aren't you?"

"Oh, yeah."

"We're not engaged." Alex spread his arms wide, palms up in a sort of reverse *ta-da* gesture. "It's fake."

James slapped a fist against the chair arm. "I knew it! I can't wait to tell Matt."

Uh-oh. Was their secret not holding up? Going for casually confused rather than panicked, Alex said, "The chief?"

"Yep. We had a bet going. Thanks to you coming clean, I just won ten smackeroos."

Good to know the chief wasn't so much of a tight-ass about the law that he wouldn't engage in a friendly wager. *Bad* to know that he'd jumped onto the *Alex and Sydney are faking it* train.

"He's suspicious, too?"

James tipped his head up to the sun, propping it on the arched wooden back. "Don't get worked up about it. Being suspicious is literally his job. Matt looks at everything through a doubting lens."

Okay. Matt's suspicion made sense.

But not James's.

They'd been a picture-perfect couple when they visited his classroom. And every other time they'd stepped out in public. Including PDA. Alex didn't expect an Oscar, but he knew he'd pulled it off.

Knew he'd looked at Sydney with equal parts lust and interest in his eyes.

Because, God help him, that hadn't been an act. He wanted to know...*everything* about her. The basics they still hadn't gotten to, like her college major. Along with the more complicated stuff that defined her as a person. And the fun stuff.

What band did she listen to when she needed to be cheered up?

What did she drink when she wanted to relax?

Where was her favorite spot to be kissed?

After gulping in air, Alex asked, "What gave us away?"

James hooted. "Are you for real? Frigging logic. What I just said. The facts don't line up in a way that's remotely believable."

Yeah. He'd said that from the start. And yet... "The whole rest of the town believes." Nobody had questioned either of them. Just offered congratulations.

"That's because they *want* to. They love the idea of your romance. They don't want to look closer and see all the holes in it."

"Are you saying we're bad actors?"

"Dude." James raised his arms, then locked his hands on top of the black ski cap he wore. "The *facts* aren't believable. But you and Sydney being nuts for each other? That's real.

As obvious as a preacher's kid in a biker bar. That's *why* people are buying it hook, line and sinker."

Great. That meant he had two problems.

"Once you get your payout from Matt, can you nail the lid back down on this thing?"

"Not gloat publicly about my win? That's as good as the cash."

"Not gloat. Not talk about it—or us—at all. Except in glowing terms of true lovebirds. We're only doing this to distract her grandmother during chemo."

"That explains it. Miss Daisy's a die-hard romantic. Always trying to set me up with the other teachers. Yeah, I'll keep my mouth shut."

Crisis averted. "Feel free to start a rumor about the bachelor party. You're invited."

"I'll hold you to that. Once Sydney leaves, we'll all go out and party hard. We could take the ferry to Atlantic City for the weekend."

"Fun idea. But if we do this right—" Alex circled his hand widely to encompass the inn, its grounds, and the cottages "—Teague and I won't have any weekends off for a good long time."

"AC is open on Mondays, too. I get Columbus Day off."

"Point taken." Man, it'd be fun. Something to look forward to if they had decent bookings all summer. "It's a good idea."

"So you want to keep faking it with Sydney?"

Did he *ever*.

"We're making a not-dying-anymore woman happy. So, yeah. I visited her yesterday during her chemo treatment. She looked so pale and sick, you know? Until we went in, talked to her. Daisy perked right up. Full of sass and spirit."

James nodded slowly. "That's our Miss Daisy."

"I'm not saying we're a magic pill. But as long as this engagement distracts her for even ten minutes a day from being scared and miserable? I'm all for keeping it up."

"*Just* for Miss Daisy's sake? No other reasons? That's your story?"

"And I'm sticking to it."

The trouble with James was that he'd finely honed his bullshit detector to see through whatever excuses and lies kids tossed at him.

Of *course* he could tell that Alex 'liked' Sydney. That he wanted more than a fake relationship.

That he wanted…her.

James leaned forward, draping his wrists over his knees. "Don't worry. I want Miss Daisy to feel better, too. I'll tell Matt to keep his lips zipped."

"Thanks." It was a relief. He'd still have to tell Sydney about their close call, though. Warn her that others might see through their secret, too.

"As long as I can hassle you and Sydney in private."

"Seems fair." Seeing Brody loping across the lawn clutching a big box, Alex added, "Don't tell the kid."

"No chance in hell. Give someone his age any scrap of leverage, and they'll use it to bring you to your knees. I wouldn't do that to another adult."

"I found 'em!" Brody yelled.

"Great!" Alex stood to look into the box. They weren't painted, but the balusters were a perfect match to the ones on the porch. "I like your initiative. We'll see how the next few months go. But I want you to know that we'll need some help once we open. And it'll pay." Not a lot. Probably enough to keep a teenager happy, though.

"Thanks, Mr. Alex. I'll impress you. Just you wait and see."

A confident, smart kid. A new friend who'd keep his secret. And a box that just shaved at least twenty hours of work off his list.

His butt was numb from the cold chair. His fingers were cold. But Alex mostly felt…*hopeful.*

It was exciting.

He wondered how long it'd last…

Chapter Thirteen

"SANJAY, I KNOW you didn't call me to gossip," Sydney said. Yes, she was FaceTiming her former colleague. No, it didn't stop her from walking away from the laptop to peruse her closet.

Well, her *sister's* closet. Since she was staying in her sister's house while Kim was doing her stint in the Peace Corps. And by 'stint,' Sydney meant elopement and extended honeymoon in a very desolate and underserved portion of Malawi.

She and her sister had very different takes on both romance and honeymoons.

Not that Sydney spent time thinking about a someday honeymoon. She wasn't one of those people who fantasized about wedding dresses and bouquets. But she did want a basic romantic gesture or two from a guy and, oh, running water.

Luckily, the Peace Corps frowned on bringing an extensive wardrobe along. Sydney had a ton of choices for her second very public and official date with Alex. To someone who lived out of two suitcases? Kim's walk-in closet might as well be Aladdin's treasure cave.

"S, you know I'd walk over hot coals to gossip with you.

Remember that time we walked on coals in Mexico? Then had to sit with our feet in that tide pool all night to cool off?"

That coal walk had been one of her worst ideas ever. Yes, it was possible to scurry across in seven seconds and not feel anything, just like the *purported* Aztec shaman had promised.

It was what happened *after* those adrenaline-filled seven seconds that he hadn't bothered to fill them in on. The pulsing pain and blisters. Thank goodness her team had been there, suffering alongside and laughing with her through the tears.

"You're right. Let me rephrase. I know you wouldn't call me *only* to gossip."

"True. I'm here to make you an offer you can't refuse," he said, in a horrible imitation of Marlon Brando.

Doubtful.

Before she'd taken her sabbatical—unpaid, no thank you very much to her boss who evidently had zero sympathy for her helping a sick family member—she'd been Sanjay's superior.

It was, admittedly, a fine line to draw. She'd been the producer on their travel show, while Sanjay operated the camera and Reggie did sound. Their working relationship had been more of a totally equilateral triangle. And their thoroughly unprofessional show host had been like an annoying fly careening around the edges of the tightly honed triangle.

But since Sydney often had to pull rank and use her title to get the diva, snotty, *whiny* host to fall in line, she knew where she stood on the official ladder.

"There's nothing you can offer me. Unless you finally worked your contacts to get us a comped suite at the Shangri-La in Dubai."

"Fat chance. Although I'll never stop trying."

"That's the spirit." Oooh. Sydney pulled out a navy ombré sweater covered in glittery stars. Gorgeous. Probably too much for casual pizza night on the Eastern Shore, though.

"Look, I'm an…intermediary. A way to get things done without going through official channels."

She didn't bother to bite back her laughter. "Now you've gone from Marlon Brando to a secondary character in a Bond film. Clearly you've been stuck in an airport binging Netflix for far too long."

"Sydney, pay attention. This is real. I need you to listen to me."

His sharp tone had her abandoning the closet and returning to the laptop. Sure enough, Sanjay's thick brows were drawn together in an uncharacteristic scowl. He never looked that serious unless the star of their show was screwing up a take.

"Okay. You've got me intrigued." Sydney perched on the edge of the bed. "What's this offer I can't refuse?"

"You're still under contract with *Excursions 365*, right?"

"Yes. Contracted but not drawing even a portion of a paycheck." The bitterness oozed over her words like lava flowing down a volcano.

She'd worked for them since the day she left college. Years of dedication, overtime she never charged for, food poisoning, lost luggage—all the hassles of constant international travel. She'd bent over backward to give everyone else on her team the best experience possible. Other people in the company took sabbaticals at sixty percent pay. But Sydney's boss had refused.

"I still can't believe they made you take an unpaid sabbatical."

"I did wring one concession out of them. Once I threatened to mention to other producers how unsympathetic they were to my grandmother's situation. They're supposed to toss me some editorial work when it comes up."

"Like you're a newbie," he scoffed. "Insulting."

"Yes. But money is money, no matter how you get it." Her boss had refused to pay for the massively expensive trip back to the States. That took a chunk out of her savings.

Sydney refused to let her father pay her any wage at all for her hours at the Merc. He might need to hire extra help once she left, depending on how well her gram bounced back. Better he save his money for that. Her time was the best gift she could give the both of them.

"What if you could get it a different way?"

Aha. They must be getting to the meat of the conversation now. "I'm not going to deliver pizzas," she joked.

"*Wanderlust* heard you're…semi-available. You remember that Yuri Kim jumped ship to move to their channel last year?"

"Of course. We threw her that party in…Prague?" Someplace with beer as dark and heavy as tar.

"Budapest. You worked with her for two seasons. Your rapport was seamless."

"I can't take all the credit. Yuri's pretty great to work with."

"Well, she's *giving* you the credit. Yuri heard about your sitch from a little Indian birdie—" Sanjay put his chin in his hands and blinked innocently "—and immediately went to her superiors. Told them this was the opportunity to snatch you up."

"You what? You know I'm not supposed to talk about my sabbatical. Not if I want a shot at getting a show of my own." It had been her dream. What she'd worked toward for so many years.

Except…

Sydney glanced over at the blown glass suncatcher in the window. Its orange and yellow glow warmed her as much as the radiator beneath it. Simple, beautiful and homey, it was one of the little touches of comfort that she hadn't realized she'd missed while she'd lived in hotel rooms for so many years.

Except that now she didn't trust the company that had treated her so poorly. *And* almost fired her entire team when the powers-that-be discovered just how awful and incapable the host was.

Strangely enough, being home wasn't making her itchy to leave again and travel more. No, she was settling into the whole idea of it. Settling into not being jet-lagged. Not being lonely. The…security and ease of having a routine.

But that wasn't reason enough for Sydney to give up on her dream.

She was merely enjoying the novelty of it. No different from enjoying the novelty of hummus for breakfast in Lebanon. Great while she was there. *Not* something she wanted to do every day, let alone for the rest of her life.

Sanjay tapped a spoon against a dish to get her attention. She wasn't sure which time zone—or continent—he was in, so it could be a dish of cereal or ice cream.

"You don't owe *Excursions 365* any loyalty," he said firmly. Then he stabbed the spoon in the air to punctuate the fact. "Not after how they treated you. Not after you did everything to save our show, save our team, and your reward was watching them put in somebody else to take over."

"Thanks for that. Believe me, I'm not brimming with loyalty. Or even trust."

Because their host, their big *star*, had been an alcoholic, unreliable train wreck. Sydney had bent over backward to cover for him. Until he'd screwed up so badly, so publicly, that it couldn't be hidden from HQ.

Which was when she'd taken her shot. Asked to take over as interim host, rather than tanking the show immediately. It'd save the rest of the crew. The dude-bro-centric theme of the show couldn't be hers permanently in its current format, but she thought it'd buy her time to pitch a way to make it more accessible to both genders. And buy her team time to keep getting paid.

Instead, they'd given her a final test to pass. A final hoop to jump through. They'd made her write that ridiculous magazine article as final proof that she could 'make anywhere interesting.' Which was an insult, making her do the backward leap from television to magazine. They'd been sure she'd refuse to even turn in the assignment. And it ran the risk of them officially cycling her back to the magazine side of the media company.

It was a risk she was willing to take to save her team.

Sydney had passed with flying colors.

Timing wise, though, she'd failed. Right after, she learned about her grandmother. And asking for three months off had resulted in losing her shot at hosting the show she'd held together for so long. Her team was safe, but with a new host. One they intended to keep in that spot even after she returned.

And now she was all kinds of skeptical and hanging waaaaay out on a limb.

"It doesn't matter if *Excursions 365* doesn't offer you a show. Not if *Wanderlust* beats them to it. Rival companies do this sort of thing all the time. They're always in competition for the same talent. You use that to your advantage. You play them off of each other. Then you end up the winner, with a fat salary and a gorgeous new show."

The logic of it played in her head. That was about six hundred miles away from signing a contract and popping champagne, however. "Is this you just stirring the pot? Or did *Wanderlust* truly say they wanted me after Yuri pleaded my case?"

"There was no pleading. This isn't a pity offer."

"But it *is* a legitimate offer?" she pressed. Because Sanjay was known to share speculation and innuendo as though it were fact. The truth, to him, was whatever was the most interesting.

"Yes, for God's sake," he exploded. It was hard to tell which was more expressive—his hand gestures or his eyebrow gymnastics. "Syd, that's why I implored you to listen the first time around. What's wrong with you? You're all over the place. Distracted. Is it your grandmother? Did she take a turn for the worse?"

"No. I mean, sort of. Chemo's certainly making her sicker than she was a week ago. But that's to be expected. It'll pass." Sydney had been shaken by the level of fragility in her grandmother's still body at chemo.

Whenever they'd video-chatted, Daisy was bright and energized. A once a week chat, however, didn't show the full picture, no matter how strong the Wi-Fi. Being here with her was sobering. A stark reminder that, while the cancer hadn't killed her, old age was certainly making inroads far faster than Sydney had realized.

And that she was running out of days, experiences, *time* to share with her.

"Then what is it, Syd? Frankly, I thought you'd be doing handstands and offering me your metaphorical firstborn at this news."

What was she supposed to say?

That while Sanjay was offering her a dream job on a doily-lined silver tray, she'd been using more than half her brain to plan an outfit that would put that wolfish, hungry look in Alex's eyes?

She rubbed at the sore spot just above her eyebrow. It came from stress. Clenching her teeth. Really just a headache spin on the old chicken and egg argument. "I'm sorry. I am distracted. Being back here isn't…it isn't what I'd expected."

"Is it worse? Are you miserable? Is your dad making you sweep the floors?"

"Worse—he's making me cook."

This time it wasn't just Sanjay's face that convulsed. It was his entire body. In *laughter*. "Get out of town! No, really—before you poison someone, you'd better pack up your tent and get the heck out of Dodge."

"I'm not poisoning people."

"But you don't cook. Even when we were holed up in an Airbnb, you offered to shop and clean, as long as we didn't make you cook."

True. Which had been an old habit. A leftover, knee-jerk reflex to the days her family had tried to stick her behind the counter at the Mercantile. A childish *I won't do it and you can't make me* sticking out of her tongue over and over again across the miles and the years.

Which was foolish. More of a cutting off her nose to spite her face gesture.

Sydney could change a tire. She was certified in advanced first aid, and had even splinted a broken arm halfway down an Argentinian mountain. She damned well ought to be able to sustain herself on more than takeout.

And learning from her grandmother now? It was a privilege. Removing that stubborn, auto-loathing of it and treating it as yet another topic to educate herself on had changed everything.

"I never used to cook because it felt like an obligation tied to the store. But now? It's *fascinating*. Something new to learn, and oh, Sanjay, there's so much I want to figure out how to do. With all of my travels, I'm already familiar with flavor combinations and profiles. Now I get to discover how to create them myself."

"What can you cook?"

"Grilled cheese. Perfectly golden without a single burnt crumb."

He blew a raspberry. "That's not cooking. That's what kids do in a dorm room with an iron and tin foil."

Echoing her grandmother, Sydney said, "You have to start with the basics. That's how you develop good habits and better instincts. Besides, we charge eight dollars for that grilled cheese with bacon in the middle."

"Are you moving on to Cup O' Noodles next?"

"All right, I deserve that. I'm concentrating first on what we sell at our store. I made a chocolate coconut banana bread that's delicious."

"It does sound tasty," he said grudgingly.

"And I've got a stack of cookbooks I'm reading faster than you go through anime. I'm going to try making a Spanish spaghetti with olives for…a friend."

For Alex.

Because he'd visited her grandmother, unasked. Because he'd brought Daisy gifts and made her smile.

Because he made *her* smile.

It seemed only fair.

"Good to know you're still exercising your brain during your sabbatical. You'll need it to be in fighting shape when you take this job. Stock up on sleep, too. You'll be on the road nonstop."

"Sanjay, you've given me zero details."

"Your own travel show. You as the host, not producer. A brand-new show, that you can mold into whatever you want. There aren't details because the sky's the limit. They want you. Whatever it takes to get you."

"That's flattering. Probably too good to be entirely true. You know I can't say anything, can't decide anything until

Gram finishes chemo and gets cleared to go back to work. I've committed to that. In the meanwhile, I'm open to a conversation. So get me some actual details. Oh, and I love you for reaching out on my behalf. You're the best."

"Remember that when you need to hire a crew for your new show."

Once they'd hung up and Sydney went back to rifling through the closet, she had to grab hold of the shelf unit full of sweaters and jeans as shock washed over her.

Why hadn't she just said yes?

Jumped at the chance to get everything she wanted, including an excuse to leave Chestertown ASAP?

When had her enforced ninety days of torture turned into more of an…interesting vacation? One that she wasn't ready to walk out on?

Or was it the *people* here that she wasn't ready to leave?

ALEX PUSHED UP the sleeves of his forest-green crew-neck sweater. It exposed veiny forearms with dark hair that made Sydney's mouth water.

Forearms were her sexual Kryptonite.

A body part always obviously more masculine with the hair and broadness and *competence* they exuded. That stretch of arm between his fancy black and gold watch and where his sweater bunched in the crook of his elbow was *everything* sexy to her. Pecs and washboard abs were all well and good. The forearms, however, were the door that invited you in to all the other stuff.

Coming to a make-your-own pizza place had been a brilliant idea, if she did say so herself. The seven-hundred-degree wood-burning oven not only banished the mid-January cold, but also forced Alex to show off her favorite bits.

"Why can't they regulate the temperature in here? I'm burning up," he groused.

"Well, our table is close to the oven. See all that wood and bright orange fire?" she teased.

"We should ask for a different one."

The grumpy mood was quickly eclipsing the studliness of his forearms. Was it already so onerous a task to fake-date her, after only two weeks?

Technically, that was his right. Alex was the one doing her the favor. But common courtesy should count for something. She'd give him one more chance to be a decent human.

"Alex, it's Saturday night." Sydney stated the fact with all the patience in the world. "This place is SRO. If you want a different table, we'll probably have to wait half an hour for it. Just take off your sweater." She could see the neckline of a button-down shirt underneath. It should be a no-brainer.

"That solves my problem, not yours. You can't strip off your top." He waved a hand at her deep purple argyle sweater. Its low-vee neck made it easy to see that Sydney was *not* layered up like him.

Unless a fancy—and probably too aspirational—black and purple lace bra counted as a layer.

"I'm not the one complaining about the temperature!" Whoops. A whole lot of impatience vented itself with those louder-than-intended words.

"God. I'm sorry. I'm being a beast." Alex scrubbed his palms up and down his face, as if trying to wipe away his gruffness.

"I won't disagree," she said with more sweetness than a jelly doughnut.

"I'm in a foul mood. I thought I'd washed it away with my shower. Instead, it just nested in my brain, waiting to go off like a ticking bomb of brutishness."

"You redeemed yourself a little bit just now with the al-literation?" Sydney held her breath, hoping he'd get the humor. If he didn't? They'd give up their table right now and call the night a bust.

Alex stared at her. His eyes started to squint, and she was positive that was a harbinger of an explosion.

And it was.

Of *laughter*.

He laughed and laughed, so hard and so long that he had to grab on to the edge of the rough-hewn wooden table.

When he finally got himself under control, he took off his sweater and draped it over the back of the chair. "Thank you. Both for the common-sense suggestion and your patience with my crap mood."

"I wasn't planning on staying patient much longer," Sydney confessed. Better for him to know that her tolerance only went so far.

"I should hope not. You didn't deserve to be on the re-ceiving end of my frustration." He skated his fingers through his hair, resettling what the sweater removal had disturbed. It gave the careful gel at front a less polished, more rugged look.

More of a lying in bed on a Sunday morning look.
Yum.

Sydney put both of her hands in her lap to keep from carrying through on the urge to reach over and tousle all that thick brown hair that glinted red at the tips from the fire's glow.

"Oh, I'm perfectly happy to listen while you vent about whatever *caused* your frustration. As long as you don't take it out on me."

"Duly noted. Again, I'm sorry I was a jerk."

"Also duly noted," Sydney said with a small grin. "Getting it off your chest with me is probably safer than letting loose with your partners. Because I assume this is all inn-related?"

"Seeing as how that's my entire life now, in a word, *yes.*"

His 'yes' was so emphatic that it almost blew out the candle sticking out of a raffia-covered Chianti bottle in the center of the table.

Sydney realized there could be more gusty sighs coming from him. As the waitress delivered their glasses of Cabernet, she moved the candle over to the far edge. "We'll be slow-rolling it tonight. We won't be ready to order for at least another ten minutes."

With a cheery nod, the waitress said, "No problem. I'll check back then."

She leaned back in the chair. "I've negated the fire danger, removed the need to make any immediate decisions, and we have alcohol. I think that means we're ready for you to safely vent."

"You're adorable." Then Alex's eyes widened.

"That…just fell out of my brain. I didn't—"

"Didn't what? Mean it?"

"No." He leaned forward, keeping his voice low enough that the surrounding tables wouldn't overhear. "Of course I meant it. I didn't mean to, well, weigh you down with flirting and expectations. Because of how this isn't real."

Enough was enough. They'd been dancing around this almost from the day they met. Trying to stay true to the simplicity of their agreement. Trying not to blur any lines.

Except all they *did* was exist in that blurry spot between real and fake. They'd packed so much into the last two weeks. Intertwined their lives. And given in repeatedly to the truth that couldn't be denied between them.

Sydney grabbed for her wineglass. Cradled the big goblet in both hands just to keep from nervously tapping—or grabbing for him. Because she was about to take a scary leap. It'd sure be nice if Alex caught her.

After taking a deep breath, she said, "You know what, Alex? It *is* real. The engagement, no. But whatever keeps sparking between us, no matter how many times we claim that we shouldn't or we can't, well, that's very, very real. To me, anyway."

He gently unfolded her hands from around the glass. Set it aside. Then he laced his fingers through hers. "To me, too."

Whew.

"So let's stop pretending that we don't feel anything. The whole town thinks we're engaged anyway. Why not go along for the ride and enjoy it? Enjoy each other. Guilt-free."

Alex's chair squeaked against the red-tiled floor as he

scooted even closer. This time, his voice wasn't low to avoid eavesdroppers. It was low like a banked fire, full of heat and those sparks she'd mentioned. "If we stop throwing up barriers, it could get dangerous."

"How? We both know it's over, no matter what, in two and a half months. I'm only here as long as my dad and gram need me to sub in for her. Knowing that removes all the danger. Protects both of us from getting hurt."

"It's dangerous because there's nothing to stop me from throwing you over my shoulder and taking you back to your house right now and getting you naked." The intensity in his tone should've made the candle flare and the glass beneath it explode.

"Sure there is," Sydney said in a voice so breathy it was ninety-percent panting. "You think I'm a woman who hops into bed after two dates? I have to not just *want* you to move to the next step. I have to *need* you like I need my next breath. You gotta work for it."

With an abruptness that shocked her, Alex leaned back, clasping his hands over his belly. "You ready to hear about my day? It started out great, but then took a huge U-turn in the afternoon."

Sydney had expected him to make a move. To plant a line of kisses up her arm. To trace lazy circles in her palm. Something physical. Something more. "Wait—*that's* your strategy? To continue with the date? As normal?"

"You bet it is. Got me this far, didn't it?" Alex was smug, roguish and adorable and…probably right.

"Save the good stuff as a mental palate cleanser. Hit me with the bad."

His hand drifted up to rub his temple where a stress headache undoubtedly pounded. "Got an inspection of the roof and chimneys. We have to reline two of them. To the tune of ten thousand dollars."

"Ouch. That sounds like…a lot?" Who knew how much chimney care cost? The bottom line was that the dollar amount was *big*.

"It is." He nodded, wincing. "We're bleeding money. I was certain I'd budgeted more than enough. Didn't count on it adding up so fast, being so bad."

While today's price tag stung, Sydney didn't believe they were already in horrible shape. "Is it *so* bad, though? If you shake off today's setback and look at the big picture?"

"Because you have a spare $10k next to the lint in your pocket?" This time he wasn't snappish, though. Just teasing.

Sydney tapped on the rim of his wineglass with two fingers. "Because you only mentioned the *two* chimneys. I've been out there. I know there are more."

"True." Alex gave a wry twist of his lips. His kissable, well-formed lips. "Only two *is* better than all of them. The roof's surprisingly fine. But if anything else big goes wrong we could be in trouble. And it's only been two weeks of discovering things."

Sydney remembered the idea she'd had while rooting through her sister's closet and stumbling across a pile of quilt squares. "Let me help."

"You know how to reline a chimney?"

"No. Nor do I want to learn. I do, however, have another brilliant plan for you to cut corners. Like with the help from the high school students."

"Color me intrigued." And Alex not only looked intrigued, but more relaxed as well. As if talking through it with her *was* helping.

Sydney was very glad she'd given him one more chance and stayed. An intrigued, interested Alex was, well, *intriguing* to her. "Why not have the retirement village help with your linens?"

His index finger shot up. "One—what retirement village and two—" another finger shot up "—we have linens? You mean the bed sheets?"

"You're such a *guy*. Even with all your planning and list-making. I'll bet Amelia and Everleigh would know what I'm talking about."

"Enlighten me," Alex said, picking up his wine.

"You'll need chair cushions in the dining room, as well as some of the sitting rooms. New throw pillowcases. Multiple sets of place mats. That's the sort of fun but basic sewing my gram's friends would love to do. Do you realize this town has *four* quilting clubs? Fixing cushions and pillows is practically the same thing. It'd be a fun change in routine for them."

"Wow. I did, in fact, have all of that on my list. As things to purchase. Your idea—if they go for it—would be better. You're really good at thinking outside of the box."

His praise warmed her even more than that giant oven at her back. "Let me keep going. What about Teague?"

"He can't sew," Alex deadpanned.

"Can he help with the money? You cashed out your retirement funds. Would he do the same?"

"No." He firmed his lips, flattened his palms on the table as if drawing a line in the sand. "I mean, I won't ask him to.

It's my responsibility alone. I got them into this."

Darn it. That annoying sense of obligation Alex wore like armor—or a hair-shirt—wasn't good for him. No matter how admirable she found it. "Who says you're responsible for everyone and everything?"

"I do."

Clearly that was a bigger conversation to push another day. She'd already pocketed the wins of fixing his mood and the linens idea.

"Good thing we're at a make-your-own pizza restaurant, then," Sydney said to lighten the mood. "You're entirely in charge of your topping destiny tonight. That should make you comfortable."

"The toppings can wait." He pushed aside the menus to half-stand and plant his hands in the center of the table. "The only thing I want to taste right now is you." Alex leaned over to brush his lips across hers once, twice, and then sank in to linger on the third pass. "Thanks for listening. And helping."

Yes, he'd definitely redeemed himself from the way the date had started. "Thanks for sharing. And being open." Sydney poked him with the menu. "Now give me a glimpse of who you really are—a pepperoni or a sausage man?"

Not that it mattered. She'd end up kissing him more tonight even if he preferred a weird combination like broccoli and ham. Alex had shown her his heart, with that single sentence of refusing to even ask Teague to pay in anything.

And she'd fallen head over heels for it.

Chapter Fourteen

ALEX REARED BACK as Amelia tapped a fingertip right between his eyebrows. "Why are you poking at me? I thought we quit all that back when you were a tween."

"Oh, I reserved the right in perpetuity to poke you if you annoy me. Or do something stupid. Or eat the last of the ice cream." She bounced on the couch cushion in his cottage as she bumped his thigh with her own. Obviously to drum in her point.

"That's patently unfair. And untrue. I've done nothing."

And while Alex took that stance on principle in every argument with his sister, this time it was true. Definitely.

He hadn't even seen her all day. They'd been working in different buildings. He'd just gotten out of the shower when she'd bounced in—without knocking, just like when they used to live together—and demanded he sit down with her.

"Incorrect. You're squinting." She managed to get in another tap before he elbowed her away. "I'm sorry if the details are hard to read. I would've printed all this out in glorious Technicolor, but I'm being mindful, per your instructions, of any extraneous expenses, no matter how small. Hence, no pricey color printing, and you're stuck squinting at my laptop screen."

Man, it took her a year to get where she was going with that. Including a rest stop at *I deserve a medal for not spending money*, and another at *I deserve a second medal for following your orders*.

Alex scrolled up and down three more pages before landing back on the spreadsheet that tabulated everything.

Yowza.

He might as well have landed on a cactus, it stung so much. "I'm not passive-aggressive squinting about the small font."

"Okay. Sorry. I'm nervous." She traced around the edge of the screen with a finger that bore splotches of grout. "I've been working on this mock-up for the gardens every night. Four different, complete versions before I landed on this one and knew, for sure, that it was perfect. Except that now I need you to say you think it's perfect, too."

Fat chance.

There was a glaring, bottom-line number that kept it from circling anywhere close to perfect.

"I'm squinting because I can't believe the cost." Alex flicked at the screen, dismissively. Well, *wishing* that he could dismiss the numbers with a flick. "This is more than we talked about, Amelia. What's the point of having budget discussions if you're just going to ignore them?"

If nothing else, that got her to move off of his cushion all the way to the end of the green and white plaid sofa. "Alex. You were a manager. Small crews all the way up to an entire hotel. Didn't you ever learn to lead with praise before attacking someone's hard work?"

Hell.

Yes.

He set the laptop on the coffee table. Adjusted diagonally to face her fully. "I'm sorry. You're right. I had you firmly in the sister zone for that response."

"I'm your colleague, though."

While Amelia was correct, he wasn't taking all the blame. Trying to keep his tone even and non-antagonistic, he said, "How do you expect me to treat you like a coworker when you're treating me like a brother?"

"What? I gave you a full presentation. Spreadsheets and pictures. The same quality I gave my clients back in Pittsburgh."

But not delivered in the same *way.* Alex hooked a thumb over his shoulder toward the door. "You barged into my cottage without knocking."

"Well, yeah. You're my broth—" She cut herself off. Then Amelia restarted, but with more sulky defensiveness. "It's Teague's cottage, too."

"Nice try. How about the fact that I'm only wearing fleece pants? No shirt? Bare feet? Did you ever walk in on your boss when he was shirtless? Or hold meetings with your clients shirtless?"

"Of course not. Fine. You win. We're equally to blame for treating each other...like we have our entire lives. Happy?" She scurried into the bedroom and grabbed the matching shirt from the bed. And executed a perfect toss to land it right on his face.

"Of course not," Alex echoed with a faint smile, tugging it over his head. "We have to do better. Kick old habits. Be co-innkeepers for at least eight hours a day instead of siblings."

This time, she sat down in the chair. No bumping or poking possibilities. "We should have a chart. Like the old swear chart Mom used. You get a tick mark every time you treat me like your little sister."

"Mom started with a hundred-dollar reward and took away a dollar for every tick mark. What's your reward system?"

She scrunched up her nose. "Aside from better working conditions?"

"C'mon, that's not a true incentive, and you know it. That's logical. We need something to fire up the pleasure centers of the brain. A week ago, James promised me a trip to Atlantic City."

"Hmmm. That's definitely a guy trip."

"You weren't invited." Maybe they *wouldn't* be able to tone down the sibling banter.

One step at a time.

"We'll need to think of something good. I'll ask Everleigh. Pleasure's kind of her *raison d'être*. In the meanwhile, are you in?"

Amelia's idea was sound. A little fun, too. Competition was a great way to get them into shape. "Yes. There's a chalkboard in the breakfast room. We'll use that. Obviously to be erased before any guests arrive."

"Deal." They shook.

Propping his feet on the table, Alex picked up the laptop again. Her talent blew him away. Every page looked like it belonged in a magazine, or on a brochure. "Your designs are beautiful, Amelia. There's no doubt they'd improve the grounds a million times over. You did a spectacular job. But they're still more than we can shell out."

"They wouldn't be implemented all at once. For example, the fall mums and winter cabbages we wouldn't be purchasing until we have a full season of cash in the drawer."

Alex didn't know a ranunculi from a rhododendron, no matter how many times Amelia rattled off the plant names. But he *did* know that it was too late to plant bulbs. She'd bemoaned that fact just a week ago. Which meant all their spring flowers would have to be purchased. Bloom-ready. *Aka* pricey.

"You've got tons of blooming flowers on here. That all costs." And it wasn't like they were starting from a bare plot of dirt. "What about the bushes that already exist? Trim 'em up and they'll be fine for a year."

The corners of her mouth turned down. She plucked at the ties hanging from the neck of her sweatshirt. "Fine? We're building out our dream here. Since when is 'fine' good enough?"

"Since we have to cut corners somewhere."

Which hurt to say. But the deeper into this they got, the more Alex was coming to accept that it wouldn't be their fully fleshed-out dream hotel that opened this spring. That version could take several years to get to.

"Not on the gardens," she shot back. "You say the view of the river will be the money maker. So will small weddings in our beautiful, lush garden. Same as looking out the breakfast room window into a blooming garden. It'll give people something to wander through slowly as they walk off breakfast. It'll be good for the soul."

So dramatic. So over the top. So *not* what he needed at the end of this long day. "We're not in the business of souls, Amelia. There are two churches on every corner of this town that take care of that."

"I'm taking a stand, Alex." And, oh, geez, she *literally* stood. Fisted her hands on her hips. "The gardens are every bit as important, as show-stopping, as 400 thread count sheets or those rain showerheads you're installing in every bathroom."

Alex curled his hands around the faded-to-ivory throw pillow. Which reminded him of Sydney's excellent plan to save money on replacing them.

"How about we compromise? I'll try to figure out where we can shift some money to cover this grand scope. In the meanwhile, you have to break out which part of the year all these expenditures will hit. And shave twenty percent off."

"That's impossible. Five."

Guess he should count it as a win that she didn't stamp her foot. See? They could be professional.

"I can't make it rain, Amelia. Not unless I go out there and work as a stripper for bachelorette parties."

"Ewww." Laughter broke her stiff, stubborn pose. She collapsed back into the chair. "Both as a colleague and a sister."

"Made you laugh, though. That's how a good manager ties off a conversation."

She waggled a finger at him. "We're not done, though. I didn't get to the best part."

Oh boy. "If it's adding in a Christmas tree budget for the inn, I'm putting up a fight. We can have a tree in the ballroom *if* there are events booked for it. One for the library and a small one for the breakfast room. That's it."

Because he knew his sister and her predilection for all things Christmas. She'd put one on every sink, dresser and landing if she wasn't reined in.

With a dismissive wave, she said lightly, "We'll circle back to that another day."

"The hell we will."

"I bring something to the metaphorical table that will fix all our money woes. Okay, not all of them, but it'll kick off fixing them." Amelia covered her mouth with her hands as if preparing to share a deep, dark secret. The words coming out in a rush, she said, "I booked our first client."

He had…no words.

Surprise knocked anything resembling vocabulary right out of Alex's brain. Getting up, he paced to the fireplace. Grabbed on to the wide, wooden mantel for support.

"What?"

"I know—amazing, huh?"

"Who…how did this happen?"

"Last week Sydney and I were at the library. Chatting about the inn, because, well, that's our number one and only topic lately. The librarian, Annie, heard us talking. She basically begged me to hold her wedding here. April 10."

"Why would she beg you? Why here?" Alex was still caught off-guard by the announcement. By the single-handed way Amelia had just committed them to an opening date, ready or not. By…all of it.

"She's pregnant and needs to get married before she pops." Amelia patted her tummy. "You can't even see her bump yet, but I guess we will by April. She just found out. Other places are already booked. And she *loves* the inn, Alex. It's both an accident and a dream come true for her."

"So…you're just at the talking stage."

"No. We've had a couple conversations. I laid out how she wouldn't have full access to everything, which is fine. She ran it by her fiancé. Then this afternoon, she committed. I need you to write up a contract. Our *first* contract, Alex!"

Her enthusiasm was great. Exactly what he wanted to see from her…down the road. He just wasn't there yet. Not anywhere close.

Because he was *pissed*.

Alex stalked to the mini fridge hidden behind decorative paneling. Yanked out a water. Guzzled down half of it. Used that time to remind himself that he couldn't yell at his sister. He had to stay professional. Be calm.

Angry, but calm.

Steely, but calm.

Patient *and* calm.

So he guzzled the other half of the water. Returned to the stability of the mantel. With a tiny corner of his brain, noted that it needed…something. Some antique-y tchotchke. Or something artsy. Just…something.

All the rooms would need little touches like that.

Eventually.

After he paid for her damn gardens.

His hand tightened around the flourish carving that pointed up in the center. Better be careful not to snap it off. "How could you lock this down without talking to me first?"

"Well, I *thought* we were equal partners?" The uplifted

223

question in her voice showed that yes, he had remained calm and no, Amelia didn't realize he was furious. "The sooner we start making money, the better, right?"

"Technically, yes. In reality, there is such a thing as too soon."

"Don't be so negative. We'll get it done." And then...*then* she had the temerity to twirl her sweatshirt string at him in dismissal.

So much for calm.

"April 10, Amelia? That's earlier than we're on track for. By three weeks." Yeah, his voice was getting louder and louder. "And if she wants to use guest rooms too, that's an even freaking harder target to hit." Alex threw his arms up in the air.

"They'll hire a caterer, and a bathroom trailer, if need be. We went over all the things they *can't* have. Zero objections. They just need our gardens and ballroom."

Doubtful. They'd want the stairs and the library for pictures. Guest rooms. And a fully functioning kitchen, which meant inspections and permits three weeks early. "You're not listening. Plowing ahead and assuming everything will work out—well, more times than not, it doesn't. Timing and priorities—we can't paint any of the outside while it's so cold. Or when there's snow or rain."

"I *know* all of that."

"Do you?" He had to pace. Walk off the anger tingling through his system. Suddenly, Alex felt very alone in this endeavor.

Except for Sydney.

She truly listened. She knew how dire their cash flow situation was.

Right now? Part of him was ready to admit that she'd had a point, asking him to tell the others. To tell them that there was no safety net, no backup for emergencies because he'd *already* tapped it.

"Yes, Alex. You've gone over all that." Now his sister was up. Jittering a little on the balls of her feet. Obviously annoyed at him right back.

"Because you, Ever, and Teague all seem to tune out when I start hammering through the schedule details. That's how problems like this start. That's how you back us into a corner. Damn it, Amelia. You can't make a commitment like that without running it by me first."

Her hands dropped to her sides. Her entire body stilled.

In a voice as cold as the ice that bumped up against their land on the edge of the river, she said slowly, "Don't you mean by *us*?"

Uh-oh.

Talk about a major slip of the tongue. Not even one he'd meant...*really*.

"Yes. Of course."

But Alex wasn't sure she bought it. Nor was he entirely sure he did, either. Had that been his subconscious poking through? Or just the worry that he was the only one who comprehended the scope, the breadth of what they were trying to do?

Amelia crossed her arms over the giant sunflower embroidered on her chest. "Are you seriously mad at me?"

"Yes. Of course," he repeated.

"Well, that's lousy. And hurtful. Just because *you* didn't

make it happen doesn't make the booking useless."

It would've been far preferable for her to be mad back rather than being hurt. That was so not his intent. Ever.

Alex-the-brother felt lower than low. Regretful.

Alex-the-innkeeper knew he had to get his point across to her, no matter how much it hurt. This was a teachable moment, a turning point.

This was *business*. Even if he still didn't have any socks on and his feet were freezing on the hardwood floors.

The compromise Alex negotiated between his brain and his heart was to soften his tone. And to sit back down in an effort to appear as nonthreatening as possible. "I didn't call it useless, Amelia. It's…ill-considered. Not strategic."

Amelia stayed standing. Like a fighter in the ring, poised to jab back. "Opportunity knocked, Alex. I've got a pretty strong feeling that if I'd turned Annie down? Told her we wouldn't be ready? You'd be yelling at me for saying no without running it by you."

"Maybe."

She had a point.

She just didn't get *his* point. It wasn't about ownership. It wasn't about getting credit. It was about his years of experience and knowledge in the hotel business, versus Amelia's zero years of either.

They would all learn so much as the months went by. Alex absolutely believed that by the end of the inn's first season, he'd trust his partners with almost any decision.

Right now, though? A couple of weeks in?

With their only acquired knowledge being about sanders and wallpaper removal? No, Amelia flat-out did not know enough to make this decision unilaterally.

Alex braced his forearm on his thigh, leaning into her. "You realize that you made this decision for all of us. To commit to Annie's wedding."

"Yes. I anticipate the others dancing a jig of joy about it. Our first booking, Alex!" She thrust her arms into the air and added jazz hands. "We should be celebrating, not arguing."

If only...

He continued as if she hadn't said anything, jabbing his fingers into his sternum. "But *I'm* the only one who can figure out how to make it work. Where to cut corners, where to juggle timelines, and how the hell we can pull this off."

Amelia tossed back her hair, jutted out her chin. "We can," she insisted.

"You don't know that. God, aren't you listening? Your decision was irresponsible. What if we gouge the ballroom floor and have to redo all the wood? Or discover the wiring sucks? Most importantly, getting the permits in time, which is always a crapshoot. Hoping and wishing doesn't cut it. Especially not with the amount of money Annie's about to lay on the line."

Her teeth bit into the side of her bottom lip. "I...might have mentioned a discount for being our first customer," she said sheepishly.

Alex slumped back against the cushion. Stared into the fireplace and imagined that banging his head into those bricks would at least put him out of his current misery. "Of course you did."

"But I didn't say how much of a discount. I didn't know *exactly* what price to quote. We hadn't talked yet about what we'll be charging."

"You're just digging your hole deeper," he muttered. "So now, if I quote her something she thinks is too high, I'll have to drop it to not look like a jerk. Because you promised her a discount on an imaginary number."

Maybe it was sinking in how badly she'd screwed up. Because Amelia backed away. Past the chair all the way to the door leading to the screened-in porch.

She worried her hand across the door handle. "Annie's local. You keep saying that we need to strengthen community ties so they talk us up."

"Yep. She's local. So if we do screw up, *everyone will know.*" Alex never would've chosen someone local for their first guest. Might as well invite the whole town to watch the wedding. Heck, give 'em all binoculars so they wouldn't miss a single misstep.

"We won't screw up."

"It is guaranteed that we'll screw up. Even events at the Ritz have screwups, and they have fully trained staff. The burning question is how badly we'll screw up."

"As long as it's here, Annie will be happy."

"I hope that's true. Because *I'm* the one who'll yes, have to write up a contract knowing that we may not be able to fulfill it. That she might not have her dream wedding if we don't meet this accelerated timeline."

Alex couldn't wait to tell Sydney about this twist. Or rather, he couldn't wait for her to sympathize with him.

Amelia grabbed her laptop, stuffed her phone in her back pocket. "Why are you being so insufferable? My God, didn't you ever have to delegate back at the Orion? Let go of a little control?"

That was the wrong button to push.

And she should've known better.

Alex straightened. He couldn't believe that he had to re-mind his sister that he'd lost his job—and been unable to find another one—because he'd loosed control.

All the pain at being betrayed by Elena, all the bitterness at being fired because of what she'd done, cascaded through him again as if it'd just happened yesterday.

"Yeah. I did delegate." Somehow, the words clawed their way out of a throat as dry as sawdust. "Put my trust in others. And look what happened. Someone I trusted *stole* from the hotel. From me. She abused that trust. Elena could've asked me for help. I would've found a better solution."

Amelia shifted her laptop awkwardly. Shifted her feet, too. Basically, her entire demeanor turned awkward and stiff, proof she knew she'd gone too far. "You don't *know* that, Alex. Hindsight is twenty-twenty. If Elena had told you she needed to run away from an abusive situation, what would you have done?"

Oh, he had the answer. He'd thought about it day and night for weeks once she left. "Given her my own money, for starters. Steered her to the safe houses already set up to protect abused women. One of which was *three* blocks behind the Orion. She could've walked there."

A silence fell between them, as palpable as a curtain dis-secting the room.

Finally, Amelia pressed her lips together into a single, pale line. "Well, we're not going to steal from you, Alex. You have to trust us."

"I trust you won't steal. But after this stunt you pulled today that will *unquestionably* cost all of us? Money, time, and stress? I'm not feeling replete with trust in your judgment."

It was harsh.

It was true.

She opened, then closed her mouth. Marched to the door. Hand on the knob, she turned back around. "Teague's right. You *do* need to get laid. You're a wound-up grump. This booking? It's a good thing. I'm going to go celebrate it with everyone else. Oh, and *you* are not invited."

Fine.

Alex had his own party to go to.

A pity party. For one.

Chapter Fifteen

WAS IT AUTOMATICALLY a date if you'd shaved and lotioned everything?

Even when your fake fiancé clearly had *not* shaved in two days? Nor seemed anywhere close to being in a 'date' frame of mind?

Sydney wasn't sure.

They'd canceled their standing, official, *let the town see the lovebirds in action* date on account of snow. No point going out if everyone else was staying in.

Marylanders were terrified of snow. They were happy for about the first twenty flakes, and then acted like everything falling from the sky was laced with radiation. Or would immediately smother them.

Sydney had trekked through *feet* of snow in the Himalayas. Schussed through it in Switzerland. Learned to drive in it. She wasn't scared of the forecast.

Neither, it seemed, was Alex. Because after they canceled going out, the little dots in her texting screen kept going. A single line. *Can I come over anyway?*

She'd agreed—after giving a time window that allowed her to buff and polish and primp long enough that you could de-wrinkle linen from all the steam in the bathroom.

To be fair, Alex hadn't said he wanted to come over *for* a date. He'd come in, sat on the embarrassing futon that her sister refused to upgrade, and stared moodily across the room.

It could be the elephants.

Kim had an obsession with them. It probably inspired her desire to sign up for the Peace Corps in Africa. Yay for selfless volunteerism! Unfortunately, it translated into a less than adult decorating scheme. The living room alone had a stuffed elephant footstool, shellacked and framed elephant puzzle, and numerous throw pillows that followed the theme.

It was like living in a zoo gift store.

Maybe Alex needed to be distracted from them?

"I got a job offer," Sydney blurted out.

Probably not the best icebreaker, but it had been the only thing on her mind for days. She knelt to rummage through the antique ice chest that held all of Kim's liquor.

"Are you looking for a job? Or is this an annoying headhunter thing?" Alex shook his head. "I just realized we've never talked about your job since that night on the porch. Well, your job before you started at the Mercantile."

Her head twisted around faster than that possessed girl's did in *The Exorcist*. "That's not a job. Not for me."

Alex let out a low chuckle. Which sounded normal. Maybe she'd imagined his lack of being in the moment? "You do it for eight hours a day and get paid, right? What do you call that?"

"My dad calls it a labor of love. And no, I'm not getting paid, so that description works. I'm laboring—happily—

because I love them. Long overdue payback for he and Gram nursing me through chicken pox, a torn ACL, and, you know, being a teenager."

It wasn't the stock answer she would've given a month ago. One based on years of running away.

Habit. Resentment.

But it was the truth now. Which was confusing. A core belief was changing. Had changed.

What was she supposed to do with that awareness?

She angled out the bottle of peppermint schnapps. How the night would unfold was still undetermined. But a snowy night called for spiked hot cocoa, no matter what else happened.

Alex tugged a corduroy elephant from under his hip. Underhanded it across the room onto a high-backed rattan chair. "So are congratulations in order?"

What a loaded question.

"Unclear," she said tersely. Sydney poured hefty shots into both steaming mugs.

"It isn't a good job?"

"It's a very good job. A dream job." Damn it, they'd barely begun discussing this, and already she was forced to disclose a scary revelation. "I'm just not sure if I want it anymore."

He cocked his head to the side. "Funny. You don't look old enough to be having a mid-life crisis."

"Thanks for that." Guess it was a good thing she'd put on the red, fleece-lined cold-shoulder top that laced up the back. And kept slipping off one shoulder. "I just...it would...I'd have to be away from here if I took it. All the time."

"Here?" Alex's brows shot up, incredulously. "This tiny town you warned us to get out of immediately?"

Smart-ass. Shouldn't they have to date for at least, oh, a year before it was safe for Alex to fight by throwing her words back at her?

"Yeah, yeah." Sydney brushed aside the needlepointed elephant family pillow she'd painstakingly made for Kim a million Christmases ago. Sat down next to Alex with one leg curled under her. "I've had a change of heart about being gone so much."

"Ah. Your grandmother? Her brush with death hit home? You're re-evaluating the time left you can spend with her, along with the rest of your family?"

Darn it. The man wasn't just a smart-ass. Alex was simply *smart*.

"Huh. That makes me realize we've never talked much about your job pre-inn, either. Any chance you were a hotel psychotherapist?"

He bobbled his mug, he laughed so hard. Barely kept from spilling cocoa onto the sea-grass rug beneath the table. "No. No chance whatsoever."

"Why's that funny? Aside from not being a real thing, except for maybe in Hollywood. Are you anti-therapy?"

"Not at all. I, well, I don't have a college degree. My parents died when I was a freshman. Had to drop out to be Amelia's guardian."

It was much more poignant and powerful to hear straight from him than when Amelia had told her the story. She'd never imagined that he hadn't gone back and finished the degree. Talk about loyal. And selfless. Because it was quite telling that Alex didn't say he dropped out because of money. No, he did it to help his little sister finish growing up.

"You're a good man, with an amazing heart," Sydney said softly.

"I try. That's all any of us can do, right? So without a degree—merely my observational skills—was I right? About your family being why you won't take the dream job?"

Maybe. Not that she'd decided yet.

Maybe not? The only thing Sydney knew for certain was that she was confused.

So she deflected. Not at all artfully. With, in fact, the subtlety of a sledgehammer through rice paper. "This is a topic I'm not prepared to think about, let alone talk about. Let's shift focus. You…do you want to be here right now?"

Alex slurped at his cocoa. Gave an approving hum at the schnapps addition. "Yes. Why?"

"I wasn't sure. When you first got here. You seemed very in your head. Or maybe I don't know you well enough yet to read you right?"

He took another slow sip before answering. Equally as slowly. "Believe me, Sydney. There's nowhere I'd rather be than here with you."

The snail-like tempo he'd suddenly adopted said otherwise. At least partially. "While I want to believe that's mostly seduction talking? It feels more like there's someplace you definitely *don't* want to be."

Slurp. "You mean my inn? Back with the people I care about most in this world? You couldn't be more right."

Now they were getting somewhere. "Rough day?"

"Rough nineteen days."

Hmm. That corresponded to the number of days since they'd moved to Chestertown. Coincidence? Heck, no. Talk about not needing a degree in psychotherapy to see right through that one.

"Something went wrong?"

"Some*one* went very wrong. My sister. She made a unilateral decision without involving the rest of us."

C'mon.

Sydney sympathized with whatever had pissed him off, but didn't come close to believing it. Amelia adored Alex. Loved the inn, too. She wouldn't anger him or sabotage the inn.

Had to be a small thing that just rubbed him the wrong way on a challenging day. Sydney patted his thigh. "Bad paint color choice for the cottage bathrooms? Or something worse?"

"If by worse you mean catastrophic, then yeah. That one."

"Uh-oh."

Alex set down his mug so he could gesticulate—in a very large manner—with both arms. "She booked our first event. A wedding. Three weeks earlier than we're projected to open."

Okay, that *was* bad. No wonder Alex looked like he'd been possessed by a stress monster. It also explained why he didn't want to be back home. And it gave Sydney a flush of warmth that he'd sought solace with her.

"Yowza."

"Exactly my feelings." He pressed the heels of both hands to the underside of his brow bone. "But with more internal swearing."

"I'm really sorry. That was…not strategic of her. Not at all." Enthusiastic and optimistic, but with zero sense of the business ramifications.

Amelia could buy blooming flowers to stick in at the last second for her portion of the rehab. It'd be expensive, but doable. What she couldn't buy was the time to finish larger projects. Like…oh, repainting the entire outside. A big job *and* wholly weather dependent.

Obviously her heart had superseded her head. Which had to make list-driven, deadline-obsessed Alex absolutely nuts. As someone who equally planned everything down to a tee *and* came up with three contingency plans for her own assignments, Sydney more than sympathized with Alex's anger.

"That is, word for word, what I said." He laid his palm in the center of his gray plaid flannel shirt and gave a half bow. "*Thank* you for recognizing the problem. It's a massive complication on an already complicated project."

Agreed. And not with a guaranteed light at the end of the tunnel. More like a semi-guaranteed plunge off a cliff at the end. Sydney pursed her lips, considering all the things that could go wrong. "Worse yet, what if you bust your ass trying to get ready in time and don't make it after all?"

Alex grabbed her hands, kissing the backs of each of them in turn. "You are the *best*."

"For pointing out that you could be royally screwed?"

"For seeing my side of it. For confirming that I'm not

just a self-centered jerk for yelling at her. For understanding that this booking could tank the inn before we even open."

A little weird, a lot honest. That was Alex in a nutshell. And she could barely breathe from the icy burn of his eyes into hers. "That compliment was deeply rooted in a dark sadness, but I'll take it."

"I knew talking to you would make me feel better. It…it's so strange." He pushed up to walk a circle around the room, hands jammed in his jeans pockets. Clearly he needed some physicality to slough off his temper. "I was furious with Amelia. I didn't sleep it off, like usual after our arguments. Woke up this morning still pissed. Again."

"Justifiably so."

An apology wouldn't make this right. Nothing would make it right until they successfully pulled off this wedding. That was a long time to hold your breath and cross your fingers.

He kept stalking around the room, reaching out to occasionally touch the edge of a bookcase or the upraised trunk of the glass-blown elephant under the lamp. "Yeah, but that's not me. Until a few weeks ago, I was known for being unflappable. For being the one always propping other people up. Pep-talk guy. The man who insists there's a solution to every problem."

Aside from his intermittent and understandable crankiness, that *was* what Sydney saw in him. He needed to cut himself a break.

She glanced out the window. The flurries had picked up into a genuine snowstorm. It already coated the corners of the windows like frosting. Ha! He needed a snow day from his stress. From feeling so responsible for everyone and everything.

"Alex, you turned your life upside down. You're opening your own business. Putting all your savings on the line. Figuring out how to be a partner with your friends. That is a *lot*."

"I know. But I like to think I can handle things. Handle anything." He sloughed a hand through his hair. Standing there, all rumpled and rugged in his flannel and filling the room with his sheer presence, Sydney believed it.

She settled her hands on her knees. Yes, knowing that it'd let her top slide down her shoulder. Because she could think of a far better way to work off his mood than just pacing. The only trick would be to get Alex on board.

"I'd say if you raised Amelia by yourself, barely out of your teens, you've proven that to be true."

"I thought so." A vertical line crinkled between his brows. "But I'm off-balance. Since we moved here, my world's been upside down. You know when I feel right-side up? When I'm with you."

The smooth and sultry strains of Melody Gardot crooned from the Echo in the corner. That proved that time kept ticking. That and, oh, the elephant clock on the wall that used the trunk as a pendulum.

But Sydney felt frozen. Absolutely pinned in place by the gift of his words. To her surprise, Alex, too, looked frozen. Braced, actually, as if unsure how she'd react. As if holding his breath with his entire body.

"I'm selfish, Sydney." He didn't bother walking around the coffee table. No, those long legs stepped right over it to put him next to her. But he didn't make any other move to touch her. His arms hung at his sides, still waiting for her to respond. "I came here tonight seeking comfort. From you."

Sydney broke out of her reverie. Out of wallowing in the moment. She could remember it later. Hug it to her heart later as truly special. As feeling more needed than perhaps ever before in her life. Instead, she dove *into* the moment.

"It's not selfish, Alex. Not if that's what I want to give you."

He inched closer. So close that she had to tip her head back to maintain eye contact. Close enough that his breath stirred the wisps at her hairline. How could a sensation so infinitesimal send such a surge of arousal through her?

"Do you?" His voice wasn't much more than a gruff growl.

"Very much so." Guess she wouldn't have to work very hard to get him on board after all.

The backs of his knuckles slowly grazed down her cheek. "You know what Amelia's parting shot was? When she stormed out? She agreed with Teague that I need to have sex. They're all convinced I'll be a better partner, more relaxed, if I just have sex."

That was unexpected. At least, coming from his sister. "What do you think?"

His right hand flipped over to cradle her jaw. The side of his thumb brushed across her lips. Which automatically parted at the calloused touch. "That I need to have sex with *you*."

Oh, thank goodness.

"Then I'd say that your sister's strategic judgment increased by leaps and bounds by the end of your conversation."

His left hand came up to cradle the other side of her face. "Do you want to finish our drinks? Have dinner? Try to fake our way through conversation?"

"Depends." Sydney grabbed on to those muscled forearms. She already knew what her vote was. But she wanted to hear his option. "What's the alternative?"

"This."

Alex tilted her head back. Then he fell on her mouth with a ravenous hunger. Sydney kept her grip on his arms because otherwise she might've lost her balance as desire swirled through her.

She crooked her leg around his calf, hitching them closer together. In just thick, fuzzy black socks rather than shoes, their height difference was more noticeable than other times they'd kissed. It pressed his erection against her lower belly.

And, oh my, it was *sizeable* already. After one, long, extended kiss.

Well, good. She was already primed, too, just from hearing that he needed to be with her.

Words were a powerful aphrodisiac. And she and Alex were extremely good at sharing words.

Sydney wanted to find out what other ways they were good at sharing with each other.

He broke off the kiss. Let go of her entirely. Stepped back. Crossed his arms with the smuggest grin she'd ever seen. Yeah, he'd felt her melt all over him. Probably heard the sigh when they'd unlocked lips.

Either Alex was insistent on getting consent every step of

the way…or he was teasing her. Sydney felt like she knew enough about him now to assume it was actually both.

"Well?" he asked.

Well, she could tease this out, too. Sydney dipped down to take what she was sure would be her last sip of cocoa for a while. "What's the name of the bride-to-be for your uncomfortably early wedding?"

"Annie. The librarian."

She took a few steps backward. To the edge of the wide doorway into the hall. And thus, to the bedroom. Then she shrugged her shoulder to dip the top even lower onto her arm. And was gratified to see Alex's gaze track its movement.

"It seems like, for Annie's sake, and Teague and Everleigh and Amelia, that I need to take one for the team. That my contribution to the successful reopening of the Three Oaks Inn will be to take you to bed."

To her delight, he stretched out the teasing even further. "You didn't win the lottery with us. You're not *required* to help."

"Oh, but I think I did win the lottery. The day you agreed to be my fake fiancé." She held up and waggled the finger with the paper clip ring. "This is my winning ticket."

"Let me take that off for you." Alex more than circled her wrist with his hand. Then, with the most sultry, half-masted bedroom eyes, he put her entire finger in his mouth. The light scrape of his teeth raced chills up her arm and down her spine. A few moments later, he held up the ring triumphantly before tossing it onto the coffee table. "In fact, why not let me take *everything* off for you?"

"It does seem to be a particular talent of yours," Sydney

agreed. "But not in here. Not with Chauncey watching. It's just creepy."

"That thing?" He pointed at the five-foot-tall plush elephant with a circus ruff. "Agreed. Please tell me there aren't more in the bedroom."

Sydney led him down the hallway. "Don't worry. My sister's fiancé made her clean it out, apparently, after the first time he stayed over. Nothing stuffed, no statues, and plain white sheets."

"There won't be anything plain about the sheets once you're lying on them."

Oh man, Alex was *smooth*. And every compliment he dished out was layered with absolute veracity.

She'd lit a big balsam jar candle earlier, left over probably from Christmas. It suffused the room with a woodsy scent and a warm glow. Sort of like lying under the tree with just its lights on. "Do you want me to blow it out? Turn more lights on?"

"It's perfect. I want to be able to see you *and* feel you. Starting with this tantalizing thing that's been driving me crazy since I walked in the door." Alex tugged at the wide black ribbon that crisscrossed her back. "How'd you tie this, anyway?"

"Not easily," she admitted. #understatement. Sydney had all but dislocated her shoulders. But the burn of intrigue in Alex's gaze was worth it. "That's why it's so loose."

"Aww, here I thought you were shirt-flirting with me."

"That, too. We'll call it fifty-fifty."

"I call it both clever and maddening." The more he undid the lacing, the more the shirt gaped open in the front.

"Holy hell, you're not wearing a bra."

"Nope." About time he noticed!

"That's some next-level shirt-flirting, right there."

"Well, you're my fake fiancé. I figure that's earned you a little more effort on my part."

Alex's hands pushed up under the top, from her waist. Fingers splayed wide, he slowly dragged them along her sides, around her rib cage, up to cup both breasts firmly. "That effort is very much appreciated, believe you me."

He was *so* warm. His hands were so big, covered so much ground. And yet Sydney still arched her back, angling even a millimeter more of her flesh under his touch.

At the same time, it was maddening that she couldn't touch him. Sure, she'd reached behind to grab his hips, but it wasn't nearly enough. Dating in winter meant that she'd hardly touched any bare skin, covered in crisp hair.

Time to change that.

Sydney spun around to work on his shirt buttons.

"Whoa," he protested. "I was in the middle of doing…things. Sexy things. Hopefully good things."

"Very good. Very one-sided, though." She spread open the shirt. "Gimme." Oh, yay. Just the right amount of black hair marched in the sexiest of lines from his navel to disappear into the waistband of the low-slung jean. Exactly as she remembered.

Sydney couldn't wait to lick it.

She circled her hands up, down, and around his chest, delighting in the ripples of muscles in his abs and pecs. Clearly the man hadn't developed this toned body in the last few weeks of manual labor. Alex was lean, but super defined.

And at what she'd guess was easily six three, his extra height made her feel ultra-feminine.

He nipped at the crook of her neck. "I was all for taking my time, but if you want to speed things up, I'm good with that, too."

Centering her palms over his hard nipples, she slid back and forth. "We've got all night. This snow means we're not going anywhere. If you've got the stamina…"

"Is that a challenge? Or are you trying to pick a fight so I'll go all caveman and do this?" Alex bent his knees, put a shoulder at her belly and lifted her up, one hand banded across her thighs.

Sydney shrieked, then giggled. Even though it only lasted six steps, she enjoyed the hell out of being carried. Then he flung her onto the bed. "Yes. Yes to everything."

He shucked out of his shoes and jeans while she did the same and got under the down comforter.

"Oh. There's condoms in that porcelain box on the dresser."

"And I'm sure we'll get to them. But a gentleman doesn't come unprepared to a date." He waved the blue foil packet in the air. "I've got this first round covered."

See? Responsible. Leaving nothing to chance. That's where she and Alex were so similar, and Sydney appreciated the heck out of it.

She held up the covers for him to get in, but he only planted one knee on the mattress. And *stared*. Ogled.

"This has to be said before we go any further. You're beautiful, Sydney. A vision."

Okay. If he could stare, so could she. Black boxer briefs

barely contained a bulge that made her mouth water. Legs that went on forever were well muscled and just hairy enough that she couldn't wait to feel their roughness rub against her.

"You're easy on the eyes yourself."

As he climbed in, he angled down, running his hands up her legs. The outside first, sweeping from ankle to calf. And then, more slowly, the inside. His head disappeared under the covers to kiss the tender, sensitive spot behind her knee.

Alex lingered there, biting and sucking until Sydney writhed and tugged on his hair. Finally, *finally* his teeth nibbled up her thigh, slow inch by slower inch. When his mouth closed around the edge of her panties, she sighed in relief.

Until he kept up the teasing pace, tugging barely at all down one hip, then the other, and back again. Each time he switched sides, his mouth grazed her core and sent her pulse into triple time. His hot breath fanned the flames just as much. When he finally hooked his fingers in to pull them down her legs, Sydney almost did a fist pump.

Alex pressed a kiss that had her hips bucking. Then a long series of licks that had her fisting the sheets and moaning. She reached for his shoulders, trying to get him to move back up before she combusted.

"You ready, sweetness?"

"I was ready back in the living room. I'm eight miles past ready. I need you, Alex."

"Right back at you."

The seconds it took for him to strip and put on the condom felt like a hundred years. When he crawled up her body,

Sydney latched her arms tight around him.

When he slid inside her with that same painstaking patience he'd displayed all night, she bowed off the bed and let out a moan of utter satisfaction.

Moans and pants that didn't let up as he pounded rhythmically into her. Alex whispered encouragement and praise in her ear nonstop as she clawed at his back. And it was only after he let out a deep growl as she broke into shimmering bliss that Sydney realized what she'd said.

That she *needed* him.

What if that was true? For more than sex?

What if her plan for no-strings fun—with the guaranteed end date—had just backfired horribly?

And why was she kidding herself with what-ifs when she was utterly certain that they'd crossed a threshold and she did, in fact, need this sexy, thoughtful, wonderful man in her life?

That wasn't what he'd signed up for.

It definitely wasn't what she could ask for *or* deliver.

Chapter Sixteen

A LEX'S HAMSTRINGS TWINGED as he rolled the ever-growing ball of snow. The last time he'd made a snowman had to be close to ten years ago. It'd seemed a million times easier when he was a kid.

Probably because kids were so short they didn't have to jackknife in half like he did.

Kids also didn't spend a day and two nights engaged in enthusiastic, gymnastic sex nonstop like he did.

Alex regretted *nothing.*

The big snowstorm did, indeed, give him and Sydney an excuse to stay hunkered in her house. But he was sure they would've manufactured an excuse, regardless. Once they started, once they broke the seal on all that pent-up lust, they couldn't stop.

It wasn't just the sex, though. He paused to yank off his hat and fling it like a Frisbee toward the cottage. It was Sydney's...verve? Was that a thing? She threw herself whole-heartedly into whatever she was doing.

He'd been amazed to discover the towering stack of cookbooks. It made him apologize again for his snarky remarks on that first day. But she wasn't just trying to learn how to make a better panini. She'd decided to learn how to *really* cook, balls to the wall. Judging from the more than decent pasta she made the first night, followed up by a golden and not at all burned grilled cheese for lunch that made her squeal with joy, when Sydney put her mind to getting something done, it happened.

Alex was the same way. Probably why they clicked so well. Along with a dozen other similarities that just worked between them.

And when they butted heads? Like whether or not the *Halloween* reboot needed to happen? She argued just as vociferously as he did for her viewpoint.

He freaking loved that she stayed strong to go toe-to-toe with him.

"Alex? What is that?" Amelia stood in the open doorway of her and Everleigh's cottage, shoving her arms into her coat.

The base was already formed. He was deep into creation of the second ball. Plus, a carrot and two Oreos lay in the snow by his scarf. Dead giveaways. "If you don't know, then I'm not doing it right."

She ventured closer. Today she was as bright as the sun glinting off the two feet of snow, mounded higher in drifts along the edges of the buildings. Amelia wore red jeans with a hot pink sweatshirt, topped off with a red knit cap with a poof ball on top. "Is that...a regular snowman? Or an official, throwback *apology* snowman?"

Ah, so she had worked it out. And was willing to talk to him. They were off to a strong start.

"Well, it worked when we were kids. When Mom forced us to apologize and we weren't ready to let it go, an apology snowman always fixed things. I figured it was about time to resurrect the tradition. The situation called for it."

"Indeed." She circled the big ball. Patted it with mossy-green mittens to test if it was sufficiently tightly packed. "But we aren't children anymore. The snowman's a nice gesture. I'll need more, however."

Yup. Exactly what Sydney had predicted when they'd talked it through.

Alex had vented. Gone into more details of their argument. And had been ready to pat himself on the back for remembering the apology snowman. He told Sydney it would smooth everything over.

She'd laughed.

Hard.

That hadn't thrilled him.

But then Sydney pulled his head into her lap and stroked soothing, wave-like patterns through his hair. It put him in a receptive state of mind for her explanation that Amelia deserved a full-blown apology from him.

She agreed, whole-heartedly, that his sister had dropped them in the shit with this early booking. That Amelia should've brought it to the group before extending the offer.

However...Amelia had been *hurt* by his words. Saying them in the heat of the moment didn't let Alex off the hook for apologizing.

What he'd meant, how right he was—that didn't matter. Not when stacked up against how he'd dismissed her efforts.

And oh, how right Sydney had been.

Alex gave a final shove to the ball, then clapped his hands to get the excess snow off of his gloves. "The snowman was the lure to get you out here and talking to me."

"Okay, so talk."

"I'm sorry."

She picked up the carrot. Jabbed it at him. "About?"

Alex had been rehearsing this list the whole time he'd been out here. "My tone. My choice of words. Losing my temper. Here we'd just finished a conversation about agreeing to treat each other like colleagues instead of siblings, and then I sniped at you. It was unprofessional in the extreme."

"What about when you called me irresponsible?"

"See, here's where I have to nitpick. Not to start a fight again, but to clear the air so we can move forward. I didn't call *you* irresponsible. Because that wouldn't be true. You're a hard worker, you stick to deadlines, and you never slack off. I'll stand by calling your decision irresponsible."

She dug the toe of her green Sorel boot into the snow. "It was...a little risky."

The last thing Alex wanted to do was belabor the point and drive them into another argument. 'Risky,' though? Not enough. For him to trust her, she had to acknowledge that it was a poor decision. His reaction had been equally poor, to be sure.

"Amelia. I need you to hear me, to understand. You were right that I shouldn't have said you had to run it by me. That was stupid. Self-centered."

"Egotistical. Pretentious." At least she grinned while she called him out.

"But what you *should* have done was, sure, hook her interest and broach the subject with Annie. You should've promised her nothing more than you'd bring it back to your

251

other three partners and see if her date was feasible. Together, we could've adjusted our timelines and made sure not to commit to something we couldn't provide."

She sucked in a deep breath, as if winding up for the requisite apology. "So we were both half right?"

God. Amelia's stubbornness was legendary.

Fine. She didn't need to apologize. Admitting she'd only been half right was the same as admitting that she'd been half *wrong*. "Sure. It was great that you took the initiative in talking up the inn. Our first leap forward in marketing. You just went too far."

"I get that." Then she put a hand on his arm. "Is it really an impossible-to-hit date? If so, I'll break it to Annie. I got us into this, I'll get us out of it."

Awww. She might be stubborn, but she was also fair. And tried to protect him as much as he did her.

Alex folded her into a bear hug. "I love you so much."

"Ditto."

The hug finished what the snowman had begun.

If only getting through the next few months went as well…

Alex stepped back, squeezed her shoulders. "Straight talk? It'll be tough to finish in time. I'll lay out in the contract what we can absolutely have ready for Annie. Then I'll make a separate list of what we'll try like hell for but can't guarantee. We can go over it with her. Together. Line by line, to make sure she's clear before she signs."

"The 'together' part's the best part."

"Yeah." It always was. It was why he didn't have a moment's hesitation of going into business with her, with all of them. "Now, do you want to help me finish this snowman?"

"I just have to do two things first. I was prepping a big pot of chicken and dumplings. That way we can just pop it on the stove when we're finished working later. Let me go in and finish that, then carry it over to the main kitchen."

It sounded great. But… "What's the second thing?"

"This." Amelia pulled back the collar of his coat and stuffed a handful of snow down it. Most went harmlessly between the coat and sweatshirt, but enough trickled down his back to make him swear and squirm. "*Now* we're all square."

Her laughter was as crystalline and pure as the snow.

"Brat," he yelled as she went back into the cottage. But Alex was smiling as he shrugged out of his coat to scoop the wetness away.

They'd gotten over this hurdle. There'd be more, no doubt. Just like there was no doubt they'd get over those, as well.

Alex felt…good. Really good. Even with the adjusted timeline. One that, despite his voiced concerns, he mentally planned to hit, come hell or high water.

C'mon. There was no way he'd let a bride down. Especially not a *pregnant* bride. He wasn't a monster. Or a slacker.

He *was* a planner. Organizer. Scheduler extraordinaire. And, thanks to Sydney, in a good enough mood to believe that anything was possible.

The creaky screen door to the breakfast room slapped closed behind Teague.

Yeah, it needed to be oiled. Yeah, it'd only take five

minutes—and that included the time walking to the solarium, which they'd set up for now as their tool and chemical holding room. No, he couldn't be bothered to deal with it yet.

"Are you alone?" Teague asked.

They weren't hiding in a corn maze, for crying out loud. Alex exaggeratedly looked left, at the wide-open expanse of snow-covered garden, then right at the empty area in front of the cottages. "Who else do you think is out here? Mr. Invisible? That's a superhero, right?"

Teague marched over, his boots sinking under all the powder. "You're thinking Sue Storm. Fantastic Four. And it depends which version of the movie you watch as to whether or not you'd call her a superhero."

"Okay. If you can't see Sue Storm, then assume I'm alone. Aside from my Frosty-In-Progress here." Alex patted the round ball. Flattened out a spot at the top to hold the next one. But he'd wait for Amelia to come back to go any further. Like she'd said, the best part was doing it together.

"I need to talk to you."

Teague was acting…weird. Which was not something he so much did. At all. Teague had two settings. Focused or chill. Now he was all awkwardly stiff. Snapping words out. Like he expected a surprise inspection from his colonel at any second.

Make that his *ex*-colonel who was about…what…six thousand miles away in the Middle East?

What was with him?

"Are you having trouble sloughing off the military? Do you need me to give you permission to approach?"

Teague scowled, his brown eyebrows coming together into almost a single line. The three days of scruff covering his face only added another layer to his pissed-off demeanor. "The *last* thing I need is you telling me what to do."

"Okay. Geez. It was a joke." Now that he wasn't engaged in snow cardio, Alex felt the cold. And not just the emotional Arctic front pumping off his best friend. He shoved back into his coat.

"I don't like what just went down."

Had Teague been watching out the window?

Not that Alex cared. No chance it was a secret that he and Amelia had a dust-up. He'd texted all of them so they knew not to worry when he didn't come back during the storm. Amelia for sure had vented to the others the moment their fight ended.

Besides, there shouldn't be any secrets. They'd agreed to that back when news of his fake engagement broke.

But how was him clearing the air with Amelia *not* a good thing?

"Uh, I don't know what you think you saw, buddy, but we just made up. Groveling went down on both sides. Big hug. We're all good. She's coming back out to finish this snowman with me in a few."

"Glad to hear it. I'm talking about before that."

Having zero clue, Alex lifted his shoulders to his ears. "What?"

Teague crossed his arms across his fleece-lined denim coat. It was identical to the one he'd worn constantly in high school—just upgraded in size a couple of times since then to make room for his Special Forces honed physique. "You hurt her. Amelia."

"I'm not denying it. Hence the groveling."

Teague's usually bright hazel eyes were now a flat, muddy brown. Almost as flat as his tone. "You yelled at her. You made her feel small and stupid."

Ouch. It was true. Hearing it laid out like that made Alex regret *how* he'd done it even more. Didn't at all impact his feelings that the talk had been necessary; just that he'd done it in a half-assed, poor choice of a way.

"I know I was wrong in the manner I shared the information. I should've communicated better."

Teague's mouth dropped open in a soundless laugh. "You think what you did was communicating?"

"Well, it wasn't my best stab at it. Which is why, I repeat, I apologized."

Why was this so hard for his friend to absorb? Yes, Alex had screwed up. But he wasn't making excuses. He wasn't shifting blame. He'd acknowledged the mistake and made amends. What the hell else did Teague want from him?

"You questioned how much you could trust her. Your own *sister*." Teague's right arm swept sideways, pointing over at Amelia's cottage. "You basically told her she had no business making decisions without your approval."

"That was a slip in context. I meant that she shouldn't make a unilateral decision. Something that big as committing to an event prior to our scheduled opening? It needed to be run by all of us. Period. I'd say the same to you and Everleigh."

Teague licked his lips. Then slowly worked his head side to side. "Man, I've known you two for most of your lives.

You've *never* talked to your sister like that. I sure as hell hope you never talked to a colleague like that. It's not cool, Alex."

Hands up, fingers spread, he said, "I know."

Sure, there was a chance Amelia had, well, exaggerated what went down. Her side of the story probably had a different shading to it than the one he'd told Sydney. Which was to be expected.

He just hadn't expected the shading to paint him into as fully evil a villain as Teague seemed to think.

Alex knew he deserved recrimination. But Amelia had forgiven him. Why wouldn't Teague do the same?

Alex put his hand to his heart. "I swear it won't happen again."

"Damn straight. I won't let you treat her like that."

This was morphing from weird to surreal. Why was Teague suddenly her self-appointed champion? He and his sister had managed to work things out—like they *always* did. Without any commandment to do so from Sir Teague, Defender of Womankind.

He'd had enough. "Stop pushing."

"Oh, like you've done every second since we got here?" Teague shot back.

What the hell was that? Was Teague mad at him about something else entirely? Using this situation with Amelia to get it off his chest? "Do you have a problem?"

"Pretty sure I made myself clear. My problem's with how you pushed Amelia around."

"Anyone else?"

Teague shoved his hands in his back pockets. Stared up at the sun for a bit, cracking his neck. "Yeah. You're pushing all of us around."

"I'm pushing, sure. But I'm pushing myself just as hard. You know that."

"I know that you put in the hours and effort. I also know that you're on some sort of messed-up power trip, ordering us around."

"What?" Had Teague lost his mind? Too many artillery explosions overhead during his tours scrambled things in there? "You think that's fun for me? I *hate* telling you all what to do."

"Right. You hate it as much as you hate diving into a cool pool on a hot day."

"Dude. Seriously. We're all used to having fun together. Hanging out, joking around. Forcing us into checklists and work schedules isn't fun. Not one bit. You know why? Because I can tell you guys *hate* it, and me, when I do."

"Then ease up." Teague barked out the order.

Alex braced his hands on his thighs. Stretched out his back and sighed. He understood where the request came from. But the *why* didn't matter. This was one of the times when you just accepted that life would be hard, miserable, thoroughly suck for the next three months.

You buckled down. Gritted your teeth.

Kept going.

"I can't let up, T." Alex let his genuine regret color his voice. "Especially not now. Not with our deadline suddenly leapfrogged forward."

"Sure you can. Drop the dictator routine. It's that simple."

No. It wasn't. Not if they wanted this business up and running. It was *that* simple. "If I don't push, if I don't tell you what to do when, then who will?" Alex spread his arms wide as he ended on a near-yell.

"We'll figure it out."

"We don't have the luxury of multiple attempts and wasted time while we 'figure things out.'" How did this man who'd suffused himself in military life for over a decade, following a chain of command and meticulous planning for every engagement, suddenly feel it was okay to be so loose?

"What you're doing, how you're acting, led to what happened with Amelia. I won't stand for it, Alex. Something has to change."

What bug had crawled up Teague's butt about his sister? "Yeah. Change is right. Thanks to Amelia, we have to ramp up our efforts even more."

"No," Teague said flatly. "We'll bust our asses, but you need to dial it back."

"I can't."

"Why not?"

"I don't want us to fail."

"So what if we do?" Teague huffed out a breath. Then he stomped forward to poke Alex on his sternum. "In my last job, if you screwed up, people *died*. Use that for some perspective."

Then he marched back into the main building.

Without Alex explaining that if they failed, there was no plan B.

No backup.

No nest egg to use to restart somewhere else.

And no chance that Alex would be able to protect his friends from the fallout...

Chapter Seventeen

SYDNEY THUMBED THROUGH her iPod while waiting for Everleigh.

Yes, she was fitting back into Chestertown a million times better than anticipated.

No, that did *not* mean she was okay with the local music stations. There wasn't much choice here in the radio no-man's-land of the Eastern Shore. And the stations that did come in were…bland. Vanilla. They made elevator music sound revolutionary.

The upside to constantly traveling the world? Sydney had amassed her own substantial music library. But she'd tried to be fair. Give the locals a try, just like she did everywhere she went.

Of course, she was more than a little biased against the station with the DJ who kept sharing her engagement and dating stories. But his constant engagement updates provided an extra layer of believability to the story for her gram, so Sydney hadn't complained.

She hit play on some old school U2 just as Everleigh yanked open the door.

"This is such a fun car," she exclaimed.

"That's one word for it. My sister's…um…eclectic. Prefers to recycle and reuse rather than buy new." Which meant Sydney, for the duration of her stay, was stuck tootling around town in a 1989 Cadillac Eldorado in bubble gum pink with a black rag top. Kim had gotten it when the Mary Kay saleswoman who won it died. Of embarrassment? Maybe. Apparently her family had been eager to give it away for a song.

Everleigh settled her water bottle in the cup holder. Took off her gloves and stuffed them in her pockets. Fluffed her hair. Pulled down the mirror and re-fluffed while looking at it. By the time she actually got around to fastening her seat belt, U2 had moved on to the next song.

She wouldn't last a day in Sydney's world, with the breakneck travel schedules and constant—and often literal—running.

But was it really so bad to sit here for a whole extra three minutes? Slowing down her pace a notch so that her new friend could feel...*comfortable*...wouldn't steer Sydney's day off track.

So Sydney rejected her knee-jerk impatience. Looked at the snow-dusted bushes and admired how they reminded her of a sugared fruit centerpiece at a Christmas tea in London, oh, a dozen years ago. A good memory that wouldn't have popped up without this brief pause.

She was still relieved when the other woman patted her lap and gave her an expectant raise of the eyebrows.

Sydney gunned it down the path so fast that snow fanned up and out in a crystalline train behind them.

"This car—I feel like it needs a name—certainly stands out." Everleigh patted the top of the gear shift, which was also Pepto pink.

"Yeah, if I want to be the main attraction in the Memorial Day parade." Sydney was grateful Kim had left her the keys. Grateful she didn't have to rent, or juggle borrowing her dad's. But geez, it was *not* what she'd been craving to get behind the wheel of after using taxis to get everywhere.

"Do they have one of those here?"

"If it's a holiday, we throw a parade. Same people every time, more or less. Only the decorations change. There's even a lit boat parade down the river in December."

Everleigh sucked in a breath so deep it was a miracle the vents didn't reverse direction. "Every year?"

"Yep."

"Down *our* river?"

Sydney waved an arm in the direction of the Chester. "If you mean the one that goes behind the inn, yes."

"That's spectacular. We can plan a whole special weekend around it. I mean, how many people get to see lit boats in winter?"

"In Maryland?" Sydney chuckled. "A ton. You know we have more coastline than any other state. Than even the big, obvious ones like Florida and California."

"That's a sneaky bit of trivia." Everleigh dug in her bag for a notebook and pen. "This will fill the inn during a down month. We'll line up the Adirondack chairs along the river's edge. Provide blankets for everyone, and spiked cocoa, and mulled wine. Maybe even do a dinner afterward."

"You guys have a cook?" Alex hadn't mentioned that addition to her. Plus, Sydney happened to know that it wasn't on his list for another month. Because they'd *absolutely* gone over his list together.

She'd thought it would skyrocket his stress every night, to see how much still loomed to get done. But it soothed him, making sure that every last detail was accounted for. Sydney enjoyed sharing it with him. Enjoyed hearing how his mind worked through the puzzles and problems, and bouncing ideas back and forth.

Everleigh made a raspberry. "No. Not yet. But we will long before December. Oh, this is marketing gold. Thanks, Sydney."

"Happy to share. Especially when all I really did was snark about my sister's car."

"Look on the bright side. You'll have no trouble finding it in the parking lot of the retirement village." Everleigh beamed at her as Sydney pulled away from the inn. "Thank you *so* much for taking me."

"Can you explain why our visit had to be today? I mean, I mentioned it to you a while ago. And I had to swap shifts with my dad to do it. Not a big deal," she rushed to clarify. "I'm just curious as to your sudden need to make it happen."

"Today marks exactly one month since we arrived."

Ah. Was Everleigh one of those people who celebrated random, unremarkable anniversaries? Like the last time she sprained her ankle? Or how many months since her fave lipstick went off the market?

Sydney had no idea which way to go with a response. "Congratulations? I think? You like it here, right? Or are you just putting on a brave face? Do you and Amelia bitch when you get in your cottage every night?"

"Of course we bitch to each other. That's what best

friends are for." Everleigh clicked her tongue. "Sydney. We really need to loop you in on the rules and regs of female friendships."

"I think I need a manual. Or a workbook. Like Mad Libs, but where I could put gold stars."

"We complain about tiny, insignificant stuff. It just unloads anything that happened during the day. Sort of like washing your face. Then it's gone and the next day can start fresh."

Precisely what she did with Alex every night now. See? She'd earned a gold star and didn't even realize it. "Just to be clear, that's a thumbs-up to one month as an innkeeper?"

"It's a thumbs-up to this adorable town and to you, my new wonderful friend." She leaned over to rest her head on Sydney's shoulder for a few seconds. "I've got no idea yet what it feels like to be an innkeeper. Right now I'm an official grunt-worker. At best."

"It'll get better."

"I know. That's what keeps us going."

"I still don't understand what the retirement village visit has to do with your month-i-versary."

"We always said that we'd officially kick off the inn's marketing after a month."

Sydney swallowed down a laugh. That was absurdly punctual of the woman. "Oh, well, I don't think anyone would hold you to the *exact* date."

"You're right. They wouldn't. Which is why I *have* to. Myself." She double-thumped her chest. Which just sounded like thumping a bed pillow, through all the fluffy down in the black parka. "Kick myself into gear."

"I...am still lost." Alex never complained about Everleigh, or called her a slacker. He *did* often compliment her hard work. Where was this coming from?

"I don't want to screw up."

"Nobody does, hon." Sydney patted her knee. "Worry about that is what keeps us focused, gets us to the deadline. It doesn't mean people expect less of you."

"I know. Except that I *do* screw up. All the time. It's kind of my M.O."

Sydney never would've guessed that the cheerful, approachable, warm, stunning woman in her passenger seat lacked confidence. Had to be it, though. Since there was no way she was as bad as self-described.

She turned down one of the long lanes that cut between soy fields, brown now, with only the giant sprinkler machinery sticking up more than an inch from the ground. "Look, we're all self-conscious. We beat ourselves up far more than the rest of the world ever would."

"Go ahead. Ask your 'fiancé.'" Everleigh used finger quotes and gave her an openmouthed, oversized wink at the word. "Or ask Amelia. She's my very best friend in the world. And she'll tell you that I'm a mess. Horrible at follow-through. My parents, in fact, would gladly fill your ears for hours of all the ways I'm a disappointment. I'm whatever the opposite of a magnet is when it comes to sticking to things. A...flibbertigibbet."

Oh, no. Sydney was awash in sadness that Everleigh thought that's how the world saw her. Her parents, too? That was the worst. She disliked those people, sight unseen, for being so unsupportive to their daughter.

Trying to balance with a bit of levity, she said, "Wasn't that what they called Maria in the nun song in *The Sound of Music*? So either you're the kind woman who ends up marrying a…naval captain with seven children? Or you're a nun?"

"Well, I'm no nun. That's fairly well established, too."

There were *clearly* a lot of stories to mine here. Sydney was engulfed with curiosity. But you didn't jump on someone right after they revealed an intimate secret with an eager 'tell me more.'

"Forget whatever happened in the past. This is your fresh start."

"That's what I'm thinking. We were all at our lowest low when this lottery win happened. I'd lost my job and my boyfriend *and* where I was living."

Sydney took a wild guess. "Were all three things related?"

"That obvious, huh? Well, to everyone but me. Yes. So even though this is a great opportunity for all of us—to work together, to stay together, as a unit—selfishly? This is great for me. Something completely different. A way to start over where nobody knows me. Where I can transform into the Everleigh I always wanted to be, but could never figure out *how* to be."

Wow. Quite a speech. Quite a life-turnaround. "I have faith in you."

"Thanks. That means a lot. Anyway, that's why we have to start today, on the precise day we're supposed to. Asking the retirees to help with our pillow and linen needs will automatically get them excited about the inn's reopening. They'll talk it up to everyone."

"That they will. Not just everyone in town, but everyone they know *outside* of town." Sydney hadn't connected the dots that way, and it had been her idea. "That's smart, Ever."

"Theoretically, anyway. So I get off on the right foot and impress everyone with how well I do it. With your help, of course."

"The only thing I'm going to do is introduce you to my gram and a few of her friends. They'll adore you. And my work will be done."

"No, Sydney." Ever grabbed at her arm, which made Sydney's grip on the steering wheel veer the car practically off the shoulder. Her touchy-feeliness was heartwarming, but a little bit overzealous. "You can't abandon me. I need your help. I need you to stick with me and watch. Stop me if I put my foot in it, or say something totally off the rails. You're so smart. I think you could help me, um, level up. If you don't mind."

Sydney's first instinct was to remind Everleigh that she'd be out the door in precisely fifty-nine days. Sticking around was the *opposite* of her plan.

But as long as she was still here, she'd help her all she could. Starting with a pep talk.

"You have to be more confident. That's the starting point for you. Do you remember that movie about a guy who built a baseball field just because a voice told him to?"

"*Field of Dreams.* Yeah. 'If you build it, they will come.'"

"Well, the hot farmer believed in himself, in what he was doing. You have to do the same. Believe that as long as you work hard, you'll get your dream."

Or so she used to think.

Before *Excursions 365* screwed her over after making her bend over backward to write that article as one final hoop to jump through for the promotion that never came...

Everleigh sighed. Swiped her hands back and forth against the blush-pink dashboard. "You and Alex really are a good match. He used to tell me the same thing. Dig in, do the work, and you'll get rewarded."

"See? We both say it because it's true."

"But then he got fired and blackballed by the hotel he managed back in Pittsburgh all because of a stupid magazine article. *And* they got the facts all wrong. *And* he wasn't a screwup at all. So what shot do I have?"

Sydney barely stopped herself from veering into the shoulder again at Everleigh's words. She did manage to hork up a banal platitude through her shock. "Cut it out. Fresh start, remember? You'll do great. No more self-doubt."

Then she turned up the volume and let U2 blast through the car.

Because she had to think.

Hard.

What were the chances that the facts Everleigh tossed out added up to *Alex* getting fired because of something *Sydney* had done?

This was very, very bad...

"GRAM, THIS IS my friend Everleigh. She's one of the owners of the Three Oaks Inn." Sydney had warned that her gram wouldn't shake hands because of the risk of germs while under treatment.

But her hazel eyes sparkled with warmth, and she clapped her hands as she beamed at them in her small living room.

"Aren't you the lucky one?"

"Ha!" Ever followed that up with a snort. "Not generally. But I'm okay with all the luck I'm supposed to get in my whole life being lumped together to give me the inn. That's enough."

"Gratitude is good. You'll do fine. And I'll bet you haven't run out of luck quite yet." She adjusted the green felt cap accented with a black leather edging. Gram didn't want to be 'one of those sad sacks with handkerchiefs on their head.' Sydney had scoured eBay with her three nights in a row to amass a collection of jazzy, spunky hats.

"Where's your quilting bag, Gram?" She was antsy to move them along. The need to do some immediate detective work to determine what had actually happened to Alex—and her part in that—had Sydney jittery and restless.

And, well, *scared.*

"Don't need it. I do need my wallet for my mahjong club. Be a dear and grab my purse from next to the recliner."

"Uh, you were going to introduce Everleigh to your quilting club. So they could help her?"

"Hon, they're too small for what you want. *Everyone* in the village comes to mahjong. Not just quilters. Women who embroider, or crochet, or sew their own clothes. That's what you need, and that's what I'll deliver."

Sydney and Everleigh exchanged amused glances over her head. Gram...gambled? Over a tile game? How wild *were* the residents of Egret Bay Retirement Village?

Desperate for five minutes alone, she squeezed her grandmother's arm. "You know, before we go down the hall, I'd love if you could have a little talk with Everleigh. She's new here, but she really wants to connect to what makes Chestertown so special. That way she can talk it up to potential inn guests. Will you tell her why you decided to stay?"

The warmth leached out of her eyes, replaced by a flatness. "You mean in this 'speck of dust on a map'? Isn't that what you called it?"

Geez. Family never let you forget a single misstep. No matter how many years—and years of maturing—elapsed. She handed over the hot teal purse. "Yes, Gram. When I was fifteen I said thoughtless, hurtful things about Chestertown to you. I lashed out. And I know I was wrong. How many times do I have to apologize?"

"Oh, you've covered that enough, hon." She tucked an errant lock of hair behind Sydney's ear. "But you haven't apologized to yourself yet."

Sydney lurched backward, butting her into the wooden chair that paired with the small bistro table. "What? Why would I do that?"

"Because running away from here put a distance—real and figurative—between you and your family. You hurt yourself with that."

A charged moment froze Sydney in place even more than the chair…and then sent her running.

Because that was her comfort zone.

It was what she knew how to do. It was easy.

Easier than continuing this conversation, at any rate.

"Sorry." She pulled her phone from her back pocket and waved it in the air. "I have to make a call. Work thing. Shouldn't take long. You two chat."

Rather than going into the bedroom, Sydney went out the front door. No way would she risk Everleigh hearing even a smidge of this conversation. She hustled down the length of the hall to the lobby area while the phone rang.

She and Sanjay usually pinged each other on G-chat. That way if it was the wrong time zone or in the middle of a shoot, it wouldn't wake you up. But this was an emergency. She couldn't wait for what might be a convenient time for him.

She had to know.

Had to confirm whether the churning in her stomach was paranoia, or dread at how everything between she and Alex was about to change.

How *stupid* and lax she'd been.

It had been lovely to exist in a bubble with Alex. One that had nothing to do with either of their pasts. Where anything that happened outside of Chestertown wasn't even a factor.

Sydney had done it out of pique. Frustration at *Excursions 365* promising her a promotion if she jumped through the right hoops, and then reneging. At treating her so poorly. This sabbatical with her grandmother gave her the chance to step away, clear her head.

Submerging herself in the bubble of right now, of living only in the moment, had been a relief.

But Sydney *knew* better. Basic dating safety as a woman

271

in today's world. Don't sleep with a guy unless you know his last name.

Had Alex introduced himself with his full name, that first day in the Mercantile? Sydney just couldn't say for sure. Maybe? She'd been frustrated, then he'd pissed her off further. And then...they were suddenly way past formal introductions. Especially with the whole town believing they were engaged. And Chestertown was a call everyone by their first name kind of place. There were no strangers.

So stupid.

Sydney dropped onto a cushioned chair patterned with the namesake egrets of the village.

Sanjay finally answered. "Hey there. Does this mean you've decided to take the next step in that awesome job offer?"

Hardly. "I told you I needed time. No. I won't leave until I know Gram's out of the woods. Everything else has to wait—even my career."

"Then what's with the call? Are you okay?"

"I'm...not sure. Remember that story I broke about that Pittsburgh hotel?"

"You mean the one that should've earned you your own show? The one they challenged you to write as proof that you could make anyplace, even the Steel City, interesting enough for viewers?"

"Yes." The insulting wording had made Sydney cringe— Pittsburgh was a perfectly interesting city, full of museums and culture and great food. But she'd taken the assignment to prove that if she was a host, she could find a *deeper* story in any location.

"Duh. Of course I remember."

"Do you know if legal got poked about it, after the fact?"

"Why would you assume I know?" His innocence was as wholly believable as a child caught with chocolate-smeared hands insisting they hadn't seen any candy.

"You're a gossip of the highest order. Every moment you're not filming, you're tweeting and DMing for the latest dirt." Sydney oozed some complimentary warmth as she continued. "You know more about what's happening in *Excursions 365* than the CEO."

"Thank you for recognizing my vast knowledge," he preened. It was easy for her to picture him smoothing back his lustrous black hair in its pompadour. "Fine. I didn't want to tell you. I wanted to protect you. And since you're on this hiatus, I thought it'd blow over and you'd be none the wiser once you returned."

Sydney's heart picked up the pace. To more or less the same triple time as when she'd kicked the mugger in Bolivia right in the nuts and then escaped *with* her purse while he whimpered in the fetal position.

"That doesn't sound good. I mean, I appreciate your instinct, but why would I need to be protected? What happened?"

"I heard someone got fired."

"Because of the article I wrote?"

"Yeah. The hotel manager. That Kirk guy."

Now she remembered. Kirk Kirkland. She and Sanjay had laughed at the double name. See? Not Alex. Kirk. Although…maybe Kirkland did fit.

And the more Sydney thought about it, Kirk Kirkland

was too coincidental to be a real name. It had to be a nickname. "Why'd he get fired? When I wrote the article, he still worked there."

"They needed a fall guy, a scapegoat, to reassure guests. I guess they'd been trying to sweep it under the carpet, but your article shone a very bright spotlight on their mess. Their way of cleaning it up was to sack Kirkland. Why?"

Sydney swallowed hard. Then regretted it, because her mouth was as dry as a cotton ball. "I think I met him."

"Huh. Small world. Is he as nice as everyone you interviewed said he was?"

"Yep. He's very nice. Responsible. Hardworking." She stared out the window at the enormous magnolia tree in the courtyard. "In fact, I'm worried that I didn't do him justice. That he might not actually be to blame."

"That's a shame. Too late to do anything about it now, though. Hey, Syd, I gotta run. We're ready to roll."

"Thanks, Sanjay."

Sydney dropped her phone onto the cushion as if it was on fire. It was so simple to fit together Everleigh's nonchalant bomb-drop about Alex's old life with what she remembered. His experience as a hotel manager also explained why he was so certain he could get the inn up and running.

It had to be him.

He had to be the manager of the Grand Orion that she'd eviscerated in her article.

Which meant that she'd gotten her boyfriend fired.

Sanjay had been correct. It was too late to do anything about it now. Right? *Right?* Job or no job, he undoubtedly would've quit as soon as they won the lottery. But...maybe Amelia wouldn't have bought him the ticket if he hadn't lost his job.

And he wouldn't have been forced to cash in his retirement to fund getting the inn off the ground. He wouldn't be working crazy hours and worrying himself silly about making it a success.

This was all her fault.

She couldn't tell him. What purpose would it serve? Except, of course, to make Alex hate her.

But Sydney wasn't sure how she could live with herself if she *didn't* tell him...

Chapter Eighteen

A FIRE BLAZED in the library. The chimneys were official-ly relined, and it was still below freezing, so they'd decided to test them out. Logs crackled. Just enough smoke tinted the air with coziness. Aside from the cottages, this was one of the rooms with the least left to redo. It made it easy for Alex to picture it, filled with guests relaxing in the afternoon.

Even though his always list-making eye noted that new curtains were imperative.

The original yellow valances were streakily faded to al-most eggshell. Along with the throw pillow project that Everleigh was spearheading with the retirees. Blue ones for the couches with their brown butterfly and leaf patterns to tie together with the solid blue side chairs scattered by the windows.

It still made him feel good.

It gave him a surge of hope.

Didn't hurt that he was rubbing Sydney's shoulders while she huddled over a laptop with Everleigh.

Being with her made Alex feel like he could finish the inn. Not just on time. Maybe even early. She didn't just give him a verbal thumbs-up like the rest of his crew. No, she logicked through things with him, and only *then* reassured him that his planning made it all doable.

"It's nice of you to help Ever set up our website." He dropped a kiss on the top of her head. Relished the silky play of hair under his lips.

"You'd be amazed what I'd do as long as you keep rubbing out my knots like that. Who knew being bent over a cutting board, only pushing a knife through bread would kink up my muscles so badly?"

"It's not an ergonomically sound workplace situation," Everleigh said, with earnest concern coloring her voice.

"I'll notify the management," Sydney said, tongue in cheek. "I'm sure Gram—who is three times my age and has been doing it all her life—will be chock full of pithy comments about what I can do with my need to be ergonomically correct."

Alex dug his thumbs in at the base of her skull. "I'm happy to keep running my hands all over your body—"

"Hey, hey, have a little consideration for those of us still obeying your celibacy command," Ever snarked.

It wasn't like he'd gone out and selfishly hunted down a one-night stand. He'd gone into this fake engagement as a *favor*. Alex certainly hadn't expected to get anything for himself out of it. Let alone such an amazing woman *and* fantastic sex.

That was all purely accidental.

"If you'd let me finish, my point is I don't think a backrub is enough compensation for you helping to build our site."

Sydney waved away his concern with one hand. "I've got

a knack for writing. Things like this always get done faster and better with two heads. Especially if one is creative and the other editorial."

Ever raised her hot pink pen. She claimed it made everything she wrote down look more exciting. "Which one am I?"

"You've got the vision, Everleigh. You're very creative. I'm just wrangling all your good ideas into a cohesive flow."

Awww, Alex loved to hear Sydney pumping up his friend. He'd certainly tried over the years. But getting past all the cool disdain her parents heaped on her was almost impossible.

"Thank goodness." Everleigh wiped the back of her hand across her forehead in exaggerated relief. "I don't know how to edit—and I'm almost certain that I'm rarely cohesive."

Sydney rapped her on the knee. "What did I tell you about negative comments like that?"

After letting out a prolonged sigh, she responded, "That they're as bad for me as scarfing down six donuts followed by an entire pizza. I remember. Changing habits is hard, though. Even when it's for my own good."

"Are you kidding? Those are always the *hardest* habits to make stick. It takes an average of sixty-six days for one to become automatic."

"That's optimal timing. Right when the inn opens, I'll be brimming with self-confidence. But today? I have to echo Alex. No matter how good he is with his hands—and please don't give me details—it isn't enough for how much you're helping me."

"This makes me feel useful before I have to go sit with

Gram tonight. She wants to watch *The Fast and the Furious.*"

That sounded like a night Alex wanted to get in on. "Which one?"

"All of 'em," she said grimly. "Or until the chemo nausea passes. It'll be a mindless, miserable night."

Yeah, no. He'd pass on inviting himself to that. Better to stay here and work on the warped windowsills in the ballroom. "It'll be a big win for your big heart, though. You being there will definitely put your grandmother at least a little more at ease."

"I hope so. I feel really useless. Holding her hand and putting cool cloths on her forehead doesn't feel like nearly enough."

"Circling back around to enough, I insist on paying you for your website development services."

"Alex, no. I'm helping a friend. I won't take money for that."

"Good. Because I was going to barter for it." He moved his hands to her head. "Scalp massage. Foot rubs." He bent to whisper in her ear. "Other, more...*comprehensive* services..."

"Geez. I can still hear you," Everleigh complained. "I'm going to refill my tea. Get all your sexy-talk out of your system by the time I get back."

That was the problem. Alex wasn't getting Sydney out of his system. Being with her wasn't scratching an itch. The more time they spent together, the more time he *wanted* to be with her.

"Hey, Alex. Can you come out here a sec?" Amelia called from the hallway.

"Be right back." He kissed the nape of Sydney's neck, then rearranged her hair over it so she wouldn't feel a chill. "What's up, sis?"

She led him around the corner into the long solarium. The *unheated* solarium, so this had better not be long and involved. Amelia handed over an envelope with the familiar black and gold crest of the Grand Orion as the return address.

Wow. Talk about unexpected.

As she stripped off her gloves, she asked, "Do you think it's a check? Or them begging you to come back?"

"Hardly. They probably had a couple of rough weeks back when they fired me, but were over it before we moved. Everyone's replaceable in corporate America."

"Good thing we're not corporate, then. Because you're irreplaceable to me." She went on tiptoe to kiss his cheek, and then dug her fingers into his ribs in an oft-repeated one-two punch of affection.

Alex ripped open the envelope to find another inside, postmarked New Mexico. A sticky note explained it had come to him at the hotel, and they'd been happy to forward it to him.

"Who do you know in New Mexico?"

"No one." This kept getting more and more odd. Until he flipped to the back of the letter. It was from Elena Vasquez. The woman whose actions had led to him getting fired. He sat on a wobbly rattan lounger and held the letter so Amelia could read it with him.

Dear Mr. Alex,

I'm sorry. I'm not sorry I stole all the hotel's money, because I needed it to get my children to safety. But I'm sorry I used you to do it. I'm sorry I used your override code. You trusted me with it to be nice when I said I hurt my ankle and couldn't get down to the locker room to change. I lied, though. I wasn't hurt. I just needed the code. I knew you'd change it immediately. I ran like the wind to clean out the cash registers, so scared you'd catch me.

But I was more scared of my husband. Of how bad he'd beat me when I got home. Of how he'd hurt my son, who already had a bruise on his face I couldn't hide from where Ronaldo threw him into the refrigerator the night before.

You saved my life. I know you didn't turn me in to the police right away. Or else they'd have caught me. And now I heard that you lost your job because of it.

So I'm sorry. I can't ever make it up to you. All I can do is apologize. And tell you that we're safe. We're not in New Mexico. Don't try to find us or anything. We have new lives, and I have a new job that is better than I dreamed I'd find. My boss isn't as kind as you, but she's good to me. We aren't just surviving anymore. We're thriving.

My kids and I pray for you every night, and always will. Thank you.

Elena Vasquez

Alex sucked in a shaky breath. Realized he'd been holding his while reading the whole thing.

"Wow," Amelia said softly. "That was nice of her."

He stared at the lined notebook paper. "Was it?"

"Alex, she's letting you know she's okay. And an apology is always a gift."

"I'm relieved to hear they're all fine, of course. But she left me a letter the night she ran away, too. That's *why* I held off on alerting the police. I didn't need another one."

"Sounds like you don't *want* another one. Why is that?"

It'd been such a visceral reaction of anger that he had to dig deep for a couple of seconds to figure out the answer. "It's a reminder. A reminder of my entire life getting stolen away, along with that money."

"Not by her. By whoever wrote that magazine article."

"Chicken or the egg, Amelia. Wouldn't have one without the other. Now she's thriving. Yeah, that's great. But it brings to the forefront that we're barely hanging on. Which is shitty."

No nice boss for him. No guaranteed weekly paycheck. No guarantee of anything. Aside from the guarantee that no other five-star hotel would ever hire him.

Which Alex tried really hard to shove to the back of his mind every day. To focus on the positive, on what *could* be at the end of all this backbreaking work and worry. But this letter opened the mental gate and spewed it all right up in the front of his consciousness.

Amelia snatched the letter and both envelopes from him. Stuffed them deep in her coat pocket.

"I'm sorry, Alex. I get it. You're the one carrying the biggest burden of all of us. You're the one who lost the most.

Ever and I didn't care that much about our jobs. Heck, Teague didn't even have a new one, or know what he wanted. But you loved the Orion, and you'd worked so hard to earn that manager spot. I know losing it devastated you. Especially losing it when all you did was protect someone who needed the help."

Thank God she understood. "I swear I'm over it. Most days."

"Mmm-hmm." She threw her arms around him in a tight hug. Then Amelia stood, pulling him to his feet as well. She kept her hand in his as they walked back to the library. "Get out of here. Go distract yourself."

"Fat chance. You want me to take the afternoon and go to the movies while you all keep your noses to the grindstone?"

"Yes. Not a movie *I* want to see, but yes. You need it, Alex."

"What does he need?" Everleigh asked, looking up from the laptop.

"A distraction. He, um, got a letter from an old friend. Back home. Now he's in his head about it."

Good that she'd kept the explanation vague. He sure as hell didn't want to explain to Sydney that he'd been fired from his last job. And that the whole world thought it was his fault, thanks to a totally wrong article that airplane travelers nationwide had tucked in front of their knees.

It was embarrassing.

And what if she didn't believe his side of it? Since Sydney would be bugging out on him in a matter of months, there wasn't a burning need to share all his deep, dark secrets with her.

No matter how much he sort of wanted to...

Even though he wouldn't tell her, it was nice to see Sydney here. Smiling at him. Tipping her head back in anticipation of the kiss he gently laid on her lips. That alone soothed the top layer of agitation from the letter.

Teague came in, carrying fresh mugs for the women and a steaming travel mug for himself. "Hey, there. You ready to get back at it?"

Sydney blinked at Teague. Then she looked over at Alex. A slow smile broke across her face. "Oh, I know what you can do. Guaranteed to get you out of your head."

Teague made a time-out sign with his hands. "No bedroom breaks in the middle of the workday."

"Absolutely not," Sydney said solemnly, crossing her heart. "They're decorating the historic downtown for Valentine's today. All the businesses. They always need people to pitch in and help. Especially tall, strong people. With their own ladders."

Amelia laughed. "That's a little sexist and a lot specific."

"They're hanging things on eaves and lampposts. Height matters. I'm sure they'd welcome my help, but what do you top out at? Five feet and change?"

"Three inches of change, thank you very much," she huffed. "But I get your point."

Getting away from the inn was tempting. But also guilt-inducing. Alex couldn't justify it. "I can put my own ladder to good use *here*."

Surprisingly, Everleigh shook her head. "You and Teague should absolutely go."

Teague raised one eyebrow. "Are you sick of us already?"

"Occasionally," she sassed back, sticking out her tongue. "But this isn't just blowing off steam. This is inn-related networking. You'll meet other business owners. Go play nice, boys."

"Plus, doing something different always helps your brain get back on track. That's a brilliant idea, Sydney." Amelia tugged on his shoulder until he bent down, putting his ear at the level of her mouth. "It's okay, Alex. You need this. Go hang with Teague."

It was better than staying and feeling guilty about not coming clean to Sydney about why he was twisted up. Plus, since Teague had yelled at him two weeks ago, they hadn't so much as hung out. The air had cleared between them. But at night, either the four of them hung out as a group, or Alex went over to be with Sydney.

Guy time with his friend would be great. Alex would've preferred it with beer bottles and a pool table between them rather than Valentine's decorations, but he was desperate.

"Well? You want to go decorate with pink hearts?"

"It's like you're a genie, granting my deepest wish," Teague said dryly. "I'm sure we'll be back in a flash. How much can there be to do?"

"THIS IS…" ALEX waved one arm in ever-increasing circles. Because he couldn't come up with the words to describe the scene in front of them.

"More than I expected," Teague muttered.

"Yeah. That."

Because the historic downtown was as decked out as the most festive Christmas street ever. The only difference was swapping green and red for pink and red, and replacing images of presents and pine trees with hearts and chocolate.

There were banners arching from every lamppost and traffic signal. The window boxes still full of their purple winter cabbages were draped with pink and white bunting.

Above them, matching lights were strung along every single roofline.

Painters were spraying the windows of shops and restaurants with fuzzy, bubble lettering like cheerleaders used on spirit posters, wishing everyone happy Valentine's Day.

Even the municipal trash cans were slipcovered in white plastic printed with purple and pink hearts.

Alex turned in a slow circle, taking in every over-the-top detail. "It's…a *lot*."

"Dude, this is ten miles past a lot. I spent the last year in a tent. The only decoration on its walls was a streak of red where I wiped my bleeding hand after a dressing came loose overnight."

Alex looked down at Teague's gloved hands. His friend hadn't mentioned any injuries while gone. It was a stark reminder of how much Teague held back. Some, probably, due to NDAs. Some, probably, from not wanting to dwell on pain and fear.

He wished he'd known. Wished he could've helped, somehow, even from half a world away.

Instead, all he could do was make sure Teague's new life worked out right. That it satisfied him. And was successful.

Another layer of pressure tightened around Alex's head. He couldn't let Teague down. He *had* to make sure the inn relaunched in grand style.

He couldn't afford a single screwup.

Alex mustered a jovial tone. "Then you're overdue for some gooey, emotionally marshmallowed decorations, aren't you? This should more than make up for what you've missed over the last ten years."

"I hate marshmallows. As bad as mainlining Pixy Stix, but with the added un-bonus of sticking to your teeth."

Alex didn't disagree. "Play nice. Network your ass off. Say nothing bad about the theme. And tonight, when we get home, I'll let you kick my ass at Grand Theft Auto."

"You'll *let* me? That's hilarious. You know I'll beat you regardless. How about you won't bother pretending it's even a contest?"

James waved at them from a stage being fitted out with what looked like sound equipment for a DJ. Even though the temp was hovering right at forty. He held an iPad and…

Holy hell.

His black eye patch was different than the last time Alex had seen him. This one was painted with a red rose, shot through with a black cupid's arrow.

Clearly there were no limits to how far this town would go to celebrate a holiday.

Their guests would *eat it up.*

"C'mon up. Are you here to lend a hand?"

"Four of 'em."

"That's great. Everyone will be glad to see you. There's been as much curiosity about the new innkeepers as there is overkill with these decorations."

All three of them laughed together. An uncomfortable laugh, that revealed how out of place they felt surrounded by so much romance.

"We're looking forward to the Chamber of Commerce meeting. Get to know more folks."

"Today should take care of that. Our turnout's good. We try to get it all over with in one afternoon."

"James, I need more juice. This extension cord's no good." Sydney's brother approached the stage, waving a giant saw. "Hey, Alex."

"Good to see you, Cam. This is my friend Teague. He's one of my partners."

"Yeah, I've heard all about him." He switched hands with the saw to shake Teague's. "My sister says you're a veteran."

"Is she doing a background check on me?"

"Worse. She's engaged to that guy. Or at least, faking it real well." He pointed with the saw. Alex managed not to flinch. Who needed a five-foot saw to hang banners?

"Ah. Sydney." Teague's grin widened from polite to genuine. "Despite her taste in men, I think she's pretty great. And she's right about the vet. Just got out a couple of months ago."

"Well, I want to thank you for your service. People take it for granted. But you signed up, left everything and everyone you knew behind to risk your life to keep us safe here. I damn well appreciate it."

Teague almost went into parade rest—his comfort stance. His feet shifted wide. His arms started to cross behind his back. Then he fig-leafed them instead. He never took compliments well. But Alex was sure that this one mattered to him.

"It was my honor," he said gruffly.

Alex knew it was his duty to shift the spotlight off the uncomfortable Teague. He gestured at the weapon Cam held so easily. "What's with the saw?"

"Come around and look. We're building ice thrones for the King and Queen of Hearts." Cam waved the saw at the enormous pile of ice blocks. "And if I can piece it together, an igloo out of the leftover bits. Just for fun."

Two sentences Alex never thought he'd hear put together. But…an igloo *did* sound like fun. "Who gets the frozen butt from sitting on those things?"

"The high school votes a King and Queen of Hearts. There's a whole ceremony here, on Valentine's Day. They'll use the thrones then. That night, they'll lead off the dancing."

"Well, we'll be sure to come and watch it. Do a deep dive into Chestertown Holidays 101." Teague had been homecoming king at their high school. Twice. As well as prom king. Everyone liked the star quarterback—go figure. His friend definitely had a soft spot for a crown presentation.

Cam put his oversized work gloves back on over regular ones and wiped away a layer of snow dust from a throne arm. "You're coming to the dance, right?"

"A high school dance?" That was hilarious. "Are you hard up for chaperones?"

"Nah. It's a whole-town dance. Over in the Armory. You're taking Sydney, right?"

Uh, no? Alex scrubbed his hand through his hair. "I didn't know about it until just now."

"There's no way Sydney forgot. The posters for it are up all around the Mercantile. Maybe she thought you wouldn't want to be stared at by the entire town?"

"More likely that she knows how swamped we are with the renovation. Taking off a whole night for a dance isn't so much on the schedule." It proved how tuned in she was to his demanding lists that she wouldn't have even mentioned it. Which Alex appreciated.

"It's a good time. The high school band director, the Methodist pastor and I do a jazz band."

"Are you available for weddings?" he joked.

"Damn straight we are. We jump on any chance to play. And we're not half bad. You can judge for yourself. And then talk us up to every couple that plans a reception at your inn."

This was the kind of natural networking Alex liked best. Unforced. Not like the idiotic icebreakers he'd gone through at the monthly meetings back in Pittsburgh with the National Association of Catering Executives. This was...easy.

But an afternoon lifting ice blocks was all they could spare. Or at least, all he'd commit to right now. Because he'd overlooked the option of Sydney maybe not *wanting* to go to the dance? At all—or with him?

Suddenly it felt very, very high school-esque. Alex clapped Cam on the back. "If Sydney vouches for your talent, that's good enough for me."

"Look, you want to be accepted? To get word of mouth pumping in the right direction? Then you've gotta leave your property more often. Become a part of the town. Not just a long-term visitor."

Guess he was as good at dishing out no-nonsense advice as his sister.

"We're here for good," Teague assured him in a firm voice. "Putting down roots."

Huh. Alex hadn't heard him verbalize it like that before. But after being shunted around the globe at the government's whim for a decade, yeah, the guy probably craved roots. Maybe even more than the new job the inn provided.

Yes, the to-do lists mattered. Finishing on time mattered. But that wasn't all it would take to make the inn a success. Alex couldn't do it alone—as Teague and Amelia had pointed out to him—or by sheer force of will.

He'd need to trust again. To trust this community to embrace his, no, *their* vision. Not to just let them put a stack of brochures in a wall holder. Alex would need to trust these people to be invested in the inn, to care about it.

Which, oh hey, was exactly why Sydney had sent him down here to pitch in.

Man, she was a good partner for him.

Man, it'd *suck* when she left.

Cam pointed across the street to a man pumping up a giant inflatable heart. "See that guy? That's Duncan Wickes. You need to introduce yourself. He approves all the permits."

"Wickes?" It was a small enough town that the recognition Alex felt couldn't be a coincidence. "Any chance he's Brody's dad?"

"That's right. And a real good way to ingratiate yourself with him is to compliment his son."

"That'll be easy. Brody's great. He's been helping us out."

"Has he? Maybe you are one step ahead, after all."

Teague had begun hefting ice blocks and fitting them onto the base circle Cam had begun for the igloo. He grunted. Something. Probably not good. "Trust me, we're barely treading water. We'll take all the advice—and intros— you can give."

They'd start with Duncan. Then all four of them were damn well going to the dance. Because Alex had it all wrong on his list.

It wasn't about networking. It wasn't about making useful business connections.

It was about making *friendships*.

How lucky was he that Sydney and her brother took the time to make him see that?

"And we'll be at the dance, Cam. Hopefully I can convince Sydney to let me take her."

Alex still loved that she hadn't mentioned it. Just as much as he *hated* that she assumed he wouldn't go. There were less than two months left to stockpile memories before Sydney left. This sounded like it'd make a cheesy, romantic one he didn't want to miss.

Chapter Nineteen

SYDNEY CONSIDERED HERSELF a seasoned traveler. She'd had to get a new passport long before it expired for the simple reason that it was full. Her job didn't have her globe-trotting—it was more like globe-*sprinting*.

And yet, when she walked into the drill hall of the historic Armory, Sydney knew she'd just done a whole different type of travel. Time travel. Because apparently the Chestertown Valentine's Dance never changed.

Maybe the pink, red and purple crepe paper streamers got freshened every year. But they swooped and draped from the balconies exactly as they had when she'd last helped decorate it, a dozen years ago. The eight-foot-tall inflatable heart arch she walked under to enter was printed with the same cotton-poofs of white hearts.

High-top tables were swathed in pink satin, and the younger crowd clustered around them. Low rounds were draped in white satin, and their chairs were filled with the…more *seasoned* members of the community. The stage for the band was at the end surrounded by all the flags— U.S., Maryland, National Guard, Navy, Coast Guard.

The only surprise? That the sameness was…not at all annoying.

"Wow." Alex's warm breath stirred the hairs around her ear. "Your hometown really, really loves this holiday."

"It's more that we're enthusiastic about *every* holiday, but yeah. There's something special about Valentine's Day. Maybe because it breaks up the monotony of winter?"

Everleigh had zipped ahead while they'd waited their turn in the coatroom. The woman looked like a movie star, with her long hair pinned back with a pale pink rose. Tiny straps barely held up her slip of a dress. It poured over her generous curves like paint, ending in a sassy ruffle at the knee. Sydney could practically hear the necks cracking as most of the men turned to ogle her.

"C'mon, there's a photo thing!" She circled her arm, beckoning them faster. Her breasts bounced *almost* out of the low-cut bodice. For a heartbeat, Sydney wished she had a body like that.

But then she felt Alex's arm around her waist. He was clearly more than content/borderline obsessed with her longer, leaner body type. His hungry looks and insatiable touching made her feel more beautiful than ever before. Sydney had cobbled together an outfit from her sister's closet of a starched white shirt paired with a short red taffeta skirt. And when Alex had picked her up, he'd taken one look before backing her against the wall and kissing her senseless.

"I'm always up for a photo op," Teague said, straightening his tie. "Good chance to put every other guy in the room on notice. I'm here. Which means even their A game won't be enough. The women will flock to me."

Sydney's jaw almost dropped. Teague had never given off so much as a hint of typical male jerkitude before. "Please tell me you're joking. That you aren't one of those alpha types who doesn't put in any effort to get a woman."

"Nah. I put in the effort, because I respect women. That's my choice, though. I don't *have* to lift a finger."

"Cocky, much?"

"Just stating the facts."

"If that's so, then why aren't you my fake fiancé?"

"There's a code. Alex saw you first. I deliberately tamp down my charm and magnetism around you because of it."

He was outrageous.

And probably right.

She'd only seen him head-down, sanding and scraping and end-of-day exhausted. And Sydney liked that version of Teague. He was a good guy. But the version she was seeing tonight? The slick, studly version? He *did* exude a palpable magnetism. Those Special Forces muscles were evident even through his sport coat.

So Sydney laughed, patted him on the arm. "I appreciate your restraint. It can't be easy."

"Well, Alex is my best friend. I'd do anything for him."

"Then how about you stand on the opposite side of Amelia. As far away from my beautiful date as possible," Alex ground out between clenched teeth.

"Oh no, it should just be the four of you in the photo. Something to commemorate your first time here." Sydney tried to edge away from the backdrop without hitting the overflowing vase of red roses on a table.

But Alex held firm to her hand. "My first time here is with *you*. That's what needs to be commemorated."

God. How did two single sentences manage to spear into

her heart so deeply?

She'd have to buy this photo. The one with Teague tickling Amelia to get her to smile. Everleigh laughing at them, and she and Alex gazing like goofballs into each other's eyes.

"I'm hitting the bar. Need a place to assess my hunting ground," Teague announced.

Now Sydney *knew* he was kidding around. Mostly.

"First you'll get us all drinks," Amelia corrected. "I'll help you carry."

"I have to start with a dance. And with this music, I'll need to nab a partner. It's been too long!" Everleigh, in fact, danced her way over *to* the dance floor.

Bing Crosby crooned through the speakers. They always started the dance with fifteen minutes of music per decade, so that the older people could enjoy some nostalgia. The band would kick in with recent hits later, once they'd cleared out and the younger people were ready to get wild.

"Tell me you dance," Alex said. "I want an excuse to keep my hands on you all night."

Sydney licked her lips. Resisted the impulse to just melt against him. "I really like that plan. But I have to make the rounds first. Say hello to my family—"

Alex cut her off. "Trot out our engagement, you mean."

A few weeks ago, she would've agreed in relief at his readiness to play along. But now? His comment felt...wrong? Cheap? Not at all fair to how far they'd grown together aside from the act they put on for the town.

Which was her own problem. Of her own making.

"A little. Mostly, it's Gram's first big event, so I want to check on her. Be sure she's not pushing herself too much.

And…" Her gaze flicked past her grandmother ensconced at a table with Hazel and all her other Egret Bay cronies to the side wall, lined with tables. "I want to assess the competition."

"There's a competition? Were we supposed to work up a routine? Sydney, I would've smoked everyone else. Why didn't you tell me?"

Ah, Alex had every bit as much swagger as Teague. The pair of them were irresistible. "No, this is *not* your wheelhouse. It's the annual brownie competition." She pointed at the tables overflowing with pyramids of chocolate goodness.

"You entered?"

"Yes." A decision Sydney had second-guessed. And third-guessed. All the way up to about forty. "I mean, just to give myself a goal to hit with learning how to bake. Gram's won the last three years in a row. She gave me her spot."

Alex lifted her hand to his mouth and pressed a kiss against her knuckles. "I'm so proud of you. You've come so far in six weeks."

Wow. She didn't need a red ribbon with support like that. "Alex, I'm not going to win. I spiced mine up with some chili powder. People may hate them. I'm basically terrified."

"The winning doesn't matter. I'm proud of you for learning something new, for not giving up. I plan to eat at least three."

"Maybe start with one. There's a lot of deliciousness here, which you don't want to miss." She stopped abruptly. "You know what? Let's dance first."

"Cold feet? C'mon. You've got me all primed for something dark and fudgy." Alex tugged, but Sydney didn't budge.

"Nora's over there."

His eyes iced over as he stiffened. "The snooty bitch Amelia and Ever rescued you from?"

"Well, I mean, I didn't *need* to be rescued, but yes."

"The one nursing some grudge against you from high school? C'mon. That's nuts. Go smooth things over."

"Why bother? Nobody needs to see a catfight on Valentine's Day. And I'll be leaving soon."

Shoving his hands deep into his pockets, Alex asked, "Yeah, but...won't you come back? Soon? Not wait for someone in your family to almost die again?"

It was a more charged question than Sydney was prepared to answer.

And oh-so-complicated now with far more layers than when she'd arrived. Her job was uncertain. Especially since she was uncertain how hard she wanted to fight to stay in a company that didn't support her. Nor did she want her last memories of her gram—hopefully many years from now—to be through the small pixels of an iPad.

Not to mention the complex situation with Alex. She'd promised him an exit from this fake engagement in a month and a half. So if she did come back to visit at, say, Christmas, they'd officially be broken up. How awkward would that be?

But Alex was right that it was absurd to avoid a table full of brownies because of some leftover, ancient snark. Sydney remembered how good—albeit unnecessary—it had felt to have Amelia and Everleigh righteously at her back during the last confrontation.

Sure, she could go over there by herself. Clear the air.

Sometimes, though, maybe *knowing* you could handle it alone was enough. What was wrong with taking an easier route? Like driving to the grocery store in air-conditioning in July, instead of sweating your way down a road, shoulders burning from carrying the bags?

Her advice to Alex was often about sharing his burdens with his friends. Delegating. Not trying to do everything by himself. It was time she took her own medicine.

With a squeeze to his hand, she said, "Come with me."

"You don't need me."

Wow. He didn't even hesitate to back up her strength and independence. Sydney so very much appreciated that he saw her that way. "Maybe not. But I *want* you with me."

With a wink and a rakish grin, he replied, "Good enough. As long as I get a brownie to eat during the show."

So she swung them wide through the crowded tables, smiling and nodding at James and the band, her brother at a table full of fellow fishermen, and even Brody with the teen crowd in the darkest corner, to the far end of the four tables swagged in red tulle. Seven plates down, she spotted her gram's pink depression glass cake stand.

"Those are mine. Take one. And buckle up. This could get messy."

"Can't wait to watch you take her down."

Except that Sydney didn't want to do *that*. Honestly, she was mostly curious. Whatever had or hadn't happened in high school, why on earth was Nora still so peeved about it now? She'd happily apologize for whatever stupid slight she'd inflicted as a teen. It simply didn't matter anymore.

Nora wore—oddly enough—all black. Sure, the little black dress was ubiquitous, but not here at the dance. Color was king, and even the most old-school, macho men rocked a pink or red splash of color somewhere. Her hair was in an elaborate updo. Diamonds shimmered in her ears, and at her wrists.

She looked elegant. But also cold. Unapproachable.

Sydney had busted her hump up some frozen-ass mountains in Tibet. Cold and unapproachable did not stop her.

"Nora. Can we talk for a bit?"

The woman didn't even look up to acknowledge her. She kept her focus on the array of brownies. Added not just one to her already filled plate, but three. "Sure."

"This is a small town. We're bound to keep bumping into each other. I don't want it to be ugly like last time."

"I recall you gave as good as you got, Darrow."

Really?

Using her last name? That was *definitely* a precursor to a fight.

Sydney had no intention of letting that happen, though. "Probably so. You caught me at a bad moment. Chances are good I would've bitten the head off someone offering me a free pizza right then. I'm sorry."

Nora still didn't look up. Just bit into a brownie that dripped caramel down her fingers.

All right. Conveniently, Sydney had a magic weapon at her side. Handsome, witty, and the man everyone in Chestertown wanted to meet. Tonight he was rocking a fitted black suit with a deep burgundy tie. He looked like he belonged in a perfume ad.

"I'd like to introduce you to my fiancé."

"He's clinging to you like lint. *Obviously* he's your fian-cé."

Alex was suave. Self-assured. He did not cling. Although she did hear him make a muffled snort at the assertion.

Enough was enough.

She could take Nora's jabs. She would not, however, stand here and let her poke at Alex. "Just tell me, already. A blanket apology's meaningless. Tell me what I did that so infuriated you back in high school that you refuse to let go of it after twelve years. Give me the details so I can grovel and mea culpa to your heart's content. What the hell is making you so upset?"

The plate of brownies fell to the ground as Nora whirled around to finally face her. "Everything!" she yelled. And then she crumpled over, sobbing.

Oh boy.

Sydney was suddenly quite sure that this wasn't about her at *all*.

Alex exchanged a look with her. Because he was an utter gentleman, he put an arm around Nora and hustled her out of the room before too many people noticed her meltdown. The door he pushed through led to the staircase. It was colder out here, but at least empty.

Sydney took her from Alex like a rag doll and gently settled Nora on the steps. Instinct was to sit next to her, try to provide comfort. As a fellow woman, if nothing else.

But Nora was prickly, if she remembered right. Getting her away from the view of an entire town that lived on gossip should be comfort enough. She'd probably prefer to sulk without anyone infiltrating her space. Instead, Sydney sought her own comfort in the crook of Alex's arm.

Nora pressed her impeccable manicure to her forehead. "You can go." The sobs had cut off pretty fast to just sniffles.

Tempting, but no. "I'm not taking orders from you. I'm also not abandoning anyone who is clearly not okay."

"I'm getting used to it. To nothing being okay."

That sounded ominous. Dramatic, but with a bitter tinge. Clearly Sydney's grandmother had forgotten to pass on a major story.

It also sounded sad. Sydney realized the woman had been standing alone at the brownie table. No squad with her, and no husband.

No wonder she was willing to spill her guts to a stranger and a nemesis.

Alex cleared his throat. "Would you like me to leave, Nora?"

"No." Her head dropped even lower as she circled her knees with her arms. "I mean, you don't have to stay, but you don't have to go, either. This isn't a shocking reveal. You're the only ones who don't know about me."

Yep. She kept tiptoeing up to the edge of sharing, and then stopping. Like when a sneeze got to the bridge of your nose and then just melted away.

That was a horrible feeling. "I don't want to pry. But I think you need to let something out. Let's call a truce. Just talk. No sniping, no judgment."

"Everyone judges."

Ouch. Her pain was a palpable cloud hovering a layer just above her perfume. Sydney did give in and perch next to her, then. Took her hand. "I won't. I promise."

Fat tears still hovered along her lash line when Nora raised her head. "Bill left me."

"Who's Bill?" Alex asked.

Thank goodness. Sydney didn't want to come off as insensitive for not remembering every random man in town and their connection to her.

"My husband." Then her head snapped to the right, with quite a bit of the usual heat in her eyes. "Sydney's ex."

Aha! She wanted to do a fist pump at the discovery. Finally, the cause of the bad blood revealed. Only... "Bill? Bill the, um, defender on the lacrosse team? We only dated for a month."

"He took you to prom."

"It was a group thing. With the girls' and boys' lacrosse teams."

The ancient accusations kept spewing out. "You only broke up because you left for college early. He pined for you."

Sydney's not-stellar memory of Bill was of a guy who lived and breathed lacrosse, and basically only dated for the, um, physical perks of it. They'd had fun. They'd been *nowhere* close to serious. She doubted he'd know what pining *was*.

"Well, Nora, you say he's your husband, so obviously you won. Sorry if I was a speed bump on your path to the aisle."

Alex wiped a hand across his mouth, clearly hiding a smirk. Whoops.

Could she have been more sympathetic? Maybe. But this

was sooo not her fault.

"It doesn't matter. Bill left me. My therapist says I lashed out at you because I can't lash out at the little skank who stole my husband. Transference? Something."

The missing pieces were starting to fill in. Sydney didn't need the details to know that it takes two to cheat. Bill obviously bore the blame, too. Too bad Nora hadn't moved through the grief to the anger stage against him yet.

"I'm sorry he hurt you. This has to be a horribly hard time."

"I'm reeling. Did you see how many brownies I piled on my plate? But eating my pain is safer than drinking it away, right?"

"Or you could try running?" Alex suggested in a super casual tone. One that carried zero judgment on her brownie totals and simply offered a different option.

He was *good*.

"Eating's easier. I'm a chef. There's always food around."

"Really? That's awesome, Nora. Where do you work?"

"Maybe nowhere." And the sobs began again.

Sydney exchanged a panicked glance with Alex. It did feel good to have that wordless communication with him. "I'm really sorry, Nora, but I don't know what I said to set you off."

"Bill and I own The Lighthouse restaurant. He runs it, and I'm the head chef. Except he wants to buy me out. Get me out from underfoot. He's already interviewing new chefs."

That made sense. The low-life cheater undoubtedly got a guilt ulcer every time he looked at her. "Nora, you don't want to have to see him every day. This is a good thing."

"Make sure the offer's fair, of course," Alex added. "You have the high ground here—and hopefully a take-no-prisoners lawyer."

"I do. I went all the way to Baltimore to hire a cutthroat who doesn't know him or his family."

"Good."

"It's not. If I leave The Lighthouse, what will I do with my days? Bill's family has their fingers in so many businesses here in town."

Sydney almost shielded her eyes from the metaphorical lightning bolt that struck her brain. The three of them, being together right now? It was meant to be. She could solve Nora's problem. More importantly, she could solve *Alex's*. Which would lessen her guilt—at least a little—about the part she'd played in him getting fired.

Maybe then she wouldn't have to tell him?

She patted Nora's hand. "There's an obvious solution. You should go work at the Three Oaks Inn. They need a cook."

Alex had been slouching against the wall. But at her words, he shot up straight, pulling his hands out of his pockets. "Not yet, we don't. We can't pay yet, either. Once we can, it sure won't be at executive chef rates."

"Nora, give us two seconds. Three, tops." Sydney beckoned for Alex to follow her up the stairs. Then she pushed through the door to the balcony.

The music was louder up here. Sinatra. She hoped Cam had their grandmother on the dance floor for this one.

Sydney gave Alex a doublet hump on the chest. "Here's

where you thank me. This is the perfect solution."

"Hardly."

How did he not see the brilliance of this plan? "She needs you as much as you guys need her. It's doubly perfect."

"Sydney. I get that you want to snap your fingers and fix her. Life doesn't work that way, though."

"Says the man who won a hotel lottery."

"Yeah, yeah. Look where I am now—stressed and strapped for cash. There's no easy wins. There's *always* a catch."

Oh, she knew all about the false promise of an easy win. It was precisely what *Excursions 365* had snatched away from her when they hadn't given her the promised hosting gig.

This, however, was serendipity.

Sydney couldn't give Alex his old job back. But she *could* help fix a gaping hole in the plan for his new job.

"Look, Nora just needs a place to go every day."

The nonchalance in his shrug made clear how much that was her problem, and not his. "Then point her to the coffee shop over on Washington, by the college. This is a trained chef we're talking about. A professional who will expect to be compensated appropriately. Not a kitten to be fostered and left alone to roam the inn."

"I guarantee you she doesn't need the money. Bill's family has loads of money. Even a lawyer with the ink still wet on his degree could empty Bill's pockets with cheating as the cause. Nora hasn't flounced out of town. She wants to stay. She just needs someplace new to root herself."

His eyes closed. Alex dragged a palm down his jaw. "You mean like the four of us are doing?"

"Yup." She knew he'd manage to connect the dots eventually. "Now say *thank you, Sydney.*"

"I'll say it later. After I say how much I like that bright brain of yours. And then I'll move on to a few more things I like…"

"Let's give her the good news."

"Hang on. One step at a time," he cautioned wryly, as they descended the steps with their rubber treads. "I'll do the talking."

Nora was on her feet. She'd wiped away the mascara streaks under her eyes. "I'm sorry. This is supposed to be a romantic night. I don't want my problems to ruin it for you two. I'm just grateful that you listened to me. And I don't want you to feel pressured into hiring a stranger, Alex."

He hooked a thumb over his shoulder toward the door. "Do you have a brownie in the competition, Chef Nora?"

"Yes. Only for appearances. I always secretly tell the judges not to rank me. It wouldn't be fair, a professional against amateurs."

"That's really nice of you." Although Sydney had to make sure her gram never discovered that tidbit of information. She'd be crushed to learn she hadn't beaten a *chef* for the past three years.

"If we keep up this truce of ours, you'll see that I can be nice most of the time."

"I think we should. It should be a permanent truce. I'll rope Amelia and Everleigh into it, too. The four of us will have a do-over."

Alex opened the door. "Take me to your brownie, so I can taste it. Then come over tomorrow and we'll talk."

Aww, she knew he'd come through. "Not too early," Sydney cautioned, with a grin of satisfaction. "I'm going to keep this man up 'not talking' all night."

Chapter Twenty

"WHERE'D YOU DISAPPEAR to?" Teague asked. He pushed back a plate with only a few sandwich crumbs left on it. "You missed lunch."

"Took it with me. So I could bring you all back dessert." Pleased by the setup, Alex triumphantly revealed the plate he'd hidden behind his back as he strode into the inn's breakfast room.

Amelia popped out of her chair. She of the voracious sweet tooth circled him like a vulture. "Ooh. What's that?"

Crap. Nora had offered to write out a key, but he'd insisted he could remember everything. Sydney would roll her eyes and laugh at him later when he confessed. And then remind him that he didn't have to pretend he could do everything, all the time, all by himself.

It was a lesson Alex was trying to take to heart.

But...it hadn't been anywhere close to sixty-six days yet. The habit wasn't set into his psyche yet.

At least, that'd be his *excuse*.

"Pineapple carrot muffins, almond pound cake, maple bacon sticky buns, double chocolate walnut biscotti, and...uh...you'll know when you taste the last one." Alex guessed apple coffee cake? Could be pear, though. Or ginger?

Something cakey and delicious with white chunks. He wasn't a chef, for crying out loud.

He peeled back the plastic wrap and set it in the middle of the table. Right on top of the pile of fabric swatches. The ones the Egret Bay ladies had sent over for them to choose patterns for their 'linen needs.'

"Why did you go and get us a treat?" Everleigh's hand hovered over the plate, then drew back. And then she squinted at him. "I'm suspicious. What bad news do you have to break?"

"No bad news, knock on wood."

Obviously, Alex *actually* knocked on the wooden table. Just in case winning the lottery had already used up all their luck. He wasn't the type to read his horoscope or avoid black cats, but no point jinxing himself, either.

"Well, I have bad news." Teague crumpled up a bag and lobbed it at him. "You didn't stick around, so I finished off your honey barbecue chips."

"Ouch. That's a low blow. Can't believe I'm sharing a cottage with a low-down, dirty, chip thief. What did the Army *do* to you, man?" Alex asked in mock horror.

Amelia knocked Everleigh's wrist aside. "Who cares *why* they're here. I just want to eat all the yummy things. Sheesh." She'd popped the top off a muffin before even finishing the sentence.

Everleigh still had a laser-lock on him. "They really aren't a bribe? Or an apology? Or both?"

"Nope. Just a test run to share."

"For what?"

He toed out a chair and flopped down next to Teague.

"Nora's baking up a storm. She wants us to try everything. First, she's trying everything, then she wants us to taste it, even though I told her there's no way we can work through it all. She's splitting the leftovers between the fire station, the police, and the three churches that host the emergency winter shelter for the homeless."

"Nora?" Amelia broke the muffin in half and passed one to Teague. "The one Sydney had us make a tentative peace accord with at the Valentine's Dance? Why does she want us to eat her stuff?"

Uh-oh.

Oh, no.

Fuck.

Alex had screwed up. Royally. He knew it. Same as he knew he'd have to admit it to them in the next breath. And it would be bad.

"Because she's our new chef. Baker. For the inn."

Everleigh dropped the sticky bun. Not back onto the plate, of course. No, it landed on a fabric swatch, all gooey and trailing caramel. So that one was now ruined.

Which was probably the least of his problems at the moment...

"I'm sorry, what?" Amelia's nose, dusted with those red-head's freckles, crinkled in confusion.

The other two had jumped ahead of her, though, and clearly figured it out. Everleigh's expression was blank disbelief. Teague's...well, the town's tornado/hurricane siren should've been going off from the storm that was brewing in his hazel eyes.

Damn it. Alex shoved up the sleeves of his fisherman's

sweater. "I hired Nora. To be our chef."

"But we're not slated to hire anyone for another month?" Amelia's voice rose in question at the end. Like she genuinely couldn't comprehend him skipping ahead on the list.

Because his sister *knew* him. Down to his core.

God, he hated disappointing her.

"There were extenuating circumstances. Nora's not getting paid yet," he rushed to reassure them. "This doesn't change anything budgetarily. She's just getting a jump on things."

"*You* hired her?" Teague's emphasis was unmistakable. Deliberate. Halfway to menacing.

No point denying it. Or trying to gloss it over as a trial period. "Yeah."

"*You* did it. Without consulting us. Compounded by not even telling us for a while, judging by that pile of pastries." Teague drove the point of his finger onto the table at the start of each sentence. "When did this happen?"

In a low voice that no doubt revealed his embarrassment and regret, Alex confessed. "Ten days ago."

"What? Alex!" Amelia shoved her chair back. It squeaked loudly, both the feet scraping across the floor and the arms on the table's edge. One more item that needed fixing to put on his list.

"It was a spontaneous thing." His words tumbled fast, in an attempt to explain and fix it, fast. "She broke down at the dance. Sydney told you her story that night, remember? Rough divorce. Hard time. She's doing us a favor. She's overqualified. We shouldn't be able to afford her. Just taste these." Alex pushed the plate toward Everleigh.

He knew sugar wouldn't frost over the problem. But he had to try.

Teague swept his arm out to the side. "I don't care if she's a five-star Michelin chef who works for free. You shouldn't have hired her."

"I know. I'm sorry. It was an accident."

Amelia rolled her eyes so hard he practically heard them rattle. "You *accidentally* dropped a contract in her lap? Try again."

"Jesus, Alex, we work together all day. You and I share a cottage at night." Teague took off his Eagles cap and scratched at his mussed hair. "You've had…ten days? Two hundred and forty hours of chances to talk to us about this."

Almost under his breath, he puffed out, "I *meant* to tell you."

Crossing her arms over her yellow turtleneck sweater, Amelia said, "Actions speak louder than words. Remember when Mom used to say that to us?"

Yeah, yeah.

He'd screwed up, but he wouldn't take a dressing-down from his dead mother, once removed.

Alex couldn't just sit there anymore while they hammered at him. He got up, paced over to the window to stare out over the frozen mess of a garden.

"I meant to have you all at the interview, the day after the dance. That was the day Duncan Wickes dropped in—unannounced—to talk about the permits. We were all frazzled. It slipped my mind that she was coming over. Then you guys went on a supply run. Nora showed up. We talked through everything. She agreed to no paycheck until we

313

officially open. She cooked like a dream. It was too good an opportunity to miss."

"Okay," Everleigh said with exaggerated patience. "Then what? Then she left, we came back…and why didn't you tell us *then*?"

"Our bride came over to do a walk-through. We all sat down and talked through everything with her and Dave. It took hours. You invited them to stay for dinner," he hurled at Everleigh.

She gave him the slow, double eye blink of death before hurling her response right back. Louder than him. "Because we liked them. Because we're trying to make friends *and* network *and* make a good impression. Don't for a second act like it's my fault you didn't confer with us."

"It's not your fault. Of course not. I'm just explaining how it was like three days of stuff rolled into one so…it slipped my mind."

"Every day?" Amelia asked, pointedly.

"Yes, every day." Why didn't they get it? Why didn't they understand the sheer, overwhelming weight of everything Alex was juggling so that they wouldn't have to? "Once I mentally checked off *hire chef*, I moved on to focusing on the next hundred things to be done. I'm sorry."

"Not good enough." Teague shoved out of his chair. Went over to the window to confront Alex, toe-to-toe. "You just steamrolled through with this decision. Which is the same thing you yelled at Amelia for doing when she agreed to let Annie get married here."

Weren't they listening? He didn't deny that he was wrong. Alex just needed them to get that there were extenuating *reasons*. That it wasn't purposeful. "I know. I felt that way when Sydney suggested it at the dance."

Teague lofted his hat into the air, throwing his hands up. "So now you're blaming her? Sydney's the steamroller?"

Hell.

Alex spun away on one heel. Yes, Sydney had put things in motion. He'd been swept up by her enthusiasm and how much she'd helped him. *Them.* But he also knew that this fight was about the four of them, as a team.

"I feel like there's no right answer to that question."

"Because what you did was wrong, Alex. No excuses. No justifiable explanations." Teague straight-armed the flat of his hand against the window frame. "It was flat-out wrong. With a dash of hypocritical on top, given how you lambasted Amelia for the same thing."

In a soft but firm voice, Amelia said, "We can't work like this."

Fear knotted Alex's stomach.

Were they giving up on him? Had he made them lose faith in their ability to pull this off? Had he pushed too hard, too far?

The fear manifested, however, as defensive anger once he opened his mouth. And stabbed his index finger at the air to emphasize every point. "This is a solution. An unexpected, simple solution to a very real problem. We knew we couldn't afford a decent chef. We knew none of us could cook well enough to do it. We were stuck. At an impasse. One that I solved. It's not like any of you came up with a solution."

Yikes. 'The best defense is a good offense' was *not* the way to treat his business partners. Alex immediately knew he shouldn't have hurled that accusation at them.

Even though it was true.

Even though there was a part of him that wished they *were* pulling their collective weight a little bit more, weighing in more.

Damn it, was he at fault for that, too? Had he shut them out?

"We hadn't come up with a solution *yet*," Everleigh corrected. "That doesn't mean that we wouldn't have."

"We've been a little busy busting our humps twenty-four/seven." Teague stomped back to the table to brandish Alex's ever-present legal pad of to-dos. "On the stuff that had to happen, according to your almighty lists, right the hell now. Not a month from now."

Amelia picked up the pen next to the crossword she'd been working on. She tapped it against her first finger, clearly handing out an edict. "This is what has to change, Alex. No more passing out lists like they're freaking sacred stone tablets. More meetings with all of us. More discussions. We're *all* in this. Together. It'll only work if we do it together. As a cohesive unit. Not as minions to an overlord."

"Overdramatize much?" he joked weakly.

Because, God, Alex *hated* that she'd described him that way. No, that she'd *felt* that way about him, even for a minute. This inn was the chance of a lifetime. Not just monetarily. It was a chance to keep them all knitted tightly together.

And he was blowing it.

Everleigh handed him a cookie. And a napkin. And then she took his hand and held it tightly. "I'm just going to say now what I've been thinking since last November. Maybe this is partly why you got fired from the Grand Orion."

Alex jerked his hand back.

How *could* she say that? He hadn't done anything wrong.

The Orion fired him as a way to cover their ass with the guests, once that article came out exposing him. To make a gesture that would convince people it was safe to stay there, that the trouble had been rooted out. And in lieu of the actual burglar being found, let alone fired, they used him.

"That wasn't my fault."

"Are you sure about that?" She gently squeezed his forearm, but her words were anything but gentle. "*You* made a decision, in secret. *You* decided to sit on the theft, and the note she left you, for twenty-four hours."

"To give her time to escape. To keep her safe." What the hell was happening? Everleigh didn't do confrontations. Or arguments. Alex told her all the time that she needed to learn to draw a line and stand up for herself.

Why'd she have to start today? With him?

"Had you dialed literally *anyone* else into your plan, they would've told you to stop protecting her and call the police. For all you know, they would've kept it under wraps for her safety, too."

He broke off a piece of the cookie so he wouldn't have to meet her earnest blue eyes. "I couldn't risk it."

Amelia took over. "Except that you put yourself, and your hotel, at risk by not soliciting other opinions. Group think. Hive mind. It takes a village. Doesn't matter how you phrase it. You get more accomplished, better, faster, smarter, by dialing in other people, other ideas, other frames of reference."

"I just…Nora was here. I took care of it." But Alex heard how his excuses—c'mon, that's what they were—were getting shorter. Weaker. Repetitive.

"Yeah. We get that." Teague bit into the muffin. Chewed. "This is fantastic. I had her brownies at the dance, too. Nora can bake, no doubt. The decision to hire her was smart. We lucked into that solution. The decision to do it being made solo, that's what sucks. You went rogue, dude."

Everleigh nibbled at the scone. "It feels like you *wanted* to do it by yourself, Alex. Because you keep trying to do *everything* by yourself."

"You didn't trust your instincts after the theft at the Orion." Amelia stared him down. "You hired Elena, you trusted her enough to give her your key card, and then she took advantage of you. You haven't forgiven yourself for that. For not foreseeing an unforeseeable situation. That's why you're making so many lists and driving us all crazy."

"I'm making all the lists because we can't afford to screw up," he burst out.

Which was a *huge* mistake.

He'd just blown the lid off a secret he'd promised himself not to let out. Telling Sydney should've been enough to bleed off the frustration.

"Sure we can," Amelia said with a light laugh. "It wouldn't be the end of the world. We give it our best shot. If it doesn't work, well, lots of people blow through lottery winnings. We'll just dig into our savings for a bit and start over again."

Given what'd gone down so far, Alex couldn't lie anymore. Or obfuscate. There was no choice but to tell them the whole of it. "*I* can't. It's all gone."

"What's gone?"

How did this conversation keep getting harder? And worse for him? "My savings. My 401(k), my IRAs, the last of Mom and Dad's trust."

"What are you talking about?"

"I cashed it all in. So that we'd have operating capital to get this place off the ground."

Teague swore, turned away and paced the length of the room before slapping his hands onto the lintel and hanging from the doorframe.

Amelia folded into the nearest chair, mouth agape. "But you said…the inn, it came with the existing bank account."

"I did say that. I, um, exaggerated the heft of its value. By a lot."

Teague came back at him with the speed of a cannonball. "You lied. Damn it, Alex, you *lied*."

For their own good! He spread his arms wide, almost in a plea for them to understand. "To protect you guys. We all needed jobs. Needed a place to live. The lottery gave us both of those. It just didn't give us enough of a cushion. So I took care of that for all of us."

"That's why you're so up our asses with schedules. We're bleeding money. *Your* money."

"Yeah." Alex let his head drop. Or rather, the weight of everything they'd heaped onto him over the past ten minutes pushed it down.

Amelia crawled into his lap like she'd done when they were little. "You're an idiot. A sweet, generous idiot."

319

Pretty much what Sydney had said when he'd told her.

He was beginning to think they were right. At least about the idiot part... Because nothing was going as planned. Fighting so fiercely with these people he loved was the cherry on that shit sundae.

"We didn't know that the inn would need so much work." Grimacing, he continued after another beat. "Or take so long. Or cost so much."

Teague sat back down, as did Everleigh. Now they were all around the table again, a united circle. Which was a huge relief. Teague wiped his hands back and forth over the wood, like he was trying to sand his way down to the truth. "Be real with us. Can we make it?"

"We have enough. *Just* enough," he clarified. "As long as nothing else goes wrong. And as long as we manage to get bookings. And if at least some of those bookings choose the non-refundable deposit pricing."

Amelia curved her arm up to pat his cheek. "You're smart, Alex. Dedicated. Responsible to a fault. But you can't do this by yourself. You've got to stop pretending that you can. We don't need protecting. We're equal partners. Let us help you with problems, not just with checklists."

Fine.

They wanted him to lay out everything? To share the stuff that kept him tossing and turning all night? Even if they couldn't fix it?

Then he'd spill the other big secret he'd been hanging on to. God knew this conversation had already hit rock bottom three rounds ago.

Alex shoved the cookie into his mouth. Reached for a

second. And didn't at all mind admitting how comforting it was to have his sister already hugging him as he laid his soul bare.

"Okay—here's a problem you can take a whack at. I'm falling in love with Sydney. And she's leaving."

The silence was only broken by his chewing. For way too long. He was three cookies in before Teague finally spoke.

"You sure about that?"

"Uh, yeah. From day one, Sydney's been an open book about how much she hates Chestertown. How she's literally counting down the days until she leaves. You've heard her."

Teague nodded. "I have. I've also seen her being really sweet with her grandmother. I've seen her learning to cook so that she does better at the Mercantile. I think she's discovering that life as an adult here is different than life as a pissed-off teenager."

Alex had noticed all of that, and more. He'd just assumed she was making the best of a bad situation.

He hadn't let himself hope that it meant she was changing her mind. That would've been too big a distraction from their race to get the inn ready.

And too painful a blow if it was wrong.

"She's got a big job offer. She won't talk about it, except to say that it's good."

Everleigh cocked her head, doing a big hair swish. "Why won't she talk about it?"

"I don't know. She won't talk about her current job, either. Aside from it not being a good situation. That they didn't support her taking a break to come help her grandmother."

"Maybe if you guys talked about these things, you'd have a better picture of whether or not she's staying."

Yeah, he didn't need armchair relationship counseling from them. They didn't know the ground rules he and Sydney had established. "It's a mutual silence. I haven't told her about being booted by the Orion, either."

"Why on earth not?" Amelia slid off his lap to sit in her own chair. "I'm not saying tell her that Dad grounded you when you were twelve for sneaking out to the movies. But sharing what you've been doing on a daily basis for the last ten years? That's a Dating 101 basic."

"Exactly. We agreed from the start that this is a fake engagement, so we didn't need to drill down into life's minutiae. No backstories. That'd make it too personal. Too complicated." Feeling smug at how they'd avoided all that, how smart they'd been, Alex smirked. "We kept it locked down to the *now*. Living in the moment. Just like meditation. Kept it simple."

Everleigh burst out laughing. And then…wait…was that *pity* that drew down her mouth? "Except that you're now sharing a life. Spending nights together. She's helping with the inn. You go visit her grandmother. Your living in the moment has turned into way more than a moment. You're a couple. One who doesn't know the important things about each other's pasts."

Teague pointed at him. "You're hiding something as big as being fired from her." Then he hooked a thumb over his shoulder in the general direction of town—and Sydney. "Makes you wonder what she's happy to *not* talk about with you, doesn't it?"

Yeah. Laid out like that? It did make Alex wonder.

It also made him wonder how two smart people could've been so enormously stupid.

Oh, *shit*.

Amelia patted the table to recapture his attention. "Here's our first group advice to you. It's fitting that it's personal, not business."

He swallowed. Hard. Same as he'd probably have to do with their advice. "I'll take whatever you want to throw at me right now. No pushback, no arguing. I promise."

"*Talk* to Sydney. Not about the inn, or the weather, or whatever kinky position you guys want to try out next. Talk to her about what happened in her life outside of Chestertown. For both of you. Dip into the past so you can discover if there's a real possibility of a future."

Chapter Twenty-One

FOR MOST PEOPLE, getting a text at five in the morning meant bad news. For Sydney, it just meant that Sanjay was up in whatever corner of the world he'd parked in. He never bothered with checking time zones. Mostly because everyone in their business never stayed in the same one long enough to get used to it.

Good thing opening the Mercantile had her alarm going off at oh-dark-thirty. But she'd barely had time to glance at the text before her dad made that tsking noise with his tongue. The one that nobody in the world made *until* the day they became a parent.

"Hon, stay off the phone. You don't want to miss a customer."

Seriously? Even the worms in the bait barrels weren't awake yet. Her father still had the till open, restocking the cash drawer. "We're not open, Dad. I could jitterbug naked and it wouldn't matter."

His lower lip jutted out. "It'd matter to me, and that's the God's honest truth."

It was too early to fight with him. Besides, the text was probably just another pointed nudge from Sanjay to get her to commit to an interview for the *Wanderlust* job.

Then Sydney would have to text him back for the seventh time that she couldn't do anything until Gram's doctors cleared her back for work at the Merc. And it was too early for even that level of arguing, too.

She slid her phone into her pocket and picked up the wiping cloth to attack the fingerprints on the bakery case. "Got anything special lined up for today?"

"It depends." Neil whacked a roll of quarters to break it open. "Are you going to start another kitchen fire? Cleaning up from one of those really steers me off course."

"Ha ha. Very funny. It is March 1. I can definitely say it has been more than a solid month since my last kitchen mishap." That he *knew* about, anyway.

The issue at home, when she'd accidentally microwaved a mug with metal engraving and set off sparks? Sydney blamed that on her sister being careless enough to own said mug. What good was it if it couldn't go in the microwave?

"That's true. I'm proud of you, hon. You didn't just step up to fill your gram's shoes. You've been working so hard to improve. I appreciate it." Then his grin turned from paternal pride to pure wicked teasing. "I guarantee our customers do, too."

"Thanks, Dad."

"I don't even feel nervous about leaving you alone here while I run out to meet Devona for lunch."

Sydney did a quick mental riffle through her hometown directory. It was assumed that she remembered everything about everyone. Most of the time she politely faked it until the pieces fell into place. This one, though, was unusual enough to stick out. "Do you mean Mom's friend?"

Neil closed his eyes and firmed his lips for a second. Then he opened them and said calmly, "Your mom's been gone a long time. We just call her my friend, now."

Yikes. Sydney crumpled the cloth in her fist and hustled over to give him a hug. "I'm sorry. That was insensitive. I was trying to put a face to a name to a relationship without thinking it all the way through."

"It's fine, hon." He patted her back and released her.

"I'm glad you two stayed friends." More so than ever before. Sydney had spent so many years being active. Social. But until eight weeks ago, she'd never experienced friendships like she was building right here.

They were better. Stronger. Deeper. Not an obligation, or an extension of work. Not a potential networking politeness about who could be useful down the road. No, Sydney had zero reason to be friends with the Three Oaks crew— except for how much she *cared* for them. Treasured them as snarky, hardworking, a little zany, loyal-to-the-marrow people. Nora included. Who would've imagined that!

So she hoped, in all her adult hindsight, that her father had surrounded himself with strong friends when his life fell apart, twenty-three years ago. It made sense that her mom's best friend would've gravitated to her dad. They were both probably searching for answers.

Ohhhh.

This was her moment. If Sydney was ever going to revisit the great, unsolved mystery that was her mother's disappearance, the segue into it had just been laid out on a freaking doily-lined silver platter.

She'd stopped asking why by her eighth birthday. Convinced herself she didn't care why by her tenth. But maybe Alex and her grandmother were right. Maybe that approach had partially driven her away from Chestertown.

If she was going to come back more, she needed to remove that block.

"Dad?"

"You need help with the coffee?"

"No." In fact, Sydney was relieved at the opportunity to keep doing chores during this conversation. "Why did Mom leave?"

The cash register drawer slammed shut. After an elephant-sized pregnant pause—weren't they the animal with a year and a half gestation—he clipped out a single word. "Dunno."

Well. Not exactly on par with cracking the Rosetta Stone.

They were adults now. Couldn't he reveal whatever he knew? Was Neil still trying to protect her?

Sydney bit her lip, and then let out the question that burbled up like decades-old reflux. "Why weren't we enough for her?"

This time the silence was broken by the harsh drag in of his breath. And the slow hiss of him letting it out. Sydney felt like he could've inflated a hot air balloon with that hiss before he finally stopped and sat down on Gram's stool.

"Sometimes the *why* doesn't matter."

"Of course it does. There has to be a why. You don't walk away from your husband, your son, your daughters, unless there's one hell of a good reason."

"I'm sure she had one."

Sydney's subconscious had, apparently, spent decades working through possibilities. And now she let them fly. "This isn't Manhattan. I doubt the mob was after her. If she'd gone into Witness Protection, she would've taken us with her. If it was another man—sorry, Dad—then she would've still fought to see me, Kim, and Cam. If she was a secret CIA agent, she'd be back by now and would've stuck to her cover. If it—"

"Sydney." Her father's hand fell heavily on her shoulder to cut her off. "Stop."

She whirled around. She'd been wrong, before. This kind of confrontation couldn't be hidden behind coffee urns. It had to be face-to-face.

Even though Neil was so tall she was more or less confronting the collar of his green button-down.

"I tried that, Dad. I tried not thinking about it, not wondering, for a really long time. I more or less ran away from here to get away from the constant, niggling memory shadow of her every single place I looked. But now I'm back. I need to know. I think I deserve to know."

"Well, kiddo, I think you do, too. I think we all do." He rubbed his hands up and down from her shoulders to her elbows. "But I don't have an answer for you. Last I checked, neither did she. Believe me, I checked a hell of a lot of times. As we worked through the divorce and the custody agreement. As I kept trying to give her the benefit of the doubt and give her every possible chance to see you kids."

Sydney gasped. "So it *was* us she was running away from?"

"Nope. Not at all. It also wasn't me. Wasn't your gram.

Wasn't Chestertown, wasn't the Merc. Sheila spelled out, clear as mud, every single thing that it wasn't. Over and over again."

"But she wouldn't say what it *was*?"

"Your mom wasn't mean like that. If she could've put it into words, given me a bit of ease, she would've. Wanna know a secret?"

"Always."

"I saw a counselor. Drove over the bridge to Annapolis to do it, so nobody would know."

It made her heart hurt that he'd gone to those lengths. Especially since he'd insisted that his three kids talk to a counselor at the school district. "Dad. You don't have to be ashamed for getting help."

"Right. Now I can say that." He crinkled up his nose, as if a skunk had just walked through the memory. "Back then, right after my wife did a runner? Not so much."

"Did it help you?"

"As much as anything. Here's what she told me about Sheila. What she thought happened." He paused to scrub both hands up and down his face. "When you're not happy, you try like mad to fix it. You can't be responsible for everyone else. For anyone else. Just yourself. Because, ultimately, nobody else will be."

Sydney pondered it a minute. While it wasn't satisfying, it did make sense. "That's why she thought Mom left?"

"Yes. As selfish as it sounds."

She'd heard something in his tone, though. Seen a pointed look in his blue eyes. There was more her dad wanted her to take away from that story. Not the unhappiness part. The responsibility part.

Guess he'd picked up a few tricks in those counseling sessions.

"But...you're not just talking about Mom." She tapped at the vee-neck of her moss-colored sweater. "You're talking about me, aren't you? How I tried to save my team and fix everything for everyone."

"Yep. Your young man, Alex, too. The way you're hooking him up with so many people in town."

C'mon. That was being a good member of the community. Not trying to fix everything. "Oh, but—"

"Even this cockamamie scheme to make your gram happy with this fake engagement. Devona agrees with me, by the way. You really went out on a limb with that. Even if you did lead with your heart."

"You told Devona? You and Cam were sworn to secrecy!"

"She won't say anything. She's tickled by how hard you're trying to make your grandmother feel better."

"Well, geez, does Gram know, too? Does everyone?" Would she have to start an apology tour for lying to everyone?

"No. She's too happy about the two of you to question it. Your secret's more or less safe. Your heart, on the other had...I don't think that's safe at all."

Fine. So he *saw* things. Things Sydney barely let herself acknowledge. Because thinking about those feelings led to a whooooole lot of complications. She couldn't lie to her father again, though.

"I do care about Alex. Very much. But there's a secret—a

big one—standing between us."

He pulled out the bags of flavored coffee. "Do you know what we just proved?"

That it didn't matter her mom had left, because she had the best dad of all time?

"What?"

"Secrets always come out. You can't control that, no matter how hard you try. The only thing you can control is *how*."

She stood on tiptoe to kiss him on the cheek. "You are wasted as a shopkeeper. You should be a bartender with all this A-game advice."

"I love you, Syd. It's been a real treat having you home. I worry that if it all goes to hell with Alex, you won't come back again for a long time."

"That won't happen. I promise. Because I've so enjoyed spending this time with you, too. You're going to be stuck seeing me much more often."

As they finished readying the Mercantile to open for the day, Sydney's brain was in a single loop.

Her dad had added Devona to the list of people who knew she was lying about being engaged. Apparently Matt and James had figured it out, too, and hey, maybe everyone in town *except* her gram by now.

He was right. The truth always came out, sooner or later.

Sydney had been hiding *her* truth, about the article, from Alex to spare him the pain of a mistake that couldn't be fixed. But the pain would be a lot worse, the longer she waited. To protect any shot at happiness for both of them, she *had* to come clean with Alex. It was safer than waiting for someone else to drop that truth bomb.

But she had no idea how to tell him. Or what would happen after that. All Sydney knew was that the idea of being in Chestertown without him was lousy.

The idea of being without him at *all* was lousy.

IT TOOK SYDNEY two days to realize there was no good time, place, or way to break it to Alex. To stop stalling and follow through.

The final nudge came from the unlikeliest place—the Mercantile. They'd received the new shipment of magazines. Sydney had to stock them on the shelves. And she'd seen the glossy cover of *Wanderlust*—the magazine produced by the same company as the TV channel—with a beautiful Savannah inn as the featured article.

Three Oaks Inn deserved to be a success. The way it was being worked on nonstop, it would be. Which meant it would come to the attention of local scouts for both *Wanderlust* and *Excursions 365*. The clock had already started ticking on her truth bomb—she just hadn't known it.

Sydney squared her shoulders and walked through the front door to the inn, careful not to let it bang against the wall. Ready or not, there he was. Alex strode down the hallway, eyes glued to his list.

His work boots clomped on the wood floor. His jean-clad hips had that unconscious swagger of a supremely confident man. The weave of a black Henley clung to his biceps and pecs. And that lock of hair had flopped down on his forehead.

Sydney wanted to gobble him up.

As the screen door thwacked shut, his eyes lifted to meet hers. And brightened his face like he'd walked in front of a ring light.

"Hey there. I've missed you these past couple of days." He tossed his pad onto a console table and closed the distance between them before she could respond.

Alex wrapped his arms around her. Lifted her off her feet to kiss her with a gusto that proved how much he'd missed her, that gentled to a tenderness that was almost painful to her.

"I missed you, too," she said as he set her down. "Sorry our schedules didn't mesh up better."

"No worries. You had to stay with your gram. It's why you're here, after all. How's she doing?"

Why did he have to be so sweet? So accommodating? So low maintenance? "She's holding up better than last time."

Alex narrowed his eyes. "I thought chemo got harder on the body as it progressed. You caved, didn't you? Did you get her pot? Have you been cruising the seedy alleys of Baltimore to find a hookup?"

If Sydney hadn't already decided to tell him the truth, she would've right then and there. Because it was apparent that Alex could now read her. Like her father had. Guess that was a side effect of getting close that she hadn't factored in.

"She's not toking up and listening to Bob Marley. Cam and I helped get her a medical marijuana card. Completely legal in Maryland. She takes CBD oil in pills. By prescription. It's working great."

"I'm glad. When's her next dose?" He shot her one of his quicksilver grins that revealed a boyish, mischievous side that was probably his main personality before his parents died and he took on so much responsibility. Sydney *loved* those grins. "Your grandmother's a hoot. Can't wait to see her with a medicinal buzz."

Sydney pretended to scowl. "It's not like that. Just stops the nausea and helps her sleep. Although we did bake brownies. As part of my practice. I won't give Nora a run for her money anytime soon, but the Mercantile had a full batch of Irish cream brownies thanks to yours truly."

"Aren't you a few weeks early for St. Patrick's Day?"

"Hmm. Aren't you risking me *not* giving you this, if you'd rather wait for the seventeenth?" she teased, pulling a plastic-wrapped brownie out of her coat pocket.

He snatched it from her. "Waiting's for suckers." Alex set it on the table next to his pad. "I'll have it after dinner—unless you're volunteering to be my dessert?"

Sydney would love that.

But it felt like a bait and switch. Getting all the awesome sex and then hitting him with a potential landmine of a truth. That'd be selfish. She jammed her fists into her coat pockets. Wondered what it said that she was still *wearing* her coat for this big reveal.

"Can we talk first?"

Yikes. Going with no plan meant she'd just initiated the worst start to a conversation ever.

"What about?"

"A talk Dad and I had the other morning. He—well, his therapist, but that's another story—claims that ultimately

334

we're responsible for our own happiness."

"Sure." His glacier-blue gaze sharpened. "Is this about your job offer?"

"Yes. No. Tangentially? I…there's this thing I figured…I was trying to keep *you* happy, but it won't work long-term." Her arms moved as she spoke. Flailed, really. Which probably looked ridiculous, with her fists still balled in her pockets. "And *I'm* not happy, because I'm keeping something from you."

Alex shifted his weight from one leg to the other. An almost-smirk of bemusement flattened his mouth into a straight line. "That's a whole lot of vague, Sydney."

She didn't want to look at him. Didn't want to watch his expression change as he took in her words. But it wouldn't be right to look away. "I wrote the article."

"What article? Oh, man, did that local radio station talk the paper into doing a piece on our engagement?"

"No. I wrote the article for *Excursions 365* that exposed you and the situation with the burglary you covered up at your hotel. At least, I think it was you. If you tell me that you *didn't* work at the Grand Orion under the name of Kirk Kirkland, this whole mess can be over."

"That's me," he said slowly.

Rats. So much for that slim hope panning out.

"Why Kirk?" It so totally did not matter right now. But Sydney still wanted to know. As well as wanting to put off the inevitable storm for as long as possible.

Alex rested a hand on the carved newel post at the curved base of the stairs. Looked somewhere up, over her shoulder as he answered. "When I started, there were already two other Alexes on staff. My manager was going to call me by my last name, but it got shortened and stuck. That's how everyone there knew me for years. Once the other two Alexes left, it was too late to ask people to change what they called me."

"I like Alex better."

That icy gaze shot to meet hers. "I like having a *job* better."

Okay. Guess they'd just fast-forwarded to the fight. Or rather, the grovel that, in a perfect world, would derail the fight.

"I know. Alex, I'm so sorry. I didn't intend for anyone to get hurt. I wrote the article, in fact, to keep my crew from losing their jobs."

"Really."

She could explain. She could make him understand. "It's a long story. Short version is that the host of our show was a nightmare of a mess. A major liability who had to be shipped to rehab with handlers. I'd been working to make the jump from producer to host myself for a couple of years."

"You did this for a promotion?"

That sounded selfish. "Not entirely. There was a very real risk they'd permanently keep me on the magazine side if I did too good a job on the article. Which would've been a huge career demotion from the TV side. I risked that to save the show for the rest of my team. Only in the best-case scenario would they see it as proof that I was ready to make the leap. Then they'd give me his show—or a different one—and I could save our *whole* crew from being laid off."

He crossed his arms. "Oh, I get it. You decided to fix

your life by ruining mine?"

Wow. Alex wasn't making this easy on her. He was about two thousand miles from receptive, in fact.

But Sydney hadn't expected this to be quick or easy. And she was prepared to hunker down here and talk through it until the inn opened, if necessary. Until he understood how guilty and sorry she felt.

So she'd just have to keep going. "No. I had no idea there'd be repercussions for you."

"Isn't that the point of an exposé? To effect change?" he shot back.

"Well, in this case, I was challenged to make a good story out of a place that doesn't, well, make it to the top of the bucket list destinations. One that went beyond usual sights. Something deeper. A covered-up theft at a big resort hotel was juicy."

Dropping his arms, Alex stalked forward until he loomed over her. "It wasn't covered up. It was handled. Internally. Because a woman's life was at stake. Changes were made so it couldn't happen again. And I still had a job until you shined a freaking light on it. Then the Orion *had* to act. They *had* to publicly fire me. They *had* to give the public a scapegoat to calm their guests."

Sydney lifted her chin. But she didn't back away. No, she was here to absorb whatever he hurled at her. It was part of her penance.

It was what Alex deserved. A chance to rant and yell and get his anger out of his system. Then maybe, *maybe* they could move forward.

But it'd be better if he was truly listening. If he gave

some indication he understood that she'd done it to help others.

"I'm very sorry your situation escalated. Our MO is to drop into a spot somewhere in the world, do a story, and then fly off. I didn't think about what would happen after I put your hotel in the spotlight. I just moved on. I swear I had no idea the manager—you—was fired until a month ago."

His hand moved up to stroke down his chin, in obvious rumination. "Your name's not on the article."

Aha! Did this mean he was coming around to realizing she'd had no idea about his involvement?

Sydney shook her head, so hard that her hair whipped at her cheeks. "They kept it under our show host. I did most of his work for him, by then. He had the name recognition. If it went over well, I'd get the promotion. If it flopped, they'd tell everyone about his trip to rehab and use that as an excuse."

"*My* name's in there, though. You knew who I was."

"Well, I didn't know your name at first. It's not like you handed me your business card when we met and I destroyed your muffin. Plus, it turns out that you don't go by Kirk anymore. Your friends, your sister—they don't use that name for you ever. How was I to know?"

Alex spun away on one heel. Paced down the hallway to where it branched off into separate wings, but immediately came back. "There was a ton of public backlash. Someone must've reached out to you for a comment, for follow-up."

Good. Another chance to explain how much in the dark she'd been about it all.

Sydney shook her head yet again. "My team protected me from it. It was happening at the same time that Gram got her diagnosis. All of a sudden, instead of a promotion, I had to scramble to keep even a semblance of my job. They were not okay with me taking a sabbatical to help her. Insisted that I finish out the three cities left on our filming schedule before coming home. It was messy and awful."

"Hang on." Alex put his hand up to stop her, palm toward her. "Back up. I just processed what you said. You found out that you were responsible for getting me fired a whole month ago?"

"Everleigh *mentioned* that you'd been unjustly fired. A few hints as to the details. Enough to make me uneasy when I remembered you moved here from Pittsburgh. From there, I put it together once I reached out to my former crew for corroboration."

"A month?" he repeated in an almost growl. "You've known that you ruined my life for a month and didn't tell me?"

Sydney hadn't been sure which part he'd take hardest. The fact that she'd cost him his job, or that she'd hidden it from him.

She had not, however, bargained on him being equally furious about both things. She had not counted on him being so focused on *what* she'd done wrong that he overlooked the *why*. And that it hadn't been personal.

And she was starting to run out of different ways to express that.

"Again, I'm truly sorry. I certainly didn't know I'd end up dating you. I didn't target my future boyfriend and then vanish with a cackle of evil glee. If I could go back and change things, I would. Except…I don't need to. You came out the other side better than ever. You're living your dream here with the inn. It all worked out."

Alex thrust his hand into his hair. "I have almost no savings left. No backup plan. No safety net. This is *not* living the dream. Not by a long shot."

"Not yet. But it will be. In a few months."

His harsh bark of a laugh bit off quickly. "Sydney, in my dream world, my girlfriend doesn't lie to me. She doesn't cost me my entire life, even if unwittingly, and then hide it from me. That's a betrayal."

"Telling you would've just hurt you. At least, that's what I thought. Since there *is* no way for me to fix it, I didn't want to make you miserable reliving it. I wanted to protect you."

He shot an accusing finger–thumb combo toward her in the shape of a gun. "Like you wanted to protect your crew. Without thinking through the ramifications."

"I did decide I couldn't hide it from you anymore. That's why I'm here, today." Sydney circled her hands in the small space between them. "To clear the air. To make things right."

"Can't hide it anymore, huh? Is that what your new job offer's about? Are you going to do a follow-up on the story?"

Sydney reeled back a few steps at the accusation. "What? Of course not. I meant that I realized that no secret ever stays hidden. It was better for me to tell you than you find out some other way."

Alex jabbed at his sternum with both hands. "My sordid, scarred reputation could make this place fail. It could make people unwilling to stay. Who wants to risk a getaway under the roof of a manager who's so lax with security? Your article not only ruined by last job, but it could have long-reaching implications on this one, if I'm tied back to the Orion incident."

Yet another complication that hadn't occurred to her. She'd have to do something to fix that, too. Beg, plead, do whatever it took to get the article taken off their website. If it meant going back to work for *Excursions 365* and giving up the potential slot at *Wanderlust*, she'd do it. For him.

"I won't breathe a word. I won't do anything to cause you any more harm." Sydney wanted to reach out, to offer him comfort with her touch. But there was a nearly visible wall of anger and hurt radiating around him. "I…care so much for you, Alex."

"Right. So much," he mocked. "Just not enough to trust me." He stalked to the front door and flung it open. "I'll keep up the ruse about the engagement for your grandmother's sake, but that's it. You and I are over. Now get the hell out of my inn."

She'd apologize again, but if the first three times hadn't done the trick, mixed with a thorough explanation, well, it wouldn't matter. Wouldn't change his mind.

Sydney folded all those layers of genuine sorrow and regret into the shreds of her bleeding heart.

And left.

Chapter Twenty-Two

"DRINK THIS." TEAGUE shoved a plastic cup into his hand, foam dripping down the side.

Alex didn't take orders well. He'd rather take umbrage. "I'm thirty-two. I don't drink beer out of plastic cups anymore."

"It's St. Patrick's Day and we're in a bar called McGillicuddy's—they don't have the time or the capacity to wash glasses tonight. Have you seen the size of the crowd? The tent?" Teague gestured to the white walls decked with shamrock streamers of the enormous heated tent that abutted the bar to handle the overflow. And it was packed shoulder to shoulder at only eight o'clock.

"Yeah. It's too crowded and loud. We should probably go home. Leave our stools to people who want to be here."

"We want to be here."

"Speak for yourself."

"I am. I've been out of the country every year on March 17th since I was legal. This is my first St. Patrick's Day in an Irish pub. I want to experience it. I want to wear the stupid hat—" Teague flicked at the plastic leprechaun hat tipped over to one side "—and listen to the Irish music and get drunk with the whole town on Irish beer. Figured as my friend, you'd want to watch me enjoy it."

Crap.

Alex hadn't done the calendar calculations. He'd just let Teague strong-arm him out of the inn because it was easier than fighting with him. The plan had been to drink a Guinness or five but maintain his dour disposition.

He wasn't in a party mood.

Or a schmoozing mood, which was Teague's other leverage to get him to join the festivities.

He was in pretty much the one mood he'd maintained every day for the past two weeks. Cranky. Grouchy. Pissy.

Huh. Guess that was three moods. Nice to get a hat trick.

But he'd forgotten about Teague's far-from-normal nomadic existence with the Special Forces. Forgotten how badly his friend wanted to set down roots here.

Forgotten how to be a good friend.

He shot out an arm to clap him on the back. "Man, I'm sorry. Of course I want you to enjoy it. We'll blow it out. Get some fish and chips, some wings, some Jameson shots, and then more beer."

Relief and joy crowded for room in the smile that split Teague's face. "That sounds great." He waved his arm for a waitress. Then kept waving, because it looked like not just the residents of Chestertown, but all of Rock Hall and Tolchester Beach was crowded into the tent, too.

Alex slid off the stool to grab a hat from the nearby wait stand. Then he snapped the elastic band under his chin. "In fact, we should make a list."

Teague let his hand drop with a thud to the table, sloshing their beers. "Hell. There you go, ruining everything with the 'L' word."

Alex held up his hands, trying to look innocent. "Hey, I've checked out for the night as a partner in the Three Oaks Inn. I'm fully committed to just being in friend mode. So it'd be a list of all the things like this that you never got to do. I dunno—go down to the National Mall in DC for Memorial Day? Have a huge barbecue for the Fourth of July? Or go sailing? We can even get sombreros and have a fajita fiesta for Cinco de Mayo."

"I appreciate you getting on board. Let's take it one thing at a time. Without a list. We'll fly by the seat of our pants." Teague grinned. "Go commando. The ladies love it."

"Oh. You need me to be your wingman tonight, T?" Alex wasn't in the mood to flirt even on someone else's behalf.

But he would.

Because he'd been a miserable jerk for the past two weeks solid. Teague, as his roommate and partner, had taken the brunt of it.

"No way. Talk about a suicide mission—for me. I won't *let* you talk to any women tonight. You'd scare 'em off. But I will insist you chug that beer so you can tell when I'm teasing you."

"Right. Relieved, actually, to know there's an extra layer of protection under those jeans."

"Hey, in the desert, you want as many layers as possible between you and the sand."

"I feel like that means I should encourage you to go commando. To celebrate being out of the desert. But since we share a cottage, I can't justify giving you that advice."

Teague *almost* snorted his beer. He did huff the top layer of foam out of his cup and onto the already sticky high-top. "That's why it isn't safe for you to talk to a single woman tonight. Not even our waitress. For Christ's sake, can we stop talking about my underwear?"

"Yeah. Of course. Sorry."

James clapped him on the back. Alex caught himself on the table with his wrists. Man, that guy was strong. "What's going on over here? No apologies on St. Patrick's Day! It's a free pass holiday. Like New Year's Eve. And bachelor parties."

"Hey there." The big man had attached green braids to his beard. His eye patch bore a pot of gold decal. Alex was thrilled at his arrival—and his look. It was just the right amount of festiveness to help Teague really celebrate. "We're about to order a ton of food. Want to join us?"

"You bet. After we get a round of darts under our belt." James wriggled his eyebrows. "Watch—even with this crowd, everyone within ten feet will edge back when they notice eye patch guy holding darts. It freaks 'em out every time."

"Sounds fun." Alex paused, only half-standing. "You're going to beat us, aren't you? We're about to be hustled?"

"It's not a hustle if you know going in that you've got no chance." James laughed uproariously at his own joke. Teague joined in, and Alex almost let out a sigh of relief.

Now they had the beginnings of a *crew*. Triple the fun with three people. He'd eyeball the room again, see who else they could corral into their party.

Teague deserved a blow-out of a night. Alex would do

everything in his power to make this a night his friend would never forget—unless they hit a level of Guinness/whiskey saturation that blacked out the whole night, which would also be acceptable.

Neither one of them was a drink-to-forget kind of guy. But they'd worked like dogs since moving here.

First there'd been the whole weird power dynamic to sort out (or as Teague now called it, for Alex to figure out how to give orders without being a jerk). Then he'd sort of abandoned Teague as he started spending any and every moment of free time with Sydney. Once that ended, he'd been a miserable wreck—both internally and to anyone in his vicinity.

If anyone had earned one damn night of throwing responsibility *and* common sense by the wayside, it was them.

Especially since Amelia had agreed to drive out and pick them up when they were done for the night. There. That would officially be Alex's last responsible thought until March 18th.

Alex scanned the crowd. Between the hats, the headbands with shamrocks and the fake beards, it took him a minute to recognize anyone. But then he started seeing faces he knew.

Jed, from the hardware store, who slipped a bag of a dozen extra nails into every one of their purchases. Dwayne, the high school band director who played drums in Cam's band at the Valentine's Dance. Even their pregnant bride Annie was there, dancing what he'd generously call a jig.

It felt good to recognize so many. Solid. Rooted. If he'd been back in Pittsburgh at an Irish pub tonight, the odds were high that he wouldn't see a single person he knew. Sydney had warned him that Chestertown took their holidays seriously—big or small—and Alex realized that he liked it.

The sense of community was palpable. Yeah, he'd lost his job. Then he'd lost the seemingly perfect woman who'd *cost* him said job. Lost the woman he'd been on the verge of admitting he loved.

But he'd survive. Because of these people. Because of Everleigh and Amelia. Because of the strangers who would come and entrust their vacations to his care at his inn. Because Alex *belonged* here. Because he'd staked his claim and would carve out a new, better life here.

That didn't tamp down one bit his undeniably intense desire to have Sydney by his side while he did it.

But what kind of a fool would he be to stay with a woman like her? Who knew how badly her actions hurt him, and didn't bother to tell him? Who couldn't offer up such an important truth?

God, he missed her.

"Meet you by the dartboard. I'll get us a round of shots. James, you in for that?"

"You're drinking with an Army man and a Marine. The real question is, are *you* in for how this night's going to go?" That question came with another clap on the back. At least this time Alex saw it coming and braced for it.

James knew the truth about his fake engagement. Knew it was over, too. So Alex was able to grimace and lay his angry, bitter, pathetic cards on the table. "You guys may be tough-as-nails vets. But I had to dump the woman I loved.

So who do you think that makes more of a danger tonight?"

"Faith an' begorra, I'm not touching that!" James said in a horrible try at an Irish accent.

Teague snorted, then raised an arm. In response to his wave, Matt joined them. Amazing how the crowd sort of melted away to form a clear path for the chief. A *Kiss Me, I'm Irish* button was pinned to his bright green Oxford.

"You really Irish? Or just hard up?"

"Neither. If someone has to lean in to read it, they're probably drunk enough to pour into a cab and send home. Easier than a Breathalyzer. And not as off-putting."

"Can you play darts on duty?"

Matt scanned between the three men. "I can watch James *beat* both of you at darts while on duty."

Teague elbowed Alex. "We're not going to let that happen, right?"

Before he could answer, Alex felt his phone vibrate in his pocket. When he pulled it out, Teague groaned. "C'mon. No work. The inn will not fall down because we took a night off. There are no freaking drywall emergencies!"

"How about an actual emergency?" Alex tilted the phone to show the name of their security company flashing on the screen.

Matt's relaxed stance didn't change one bit. But his *vibe* did. Alex couldn't explain it, but the man clearly went on alert. "Are Everleigh and Amelia on site?"

"No. Nora's doing a cooking class at the retirement village on a full Irish dinner. They went along to help out."

"Good. Answer it, and tell them that police have been dispatched."

"How about I find out what's wrong first? This is a new system. What if the wind tripped a tree branch someplace?"

"You've got a big property. I'm going out there to check on it, with or without you. Because that's my responsibility. To take care of all the citizens of this town."

That was...weirdly heartfelt inside a bar with the Chieftains blaring and green beer in puddles on the straw-covered ground. Alex answered, gave his security word, and had the satisfaction of watching Teague punch James in the shoulder when the man rolled his eyes at 'Steelers.'

By the time he concluded the call, they'd shrugged into coats and were at Matt's cruiser. Or rather, his decked-out Suburban.

"I'm driving. Get in," the chief ordered.

Teague started to argue, clearly forgetting that they didn't *have* a car there. "Why do you get to drive?"

"Because I get to speed recklessly and use my siren."

"Plus, he's got weapons in the trunk," James said with glee as he climbed in the back.

Matt let out a long-suffering sigh that indicated this wasn't the first time he'd tamped back James's appreciation of his service revolver. "Let's not escalate the situation before we even get there."

There was a satisfying screech of rubber as he peeled out of the lot. Okay, maybe it was a little fun to ride shotgun in a police car. Silver lining to a break-in?

"What'd the security company say?" Teague asked.

Nothing that made sense to Alex. "That the front door opened without anyone disabling the alarm. Hang on, I'll pull up the video feed they sent."

He'd waffled on getting the security system. It was an added expense for a building they literally had to leave open much of the time for their guests. But Teague had read through a bunch of innkeeper forums—which had been a welcome surprise—that all recommended it, if for nothing else than the video feed. If it deterred the high school kids from trying to party in the barns, it was worth it.

Speak of the devil. "That little punk," Alex said under his breath.

Guess that was one downside of small-town life he hadn't considered. That you didn't just recognize the people in the Irish pub. You recognized the ones who broke into your home, too.

"Who? What'd you see?" Teague demanded, leaning forward to try and peer at Alex's phone.

"Brody, that's who." He flashed it to the back seat so there'd be no question. "Didn't break anything to do it, at least. Just grabbed the spare key from under that fugly crab planter and waltzed right in. When the alarm went off, he turned right back around and ran for his life."

"Brody Wickes snuck into your inn?" James slammed his palms into the back of Matt's seat, which earned him one hell of a dirty look in the rearview mirror. "Man, I'm sorry, Alex. This is my fault."

Teague snickered. "How's that? Is your assignment this month on cat burglary? A scavenger hunt where you're required to break into public buildings for each item?"

"Don't even joke about that," Matt growled.

Alex stared into the darkness that he knew was the marshland edging the road. Knew without even counting at this point how many stop signs Matt would streak through before turning left into the inn's drive. He knew all those things.

It was apparently *people* that he didn't know. At all.

"I'm the one who told you he was a good kid. Trustworthy." The edge to James's voice whipsawed between anger and apology. "You gave him a chance on my say-so. Even though you knew about his prank that had him in work-study detention."

"Stop it," Matt ordered. "Nobody's to blame for the poor decision-making of a teenager. Except for the said hormonal, idiotic kid. Did he know about the security system?"

"No. It's brand new." Teague sighed. "Tonight was its inaugural run."

"Okay, so he's not actually as dumb as a box of river rocks. Plus, he didn't do any physical damage to the structure."

"Should we go find Brody first?"

"No." Matt turned off the flashing lights and siren. "I want to walk around all those empty buildings on your lot, make sure he was the sole perpetrator. It *is* St. Patrick's Day, the second biggest drinking holiday. What do you want to bet he was just trying to steal some beers to impress his friends?"

"Or a girl?" James added. He sounded hopeful that Matt was downplaying it.

Alex almost didn't care what they found at Three Oaks. He was reeling. The *break-in* wasn't the horrible discovery of the night. It was the revelation of how badly *Alex* had screwed up.

He propped his elbow against the window and leaned his forehead onto his palm. "It's not your fault, James. It's mine. Hell, at this rate? Because I hired her? We'll probably find out that our new cook did ten years' hard time for poisoning an entire country club with her crab cakes."

"Nora? Bite your tongue." James jabbed an outstretched finger in the space between the seats and wagged it. "The woman cooks like an angel. Looks like one, too. Have you lost your mind?"

"Maybe. A part of it, anyway. Seeing as how it turns out I really can't trust my judgment anymore. That I can't read people worth a damn." Alex shifted to look back at his friends.

"Bullshit," Teague spat out. "Alex, you can't let what happened at the Grand Orion color everything that happens from here on out."

"My cop radar doesn't even tingle about Brody," Matt said. "I mean, I'll go through all the motions, be sure to scare him silly and talk to his parents, but my gut says this isn't as bad as you think."

James nodded, setting his green braids to shaking. "Because Brody's generally a good kid. He works hard and made one bad choice."

"Remember the things we did back in high school?" Teague added, laughing with a twinge of disbelief. "And the ones we got away with? This isn't about your judgment, Alex. It's about kids being kids."

Matt switched off his headlights as they turned into the long drive. Stealth mode. "People make mistakes. It's how they man up to being caught and fix 'em that matters." He stopped halfway to the lot. "You three stay in the car. It isn't likely anyone's still here since the alarm went off. But I want to swing past the barns on foot. Once I know they're clear, I'll come get you."

When he got out, he switched off the dome light and left the door open. Then he melted away into the shadows. Alex had to admit it was impressive watching him in police chief mode. As long as he didn't think too hard about why and where Matt was doing it.

Were they supposed to stay quiet?

It was still at least two hundred feet to the inn's front porch, and the barn was way beyond that. With the door open, the just-above-freezing temp seeped into them fast. All three pulled gloves from their pockets and tugged them on.

Teague leaned forward, keeping his voice low. "Is this wallowing freak-out just about Brody? Or Sydney?"

Damn it. Teague was a lot more perceptive than he used to be.

"You're losing me, guys. What do Nora and Sydney have to do with Brody breaking into your inn?" James asked.

It wasn't fair to keep James in the dark. Not when he'd come along as backup, without hesitation. "The short version? I had an ugly situation at my last job. A burglary, right under my nose."

Teague gave him—wow, a look he never thought he'd see on his friend's face. It was a full-on, tight-lipped, half-headshake, parental version of *you know better than that*. "She did it to escape domestic abuse, Alex. The woman wasn't just out for a quick score."

That didn't let him off the hook. "Still, I doubted myself after Elena took advantage of my trust by stealing that money. Thought that I'd lost my ability to get a read on people. In my business? That particular talent has to be overdeveloped, not lacking in any way. I'm responsible for all the people staying under my roof. I have to trust that I'll tell if someone's dangerous. Or even just up to no good."

"*You're* not responsible, Alex. We *all* are."

"Yeah, yeah. I'm not backsliding. I'm just talking about *my* problem. You're Special Forces. You've been literally government trained to sense danger a mile away."

"Trained?" Teague scoffed. "Nah. My talent's innate."

Either way, he knew his friend had instincts beyond reproach. That their guests would be safe under his watch.

"But Everleigh could be introduced to a terrorist wearing a suicide bomb strapped to their chest, and she'd still probably invite them out for coffee. Amelia knows there's a balance, but chooses to see only the good in people."

"Agree on Ever. I don't think you're giving your sister enough credit, though."

"Because of that, I need to be twice as on guard, twice as ready to spot trouble. I can't slip up again and lose us the inn."

"Whoa. I know Easter's right around the corner, and Father Mike would cringe if he heard me saying this, but—" James let out a long, low whistle. "That's one hell of a savior complex you've got going on there."

Teague clapped him on the shoulder. "Thank you! See, Alex? James is objective, hearing all of this for the first time, and still target-locks on your problem."

They couldn't be more wrong. "I don't think I'm anywhere close to the inn's savior."

"Nope. But you think you *ought* to be. For everyone, for everything. You can't be. No matter how hard you twist yourself into knots trying. And that's okay. Go ahead and doubt yourself. As long as you temper it by knowing that if you do fail, if you do mess up, the world will keep going."

Maybe…

Maybe he'd gone into overdrive when his parents died, worried about taking care of Amelia. Maybe he'd left himself revved too high on the responsibility front…

"What about Sydney? I thought I knew her. Trusted her." Alex swallowed down the thickness in his throat. Told himself it was just a reaction to the cold. "Loved her."

"You still know her. Whatever you loved in her, that's all still there."

So was the deep slash she'd left across his heart. "She got me fired."

Teague thumped his forehead against the headrest. "*Before* she met you. Sydney got a total stranger fired with the article, sure. But to save the jobs of multiple people she cared about. Kind of like how you hid Elena's burglary for a day to help save her."

"It's not the same," Alex said, shocked that his friend would make that comparison. Whose side was he on?

"Isn't it?"

No.

Maybe. But still… "She kept that huge secret from me."

On a half-laugh, half-groan, Teague said, "Kind of like how *you* kept being fired from *her*. You two set up these

355

asinine rules at the start of this whole weird fake engagement. You're both to blame for how it turned out."

Matt's flashlight beam cut through the darkness. Alex would take it as an all-clear signal. Mostly because he was desperate to get out of the car and Teague's unexpected pushback. Couldn't a guy emotionally beat himself up in peace anymore? Without having logic thrown at him like a spear to disrupt it all?

They spilled out of the car. "Let's get this over with and get back to McGillicuddy's." James took point, his feet crunching against the frozen oyster shells of the drive. "I've never seen two people more in need of blowing off some steam."

That was as good a place as any to leave it for the night.

Not knowing *why* Brody got into the inn.

Not knowing if his judgment was permanently broken.

Not knowing if he could believe what Teague had laid on him. If he could dial back his responsibility-meter.

Not knowing how to balance what Sydney's actions cost him against his feelings for her.

The only thing Alex did know was that this St. Patrick's Day would be one for the books, if it was the last thing he did.

Chapter Twenty-Three

"DON'T YOU HAVE anything better to do than sit in a hospital room watching them drip poison into my veins?" Daisy demanded in a querulous tone.

The medical marijuana might've made her grandmother's chemo rounds more bearable, but they were wearing on her, for sure. Sydney didn't blame her one bit for being out of sorts to start yet another treatment.

Didn't make her bad mood any fun, though.

Sydney tapped a finger against her lips, pretending to think. "Well, when you put it like that…no. I don't have anything better to do. It is *literally* the reason I came home, remember?"

"You came home because you thought I was dying."

"Meh." She batted away that answer like it was a gnat. "That was just the tipping point."

Daisy gave a viciously strong pull on her cranberry juice box, hollowing in the sides. "You came home to fill in for me at the Mercantile."

"Yes, but Dad could've hired someone to do that. I came home to keep you company, you crotchety old woman."

"And I'm eternally grateful." Fast as a whip crack, Daisy's mood morphed to teary-eyed sweetness. She reached over to pat Sydney's hand. "Seriously. I realize this was a big stall-out for you, my darling girl. Coming home. A sacrifice, both to your heart and your career. One I can't ever repay."

Sydney's emotions had been hovering uncomfortably close to the surface ever since Alex dumped her three weeks ago. It was sort of like having all of her nerves on the outside of her skin. The faintest brush would set her off.

So her eyes welled at her grandmother's gratitude.

"Gram, you raised me. You helped put me back together after Mom left. You taught me to use hair spray to prevent static cling on a slip. That it's okay to say no when someone asks you out. That it's okay to embrace your dreams no matter what." Sydney leaned in to whisper in her ear. "And you just taught me how to bake."

"That last one, I do deserve a medal for, I don't mind saying." Daisy cackled and slapped her leg. Then she winced when the motion pulled at her IV line. "All right. You can stay."

Sydney kicked back into full recline mode in the treatment chair. No other patients this morning meant she got to be super comfy.

And comfortable was exactly what she'd finally settled into in Chestertown.

It wasn't anything she'd ever thought she wanted. It sure felt like what she needed, though. The closeness. The sense of community. The new friendships that were so much more...*vital* and interesting and fun. They sure beat sitting cross-legged on a scratchy hotel comforter night after endless night.

It was comfortable not feeling wrecked by jet lag. Comfortable having new inside jokes with her dad and brother. Comfortable having people to turn to instead of insisting that she do everything herself.

Home had never mattered.

Now that Sydney was *back* home, she'd discovered that it mattered more than anything.

"You're wrong, you know, Gram. I thought coming home was a sacrifice. But it turned out to be a real gift."

"Because of Alex moving here?"

Yes...and then no. "Because of lots of things. I missed all of you, but I didn't realize quite how much until I was with you again. I don't want to do that again. Be so distant. I want to be a part of your everyday lives, triumphs, laughs, and losses."

"You're giving up globe-trotting?" Daisy hitched herself up on one elbow on the armrest to scowl at Sydney. "Did that fiancé of yours insist on it? That's going too far. If you want to spend every week in a different country for your career, that's your decision."

"Thanks for the empowerment. I'm not quitting. But I am figuring out how to make some changes to be an, ah, *present* member of this family."

Some might call her slowly evolving plan a step backward. Sydney considered it a step sideways. A way to have it all—a job she loved and time with her family. And if *Wanderlust* truly was salivating to lock her in? She should be able to negotiate a deal that would allow that.

"I'd be lying if I didn't admit to being tickled at the thought of you popping over to see me every week. I could teach you how to make a Southern jam cake with caramel frosting. The secret's to tip in a little bourbon."

Biting her lip to keep from laughing, Sydney said solemnly, "That's the secret to a lot of things in life."

"We could make a cake for you to take to Alex tonight when I'm finished with this nonsense." Daisy turned up her nose at the hanging bag of chemo drugs. "Nothing complicated. Just a dump cake. Whatever ingredients I don't have, we can borrow from Hazel."

Sydney realized she'd just been given an opening. One that laid the groundwork for her inevitable 'broken engagement.' Plus, she'd get to stop hiding her tear-reddened eyes from her grandmother.

"I'm...well, I'm not seeing Alex tonight. We had a big fight."

After making a raspberry, Daisy said, "Pish tosh. You'll get over it. Men will make mistakes. Again and again. As long as they keep trying to do better, they're worth keeping around."

It'd be easy to let her think Alex was the jerk. The whole thing was made up anyway. But Sydney refused to lie any more about this particular situation.

She grabbed the folded blanket at the foot of the recliner and pulled it up to her chin. "Actually, Gram, I'm the one who screwed up. Then I hid it from him. Lied—by omission. For a long time. I came clean, but he's, ah, rightfully pissed at me."

For a long minute, the only sound was the steady beep of the monitors and the IV machine. "That's disappointing to hear. You know better than that. I raised you better than that."

Oh, no question.

Trying to fix everything for everyone kept backfiring on her. It got Alex fired. Gave her mess of a host a boost with that article that went viral instead of saving her team. Even recommending Nora to Alex as the inn cook had caused a huge fight with Teague, Amelia, and Everleigh.

"I was trying to protect him, not myself. It backfired," Sydney said simply.

"Did you apologize?"

Seriously? "Of course I did. Multiple times. He's too mad to accept it, though. Which I understand. I sort of ruined his life. Or at least, made him veer off the path he'd planned to take."

"Why does it sound like you've given up?"

Because that was what mature people did. "I have to respect his decision."

Daisy hooted. Loudly enough that a nurse wheeled over on a stool to peek in the doorway. "Balderdash. Is that what you learned in all your time traveling the globe? If you make a mistake on a shoot, you just pack up and move on to the next thing?"

"Well, ah, yeah."

"That's not how the world works, hon. You hunker down, you work through things. You don't run away. Or you shouldn't, after all this time."

Wow. That was a pointed jab she had not been expecting. How had the older woman so deftly connected the problem with Alex to the problem she'd been harboring with her hometown for so many years?

They were totally different issues.

Weren't they?

Sydney looked at herself in the mirror over the sink across the treatment room. Sloppy ponytail. Yoga pants and a sweatshirt from Australia with a kangaroo crossing sign. No makeup.

She was a mess. Inside and out.

Slowly, she asked, "You think I ran away from here? When I left for college?"

"Oh, definitely. The eighteen-year-old version of a kid who packs two PB&Js in a backpack with a teddy bear and runs away to sleep in the neighbor's treehouse. And the parents know where he is the whole time. They know that he needs the space, and will come back when he realizes that home is a heck of a lot better than a drafty old treehouse."

"Gram, I love you. And Dad, and Cam and Kim. My choice was never to leave you guys. My choice was to…to…find what I wanted."

"Did you find it?"

Hmm.

She'd spent years driving herself relentlessly, working for a heartless company that wanted to punish her for taking a sabbatical (an actual entry in the employee manual) to take care of her dying grandmother. *Supposedly* dying when she'd made the request, anyway.

She'd worked her way up the ladder. Then they yanked it out from under her.

Most of the friendly acquaintances she'd made in her travels hadn't checked in the whole time she'd been here. Work friends were absolutely *not* the same level as the actual friends she'd made here.

There'd been zero effort to have a boyfriend, to truly connect with anything besides her to-do list. Here, she'd found the time. Made the effort. Against all odds and logic. She'd found love. Here.

But...her first real, serious, long-term relationship had just ended. She'd imploded it. And no, staying to pick up the pieces and fix it had never occurred to her.

Sydney was suddenly so tired of spending more than a decade chasing after everything. Alex had posited that perhaps she'd been running away from the pain of her mom's departure. Sydney always believed she was chasing whatever was *better* enough out there in the world to pull her mom away from them.

Either way, she'd had enough. Enough letting the actions twenty years ago of a selfish woman determine the course of her life.

She curled up sideways to look at her grandmother. The brave, strong, woman she'd forever regret not spending more time with. "I think I found out that I'd rather be happy than simply satisfied."

"Does Alex make you happy?"

"Yes." Sydney didn't need to think about it. The word popped right out. No need to get into the complexities and evolution of their purportedly fake relationship.

Daisy adjusted her Orioles hat. "When people are hurt, they lash out. They want to escape. After that passes? They want the comfort of home. Which isn't always a place. Often, it's a person. The one you feel most comfortable with."

Huh. Was it a coincidence that word 'comfortable' had

come up again?

Doubtful.

"You're very wise, Gram."

"It's about time you came to that conclusion," she said pertly. "Now will you please get your brother to come around to that way of thinking? He still ignores my advice on a regular basis."

Oh, she'd gotten an earful about that 'advice' since coming home. "Telling him to date your best friend's granddaughter because you two want to plan a wedding together isn't advice. It's coercion."

Daisy pointed out the door. "Take that sass out of here and bring me another cranberry juice."

Sydney threw back the blanket, but she didn't leave. Instead, she leaned over to press a kiss to her grandmother's wrinkled cheek. "Thanks for letting me keep you company. And, you know, everything."

Because now, she knew she needed a plan. Not one to get Alex back. That was entirely up to him. But one to fix the people she'd hurt, unintentionally or not. No matter how hard or uncomfortable it'd be for her.

No more running.

SYDNEY WAS GREAT at making a plan. Equally great at the execution.

And yet, she sat there, in her sister's car, not getting *out*. Just staring at what seemed like hordes of people on the grounds of the Three Oaks Inn.

James was there, looking twice as huge as usual in white painters' coveralls. He was running herd on at least a dozen of his students as they laid out drop cloths and trestle tables next to the piles of black shutters from every window on the inn.

Nora was setting up a table with coffeepots and thermoses, next to platters of breakfast treats. Matt and two men she didn't recognize were up on ladders dealing with the gutters.

The inn crew—Teague, Amelia, Everleigh, and Alex— were unloading paint cans and supplies from the back of their SUV.

Sydney hadn't accounted for an audience in her plan.

She should have. Should have realized everything would align to make this as difficult as possible for her. Because, well, *Karma*. But that was okay. Maybe the greater sacrifice, the harder this was, meant that a more positive resolution was in the cards?

Okay, maybe not. Clinging to that hope, though, would at least get her butt out of the driver's seat.

When Sydney slammed the door shut, every head turned her way. And it got quiet. So quiet that she could hear the myriad of birds squawking and chirping. Then a bellow from James had the kids refocusing on the shutters.

She waved at Matt and Nora, but beelined over to Alex. He wore a Grand Orion Henley. Seeing the name of the hotel across his chest was another quick punch to her gut. He'd belonged there. Enough to have branded clothes. And she'd taken that away from him.

But, hopefully, today would fix it.

A little.

Enough.

"Hey, Sydney," Everleigh said, without any of her usual warmth. "What brings you here?"

"Well, it's the first Saturday in March without any frost. Painting day. I promised I'd help you guys. So here I am."

"That's up to Alex." Amelia waved an arm at the people scattered across the grounds. "As you can see, we've already got a lot of help." She started to walk toward the porch. Ever and Teague followed suit.

In case Alex sent her away, she needed to flip her script. "Wait. Please don't leave. I'm also here to apologize. To all of you."

"The one you need to apologize to is Alex," Teague said gruffly. He wore camo pants and cap, an Army long-sleeved tee, and looked incredibly intimidating.

"Well, I have. I'll do it again. But I owe the rest of you an apology. For walking away. For assuming that you wouldn't want to talk to me after Alex told you what I did. I guess I thought of you all as a package deal. Until I remembered that our friendships were totally individual."

With a huge toss of her glossy black hair, Ever said accusingly, "You ghosted us. That hurt."

And she regretted it. Deeply. Looking through the lens of her gram's wisdom, it had been apparent that she'd treated them badly, too. If she could work it to spend more time in Chestertown, Sydney wanted to be sure to salvage these friendships.

Even if she couldn't manage to salvage things with Alex.

"I thought that's what you'd want. To not see me. Clearly, I have a problem with assuming what other people feel.

Or need. Or want."

Amelia tightened her ponytail. And squinted those green eyes at her. "You thought you were doing us a favor? Like how you did Alex a favor by not telling him you were behind his firing? Geez, Sydney. That's just *wrong*."

"I figured my staying away would give you peace. Space." Her gram had labeled it as yet another instance of running away. Talk about beating a dead horse. "I told you from the start that I didn't have experience with deep female friendships. You're my OGs. My starter pack. That didn't come with instructions. So I screwed up. I'm very, very sorry."

"I missed you," Amelia said softly.

Sydney put her hands to her mouth, overcome with relief. "Not as much as I missed you."

Teague lightly squeezed her shoulder. "Don't be a dumbass. You get one free pass."

"Thanks." Sydney looked down at her sneakers. "I'm going to try my best, but I might need more than one."

"Did I say one? I meant one a month." He winked at her. It was a devastating hit of charm and charisma, and for a split second, Sydney wondered how on earth Ever and Amelia had only seen him as a brother figure for all this time.

Ever threw her arms around Sydney in a tight hug. "Rule number thirteen: friends don't give up on each other."

"I'm learning."

The three of them edged away again, and Sydney didn't stop them this time.

Now it was just she and Alex, standing by his open tailgate. Alex, who had yet to say a word or acknowledge her arrival.

That didn't bode well.

"I know you're pissed at me. I respect that. But I have something important to share with you. An apology gesture. Please hear me out."

"A gesture?"

Sydney was no body language expert. But his crossed arms and stiff posture weren't encouraging. Not to mention that she couldn't read him at all behind the dark sunglasses.

"Well, I said I was sorry a bunch of times and it didn't seem to sink in to you. I get that you were fresh in the moment of feeling betrayed. There's no judgment, no excuses. Then I realized that just *saying* I was sorry didn't fix anything."

"It helped."

Sydney blinked. What felt like as fast as a hummingbird's wings. "Oh. Good. Because I am sorry. So…I got the story pulled down from *Excursion 365*'s website. I know it doesn't make it vanish in today's internet-heavy world. But if anyone goes looking for your name, it shouldn't pop up anymore."

Alex gave a sharp up/down of his head. "Thank you. That's a nice gesture."

"What?" How could he think that was all she was willing to do for him? "That's not my apology gesture. That's barely a thing. And what I should've done back in February, the moment I put the pieces together."

"Sydney, you don't have to *do* anything. You made your choice. The consequences had unintentional blowback onto me. I know it wasn't malicious."

"You do? Then…why haven't we talked in seventeen days? Why haven't you reached out to me?" She swallowed hard. Mostly tamping down her pride. "Why didn't you try to get back together with me?"

He wrenched off his sunglasses, tossing them onto the baby grass struggling to cast off winter. "Because being apart seemed easier. I can read a calendar. You're coming up on your ninety-day cutoff. When you run away from Chestertown as fast as you can. The deeper into this whole thing we got, I knew your leaving, the end to our fake engagement—that'd be so damn hard. This way it was already done."

In the time they were together, Sydney had spent a lot of time actively *not* thinking about how hard it would be to walk away from Alex. Compartmentalizing was another one of her specialties. Thoughts that scared her, that could hurt her, got locked away in a mental bunker of concrete and titanium.

Which was great when your day was spent zipping between two airports and three countries while keeping a crew together. It was not, however, conducive to an open and honest relationship.

She'd never spared a thought for how her insistence on leaving could be an open wound for Alex.

Wow, she had a lot to learn.

Nevertheless, this all sounded...positive? Cautiously, Sydney asked, "So you're not still mad at me?"

Alex dropped his arms. And held them out, open, to her. "No. I miss you too much to stay mad."

Sydney rushed forward to burrow against his chest. They stood there, entwined, hitching in breaths until their chests rose and fell in sync.

Gram was right. Home *could* be a person.

Alex loosened his hug just enough to look down at her. "I'm sorry, Sydney. I shouldn't have ended things with you. Not that way. Not over my own stupid mistake."

Oh, no. Mr.-Always-Responsible didn't get to co-opt her apology. "I got you *fired*, Alex. You said they'd shoved it under the carpet, let you stay until I told the world what really happened."

"True. But it was my bad, stupid decision in the first place that led you there. It started with me making the wrong choice. It got compounded by not telling you about it. I'm just as much to blame. It's been hammered home to me lately that going it alone just doesn't work."

"Funny—I feel like that's the big lesson life stuffed down my throat since coming home, too." Which Sydney didn't mind, because it was all better. Insisting on doing everything herself was hard. Lonely. Didn't come with any medals. Whereas sharing herself *with* people felt whole. Complete. Especially with Alex.

His hands framed her face, thumbs caressing her cheekbones. "That idea we had about not sharing our histories with each other to make the engagement easier? That was...dumb."

Sydney laughed. They'd set themselves up for failure from the start. "Agreed. The shocking thing is that we both actually thought it would work."

"The shocking thing is that we still stuck to it. Kept our heads buried in the sand as our hearts got closer and closer."

That could easily be labeled the biggest mistake she'd ever made. "I should've told you about my job. And vice versa. Alex, there's so much we still need to share with each other. Things I really, *really* want to share with you."

"I want to tell you everything, Sydney. I want to bore you silly with the verbal download of my life." Those stunning, pale blue eyes bored into hers. "Except...you're still leaving. Aren't you?"

Her smile grew so big that she could barely talk. "No. Not right away. And once I do leave, I plan on it to only be for short bursts of work, and then come straight back here, where I belong."

Alex's jaw dropped in astonishment. "How is that possible?"

"That job offer I mentioned? *Wanderlust* wants me. They want me badly enough that it looks like they'll agree to my terms of being a contractor. Doing a few shows as seasonal specials, but not living my life on the road 24/7, 365. And working on new show development the rest of the time, which I can do here. Because I have a home, people I cherish right here, that I'm not willing to be away from."

His thumbs stilled. His whole body stiffened again, as if bracing for a blow. "Where do I figure into that?"

"Wherever you want." Sydney stepped out of his embrace to take his hands. "No more hiding things, Alex. We put all our cards on the table. Which means me admitting that I want to be with you, no matter what. That I love you."

A huge smile spread across his face. It was the same smile he wore when they were in bed together—a combination of smugness and contentment. "It is downright freaky how we're on the same page. I love you, Sydney."

"No. Wait." She stepped back, waving her hands in the air like she was trying to wave off a plane barreling down the wrong runway. "You can't say that yet."

"That isn't even a little bit funny."

"You have to accept my apology gesture."

Alex shoved his hands in the back pockets of his jeans. "Hit me."

She pulled a business card out of her jacket. "That's for Langdon Crews. He works for *Excursions 365*. Stories on hot new properties. When you're ready, he'll come and shoot video, take pictures, and do a mention of you in the next episode. If you want."

Alex took it slowly, almost gingerly. "You're joking."

"Nope. He's pretty excited. Langdon far prefers old, comfortable properties to new, glitzy ones. He likes character."

"That's about all the Three Oaks has going for it." A rueful acceptance tinged Alex's words.

"Nonsense. She's beautiful. You're bringing her back. Look, I tanked your last job. The least I can do is give this one a boost."

"This will be immensely helpful. Thank you." After giving a stiff nod, Alex said, "Apology accepted." Then he lifted Sydney into his arms, covering her face in kisses as he sat them both on the tailgate. "Say it again. Say you'll stay with me. Say you'll let me love you."

"Yes." Sydney let her head drop back, giving him access to continue the line of kisses down her neck. "Now you. Say you forgive me. Say we can have a fresh start. Say you'll let me help you and love you."

"Yes."

And then his mouth covered hers, and neither one of

them said anything for quite some time...

Epilogue

Three Weeks Later

EVERLEIGH SPUN IN circles down the length of the ballroom. It made the full skirt of her blue dress billow up.

Alex knew he'd probably get branded a stick-in-the-mud. But he had to stop it. Because nothing could go wrong today. *Nothing.*

"Ever, enough of that. This is a PG-13 wedding. Please don't risk flashing your panties at the guests."

"Spoilsport." But after one more twirl and some complicated, ballet-esque leap, she stopped at the first row of tables. "I'm just so happy to be dressed up again. To feel pretty."

"You always look pretty." Alex didn't say it to shore up her ego. It was fact. His sister's BFF was a stunner. Which in no way explained her god-awful track record with men. With her looks and inherent sweetness, she could crook her finger and get any man. Yet for some reason, she always ended up with jerks and losers.

"I know I do," she said smugly. "But *feeling* pretty's different. I don't feel pretty scrubbing and sanding and painting and dusting."

"Oh, you're so put-upon. Should we start calling you

Cinderella?" Amelia asked dryly. She was at the cake table, adding sprays of fresh flowers around the bottom of Nora's lemon raspberry wedding cake. "Except, wait, we're *all* Cinderella, working our fingers to the bone."

"Yes, but you like it. You're never happier than when you're sitting *on* dirt with your hands *in* the dirt."

"True. The last couple of days have been sheer heaven. Potting up all the annuals, planting the flowering shrubs. It felt like the inn was in that scene in the *Wizard of Oz* where it switches from black and white to Technicolor. My reward for surviving the winter and all our hard indoor work. Just like wearing a cocktail dress today is your reward."

"I'll take it."

"The gardens are spectacular, Ame." Alex looked out the wall of windows overlooking the main garden that led to the river's edge. His sister had brought to life all the flowerbeds, and created a beautiful trellis at the apex of the three ancient oaks. The outside of the inn now looked just like the pictures they'd seen online when they won the lottery.

"The gardens are barely acceptable," she corrected him. "They are, at best, a *start*. And frankly, miracles were worked with that minuscule budget you allotted me."

"A budget that you and I worked on together. Don't treat me like Scrooge."

"I'm sorry. I just see how much potential this place has as spring brings more and more of it to life every day. It kills me not to be able to do all the things I can picture for it."

"We'll get there," Teague said. He didn't wear a tie, because Alex knew which battles to pick. The sport coat and dress shirt had to be enough.

"How'd valet duty go?"

Teague grimaced. "Count your lucky stars that it's a small wedding. We need to get that second overflow lot ready to go ASAP. Fill in the potholes, top it off with fresh gravel."

They'd been hoping to wait another month before taking that step. "Gravel's not free."

"Neither will the garage bill be when we tweak someone's chassis from those knee-deep potholes. We're lucky a lot of the guests are locals and carpooled."

"I hear you." Alex knew how lucky they were to have scored more event bookings for April and May. It accelerated their timeline, though, in terms of financial outlay. Thank God for deposits. "Want to take point on that?"

"Might as well. That lot's as bad as a minefield, which is, after all, my wheelhouse."

Alex white-knuckled the dainty gold back of the Chiavari chair. "Don't say anything like that in front of the guests. Please."

"You mean that the government paid me to wreak havoc around the globe?"

Teague must've had a bad set of nightmares last night. He only got morbid and snarky like that about his Special Forces days when his past paid him nocturnal, subconscious visits.

They never talked about it.

Alex just heard the thrashing and moaning from the next room. Then he'd grab a bottle of water and wake his friend. Teague would look shattered, they'd make desultory conversation about the Pirates's chances for the upcoming season, and then they'd go back to sleep.

"Yes. No flashing of underwear, and no mention of government-sanctioned violence." Alex shot his cuffs. "I can't believe I have to say these things out loud. What's next? Amelia, do you plan on breaking a mirror? Adopting a stray black cat and letting it walk in front of the bride?"

A pair of hands settled on his shoulders. Soft lips pressed just above the collar of his suit coat. "Breathe, hon."

Sydney's touch alone probably ratcheted back his stress by half. Alex turned to give her a proper kiss. Vaguely, he heard Amelia blowing her customary raspberry of disapproval at their PDA. He didn't care. Sydney's kisses were worth putting up with all the sisterly razzing in the world.

"This is a surprise. What are you doing here? Are you Annie's guest?" Then he scowled over her shoulder at Everleigh. "Or did these guys beg you to come over here and distract me?"

Ever scowled right back. "We did no such thing. Because if we had—and it would've been brilliant—we would've had her show up four hours ago when you started your day-of freak-out."

"I'm not freaking out. We have lists, we have a schedule and everything is going according to plan." So far. Which was a guarantee of exactly *nothing*.

Alex had never been this nervous. Not even on his first day as manager at the Grand Orion. He knew they'd done all that was humanly possible to prepare. He knew the parts of the inn they were opening to the public were ready.

It was what he didn't know, what unexpected wrench might be thrown into the works, that had him on edge.

Teague rolled his eyes. "Dude, you are so far up our asses today you can see the scar from my tonsillectomy."

"I'm just concerned. Anxious. Nothing can go wrong."

"Which you've said eight hundred times already. We get it. This is a big day."

"Which is why I'm here," Sydney jumped in. "To support you on your big day. Whether that means being put to work, or just standing in a corner beaming with appreciation of what my talented man has wrought."

Her thoughtfulness caught him off-guard. "That's…that's great. Thank you."

Teague snorted. "You must really love this guy to put up with him in this state."

"I do. I even love that he is this much of a wreck."

"Huh?" She wanted him to be miserable? Was this payback for the cold pizza he'd swiped out of her fridge last week?

"It shows how much he cares. You know Alex isn't nervous for himself, right? You know he's worried about something happening that you can't handle. Something that would make you feel bad, like you aren't right for the inn, or don't deserve to be here. He's nervous because he wants to protect you. Because you're his family."

"That's why you're being such a pain in the neck?" Amelia stood on tiptoe to kiss his cheek. "Thanks, bro. Which reminds me, I have one more part to your Christmas present. Be right back."

"I barely survived the first part," he yelled after her. It was impossible to tally up the bruises, scrapes, cuts, puncture wounds (including tetanus boosters for all of them) and aches they'd accumulated since January.

Sydney slid her arm around his waist. "I did run into Annie in the hallway. She couldn't stop gushing about how sweet it was for you to offer them a cottage for their honeymoon weekend."

"Trust me, I regretted it when Ever had me swapping out screens at midnight to prepare it."

"Nobody wants bugs on their wedding night. And I just noticed the hole yesterday." Ever poked his biceps. "Besides, it's a waste of breath for you to grumble. You're a softie at heart. Don't deny it."

Softhearted about the people he loved. Not about business. Nothing but cold, strategic, fiscally sound calculations when it came to business. "It's a good test for us, having a couple in a cottage. Since we open in a week."

"Not everything is a test." Ever poked him again. Maybe he'd have to give her the same speech he'd given Amelia. Professional partners in public, not the familiarity of someone who'd known you for twenty years. *Aka*, no poking.

"Sure it is. Sneaking around the night we thought Brody broke in showed where we needed to add more perimeter lighting."

Sydney gasped in surprise. "He didn't break in? The rumor mill had him stealing liquor."

Oh, yeah. The aftermath of that had been while they were split up. "Nah, he really is a good kid. He'd left his backpack inside, with an assignment due the next day. All he did was use the key to try and grab it. Brody had no idea we'd installed a security system. He was terrified."

"Here we go." Amelia bustled back in, her long pink

skirt rustling and her heels clicking on the beautifully polished—if he did say so himself—wood floor. She carried a tray with champagne and glasses. "Come over by the windows. It's time."

Sydney held back, but Alex didn't dignify that with a comment. He just grabbed her hand and pulled her along at his side. Where she belonged. She was a part of this family now, after all.

Outside, a violinist played as the bride processed down the aisle. The river sparkled, the trees had leafed out enough to shade the sun. It was a perfect day.

Which, of course, jolted Alex's nerves again.

Amelia handed around the filled flutes. "I bought this bottle on December 26th. To save for the day we opened the inn."

"We don't have the official opening party until May 2. Haven't booked guests to stay until the week after that." It wasn't *exactly* the date they'd been pushing for. But it was what they'd ended up with—and Alex wasn't complaining about having some extra days to finish everything.

"But we've let the public onto the grounds. They'll be eating and dancing in this ballroom in less than an hour. As the bride and groom start their new life together, so do we."

If he'd gone along with Sydney on her decade of globe-trotting, he still wouldn't find a better sister than Amelia.

Alex raised his glass. "To Amelia, for giving me the best Christmas present ever. To Teague and Everleigh, for being just crazy and loyal enough to join us on this adventure. I thought this place was a last chance for all of us—and frankly, I wasn't convinced we'd get to this point."

Ever looked surprised at his words. "I was. Your sheer force of will would've made it happen even if the rest of us quit."

Teague gave him a shoulder bump. "I knew you'd drag us across the finish line. Bruised and battered, kicking and screaming, occasionally mad as hell, but I knew you'd get us here."

These people—*his* people—were incredible. "I had it all wrong. It wasn't our last chance. The lottery made our dreams come true. Not as easily as expected, but what's worth it ever is? Amelia, your lottery ticket didn't just give me a hotel." He draped his arm around Sydney's neck and kissed her. "It gave me love. To Sydney, for agreeing to marry me."

Alex was the only one who touched the glass to his lips. Everyone else stared at him, Sydney included. "Wait. Do...do you mean...for, for *real*?" Everleigh stammered.

"I meant the day she proposed to me, back in January. Which doesn't really count." He tugged off the paper clip ring she still wore. No more reminder of how they'd almost sabotaged their relationship. "There's still so much I don't know about you. Like your middle name."

Sydney quirked her lips, then said softly, "It's Louise, after my great-grandmother."

"That's a good start. Maybe once you find out my middle name, maybe a few other personal nuggets get shared over the summer, we can put a ring on that finger that isn't just a placeholder."

"I'll drink to that." They clinked glasses, huddled in a tight semicircle at the window, as in front of them, a promise of forever love was made.

And the Three Oaks Inn was up and running.

Alex had his hotel and his woman and his family. Life was pretty great.

The End

Want more? Check out Christi Barth's Christmas story, *The Magic of Christmas*!

Join Tule Publishing's newsletter for more great reads and weekly deals!

If you enjoyed *The Accidental Fiancé,*
you'll love the next books in the….

Love Lottery series

Book 1: *The Accidental Fiancé*

Book 2: *Definitely Not Dating*
Coming May 2021!

Book 3: *Coming October 2021!*

Available now at your favorite online retailer!

About the Author

USA TODAY bestseller Christi Barth earned a Masters degree in vocal performance and embarked upon a career on the stage. A love of romance then drew her to wedding planning. Ultimately she succumbed to her lifelong love of books and now writes award-winning contemporary romance.

Christi can always be found either whipping up gourmet meals (for fun, honest!) or with her nose in a book. She lives in Maryland with the best husband in the world.

Thank you for reading

The Accidental Fiancé

If you enjoyed this book, you can find more from all our great authors at TulePublishing.com, or from your favorite online retailer.

TULE
PUBLISHING

3/18/2022

Made in the USA
Middletown, DE
22 May 2021

39530140R00234